# THE R.E.M. PROJECT

I0604670

J.M. LANHAM

No part of this book may be reproduced, scanned, or distributed in any printed or electronic form without permission from the author, except in the case of brief quotations embodied in critical articles and reviews. Please do not participate or encourage piracy of copyright materials in violation of the author's rights.

This is a work of fiction. Names, characters, places, and incidents are a product of the author's imagination or are used fictitiously and are not to be construed as real. Any resemblance to actual events, locales, organizations, or persons, living or dead, is entirely coincidental.

The R.E.M. Project
Trade Edition, March 2018

Copyright © 2018 by J.M. Lanham. All rights reserved.

ISBN-10: 0-9973460-4-3
ISBN-13: 978-0-9973460-4-6

Cover design by 2Faced Design

Keep up with the latest J.M. Lanham news and releases by visiting www.jmlanham.com.

For Hollis.

*Some cures are worse than the dangers they combat.*

–Seneca the Younger

# Prologue:
## Bringing in the Sheaves

It was Sunday morning at 11 a.m., and already the parking lot of Fruit of the Faithful Ministries was at full capacity, the ferocious wave of late-summer humidity doing little to stave off the determined congregation of the Reverend Jonas Perch. The aging preacher stood at the entrance to his newly-formed church and watched the heat rise and twist from the asphalt like cobras called from their charm baskets, giving him just enough time to entertain a daydream or two before the incoming hoard of parishioners broke the spell.

He quickly donned a grin that stretched from ear to ear, greeting the churchgoers with two big rows of bright-white veneers and an enthusiasm he hadn't felt in almost three decades. His once jet-black hair was now a slicked-back silvery shade of gray, and his timeworn face had earned him a hefty number of crevices, but on this Sunday morning, age was just a number. Perch was back at the top of his game, and with a faithful congregation to prove it.

The reverend's first summertime revival in almost thirty years was set to wrap up an exceptionally hot August. Droves of churchgoers filled the parking lot of the rundown strip mall in Spring Hill, Georgia, their cars overflowing into spaces reserved for nearby businesses that usually didn't open up until noon on Sundays. Men searched for a place to park while women deployed vanity mirrors to put the finishing touches on their makeup. Once parked, the faithful hurried from their cars to the narrow cinder-block cathedral on the corner. The sound of high heels and hard soles clacking across the radiating asphalt parking lot was music to Perch's ears. He emphatically greeted every member of the freshman congregation with humble nods and handshakes before ushering them inside, out of the heat and into the shade.

The space Perch had leased just two months earlier had seen better days. The glossy vinyl letters on the outer glass, advertising the chapel was now open to all, jockeyed for real estate over the faded letters of the previous print shop that had occupied the space before going out of business. Chipped paint on the interior walls revealed a layer cake of colors from the countless other endeavors that had come and gone over the years. The fluorescent lighting was glaring and bright, revealing every stain in the ceiling and every rip in the gray-carpeted floor. Even the AC struggled to keep the mercury below eighty, but compared to the triple-digit temps outside, the church was an icebox.

Seating was another setback. Rows of folding metal chairs were packed tightly together, with barely enough room for five chairs on each side of the cramped aisle that parted the congregation right up the middle. The seats filled up quickly as tardy churchgoers squeezed into the last of the empty spaces along the walls where additional chairs had been set up last minute, right by the entrance.

It was a dingy, intimate setting, with attendees standing shoulder to shoulder as they waited for the good reverend to close the doors of the church and make his way up to the wooden podium at the front. The packed house had easily raised the temperature inside another ten degrees, and was likely in violation of at least a dozen fire ordinances. But the heat was something Perch had grown accustomed to over the years, and legal violations had never been much of a concern for the 56-year-old to begin with.

For the last thirty years, Jonas Perch, arguably the most profitable televangelist during the 1990s, had disappeared into obscurity, the result of a few inquisitive journalists shedding light on his deceptive late-night television program. For almost a decade, Perch's *Power Hour of Prayer* had reeled in thousands of vulnerable, disheartened souls tuned in to the late-night program, selling the susceptible a faux path to a better life through the doctrine of seed faith. By convincing thousands of elderly, disabled, and working-poor viewers that forking over every last penny was a leap of faith that wouldn't go unnoticed by the Almighty, Perch effectively got rich off the backs of the needy—while driving countless believers to bankruptcy in the process.

The once-youthful and dapper Reverend Perch had brandished a porcelain smile and a silver tongue built to deceive countless faithful devotees for almost ten years, but like all surreptitious late-night scams, it was only a matter of time before he ripped off the wrong person. When the chairman of *Action News Atlanta* discovered his cancer-stricken mother had given up on chemotherapy at the recommendation of "*that nice young man on television,*" the career newsman decided to use his position to take decisive action. A few months of investigative reporting and one hard-hitting prime-time special later, and the good Reverend Perch was finished, banished from the public eye and forced into hiding by his victims' furious family members, out for blood.

Anyone familiar with Perch's days of preaching for profit would have thought the scam artist had gone the way of the dodo, but from the looks of the standing-room-only crowd packed into the tiny space at the Spring Hill Mall that Sunday morning, it appeared the prophecy of Perch's foretold extinction had been a little premature.

He flipped his wrist and checked his watch, then greeted the last of the stragglers.

"Good to see the family this morning, Robert. Ma'am."

Together, "You, too, pastor."

"Did the Dixons bring something to sow this morning?"

Robert patted his pocket. "Got mine right here, pastor." His wife raised her pocketbook, smiling with affirmation.

"Wonderful. Looks like everyone's prepared to receive His blessings. Absolutely wonderful." Perch knelt down to speak to their six-year-old, Katie. "And did my favorite little girl bring her singing voice with her this morning?"

"Sure did, pastor," the girl replied.

"That's my girl." Perch stood. "Y'all find you a seat inside and we'll get started."

The new digs—along with the congregation—were a fraction of the size the pastor had been used to preaching to in his heyday, but he wasn't complaining. In a little over four months, Perch had crawled from the trenches of the forgotten back into the limelight. And his followers were as faithful as ever.

Salty beads of sweat covered the reverend's face and moistened his collar, a result of the half-hour spent greeting parishioners in the August sun. He pulled a handkerchief from his suit pocket and dabbed his forehead, scanning the parking lot once more for late arrivals. No one else coming—the sheep were safely in. He shut the doors of the church and walked inside.

The room was noisy, filled with the sounds of chatterboxes and whispered voices talking amongst themselves in pitches that would rival a high school lunchroom. The loud ones stayed on innocent topics: work, sports, whose kid just got married, whose kid was sick. The quiet ones, on the other hand, murmured seedier stories. Who got caught drinking at work. Who was about to lose his house. Who was cheating on his wife with his secretary. The lower the tones, the lewder the tales.

Perch gestured to a young man at the front to hit the music, and in an instant the voices faded into the sounds of gospel hymns playing from the loudspeakers up front. He began the slow and purposeful walk toward the podium, arms crossed behind his back, smiling at random faces on both sides of the aisle while singing along.

*Sowing in the morning, sowing seeds of kindness,*
*Sowing in the noontide and the dewy eve;*
*Waiting for the harvest, and the time of reaping,*
*We shall come rejoicing, bringing in the sheaves.*

The pastor bounced a fist with the tempo as he stepped up to the podium. The singing continued.

*Sowing in the sunshine, sowing in the shadows,*
*Fearing neither clouds nor winter's chilling breeze;*
*By and by the harvest, and the labor ended,*
*We shall come rejoicing, bringing in the sheaves.*

Perch nodded a cue to his young assistant and the music stopped. All eyes were on him, every face in the room eager to hear his message. A Bible lay open on the podium, the golden pages turned to some random spot in the middle. The presentation looked good. He clenched both sides of the lectern as he spoke.

"Nothing like an old-fashioned gospel song to ring in a service, is there?"

The congregation muttered a collective "*Mm-hmm.*" Faces were blank, but attentive. No nap-takers or songbook flippers or seat squirmers were present. The pastor spoke, and the people listened.

"There's a lot of wisdom in that song," Perch said. "I want you all to take a moment and ponder on the lyrics. The meaning behind them. What do you think the writer was trying to say when he said, 'fearing neither clouds nor winter's chilling breeze?'"

Silence.

"Was he trying to say we should only sow our seeds when the weather is nice?"

Faintly, "No."

Perch explored the space behind the podium. "Was the writer saying, 'Boy, it sure looks scary out there! Maybe we should wait till things clear up a bit'? Is that the message here?"

Louder, "Nuh-uh."

"Did the writer think it was okay to sow *some* of the time, or does a good Christian sow *all* of the time?"

"All the time, pastor."

"That's right!" Perch hollered, punching the air in front of him. The audience was getting riled up now, responding with a combination of boastful amens and bless-him-Lords.

"He that observeth the wind shall not sow, and he that regardeth the clouds shall not reap. Ecclesiastes 11:4. Doesn't matter whether the winds a-blowing or the clouds are a-thundering. Whether times are good, or whether times are bad. We don't get to pick and choose when the best time to sow is, because the best time to sow is *all* the time. Can ya say amen?"

"Amen."

Perch lowered his tone. "Now, most everyone here already knows how important it is for us to be sowing. But there are some of those among you"—he tossed his hand like a man feeding the birds—"who believe a little sowing here and a little sowing there is all it takes to earn favor with the Lord. Brothers and sisters, how can you expect a bountiful harvest when you're not even sowing enough to draw interest from the fowls in the air? Pretty bad when you're sowing seeds and can't even get a bird to bat an eye, ain't it?"

The audience chuckled as Perch walked back to the podium. Well, most of them anyway. A stone-face in overalls sat near the back and caught Perch's eye, but only for a second. Perch had never seen him before, but that wasn't much cause for concern. His congregation was growing every week. He ignored the look and moved on, flipping toward the back of his Bible. "Just listen to what Paul told the Corinthians some 2000 years ago: *He which soweth sparingly shall reap also sparingly; and he which soweth bountifully shall reap also bountifully.*" He closed the book and paused. Then he said, "The word of God is everlasting."

The congregation agreed.

"God's word never changes," Perch said. "It's the same now as it was two thousand years ago, and it'll be the same two thousand years from now." He pointed to the front row. "Tell me, Catherine. Do you want to reap a bountiful harvest?"

"I do, reverend."

Perch looked over. "What about you, Evelyn? You expect to gain something from heaven by sowing a little here, sowing a little there?"

"Course not, reverend."

"That's right!" Perch said, slapping his knee. The ebb and flow of the sermon was predictable. A song stanza or Bible verse was cherry-picked to make a point, followed by two or three rhetorical questions to raise excitement in the crowd. Once the melodramatic tide reached the high-water mark, the pastor let his staged spirit flow with a boisterous round of hoops, hollers, knee slaps, and fist pumps. Then it was back to solemn tones and soothing anecdotes, letting the tide roll out while taking a moment to catch his breath.

Softly, "I want to share with you all a story about a woman I met some thirty years ago," Perch said. "Name of Annie. When I first met Annie, she was in bad shape. Her husband had passed away, her health was failing, and the IRS was after her for several years of unpaid taxes. Couldn't really blame Annie for falling on hard times. 'After all,' she told me, 'my husband used to take care of all the bills.' That sound familiar to anybody?"

The women nodded.

"Annie needed help, and a friend had told her about my ministry," he said, lips curling into a smile. "Annie sought, and boy, did she find. I remember the first time I sat down with her to give her counsel after one of our services. I let her tell her story for the better part of an hour. Didn't interrupt—just listened. When she was finished, she said, 'Well, reverend, I've told you just about everything I know to tell. Is there anything you want to ask me?'"

Perch held a finger up. "I had just one question for poor Mrs. Annie. I said, 'I didn't hear anything about sowing, just a whole lot about how you've been reaping a pretty dismal crop over the years. Tell me, sister. Do you tithe?'" He mocked Annie, raising his voice an octave. "She goes, 'Well, I used to, but not for a long time now.'"

The congregation murmured disapprovingly—all except for that one solemn face in the overalls. He stayed quiet, arms crossed, bottom lip full of what must have been chewing tobacco.

"Now, I could stand up here all day and go on about how wrong Annie was to think the good Lord was gonna bring the blessings when she didn't bring the tithe. But I'm not gonna do that, because that's not the story of God's desire to redeem each and every one of His believers from the most wicked of curses: the curse of lack. You see, just moments after me and Annie met, Annie chose to sow a seed as a covenant between her and God."

"Praise the Lord," a man shouted from the back.

"Amen," said another.

"And let me tell you something: God did not disappoint. Just like Isaac sowed his seed in Gerar, receiving a hundredfold return that same year, so did little Mrs. Annie, just a few weeks into her new life as a sower and a tither. About a month or so after our first meeting, Annie got another notice in the mail from the IRS. But instead of threats of property leans and jail time, this letter came with an apology. Turned out the IRS had made a terrible mistake and actually *owed* Annie over $5,000."

Perch took off his suit jacket and tossed it behind the podium as a chorus of hallelujahs and applause filled the cramped church hall. "Now, some of you may be a-wondering," he said, rolling up his starched white sleeves, "Just how much little Mrs. Annie tithed that day. Well, let me just put it this way. Annie hadn't tithed in years, so she had a little catching up to do.

"What would have happened if Annie had only given the bare minimum that day? Really no way of knowing, is there? But know this, brothers and sisters: the more you give, the more you shall receive." He pointed toward the crowd. "Don't you want to receive *all* the blessings the good Lord wants to give you?"

"We do, reverend!"

"Don't you want your cup to runneth over?"

"Bless us, reverend!"

"Are you ready to sow your way into God's favor?"

"We are!"

"Hallelujah!" the pastor yelled with a confirmatory jump and a clap; a motion reserved solely for collection time. Perch's assistant recognized the signal. He hit the music again, then walked to the front and stood next to Perch, a purple felt bag held tightly in his hands.

The congregation rose to their feet. Men rustled deep in their pockets, pulling out handfuls of neatly folded cash. Purse latches clicked open in concert as women searched for their checkbooks. Parents handed their children money, then ushered them up front to make a donation. Everyone was ready to tithe, save one: the sour man in the overalls. He stood and watched the spectacle, shook his head, then spit a shot of tobacco juice on the floor. Only a few folks nearby noticed, but didn't dare call him out. The man was rough, grizzled, and for a moment it looked like he might have had something to say, but he opted to stay quiet. Instead (and to the great relief of many), he turned to walk out the door.

The rest of the congregation formed a line to the front. One by one, hands dropped cash and checks into the purple felt bag. Perch kept a close eye on every donation, counting the increase while playing the part of a man who didn't care how much or how little each person tithed. He graciously nodded to each person who passed, pairing the gesture with a soft-spoken "Bless you, child." Then it was back to counting.

The reverend's excitement grew in harmony with the swelling purple felt bag. *There's Evelyn's $200, and Catherine's*

*$250 makes $3,700.* Perch checked the line. The bag was almost full, with two-thirds of the congregation still waiting to hand over money. *Jesus Christ*, he thought. *This'll be the best week yet.*

Soon, Robert Dixon walked up, family in tow. The money folds in their hands were bigger than the smiles on their faces. Even little Katie Dixon carried a wad of cash, dollar bills bursting from her tiny hands. The assistant knelt down to accommodate the young sower, and Katie dropped in the cash.

Perch couldn't contain his excitement any longer. He picked up Katie and twirled her around, planting a big kiss on the little girl's forehead. The congregation whooped and cheered and cried tears of joy.

"God bless the little children!" Perch hollered. *God bless them, indeed.*

***

Jonas Perch sat on the edge of the bed and glanced over his shoulder at the empty space on the other side. It was nights like this he wished he had someone to talk to, someone to celebrate the prosperous service that had taken place earlier that day with.

He had thought once about getting married, and for a while, the outlook was promising. Her name was Bethany, a blonde, twenty-five-year-old presenter working alongside Perch during the *Power Hour of Prayer* nightly broadcast. Perch led the majority of the service, preaching his version of the gospel well into the wee hours of the morning. Once he was finished, it was Bethany's job to follow up with a call to action, urging viewers to give their way out of debt before reciting the telephone number enough times to drive a parrot mad.

A thirty-something preacher and a choir leader would have made a formidable power couple in the faith community. Unfortunately for Perch, fate intervened in the form of a scathing investigation followed by a fall from grace. When the coffers dried up, Bethany disappeared. It wasn't long before Jonas followed her into the archives of long-forgotten memories.

Still, things were looking up for Perch. He slipped on his house shoes and shuffled to the bathroom, following the narrow path of moonlight that shone through the windows. He flipped the bathroom light and walked to the sink, reminiscing on the earlier church service. He couldn't help but laugh to himself; just four months earlier, he had been wondering how he was going to pay the light bill. Now he was depositing five figures a week into the bank account of an ironically-labeled nonprofit organization.

Perch stared blankly into the mirror of the medicine cabinet above the sink and wondered where his good fortune had come from. For decades, he had been publicly humiliated; bouncing from one low-income job to another; forced to quit and move on to another gig as soon as someone recognized him from his scandalous past.

That was before Jonas Perch bagged Robert Dixon's groceries. The meeting was uncanny. Perch remembered how Robert pulled him to the side while the clerk rang everything up; whispered to Perch that the Lord wanted him to preach again; promised that if Perch would take a leap of faith and find a place to hold a service, that people would come.

And come they did.

Now, after thirty years in purgatory, the formerly disgraced pastor had risen from the ashes, amassing a flock of faithful parishioners who were more than willing to fork over every spare penny they could muster. With each passing Sunday, more people filled the folding metal chairs, more people singing Perch's praises, and more people tithing.

Every Sunday there were more.

The pastor shook his head, laughing, and opened the medicine cabinet, telling himself it was no use worrying about why things were looking up, so long as they stayed that way. He reached for the top shelf and took down a bottle, reading the side.

**PERCH, JONAS**
**OCULA 10 MG**
**MFR: ASTERIA PHA.**
**TAKE ONE BY MOUTH IMMEDIATELY BEFORE BEDTIME.**
**QUANTITY: 30**
**EXPIRES: 07/15/2022**

Perch shook out a pill. It was the last one left. Already time for a refill.

Cool tap water sloshed in the glass as Perch carried the nightcap to his nightstand. He kicked off his house shoes and tucked himself in, then leaned over to take the pill, washing it down with a big swig.

There was just enough time for a thought or two before the medicine kicked in. He closed his eyes and took pleasure in his growing bank account. If things continued along the current path, it wouldn't be long before everything he had lost was returned in full. A big house. A fancy car. A beautiful woman to fill the empty space in the bed next to him.

His eyes grew heavy as he marveled at his newfound freedom from that wicked sin of lack. The late 90s and early 2000s had been tough. He had spent the entire twenty-first century struggling to make ends meet. Now he was back. He drifted off to sleep, content with his second chance and eager to see what tomorrow would bring.

It was 2021, and Jonas Perch lacked for nothing.

# Chapter 1:
# Pill Run

The glass door hit the bell hanging above it, sending it swinging and ringing as a customer walked into the campground store. The hipster-on-staff emerged from the back to see a grizzled-looking twenty-something making a beeline to the medicine aisle, thumbing through the hanging packets before walking empty-handed toward the coolers. The man didn't speak, but the clerk would have recognized his trademark plaid shirt and worn denim jeans anywhere.

"Ronny, my man. How ya doing today?"

"Good," he mumbled from the back. He grabbed a Coke out of the cooler and brought it to the front, setting it on the counter with a grimace and a thud.

"You're not looking too good, Ronny," the clerk said. "No offense."

"None taken. Hey, you wouldn't have any ibuprofen behind the counter, would you?" The man nodded toward the medicine aisle. "Looks like you're out back there."

The clerk bent down and fumbled in some boxes under the counter, but came up short.

"Sorry, Ronny. Nothing here, either. Everything all right?"

"Just a headache is all."

"Ah, man. That sucks."

"Eh, it happens."

"Everything else going well over on eleven?" The clerk asked as he rang up the Coke.

"Yessir. Campsite's just fine. Could use a little AC, but other than that it's just fine."

The clerk laughed. "Yeah, I hear you. Well, look at it this way, it'll be fall before you know it." He tilted his head, then asked, "Think you'll be sticking around much longer?"

The man shrugged. "Who knows. Kind of playing it by ear."

"Well, I know you don't like paying more than a week out, but you'd sure save a lot of money by renting a site by the month."

"I appreciate that. I really do. But like I said before, I'd prefer to just pay a week at a time."

The clerk pressed his lips and nodded. "All right, man. You're the boss. Just trying to save you a little bit of money, is all."

The exchange was beginning to try the man's patience. His head was throbbing and his right eye was dangerously close to swelling shut. Every sound was amplified. The cha-ching of the cash register. The hum of the beer coolers. The chatty hipster. He pretended the pain was little more than a nuisance, but even the slightest of sounds splintered the man's mind, the migraine becoming more intolerable with each passing second. A sinister part of him wanted to tell off the know-it-all hipster for consistently nosing in on his business, but he knew better. This was the longest he had stayed in one place in a while, and he didn't want to ruin it. He mustered a smile, told the clerk thanks, took his Coke, and left.

***

The drive to the nearest drugstore should have taken

fifteen minutes, but rubberneckers along the northern California two-lane slowed the pace down to half an hour. But there were worse places to be with a migraine, the man figured. He could have been sitting in bumper-to-bumper traffic in downtown Atlanta, where the only scenery consisted of towering pillars of concrete and glass, enough billboards to block out the sun, and a sea of taillights amongst a nerve-wracking symphony of honking horns and squealing brakes.

Instead, he was following a pack of slow-moving tourists through the Six Rivers National Forest, where the only skyscrapers in sight were the endless scores of evergreens overshadowing the winding asphalt road. He was a few miles from redwood country, but the scenery was still remarkable. Short stretches led through dark tunnels of Douglas firs, blocking the sun from both sides of the road, the drooping limbs coming dangerously close to cars passing underneath.

When the road did open up, there was always a notable landmark responsible for it. A Roosevelt-era bridge crossing a whitewater stream, an aging span of concrete boasting a precarious view of spring waters below on a southbound rush. A mountainside carved out and graded to make room for a road, scraggly pines clinging to what little soil they could find between a wall of crumbling gray boulders hanging on one side of the road. A rural outpost marked by a shoddy country store, with a few dated homes scattered across the distant hills.

The drive was peaceful, almost otherworldly. A line of cars would dip into the safety of the thousand-year-old woods, going back to a time when the only footprints humans left were the ones beneath their feet. Then they would emerge again, back into a world of tourism and progress and human encroachment. The man appreciated the idea behind conservation, and was thankful big-city developers had spared this particular stretch of country so far, but he knew the backwoods had its drawbacks. He was, after all, in dire need of pain relief from the headache bearing down between his ears, and a store closer to his camp would have been a godsend.

At least he would get his meds soon. After what seemed like an hours-long drive, relief was in sight. He watched ahead as every car in front of him hit its blinker to turn into the Hardscrabble Creek Scenic Area. That was the thing about tourists: they could never pass up a sightseeing opportunity, even if it was a featureless dried-up stream (an unfortunate reality of longer summer droughts).

The last car turned and the driver floored it. *Five minutes to the drugstore in Hiouchi,* he thought. *Can't get there fast enough.* He hugged the turns and feathered the pedals, sticking to the outer white line and blowing past the slow-crawling cars moving in the opposite direction.

Soon he was out of the curves and on the last straightaway leading into Hiouchi. A mile-long stretch of clear highway lay before him. He pressed the pedal to the floor, reveling in the sounds of roaring tires, ascending RPMs, and the high-speed wind blasting the campground's hitchhiking gravel dust off the windshield.

The young man rarely got out these days, and for a split second, the impromptu joyride caused him to forget all about his headache. The momentary escape, however, was short-lived when another sound joined the speedway chorus: the whirling blare of police sirens.

His eyes immediately cut up to a rearview mirror filled with flashes of blue and red. "You've got to be kidding me," he mumbled. For a split second, he considered running. If he could somehow double back into the forest, he might be able to lose the officer in the curves. Then he could ditch the car and make a clean getaway.

All hopes of escape were lost when the officer's voice blared over the loudspeaker, ordering him to pull over. He hit the brakes, then his blinker, and pulled off on the shoulder.

The man rolled down his window. In his rearview, he watched the cop walk up, quickly filling the space in the reflective square on the driver side. Soon the officer was looming overhead, his silhouette blocking out the sunlight.

"License and registration, please," the officer said.

The driver nodded and reached for his wallet, pulling out his credentials and handing them over.

The officer tilted the license away from the glare and read, "Freeman. Paul." He looked at the driver, then again at the license. "So, Mr. Freeman, any idea why I pulled you over?"

Paul knew. The officer walked back to his car to run his license, and Paul cursed under his breath. *How could I have been so stupid? Speeding through a tourist town?* He would have kicked himself if he weren't sitting in the driver's seat. He watched as the cop parked behind him, sat in his cruiser, and kept his head down. It was the focused look of an officer writing a traffic ticket.

What a disaster. The traffic stop would mean the Freemans would be moving again. Aaron was oblivious to their new nomadic lifestyle, but Michelle had already declared the last move the last time she'd had to pick up in the middle of the night to flee one campground for another. He remembered the conversation distinctly: *No more campgrounds. No more hiding. This is no way to raise a child.* Sooner or later, Michelle had said, they had to return to the world.

Unfortunately, settling back into society hadn't been that simple. The destruction of Asteria's secret research facility in Costa Rica had been the break of the century for the pharmaceutical company—and downright devastating for those who had sought to expose the company's misdeeds. After counting on Claire Connor's connections to Costa Rican aristocracy, the cooperation of Atlanta PD's Dawa Graham, and the testimonies of a dozen former employees of the facility to bring down one of the largest drug companies in the world, it had all come down to evidence of wrongdoing. Unfortunately, a volcanic eruption large enough to capture the attention of the international press corps during spring sweeps left the outliers with little to go on. Tanner and Doyle's jungle playground had ceased to exist, the truth behind their actions forever hidden under a thick blanket of volcanic ash.

With no evidence, few witnesses, and a claim that would easily top a list of The Greatest Conspiracy Theories of All Time, Paul had decided to put his initial plan of disappearing into action. Of course, that had been easier said than done. Fake IDs. Social security numbers. Auto registration. Employment records. Starting anew in a manner akin to witness protection would have cost at least $30,000—and that was per person. No family discounts, no refunds, and completely out of the question.

It also hadn't helped that Paul had been the only breadwinner in the family since Michelle had taken her extended leave of absence to watch after Aaron, or that Paul's income was tied to the very drug company that now wanted him either dead or strapped to an observation chair (which, according to his friend Claire, was worse than calling it lights out for good). Their savings account wasn't bad for a couple of twenty-somethings, but without a steady income, it would go quickly. It was clear the escape plan would have to be on a shoestring budget.

Thus, the westward migration had begun. Over the last six months, the Freemans had traveled from the East Coast to the Pacific Northwest, staying at whatever cheap motel or campground was willing to accept cash in advance without asking too many questions along the way. Going into hiding was never meant to be a permanent solution, but Paul hoped a few months off the grid would give him enough time to hunt down the other Ocula outliers while keeping his family safe in the process. Problem was, they were short on money, they didn't have a single lead, and time was running out.

This situation was dire, but at least the Freemans had their lives. Paul empathized with Michelle's grievances, and he was tired of life on the run, too. But he also knew it would make a lot more sense to emerge from the shadows with a few aces up their sleeves, as opposed to waddling out of the woods like sitting ducks, ripe for an Asteria culling.

A car door slammed shut, and Paul snapped out of his trance to see the officer returning to the driver's side window. Soon he was greeted with a yellow citation and a stern warning. Hiouchi Police had little tolerance for that kind of driving, he was told. Don't let it happen again. Then the officer left.

Paul read the notice. $200 for 14 over. He rubbed his temples and cursed the bastard. Soon the officer pulled back onto the highway, waving as he rolled past the speeder parked on the shoulder. Paul returned the gesture and cussed him through his teeth while donning the fakest of smiles.

He started once more to the drugstore, already going over the ways he could break the news to Michelle that they would be leaving again. Nothing sounded good, because nothing was good. Michelle was right: they couldn't keep running forever.

But for now, they had to. Asteria had powerful CIA connections that were undeniably monitoring any and everything connected to the Freemans. From the moment the officer ran Paul's license, the clock had started ticking. It was risky enough for Paul to waste time going on to the drugstore before doubling back, but he couldn't ignore his migraine. If he was going to be of any use to his family, the pain had to be taken care of first. Then, it would be back to the campground to pack up and head somewhere else. Somewhere far away from the traffic stop. Oregon. Maybe Washington.

Another week, another move. And not one step closer to protecting his family from the powers that be at Asteria Pharmaceuticals. Paul had plenty to worry about, but a single thought dominated his mind as he pulled up to the drugstore, hand still clenching a freshly wadded yellow citation.

"Michelle's going to kill me."

# Chapter 2:
# From Bunker to Bungalow

Snow was sure to slow the fighting down in north Estonia, but it never came to a full stop. Gunshots echoing across the Bay of Tallinn could have been mistaken for the chop of helicopter rotors, were it not for the short bursts followed by silence in between. Explosions were less frequent, rattling the nerves of rebel factions holed up on the small island of Aegna about once a week. The conflict seemed distant from the island outpost, still wild and relatively isolated from the turmoil in Tallinn's Old Town: a well-preserved remnant of the country's medieval past that represented the boiling point of the War of the Baltics. Although the heaviest fighting filled the snow-drifted alleys and cobblestone streets of the ancient precinct to the south, everyone occupying the wooded Estonian island to the north knew they could be pulled into battle at a moment's notice.

Especially Claire Connor.

The abandoned bunker which Claire called her Baltic home had a variety of guests. Estonian fighters determined to hold off the encroaching Russian Federation. Civilians seeking safe haven from the fighting across the Baltic Sea. Journalists eager to earn the title of war correspondent, naively optimistic they would make it back home in one piece. The cement remnant of a partially underground World War II facility was cold, dark, and uninviting, but to the exhausted guests taking up cots between the concrete columns it might as well have been the Ritz Carlton.

Claire sat on her cot holding a flashlight in her mouth,

hands busy working on her camera, when a soldier smoking a cigarette walked by.

"Shutter jamming up on you?"

"No," Claire answered without looking up. "It's these damn batteries. Temperature drops below freezing and they won't hold a charge past a few dozen shots. A friend told me to try insulating the space around the battery compartment, so we'll see. Maybe it'll help a little, so long as it doesn't get any colder."

"Colder," the soldier repeated. He looked around at the hissing propane heaters spread in ten-foot intervals down the corridor. "If it gets any colder, we won't have enough gas to make it through the winter."

"I thought the U.N. was taking care of all that, dropping off gas and food every two weeks."

"They were, back when the rebels still had real international support. You haven't been back on the island long, have you?"

Claire shook her head. "Nope. Just got back from a six-week tour in Old Town."

"Then you know as well as anyone the fighting is going nowhere. Russia has the east; the U.S. holds the west. Estonians are caught in the middle. Voiceless and unheard. If communications weren't down, things might be different. But, out of sight, out of mind, right? To the rest of the world, our battle has long been forgotten, so naturally, the U.N. is pulling out."

"I'm sorry, Marko. You know if I thought a headline would—"

"Do not worry, Claire," Marko said, waving his cigarette. "The work you've done here has shown the world what's happening in our streets and in our cities. It's not every day you meet a westerner who is willing to put their own boots on the ground. That's what we Estonians call *vaprus*, Claire. Courage. Bravery." He punched his abdomen. "Guts."

Claire forced a smile. She had never been good at responding to flattery. "Who knows," she said. "Maybe the world will start caring again."

The soldier took one last puff and then dropped the cigarette butt on the floor, the heel of his combat boot twisting the last of the smoke into the cold concrete. "Maybe," he said. Then he turned and left.

Claire could tell Marko wasn't holding his breath. She had been covering the ongoing battle in the Baltic State of Estonia for the last six months, and in that time she had witnessed the United Nations slowly distance itself from the growing conflict between the U.S.-backed rebels and the Russian-backed establishment. With one side hungry for territorial expansion, and the other doing its best to abstain from foreign conflicts, the international community had developed a distaste for such proxy wars, leaving smaller countries like Estonia, Latvia, and Lithuania to fend for themselves. Sure, an international military presence could be seen in the streets—red in the east, blue in the west—but for all intents and purposes, the fighting was going nowhere. Estonians were in the midst of a perpetual standoff, with no rational end in sight.

And Claire was right in the middle of it.

She examined the camera in her lap; the modified battery compartment looked like it would hold up in the cold, but she would have to test it first.

She threw on her parka and walked to the bunker entrance. A guard saw her coming and nodded, lifting the large steel lever and swinging the heavy door open. A whoosh of cold air blew in, carrying with it a flurry of snowflakes and a vicious bite that drew a scowl from every person camped out near the entrance. She made a quick exit, and the guard shut the door behind her with a heavy metallic clunk that rang out into the otherwise quiet and snowy scene outside.

Claire looked out on the horizon while she adjusted her scarf. At first glance, the northern European landscape seemed serene and peaceful. The bunker entrance jutted out from a moss-covered hill, opening into the middle of a thin grove of pines a quarter mile from the rocky coastline. She squinted as she looked out into the whitewashed landscape, spotting the horizontal streak of dark blue water in the distance that was the Baltic Sea.

Not a soul in sight. Alone. Just the way Claire liked it.

The cold still of a gentle snowfall always took Claire back to her childhood, time traveling past years of work and travel and college and grade school in the blink of an eye. The moment the chill set in, she was back in her rec-ball hoodie and Chuck Taylors, back to the field beside her parents' house in Kansas, lying in a snowdrift and staring up at the sky, watching tiny flakes growing larger on their descent before landing and melting on her rosy red cheeks.

Her parents had always warned her not to lie down in the snow for too long; cold made the body lazy, her father had said, touching on his fear that his only daughter would get too comfortable playing outside in the snow, drift off to sleep, and freeze to death. Claire could remember the first time her father had issued such a warning before bundling her up and sending her out to play; it hadn't been ten minutes before she'd hurried back inside to the safety of the wood-burning stove. But after a while, she'd pushed the limits, lying in the driven snow first for half an hour, then a full one, growing bolder while beginning to think her father was being overly protective of his ten-year-old baby girl.

Then it happened. She remembered it like it was yesterday, lying in the snow, ignoring her father's advice once again. Cold turned to warmth, and although the snow continued to gently fall, everything else became quiet and still. Her eyes grew heavy, her breathing slowed. Sleep was irresistible now, a temptation she no longer fought.

*I'll just rest my eyes,* she thought. *Just for a minute or two.*

But instead of opening her eyes to the serenity of frosty flakes gliding down from the sky while she lay there peacefully, Claire awoke to her father's face mere inches away from hers, panicked and afraid, nervously tapping her cheeks as he desperately tried to wake her up.

"Come on baby, girl, wake up," she remembered him saying. She had fallen asleep outside, nestled in a mound of new-fallen snow near the creek by their house. Had her father not spotted his daughter's motionless body in passing between the garage and the house, Claire's snowdrift ottoman might have become her eternal resting place. It was the first time—and the last—Claire ever saw her father scared.

Every time Claire stepped out into the snow, she recalled the peace she'd felt lying in the cold and billowy drifts, followed by the fear she'd heard in her father's voice. She always found it strange how two contrasting emotions always seemed to mark the most pivotal events in her life, the order in which Claire experienced such emotions never varying, not once. Calm, then the storm. Any time an internal sense of peace and well-being overcame her, the alarm bells went off, with fear sure to follow.

That made the current state of tranquility that much more unnerving. She lifted her camera, scanning the perimeter through the viewfinder with the knowledge that the still woods could turn tumultuous at any second. She only needed to take a few shots to complete her field test, then she would know if her modification had improved the camera's battery life. Either way, she wouldn't be out too long.

*Just a minute or two.*

Claire slowly panned the camera across the horizon, the telephoto lens uncovering distant details like the charcoal-colored pine bark wrapping the trees, surrounding the snowcapped ruins of a WWII gun battery a hundred yards down the road. Everything seemed in its proper place, except for a fuzzy figure sitting atop a decades-old slab of concrete. Claire stopped, giving her lens a clockwise turn to zoom in on the object.

It was a Eurasian lynx, easily distinguished from other big cats by a silvery gray coat, black spots, and dark tufts of sharp, pointy hair protruding from the tips of its ears. The cat rested on its massive webbed paws, surveying the coastline from its perch near the battery ruins, oblivious to the bundled-up photographer nearby.

Claire sharpened her focus and took a few shots, wondering if the big cat would react to the unnatural clicking of the shutter. It didn't. She tilted the camera to check the battery: 98 percent. *So far, so good.* A battery that could hold up to a hundred or more shots would be more than enough, especially since she carried several into the field.

She switched over to high-speed shooting and shot some more, her stealthy muse none the wiser. She checked the battery again; the fix had worked. Satisfied with the results, she turned off the camera, bid the lynx farewell, and turned to walk back to the bunker, when something stopped her dead in her tracks.

An explosion.

It was distant, across the Baltic separating Aegna Island from the mainland, but still enough to send shockwaves through the atmosphere. She lifted her camera to observe the pillar of smoke rising from the capital city, casting a shadow over the centuries-old architecture on its slow climb into the atmosphere.

The cloud grew and the roar continued, Claire's peaceful moment in the wilderness interrupted by violent destruction and shattered nerves. In the short moments following the blast, countless innocents had likely lost their lives. But for whatever reason, Claire's thoughts weren't with the victims. They were with the lynx.

She moved her camera back to the pile of concrete ruins and was immediately relieved. Her furry subject was right where she'd left her, unflinching and resolute, watching the smoke billowing into the air along with the rest of north Estonia. The lynx turned its head to face Claire, big eyes staring into her zoom lens, unfazed by either the human trespasser or the fiery destruction on the other side of the foamy dark blue sea.

Claire stared back through her viewfinder, disturbed by the lack of reaction from the wild creature. Finally, the lynx looked away, back to the smoke on the horizon. She wasn't sure why, but the sheer calm of the endangered animal made Claire nervous and afraid. How could it be so composed? Why wasn't it scared or frightened or running to safety, like she would be doing if she weren't frozen in place?

Suddenly, Claire felt a cold hand on her right shoulder. She jumped and turned, expecting to see Marko standing behind her, bidding her to come back inside where it was safe and warm.

Instead, she was face to face with her Torturer-In-Chief,

Dick Doyle.

His face was a cold gray, eyes milky and glazed over. Claire looked down, horrified to see a crimson hole in Doyle's torso. A thin stream of blood slowly oozed from the opening and down the front of his shirt, the mortal wound delivered courtesy of the bullet she'd put there months ago.

"I don't under—"

"Claaaire," Doyle called out, extending a feeble hand. "Time to wake up, Claire." He took a step closer.

Claire stepped back, tripping on a stone in the road and falling back into the snowy embankment. She looked up in horror as Doyle continued his slow advance.

"Claaaire."

She screamed. "Get away from me! You're dead. You can't be here. Get away! Get. Away . . . "

Doyle closed in with a darkening face that was no longer his own. Suddenly, the gray and wintry Estonian sky shifted into a white coffered ceiling, held up by canary yellow walls soaked in afternoon sunlight. Tall windows on three sides of the room cast beams of angled light across the hardwood floors.

"Claire." A Hispanic man loomed over the frightened reporter on the couch.

It was Alejandro Aguilar.

"Claire. Wake up. You're having a nightmare." He gently shook her shoulder as she came to.

"Wha—where am I?"

"In my sunroom."

"No, I mean where."

"San José."

"California?"

"Costa Rica."

Claire sat up on the couch and looked around. Not a snowflake in sight. In fact, the scene was quite the opposite. Fans hung from the ceiling slowly twirled and steered the muggy air through the room, but did little to cool the place. Claire found it odd that a man of such renowned wealth and taste as Aguilar had never invested in an efficient air-conditioning system. Perhaps he liked it warm, she thought. That made one of them.

She rubbed the sleep from her eyes as Aguilar watched, sipping his coffee.

"How can you drink that stuff in this heat?"

"Heat? I was just about to turn the fans off—"

"Please, don't."

A look of concern arose on Aguilar's face. "The Baltics again?"

Claire somberly nodded. She found her tennis shoes by the couch, kicked off in her sleep. She laced them up while changing the subject. "How long was I out for?"

"Not very long. An hour, maybe two."

"Get any calls?"

Aguilar took a deep breath. "Just one, of course."

"Ford?"

Aguilar nodded.

"Jesus, what's the deal with that guy?"

"My guess? Señor Donny Ford seeks the companionship of a smart, beautiful, fierce—"

"Oh, come on, Han," Claire rolled her eyes, and Aguilar playfully backed away into the safety of the kitchen. The Costa Rican aristocrat had never made advances toward Claire in the past, even though their relationship had outgrown its professional façade in the years since Connor's investigative reporting had led to the recovery of Aguilar's young daughter.

Aguilar was a devoted family man, and they were only friends. Nothing more.

But 2021 had been a difficult year for Aguilar, one that had changed the man Claire once knew. When she'd contacted him in February, looking for a low-key flight out of San José, the man she had spoken to had been proud, upbeat, and confident. A man of industry. The epitome of power and success in Latin America.

When she'd called a month later, seeking refuge after the case against Asteria Pharmaceuticals had fallen through, however, the man she'd spoken to on the other end of the line had been broken and alone. Aguilar's wife, Isabel, had died unexpectedly of a heart attack, just one week after Claire and Paul had snuck back into the United States aboard one of Aguilar's planes.

The charitable aristocrat had still been willing to help, hiding Claire out in his mansion outside of San José; setting her up with a fake identity so she could move around the city without popping up on Yankee radar; and helping her establish a secure home base for her investigation into the remaining Asteria clinical trial outliers.

Aguilar had always been more than willing to go out of his way to help a friend in need, but Claire suspected that perhaps this time he was the one who needed support; if anything, just to keep his mind from the crippling depression that had come from losing his beloved wife.

Claire tried to press the wrinkles out of her T-shirt and jeans with her palms but the creases were there to stay. Falling asleep on the couch had left her a disheveled mess. She got up and shuffled into the kitchen, straightening her tussled hair just as Aguilar was fixing brunch. He stopped to slide Claire's cellphone across the bar to her, then went back to frying eggs.

"I don't get it," Claire said, taking a seat on a barstool. "I tell Ford every day: when I know something, you'll know something. And still, he calls. What the hell does he expect from me?"

"I already told you what he expects."

"Be serious."

"Okay then, let's be serious," Aguilar said, his tone changing from that of a playful chef to a more familiar no-nonsense businessman. "This man Ford is a showman. Business owner. Likes to be in control, no?"

Claire agreed.

"So here is a man who thrives on the spotlight, craves attention, publicity. And he's been hiding away at his friend's . . . What was it, David?"

"Dawa."

"Yes, Dawa. Anyway, Donny has been hiding away for months now. Away from the world. Naturally, Dawa isn't going to let him out of the house, because he's risking his career just to keep him there. So, Donny is getting a little, how can I say this"—he waved the spatula—"stir crazy?"

"I'm sure that's it," Claire said. "I just wish he would pester someone else for a change."

"You know, Claire, you didn't have to contact him in the first place. You've had a new life here for what, six months now? And no sign of these people from Asteria, the CIA . . . no one. Why don't you lose the phone and forget about Donny Ford? The man is bad news, Claire." Aguilar slid Claire a plate. "And look at this: right before your very eyes, you have a man who will cook for you. Give you room and board. Keep you safe."

Claire's answer was written all over her face. Jokingly,

"Since when have I ever needed a man to keep me safe?"

Aguilar couldn't contest that. He was just about to sit down across from her to eat when Claire checked her wristwatch. 11:30.

"Shit," she said, grabbing her bagel to go. "I'm supposed to meet someone in town at noon."

"But, your breakfast, Claire?"

"Sorry. No time."

She snatched her jacket off the hook by the door, then doubled back for her cellphone.

"And I assume there's no point in asking where you're going, is there?" Aguilar asked.

Claire shook her head no, then left in her typical manic, I've-got-places-to-be fashion.

Aguilar sat, eating his eggs, smiling, and staring at the door. She was a complete mess, he thought, but it sure was nice to have some company.

# Chapter 3:
# The Fugitive

Dawa's eyes were comfortably shut, deep in meditation as he sat at the front of the large meditation room in the Vajrayãna Monastery. Incense burned as smooth lines of smoke twisted upward before dissipating into a light and fragrant cloud spread thinly below the vaulted ceiling. Maroon walls surrounded a dozen of his young students as the group sat quietly on pillows with minds far from the material desires and afflictions of this world.

Dawa had drifted far away, too, leading his students down the path toward some unknown spiritual plane a person couldn't explain to another—it had to be experienced. But, no matter how distant he seemed, the slam of a car door outside was impossible to ignore. He opened his eyes and addressed his students.

"It sounds like today's teachings have come to a close."

The students collectively opened their eyes, alert and refreshed from the half-hour session. They stood and bowed, and Dawa returned the gesture. But as the majority of students left through the double doors, two stragglers stayed behind, whispering to one another and cutting their eyes toward the teacher.

"You ask him," one said.

"No, you ask him," said the other.

Dawa called upon the older of the two. "What is it, Christopher?"

Christopher was silent, and Dawa waved him over. The preteen timidly approached.

"It's okay, Chris. Tell me, what's on your mind?"

Chris looked back at his friend, then said, "Me and Thomas were wondering when we were going to learn about the fire within."

"You were, were you?"

"Yes, teacher. Thomas said he saw a video online where this guy puts wet towels on his back, then they get so hot they start steaming up. After like ten minutes, the towels are totally dry—all from just meditating. Another guy said he survived a week in the snow with nothing but a bathing suit by practicing the fire within. So, you know, we were wondering when we were gonna learn cool stuff like that, too."

"I see," Dawa said, rubbing his chin. He placed a hand on Christopher's shoulder and walked him to the door. "Do you remember the first time you came to the monastery, Christopher?"

"Yes, teacher. You told me to be here at noon, and then you made me wait outside for three hours in the middle of January. It was so cold."

"That's right, Christopher. I remember the day well, too. Tell me, have you ever asked yourself why I made you wait in the cold for so long that day?"

Christopher hadn't.

"You see, Christopher, when your father came to me and asked if I would accept you into the monastery, I already had a feeling you would be a fine student. I have known your father for years. He is a good man. A patient man. But I had never met the son." Dawa stopped at the door and faced his student.

"Do you remember our lesson on Kshanti?"

"Yes, teacher. Kshanti is a kind of patience, right?"

"Right. Patience leads to endurance, which leads to the

discipline necessary to achieve enlightenment. It's a marathon, Christopher, not a race, so try and have the kind of patience that you showed me the first day we met. I promise that, in time, the rest will follow."

Dawa opened the front monastery door to let his student out, just as another door was opening down the hall behind him. The echo of creaky door hinges alarmed both teacher and student, who turned to see a shadowy, bearded figure step out of the room and limp across the dimly lit hallway to one of the private prayer rooms on the other side.

"Who was that?" Christopher asked.

"Just an old friend," Dawa said, ushering the young student out the door. "See you next week, Christopher. And tell your father I said hello." Christopher nodded and left.

Dawa quickly shut the door behind him, then walked briskly down the hall to the prayer room at the end. He threw open the door, the knob slamming hard into the oak-paneled wall. Sitting on a rug in the middle of the floor was Donny Ford, legs crossed, eyes closed. The wanted man-in-hiding pretended Dawa's forceful entrance hadn't fazed the first few moments of his meditation, but Dawa wasn't buying it.

"What exactly are you thinking, Donald? Didn't we discuss you making appearances in front of the students?"

Donny slowly opened his eyes, silent.

"You cannot be this careless, Donald. Do I really have to stress how much I have stuck my neck out for you here? Keeping you hidden for the last six months, while every agency in the state is looking for you? Filing warrants ranging from questioning in a twelve-car pileup to two murder cases? I have put my entire career in jeopardy for you, and you walk around the monastery in plain view, waiting for someone to recognize you as the foolish fugitive on TV?"

"They're just kids, Dawa."

The guru scoffed. "You say that like it is a handicap, Donald. Those students out there have seen your face on their newsfeeds everyday now for the last six months, and all you have to say is '*They're just kids, Dawa.*'"

Donny raised his eyebrows and pressed his lips. Dawa had him dead to rights, and he knew it. Still, what could he expect from someone who had gone from selling out crowds of thousands to an indefinite purgatory, away from the limelight, away from the publicity, and away from human contact, save for a workaholic Atlanta detective and a recent acquaintance living abroad who never answered her cellphone?

Not much more, apparently. Donny had embraced seclusion for the first few months, mainly because he had to. Broken bones had a way of sidelining the haughty and proud. But after spending the first few months on the mend, he was almost back to normal, minus a limp in his step on the days his leg decided not to cooperate.

For the most part, Donny was looking like his old self again. And now he was growing restless. A life of hiding wasn't something the old showman was built for, even if it meant turning himself in. Such an act would likely result in a life sentence; murder suspects on the lam didn't exactly fare well in court once the law caught up with them, innocent or not.

With Dawa's involvement, the situation grew much more complicated. Dawa had put Ford's well-being before his own, and now he was paying the price. If Dawa couldn't rein in his old friend, Donny's carelessness was going to land them both behind bars.

*No good deed goes unpunished.*

Never had the Buddhist-slash-detective had such a hard time reconciling his two lives than in the last six months of his life. He shook his head as Donny continued to sit in silence, waiting for one of the teacher's trademark allegorical responses.

"Look, Donald. I know being shut up in the monastery is difficult for you, but until we make some real progress with the outliers case, I'm afraid you are stuck here."

Dawa knelt to Donny's level. "That doesn't mean you have your run of the place, either. When I have students over, you *have* to stay hidden. You simply cannot be seen by anyone; the risk is too great. Not just for you, Donald. My career hangs in the balance. Do you understand, old friend?"

Donny lowered his head and said, "Yes. Of course, Dawa." It was apparent Dawa had made his reckless old friend feel like a complete ass.

*Good*, Dawa thought. If he had to shame him into good behavior, so be it.

Dawa stood to walk out when Donny spoke. "I just never thought I'd be put through such a crucible, Dawa. First, Bill dies, then Marci—I worked with these people every day. There's just no way anyone in their right mind is going to believe I had nothing to do with their deaths. All because of some stupid clinical trial I never should have been a part of in the first place."

"You know I don't believe—"

"I know, I know," Donny stopped him. "But it doesn't matter what you think caused all of this, because we already know what the result was. People I cared about are dead, and if Asteria's not behind the wheel, then they're definitely riding shotgun."

That was something Dawa could agree on. Even though he stood firm in his belief that a concoction of drugs and meditation could never have been responsible for the deaths of Donny's friends, he did believe the drugs had altered Donny's state of mind in a way no legally prescribed pharmaceutical should be able to do.

That by no means washed Donny's hands of a crime. Ford had given Dawa his word that once charges were filed against Asteria, he would turn himself in. The Atlanta detective had considered doing just that the moment warrants had been issued, but a strong internal conviction that the pitchman was innocent had kept Dawa from doing so.

Now he was harboring a fugitive.

Donny went on. "Then there's Claire. She's the only one who's gone through the same crap the other outliers have, and I can't even get her to return a phone call."

"I told you she needed space, Donald. She has just as much chance of locating the others as we do. When and if she finds out anything, I am sure she will let us know. But you need to tread lightly, my friend. If you do not stop harassing her, she may disappear for good."

"Well, what else am I supposed to do, Dawa? I've been locked away for half a year, Ocula's on the market, and we're not one step closer to bringing Asteria to justice."

"Says who?" Dawa reached in his pocket and took out a business card, tossing it on the rug in front of Donny.

"What's this?" Donny asked.

"Look on the back. There is a phone number, and an address for an old friend of yours."

Donny flipped the card over and read the note, hastily scribbled in ballpoint on the back:

*Wayne Rider, a.k.a. Fenton Reed*
*724 Peachtree Street, Atlanta*
*555-9858*

"Your online pen pal from the Ocula trials," Dawa said. "Got a hit on his real name early this morning, just before getting in."

Donny looked up, speechless.

Dawa said, "Perhaps you could use a lesson in Kshanti, too." Then he left.

# Chapter 4:
# Running Down a Dream

The single-story cinder-block motel was right off Highway 79, a meager ten rooms sprawled across a modest hundred-foot stretch of South Georgia flatland in the middle of nowhere. Seagulls harassed the tenants unlucky enough to get a room on the far end of the building near the dumpsters, and the occasional gator could be spotted in the algae-covered retention pond in the back. The rural rest stop was dated, secluded, and barely up to code. A real magnet for undesirables—or folks on the run.

Managing a motel by the highway took a healthy dose of tenacity, grit . . . even an iron gut. Rooms were trashed nearly every Sunday in the fall (a result of college game-day celebrations running into overtime). Linens took a toll every spring as the pervs came out of hibernation to shed their winter clothes, looking for something, anything, to soil after being bundled up for the cold season. If tenants weren't breaking shit in drunken tirades, then shit was breaking all on its own—and the repairs were never cheap.

Thing of it was, Manager Jerry Kirkland thrived on the chaos, handling the druggies and the cheaters and the occasional dead bodies without batting an eye. The gray-headed Vietnam vet had seen it all, and there wasn't a soul on earth he couldn't size up in the time it took for that little bell on the counter to stop ringing. For Jerry, profiling was part of the job. Meth heads had a habit of covering their mouths when they asked for a room. Cheaters kept their heads down, unable to look the hotel keep in the eyes. In the forty-plus years he had owned and managed the property, the stone-faced vet had learned to spot the problem customers a mile away.

That might have been why he was so pissed, not so much at the young man he was kicking out of his motel, but at himself. He couldn't remember the last time a tenant had gotten the best of him—if ever—but now it had happened, and at the hands of a kid barely old enough to buy a pack of cigarettes. His raspy voice crackled from behind the front desk as a pimple-faced white kid stood across from him, his slender fingers nervously twitching with palms down on the counter, desperately trying to talk his way back into his motel room.

Jerry said, "Now listen, young man. I don't want to make a scene, but if you don't get your shit and get going, I'll have no other choice but to call the police."

"So it's young man now. Come on, Jerry. I thought we had a good thing going here!"

"Good thing going? Well, I guess you did, Fenton, considering you've been living here rent-free for the last month."

"But that was all part of the agreement, Jerry. Remember? You told me I could live here rent-free, so long as I took care of the grass."

Jerry looked out the window at the narrow strip of land separating the motel from the highway. Rocks and dirt. Not a blade of grass in sight.

He set two fists on the counter and leaned in. "I'm not gonna tell you again, son. Get your shit and get—"

Jerry stopped, his brow furrowed. He watched curiously as Fenton raised two fingers to his right temple.

Persuasively, "*You don't want to kick me out,*" Fenton said.

"My God, son. Just what in the hell is the matter with you?"

Fenton slowly waved his hand from left to right.

"I said, *you don't want to kick me out of my motel room. You want to give me till the end of the month.*"

Jerry's eyes widened. He couldn't believe what he was watching. He marched around the counter, grabbed Fenton's bag, and threw it out the front door. Fenton quickly dropped the act.

"Hey, man, there's a laptop in there!"

Jerry stood with the door open and said, "You got three seconds to get your scrawny little ass outta here. Count 'em. ONE. TWO . . . "

Jerry didn't make it to three. Fenton scooted out the door, picked his bag up from the handicapped space in front of the Mulberry Motel, and got to walking, unzipping his bag to check his laptop along the way. The old man watched the young con artist straddle the white line of the highway as he moved further into the distance. Soon, he was little more than a mirage. Then he was gone.

Jerry walked back inside and returned to the comfort of the lounger set up in the room behind the front desk. He kicked back and started to reach for the newspaper, but a thought stopped him halfway.

*How could I have ever been so stupid?*

He stared into the dark knotholes of the wood-paneled wall in front of him and thought over all the years he had managed the motel. Ages had passed since he'd first opened the doors in the early 80s, back when the paint on the faded exterior was as fresh as the newly laid highway connecting Tifton to Jacksonville. A lot had changed in the time since he had traded his dog tags for a set of room keys, but one simple fact had become clear: he had never let anyone stay for free. Not once.

Jerry had never been gullible enough to let a kid stay for free for a single night, let alone an entire month. What could he have been thinking? The kindness shown toward Fenton over the last month had washed over him like some foreign, charitable spirit come to transform the hardened war vet into Mother Theresa.

He recalled the moment he'd decided to sober up some twenty years ago. An all-nighter at the local VFW had been interrupted by a moment of clarity that had led him to his first AA meeting the following day. It was the sharpest his thoughts had been since making it back from Vietnam in one piece.

That was exactly how he felt now.

Clear and thoughtful. Not like the last month; a month that felt like he had fallen off the wagon again, a bumbling drunk who had finally come to the realization that he was being taken advantage of by a freeloading wiseass.

He rose from his recliner and checked the mini-fridge. Nothing but Cokes and sandwich meat. Then it was on to the cabinets, rummaging past the Tupperware and pots and pans in search of the strong stuff. He knew he hadn't bought a stiff drink in decades, but he had to check. Had to be sure.

He looked around the cluttered office, grimacing and perplexed. In a way, he almost wished he had found a half-empty bottle of scotch in the fridge, or a pile of crumpled beer cans lying on the counter or stuffed in the trash.

Because, alcohol aside, there was no explanation for the way a crater-faced kid like Fenton Reed had pulled one over on Vietnam vet Jerry Kirkland.

***

Fenton walked the shoulder of Highway 79, thumb out, headphones in, bookbag sagging low. The laptop, narrowly escaping Jerry's wrath, had been protected by a wad of clothes packed tightly around it in the nylon bag. It was a silver lining to an otherwise crappy situation. Had Jerry busted the laptop on the curb outside of his motel, six months' worth of work would have been lost.

A part of him could have been angry with his current situation, but Fenton had learned early on that feeling sorry himself was never going to get him anywhere. He had always been short and skinny; two attributes that had made living through grade school a trial by fire. Had he not developed the ability to make everyone laugh with his quick wit and sharp tongue, he likely would have been the victim of countless meathead offenses like death by wedgy or locked-in-locker asphyxia well before junior high.

His appearance could have improved, if only he had taken the time to make an honest effort. Drawn-in shoulders and long, dangly arms were easily fixed with the correct posture and a high-calorie diet. His pale skin would have likely been olive brown like his father's, had he taken the time to step away from his computer and out in the sunlight every now and then.

But Fenton Reed had never been interested in keeping up appearances. Instead, his passion lay in combinations of ones and zeros flying through sophisticated processors and flashing across digital screens at lightning speed. Computers clicked with Fenton in a way people could not. By his senior year of high school, his obsession had landed him in hot water. While peers worked on senior projects like volunteering at the local nursing home or adopting a mile of highway, Fenton had been raising money to fund a booze cruise by hacking into the local board of education and changing the grades of underperforming classmates—for a nominal fee, of course.

Fenton was far from a mastermind, but he had a knack for breaching sites with low-end security. He had considered using his skills to book a free room more than once; would have been nice to lounge up in a clean room while sleeping under the sheets for a change. But then he would have run into other issues. Fake credit cards. Fake ID. Security cameras with image recognition technology. With everything that had happened lately, he just couldn't risk it.

Instead, he'd decided to keep a low profile, sticking to the kind of motels that offered weekly discounts for extended-stay guests while he conducted his research.

In the beginning, disappearing had been easy. His parents were divorced, both living in different states. He had lived with his grandmother throughout high school, but had moved out to split the apartment rent with a buddy living on the north end of Atlanta.

That's where the situation with Asteria had reached its boiling point. Back when he had had enough cash to live comfortably on the road. Nowadays, cash was scarce, and charity was non-existent. *At least some things are still free,* he thought, *even if they do come and go.*

A semi-truck blew by, the gust of wind like an unfriendly nudge, reminding him to scoot over. He took a few steps off the shoulder and kept walking, thinking back on the last time he had seen his apartment almost a year earlier.

Fenton had suspected he was being followed for several weeks, starting shortly after his participation in a clinical trial that promised to cure his incessant insomnia. It began innocently enough. A familiar car in the rearview in front of his apartment building. Then the same car at work. And school. And the pharmacy.

Once he noticed the driver always matched the car, he started to worry. But despite Fenton's fear of being snatched up and stuffed in a trunk, it never happened. The man watched, and waited. And the one time Fenton worked up the courage to confront the man sitting in the complex parking lot, he sped off, tires chirping, as Fenton took note of the sign stuck in the back glass that simply (and unconvincingly) stated TAG APPLIED FOR.

The stalking carried on for weeks, turning into months. Eventually, Fenton learned to ignore it. He called the police a couple of times, but nothing ever came of it. The mysterious car always left the scene well before the cops ever showed up. It was obvious the only station playing in the four-door sedan was the local police scanner's Greatest Hits.

But everything changed the night of Fenton's dream.

He hadn't had a dream in years, a prolonged bout of insomnia preventing any meaningful sleep from taking place. (When he did finally crash it was from pure exhaustion, sleeping straight through without any awareness of the time that had passed.) That night, however, Fenton experienced the most lucid dream of his life. He was standing in his kitchen, fridge door open, staring into the artificial glow like a moth to a flame. The fridge hummed loudly, the sound consuming him and ringing in his ears.

The humming stopped. Then three distinct knocks at the door.

*Knock. Knock. Knock.*

He closed the fridge and walked to the front door. Light

beamed in from the peephole before being eclipsed by the figure on the other side.

"Hello? Who's there?"

No one answered.

Fenton leaned forward, a single eye peering through the peephole. Only darkness. Black. Whatever was outside was very close to the door.

Then the door came in.

Locks busted and wood crashed as the door slammed into Fenton's face, knocking him back and onto the floor. He lay there motionless in a pile of splintered trim and molding as the shadow of a man stood between him and the door. The man's coat was long and black, his hair high and tight. Aviator shades covered his eyes, with a face harboring a distinct mark on his upper lip, like an old surgical scar for a cleft palate.

Fenton propped up on his elbows, then leaned to one side to touch his forehead. He looked at his fingers: bloody. He glanced up at the man standing over him with just enough time to see a fist coming at his face.

*BLAM.*

Then he woke up.

The first memorable dream he had had in years, and it turned out to be a nightmare. *Some sleeping pill,* he remembered thinking. The event had rattled him so much that instead of sleeping in that Saturday morning, he got up a little earlier to catch breakfast at a local mom-and-pop diner down the street. It was supposed to be nice out, seventy-five and sunny. He figured getting a little work done at the restaurant might do him good.

At the diner, time seemed to pass a little faster than back at the apartment. Several hours had already gone by before Fenton realized his morning escapade had turned into an afternoon affair. He decided to leave, packing up his laptop and taking his time walking home to watch the drivers and cyclers and other pedestrians out and about while enjoying some of that vitamin D everyone was always talking about.

He was a building away from his apartment when he noticed a figure on the catwalk near his door—a man, tall and dark. The sight unsettled him, but he was still too far away to draw any meaningful conclusions. He ducked into a side street, opting to take the long way around and approach his apartment from the north side.

After a ten-minute detour, Fenton was trudging up the north-side stairwell that led to his apartment on the seventh floor. The stairs were opposite the elevator lobby that was central to the building; if the man was watching his room with one eye, he would likely be spying the elevators with the other.

Fenton reached the top of the stairs, came to the north-side corner of the catwalk, and stopped for a moment to catch his breath (which was a bit labored for a kid his age, but then again, this was the most exercise he'd had in a minute). He slowly peered around the corner, fighting the pain in his chest to keep his huffing and puffing from giving away his position.

One look down the catwalk and his suspicions were realized. A man in a long, dark overcoat, sporting a high and tight haircut, with Aviator shades, faced his door. Fenton squinted to zero in on the details. Sure enough, the man had a visible scar, right above his upper lip.

"*No way,*" Fenton said, apparently a little too loud.

The man turned and immediately recognized his target. "You! STOP!"

Fenton didn't comply. He took off in the opposite direction, busting through the stairwell door and flying down the stairs, skipping every other one on the breakneck descent. He had already made it halfway to the bottom when he heard the same door slamming open above him.

*Don't stop. Just run.*

He reached the bottom fast, but his escape was hampered by a snagged backpack on the ground-level door handle. He reached back to unhook his bag and glanced up. The man was making time, rounding down the stairs, one hand skimming the rails, the other clinging to a gun.

Fenton was winded beyond belief, but the sight of the semi-automatic was all it took to get him moving again. Adrenaline kicking in, he freed his bag and sprinted down the street—and away from his apartment complex for good. Within twenty-four hours, he was two hundred miles away from the city, holed up in a sleazy South Georgia motel, searching the Internet and wondering what in the hell had just happened.

That was almost a year ago. Now, Fenton finally had some answers. But, one thing remained a mystery:

*Why was everyone doing everything he wanted?*

It wasn't an exact science, by any means, but there was no denying that in the year Fenton had been on the road, a lot of things had turned in his favor. The Mulberry Hotel was a perfect example of Fenton's good fortune. Jerry Kirkland was old, crabby, and couldn't have given two shits about a nineteen-year-old computer geek who had fallen on hard times. Kirkland wasn't running a charity; he was a graduate of the Old School, living by a closefisted code of pay up or get out. So why was it that he had let Fenton stay in room 110 rent-free for the better part of a month?

The question was perplexing, but Fenton was starting to suspect it had something to do with his old Ocula prescription, the bottle found in the bottom of his backpack a few days after fleeing Atlanta (however insane the idea of a magic mind-control pill sounded). He didn't have enough to last more than a couple of months if taken regularly, so he saved it for nights when he desperately needed sleep.

Some nights, it helped. Others, it did not.

On the bad nights, Fenton was left with a debilitating headache, leaving a trail of sweat-soaked sheets on the beds of whatever motel he had stumbled into the day before. Eventually, after hours of excruciating pain and retching dry heaves, he would pass out from the sheer agony of it all, slipping into a deep sleep, eyes dancing rapidly under their lids into the wee hours of the morning.

Fenton was always surprised when such bad nights led to such good fortune the following day, but that was almost always the case. A stranger approaching him on the street, placing a wad of cash in his hands. Another offering the keys to his car. Even the owner of a motel offering to put him up rent-free for a month, all following horrendous nights of migraines Fenton had never experienced prior to the clinical trials.

All the following nights had been filled with fortuitous dreams.

He walked down the rural highway, pondering the strange sequence of events and looking up into the clear blue sky. An airliner soared high above, the shiny and silvery fuselage leaving a pair of contrails in its wake.

He thought a ticket out of the country sure would be nice. So would some answers. But, like the plane flying five miles above, both were far out of reach.

# Chapter 5:
# End of the Line

"What do you mean, we've got to leave?" It was clear Michelle was not a happy camper, but they didn't have time to sit still and debate. The tent had to be dismantled, the coolers and chairs loaded up, and Aaron's junk picked up and packed into the sedan.

*The sedan. Shit.*

Alejandro Aguilar had helped Paul secure the car months ago as a personal favor to Claire. Paul had hoped Aguilar would hook him up with the entire Walter White package. New name. New identity. Cozy little cabin in the woods.

Unfortunately, Aguilar had said the car was the best he could do. And the traffic stop meant the tag was now linked to his driver's license. He would have no choice but to ditch the ride.

*Shit shit shit.*

Paul would have a lot of explaining to do along the way. He started breaking down the tent while Michelle waited for an answer.

"That's what I said, Michelle. We can't stay here. It's too dangerous now."

"Why? What happened?"

"Traffic stop," Paul said. "I got pulled over on the way into town."

"What for?"

"Speeding."

Michelle deadpanned. "You're joking, right?"

Paul didn't answer. He wadded up the tent, then

crammed it into the back of the car.

Michelle grabbed his arm. "What exactly does this mean, Paul?"

"It means we've got to get rid of the car."

"And trade it in for what, a horse and buggy?"

Silence.

"What the hell are we supposed to do?" Michelle asked. "We can't rent a car, because we'll show up '*on the grid.*' We can't call any of our friends or family for help, because we'll show up '*on the grid.*'"

Michelle's use of air quotes wore on Paul's nerves, but he let her vent. "We've been stuck out here in the middle of nowhere for the last six months, and we're no better off than we were when we left. And now we have to get rid of the car? What do you want us to do, Paul? Live off the land like a bunch of fucking pilgrims?"

Aaron started crying from the playpen nearby. She walked over to console him while Paul hastily packed. Soon the playpen was in the back of the car, along with the rest of their lives, stuffed gracelessly in the back of a weathered Mercury.

Michelle watched and judged from the picnic table, bouncing her son on her knee while staring at Paul with eyes that could cut through steel.

"And what about Aaron?" she said. "Do you think this is the kind of environment we should be raising our son in?"

"Of course not. It's only—"

"Temporary? Jesus, Paul. How many times have you told me it's only temporary? Temporary was supposed to mean a few weeks, maybe a month, just until you could find others to corroborate your story. But none of that's happened, has it? You've been dragging us from one state to the next, with no way to get us out of this mess. It's no wonder I had to pay the bills, back when we had bills to pay. You can't even remember to mail a check from one month to the next . . . Why on Earth did I ever think you could take down a major pharmaceutical company?"

Paul snapped. "Listen, Michelle. We wouldn't even be in this situation if—"

"I swear to God, Paul. If you say one more time I had something to do with this, I'll call Asteria myself."

"Well, what other explanation is there, Michelle? I sure as shit didn't sign up for the Ocula trials, and you were the one always harping on me about my sleep. You even brought it up the day I was kidnapped, for Chrissake."

"Why on earth would I drug you without telling you, Paul? And where would I even get the drugs to begin with? For you to even think I had something to do with this is a whole other level of messed up. Really says a lot about your opinion of me."

"It's not that, Michelle. It's just that no other explanation makes any—"

"Just save it, Paul." She got up to strap Aaron in his car seat, stopping halfway to put her finger in Paul's face. "You know, you can be a real asshole sometimes." She loaded up the youngster, then stormed to the passenger side and got in, slamming the door hard enough to rock the car.

Paul couldn't argue with her assessment, but he did have a point. What other explanation was there for Ocula being in his system that day? The mystery behind his initial contact with the medication was the subject of every argument Paul and Michelle had had since they'd gone into hiding.

The evidence was intriguing, but still circumstantial. Michelle's concern over Paul's sleep the night before his kidnapping; the fact that his own brother had had access to Ocula after participating in the clinical trials; and Michelle's occupation as a registered nurse. That was it. Nothing concrete, no smoking gun. But Paul still couldn't shake the gut feeling that something wasn't right. Whenever his mind found relief by defaulting to the logic, it always drifted back to something Michelle had asked him the day he was kidnapped:

*"Did you sleep good last night?"*

Simple enough question, Paul thought, at least on the surface. But the more he thought back to that moment, the more that heavy feeling of dread and doubt would creep back in. It wasn't the question itself, but the manner in which she had asked it.

Not once. But twice.

Paul hadn't really heard her the first time; his mid-morning tirade directed at the blissfully insane drivers who made up Atlanta's rush-hour traffic took precedence over small talk. But replaying the events in his head, there was no mistaking the fact that Michelle had asked him the seemingly benign question twice. It was also a question she rarely asked, if ever.

Paul knew the evidence was thin, and to some extent, ridiculous. He wanted desperately to be the good husband, to believe everything Michelle had told him. But then there was that gut feeling, pressing and tight, like an unseen hand reaching deep into his chest and giving his insides a twist every time he was beginning to feel like he could trust his wife again.

So much had happened since the kidnapping that he could no longer discern between the truth and fiction anymore. If Michelle hadn't drugged him, then who had, and why? His brother Alex had been taking the drug; had he somehow dragged Paul into this mess?

Paul would start to believe there was a corporate

conspiracy targeting the Freemans, but then he would always recall something drilled into his head in statistics class: Correlation does not imply causation. Over 2,000 people participated in the clinical trials held in Atlanta, right down the road from the Freeman clan's old stomping grounds. And ever since their father's death, Alex had been an insomniac. It wasn't out of the question to think Alex had signed up for the trials, told Michelle how wonderful Ocula was, then loaned a few out for her to try on her restless husband.

For Paul, it made a lot more sense to think family members had been swapping miraculous little sleeping pills rather than pharmaceutical bigwigs singling out the Freeman brothers for illegal experiments.

Whatever the truth was, the lack of a clear-cut explanation was taking its toll on Paul's marriage. He picked up the rest of their gear, stealing glances at Michelle in the side mirror while he finished loading the car. He could see her flared nostrils from the rear—no question she was pissed. He closed the trunk and walked around to the driver's side, taking a deep breath before getting in. They sat in silence for at least a minute before Paul spoke.

"I'm sorry, Michelle."

She stared out the window.

"Look," he said, "I don't mean to make you feel bad, or accuse you of anything. I'm just as frustrated as you are. I just want an answer, any answer. That's all. I know we've fought about this a thousand times already. Maybe I shouldn't have brought it up." He would have reached for her hand, but he knew better. He opted for something safe. "I'm sorry."

She cut her eyes over at him, then looked out the window again, shaking her head. "It's obvious you don't trust me, Paul.

Out of all the crap we've been through the last few months, that's what hurts the most."

"You know that's not true."

"Do I?"

"Michelle. *Of course* I trust you."

"Okay, fine. Let's just get a move on, okay?"

That was Michelle's way of saying drop it. Paul nodded, turned the key, and put the car in drive. Soon they were eastbound on the same two-lane highway he had been pulled over on earlier that day; only this time, they were heading in the opposite direction, far from anything resembling civilization.

The dark strip of northern California asphalt wound through the valley between two evergreen mountains, snaking deeper into the Pacific Coast range just a few miles south of the Oregon state line. Paul had no idea where he was going, but he wasn't about to stop to look at the map. He just needed a minute to think. Problem was, taking a minute to think was Paul's answer to everything. More often than not, minutes turned to hours. Hours turned to days. And in the case of obtaining damning evidence to make a case against Asteria Pharmaceuticals, a minute to think had turned into half a year.

Michelle was right. Living in hiding was no way to raise a child (if their transient lifestyle could even be called living). Something had to change. Not in a minute. Right now.

Paul jerked the wheel and hit the brakes, taking a hard left into the rest area just before the entrance to the Collier tunnel, a tight intermountain pass leading into Oregon.

Michelle grabbed the dash. "Jesus, Paul! What are you doing?"

"Something I should have done months ago."

Paul parked in front of the information center, pulled a business card from his wallet, and hopped out.

He said through the window, "I need to make a phone call. I'll only be a second."

Michelle leaned across the seat. "Do you think it's safe?"

"Absolutely not." And with that, Paul walked inside.

# Chapter 6:
# Cloak and Dagger

"It's still a madhouse . . . is that what you're telling me?" Claire sipped her coffee, an afternoon pick-me-up courtesy of the outdoor café in downtown San José.

"Sí, Ms. Connor." Carlos Vargas sat across the table, forking away at *pollo con huevos* and turning Claire's stomach with every revolting bite. The portly government official was by no means a shy eater, but she hoped that what he lacked in table manners, he made up for with information. She winced through the meal, trying her best to listen intently without focusing too much on the sweating man's poor eating habits.

He took a sip of beer, then said, "Security forces have thinned out in the area, but they are still keeping a tight perimeter around Poás Volcano. Then there is the restricted airspace, currently a five-mile perimeter. It's been sealed off tight since the blast. The government's stance remains the same: entry to the national park is strictly prohibited."

"Do you think the restrictions will loosen up soon?"

Carlos laughed. "It's been six months since the blast, and they haven't found a thing. No secret facility. No bunker. Nada. At this point, security simply has nothing better to do. Could be days, could be months. My guess is they will hang around until the next national catastrophe, but who knows when that will occur."

"You can't call them off?"

"You overestimate my influence in the Ministry of Public Security, Claire. Calling off that kind of personnel would have to come from the top."

"Who's heading up the operation?"

"Gabriel Prado. But even he takes his orders from the politicians. Poás has been declared restricted to select security personnel only. Without a direct order from the president himself, security will remain."

"Dammit." Claire shook her head and looked across the street toward the Santo Paul Hotel. The white-stucco building wasn't the most welcoming in San José, but it was popular with traveling college kids on a budget. She watched a couple of young tourists standing on the sidewalk in front of the hotel's blue-arched windows, wearing hiking backpacks and reading a map. She had a thought, then turned back to Carlos.

"What about hiking in? The town closest to the volcano is only a two-hour drive from here. If it's outside the restricted zone, I could hike in from there."

He shook his head before she could finish. "You forget one thing, Ms. Connor." He tapped his finger on the table. "*This* is not the real Costa Rica. Out there, in the jungle, that is the real Costa Rica. The guards, the checkpoints . . . those are the least of your worries. You'd be completely loca to hike in alone."

She batted her eyes, leaned forward, and in her best Marilyn Monroe voice asked, "You don't want to escort me into the jungle, Mr. Vargas?"

Carlos almost choked on his eggs.

"Relax, Carlos. I work better alone."

"That may be, Ms. Connor, but you would be ill advised if I didn't warn you against going into the jungle alone."

"Point taken." She leaned back. "Now, did you bring what I asked for?"

He nodded, and pulled a manila folder from his briefcase. He slid it across, Claire lifting the corner up just enough to check the contents.

"Good?" Carlos asked.

"Good."

He cocked his head, then said, "Tell me, Ms. Connor. Why are you so interested in the situation with the volcano?"

She played coy. "Come on, Carlos. You said it yourself: there's nothing better to do. The eruption gave the entire north face a crewcut and took out a village. Why wouldn't I want access?"

Carlos smiled, certain there was more to her story. "Well," he said, standing up, "if that settles our business, I must be going. Whatever you decide to do, Ms. Connor, do be careful."

Claire lifted her glass and nodded, and Carlos left.

*** 

"You have got to be crazy!" Aguilar walked away the moment Claire mentioned the restricted zone. She followed him into the sunroom.

"Come on, Han. I could really use your help here."

"My help here? What have I been doing for the last six months, Claire? From the moment you called me out of the blue, my life"—he pointed to a family photo—"*our* lives have been utter chaos. I have given you refuge in your time of need; helped your friend in hiding; entertained this notion of some grand conspiracy, and for what? I have a teenager who never talks to me, and a woman living with me who is not my wife. Who is doing whatever she can to get herself killed."

Aguilar sat on the couch, head in his hand, exhausted. Claire sat next to him.

"I'm so sorry, Alejandro. I know how much Isabel meant

to you. How much Eva still means to you."

"She won't even speak to me anymore," he said, looking away. "Ever since her mother died, she's been distant. I call her school, drop by unannounced, send her gifts and letters and books to take her mind off everything that has happened, and she never replies. It's like I lost both my girls this year." He turned to look at Claire. "I cannot stand the idea of losing another."

Aguilar fought back tears. It stood as a general rule that in his part of the world, men did not cry. But as he sat in the sunroom and looked into Claire's eyes, he was coming dangerously close to breaking down.

Claire knew Aguilar had had romantic feelings for her for a while now, but unfortunately for the lonely widower, the feelings weren't mutual. She felt bad for the man she considered a good friend, even regretting some of her actions of late.

Calling him Han might have been her first mistake. She had always been easygoing and affable with the opposite sex; most girls who grew up tomboys were. The problem was that men tended to interpret her spirited friendliness as a romantic advance. There was no denying there were times it helped; flattery worked wonders when chasing leads. But this was not one of those times.

She took his hand and said, "Nothing is going to happen to me, Alejandro. But you've known me for a while now, and you should know better than anyone that I'm not going to give up on a story because it might be a little dangerous. I'm just not built that way."

She let go, reached for the folder, and handed it to Aguilar. He thumbed through a stack of eight-by-eleven photos inside.

"So this is why you rushed off earlier," he said.

Claire said, "Listen, I completely understand if you don't want to go. But satellite images of the park will only get me so far. You grew up here, Alejandro. You know the terrain. You said so yourself."

He shook his head. "Yes, I know it well. I grew up in Colinas del Poás. My father was a priest in the small village there."

"I remember you telling me."

He handed the photos back. "It's been years since I've played in those hills, Claire. I wouldn't know where to start."

She shuffled through the photos and found a group labeled 10°12'54N, 84°17'54W—BAJOS DEL TORO.

"We start here," she said, tracing the proposed route with her finger. "The perimeter holds tight to the base of the volcano, making Bajos del Toro a good drop-off point. We'll hike in from there, coming in from the west and sticking close to the canopy in case we need to duck for cover. That should get us to the base of the mountain. From there, you'll lead the way."

Aguilar sighed. "It doesn't sound like I have much of a choice, does it?"

"I'm going either way, Alejandro."

"When?"

"Tonight. At least, that's when I'll be leaving the city. I want to be in Bajos del Toro by first light. Should give me plenty of time to make it to the facility by sunset tomorrow."

Aguilar stood up and walked to the shelf on the far end of the room. He lifted the lid on a mahogany box and took out a revolver, checking the chambers before sticking it in his back belt.

Claire asked, "Does that mean you're going?"

"Like I said, I don't have much of a choice, do I?"

# Chapter 7:
# Dissolution

There wasn't an empty leather seat in the executive boardroom of Asteria Pharmaceuticals that Monday morning. Board members, all white and mostly male, sat and listened to Jillian Penn report third-quarter earnings projections to a room full of suits.

"Financial milestones set for the second quarter have long been surpassed by the continued commercial success of Ocula. As most of you are well aware, the period between March 1st and May 31st marked Ocula's first full quarter on the open market. The results have been nothing short of phenomenal. Following regulatory approval, Ocula experienced a higher than expected increase in new prescriptions, refills, and total sales. Conversely, competitors' Q2 earnings posting last month reflect a drop in earnings per share that can only be attributed to Ocula's record-breaking success."

Jillian paused as a flat screen rose from the center of the polished mahogany table. She referred to the mountain chart on the LCD screen, displaying two distinct lines: one red, one blue.

"The blue line represents the Q2 projections for 2021," she said. "The red line represents actual earnings. As you can see, actual earnings beat out early spring estimates by thirty-seven percent. Should the current trend continue, Asteria will be able to move up the proposed twenty percent budget increase for R&D from Q3 to Q1 2022."

George Sturgis sat at the head of the boardroom, half listening to the highlights. Q this. Budget that. It was all boring the hell out of him. Instead, he diverted his attention to Jillian's outstanding bosom—as ample as her lengthy presentation. He cracked his knuckles, passing the time taken up by the monotonous formalities while stealing glances of the only board member without a Y chromosome.

Sturgis might have seemed a distant and disengaged CEO, but that was far from the truth. A lifetime of trust issues had prompted Sturgis to seek out answers for himself long before the minions were scheduled to report it. The information so eloquently presented by Ms. Penn was news to everyone in the room—except for the man at the end of the table, who had been monitoring Ocula's performance on a daily basis since its March 1st release.

Not that he had to. The silvery-haired CEO had a knack for picking winners. The moment he'd heard the genes responsible for insomnia had been identified, Sturgis had wanted R&D's antisense program all over it.

Predictably, the game plan had had its share of detractors. Board members had voiced legitimate concerns; concerns that tended to worry people with salaries that fluctuated with rising and falling market share prices. A successful antisense regimen could still be decades away; research and development costs might not be recovered in time to pay back investors; consumers might reject a genetically enhanced sleeping pill in much the same way they'd rejected GMOs in other consumer goods. The general consensus was that the rewards didn't outweigh the risks.

*Spineless*, Sturgis remembered thinking. Jillian read on, a distant echo in Sturgis's ears as he scrutinized the faces of each and every board member sitting around the table. Some were visibly elated with Ocula's success, grinning ear to ear and pumping fists and laughing out loud. Others were more reserved, still smiling and nodding with enthusiastic approval.

All were overjoyed. All because of Sturgis; the only one with the balls to take a risk.

*Damn cowards.* He shook his head, disgusted with their reaction to a program they'd wanted no part of just a few months earlier. They didn't deserve a seat at the table; they should have been at Sturgis's feet, kissing his soles and praising his name.

*Spineless. Every last one of them.*

He turned his attention to the glass double doors. The blinds were drawn as a shadow of a man stood on the other side. The man tapped his watch through a crack in the blinds as he tried to get the CEO's attention.

It was his CIA contact, Colin Kovic.

"Okay, everybody. That should wrap it up for the day."

Jillian said, "But, sir, we haven't had a chance to discuss—"

"Later. Everyone out. Now."

Papers shuffled and chairs squeaked as members of the board cleared the room. Kovic held a door for the exiting herd, Jillian bringing up the rear. He smiled kindly, then shut the doors behind her.

Sturgis's voice resonated from the far end of an emptied boardroom. "Kovic, it's been a while. To what do I owe the pleasure?"

Kovic approached as he pulled a dossier from his suit jacket. "Traffic analysis at our West Coast station picked up a hit on a long-term target. Control says it's legit."

"Jesus, Kovic. Speak English, would ya?"

"It's Paul Freeman." He dropped the folder in front of Sturgis. "He's been spotted in California."

"California?" Sturgis looked puzzled.

"That's right. Driver's license was flagged yesterday. Apparently, Mr. Freeman's got a bit of a lead foot."

"Is he in custody?"

"Negative."

"Well, why the hell not?"

Kovic took a seat, propped his leg up, and bounced his foot. "Read the file, George."

Sturgis's brow furrowed as he flipped through the pages. Photos of the Freeman brothers. Claire Connor. Donny Ford. Bulletins detailing last known whereabouts and possible leads. Pages and pages of social security numbers, known addresses, and next of kin. A dense, information-filled packet of Asteria Pharmaceuticals' most wanted, prepared and served up courtesy of the Central Intelligence Agency.

"There's nothing new here, Kovic. We already know—" Sturgis stopped.

He read the memo highlights out loud.

From the Office of Howard Miller

Deputy Director

Central Intelligence Agency

Washington, D.C. 20505

Stephen Cline

CIA Station Chief

Atlanta Regional Office

Atlanta, GA 30301

Chief Cline,

Your presence is requested before the Senate Select Committee on Intelligence this Wednesday, August 25th at 8:30 a.m. This will be a closed hearing.


Respectfully,


—   H. Miller


"What's this all about, Kovic?"

"Project THEIA. The CIA's affiliation with Ocula, specifically the work that was carried out at the facility in Costa Rica. The new director believes Ocula 2.0 poses a threat to national security. It's rumored she's moving to have the program terminated entirely."

Sturgis laughed. "Threat to national security? A student of Doyle and Tanner's bullshit white papers, is she?"

"Something like that."

"So when did you find this out?"

"Cline pulled me aside this morning. He wanted me to personally deliver the news to you myself."

Sturgis leaned forward, eyes sharpened. "Why should I care, Kovic? Ocula 2.0 was your project, not mine. I told you months ago I didn't want my company affiliated with any more side projects. Tanner was the last. We've got our own product to worry about, and right now things are going quite well."

"It's more than that, Sturgis. There's been talk of a push

to have Ocula blacklisted from the government formulary. Ban it from public use."

The word blacklisted had barely left Kovic's lips when Sturgis launched his leather-clad chair into the wall behind him, busting a chunk out of the sheetrock and knocking a framed certificate into the floor. Outside, employees walking by heard the noise and jumped, then briskly moved on, remembering Sturgis went off his rocker at least twice a week.

Inside, Sturgis calmed himself. He walked to the double-pane windows and looked down on the city. The buildings below seemed small and quaint, like the decorative miniatures that filled department-store windows around Christmas. Cars were little more than rolling toys clogging the streets. Asteria's executive floor was so high that pedestrians couldn't be singled out; instead, they moved down the sidewalks like a single tapestry, noticeable ripples here and there, but for the most part, gliding along as a single unit. Every time Sturgis encountered an issue, whether it was managing a budgetary crisis or combating corporate espionage, he retreated to the window. It was if he expected the world to stop every time his own little world came to a halt. He would look down and check, and the result would always be the same.

*The world just keeps on moving.*

He shook his head. "I knew some shit like this was going to happen the moment she clinched the appointment. The CIA has always been a boys' club. Hell, runs better that way. All this new administration has ever given a shit about is politics, pure and simple. Can't make the tough calls, or appoint someone who can make the tough decisions."

Sturgis looked back at Kovic, shaking his finger. "Bennett wouldn't have backed out of an agreement the moment things became politically inconvenient for him. He was old school. Ruled with an iron fist. This Lancashire woman—"

"Lancaster."

"Whatever. Lancaster." He tossed his hand dismissively. "She'll never get anywhere playing the crusader. World's an ugly place. Nothing's black and white. You'd think these people running our government would realize that by now."

Kovic shrugged. "Politics aside," he said, "we're going to have to accept the reality that our cooperation is coming to an end. Now, there has been talk of an offer for Ocula's patent. Would have to be carried out through third-party channels, of course—"

"You've got to be joking."

"The CIA's budget is $18 billion annually, and that's just what comes from the treasury. We're not joking."

"You could cut us a check for half that amount today and it still wouldn't be worth it. And what about these rogue outliers, Kovic? Freeman, Connor, Ford . . . You're just letting them go? Just like that?"

"Face it, Sturgis. They've been gone for almost six months now. If they had any solid evidence of wrongdoing taking place between Asteria and the agency, they would have come forward a long time ago. Anything they bring up at this point is obsolete, circumstantial at best."

Sturgis faced Kovic, hands on the table, gray eyes staring intensely. "And by cutting ties with the company altogether, the agency eliminates the threat of being implicated in illegal genetic experiments in the future."

"Now wait a minute, Sturgis. It's been clear for months now that the new director has had plans to take the agency in a different direction. That news shouldn't come as a shock to you."

"Don't tell me what should or shouldn't come as a shock, you sawed-off little shit!" He pushed off the table and paced the room. "The only thing that's clear here is the fact that your agency got everything it wanted from my company, and now it's trying to shut down its only competition. I've been around long enough to know exactly how you sons of bitches operate."

Kovic raised his eyebrows but kept his mouth shut. He must have known Sturgis would vent; the man was known for his boisterous temper. Fortunately for Kovic, the outbursts were usually short-lived. Sturgis regained his composure, gave his jacket a tug, and held his chin up.

"Doesn't matter," he said. "You're one agency; not the end-all-be-all of the federal government. Ocula's not going anywhere. The good folks at HHS love it, the FDA approved it, and the DEA's behind it one hundred percent. If your sanctimonious director thinks all of those agencies are just going to reverse their decisions because of a little bitching and moaning from a career politician, she's got another think coming."

"That may be, Sturgis. Cline just wanted to give you a heads-up."

Sturgis huffed. Sarcastically, "Thanks. Now, if you don't mind, I've got some calls to make."

Kovic nodded. He opened the door to leave, then stopped to look back. Sturgis was already holding the phone.

Kovic said, "I have to ask: you still believe our research was a bunch of nonsense? That the director would go through all this trouble to ban Ocula from the open market if Tanner and Doyle were wrong?"

Sturgis put his hand over the receiver and said, "What I believe in, Kovic, is the power of money. That's all this boils down to. Rest assured, I'm going to get to the bottom of it."

Sturgis returned to his call, and Kovic left.

# Chapter 8:
# Kerry's Restaurant

The lobby of the First National Bank of Savannah was heavy on opulence, light on comfort. Roman columns formed a parameter around the vaulted main lobby, the smooth stone pillars rising past the second-floor walk-around to support a crown-heavy ceiling filled with octagon insets, bronze molding, and massive chandeliers. Dark marble floors reflected the affluent features that hung from above, doppelgangers of golden lights twinkling in the rich brown, freshly polished floors below. Every square inch of the lobby seemed built to intimidate the working man—while welcoming the wealthy with open arms.

At least, that's what Arlo Vaughan thought as he waited for the loan officer to call him into his office. He patiently watched as the old money walked by, hard-soles clacking, casting double takes in his direction before quickly looking the other way. He even caught a bug-eyed clerk staring from the teller window. Embarrassed, she turned away fast, knocking her coffee off her desk in the process.

It was obvious more than a handful of bank patrons thought Arlo Vaughan was lost; that the blacks were supposed to bank on the other side of town. He hated to think that way, and typically ignored the childish behavior of a few. But as the minutes turned into hours; as old money came and old money went; as the heavy arms of the giant clock on the far wall ticked closer and closer to five, he was starting to think he might be on to something.

Or maybe it was just his nerves talking.

Arlo wasn't the type to dress in a suit and a tie, but today was a special occasion. For twenty years, he had called the Port of Savannah his workplace, and for the last two years, working third shift as a logistics coordinator had been his responsibility. It was a demanding role, getting to work at one of the busiest deep-water terminals in North America about the same time his colleagues were getting into their second beers.

But Arlo wasn't one to complain. It also didn't hurt that third-shift pay was fifty percent higher than working the nine to five. The bump in pay had helped him and his wife Kerry save up enough money to put a down payment on a dream: a creole restaurant, riverside in downtown Savannah.

They had had their eyes on the property for years. Originally built in the 1800s as four- and five-story cotton warehouses, the brick buildings lining the riverfront now served two purposes: residential condos on the top, commercial property on the bottom. Restaurants, hotels, gift shops, and pubs stretched down a cobblestone street split by trolley tracks. The pedestrian traffic alone was enough to keep businesses going year-round. In fact, local support was exactly what had kept Mary Lou's open for over a decade.

The Vaughans had originally fallen in love with the southern-style restaurant on the corner because of the food, but after countless date nights and interactions with the staff, they'd grown to also love the owner of the eponymous eatery. Mary Lou ran her kitchen like a fine-tuned machine. Her business acumen, combined with an unwavering work ethic, had turned Mary Lou's into one of the most popular restaurants on the river. Everyone loved it, and no one wanted to see it go.

Trouble was, Mary Lou had little choice in the matter. One night after closing, as she locked the front door, a strange pain cramped her shoulder. At first she thought it was the way she had turned the key. The deadbolt was heavy, and she had to put some force into it. She shrugged it off, and turned to walk to her car.

It was the second pain that stopped her cold.

She grabbed her chest as the pain quickly sent her to her knees. She listed over and hit the street, coming to rest on the left side of her face, framing the cobblestone walk ahead of her from the most peculiar angle. It had just rained, and the streetlights caused the pebbled street to glow like river rocks at daybreak. Soon the scene began to blur, then fade. Within a minute of noticing a stiff shoulder, Mary Lou was dead.

Working six days a week had caught up to the old girl. Coupled with a pack-a-day smoking habit, it had only been a matter of time before her lifestyle took its toll. Still, her death had come as a shock to the tight-knit community, and laid a heavy blow on her financially burdened family. Her aging husband Harry had already had his share of ailments, and the medical bills were piling high. Now he had funeral costs to deal with—and absolutely no interest in keeping the doors to the restaurant open.

That was why he had approached the Vaughans. Harry knew they had dreamt of opening their own restaurant for years. Now was their chance. If they could come up with the money for the lease and the personal property, the keys were theirs. It was the opportunity of the lifetime.

The timing, however, was way off.

The Vaughans had saved up for years, but they were far away from being able to afford the overhead costs associated with setting up a restaurant. The kitchen equipment alone was enough to put them in the red. Stainless steel ovens. Industrial-size refrigerators. Tables and chairs and flat-screen TVs. Even the hoods above the ranges were a grand a piece. If Arlo was going to make this work, he was going to need a little help from First National.

He rested his hands on the briefcase in his lap and waited to be called, foot tapping, his patience wearing thin. He turned his wrist, comparing the time on his watch to the clock on the wall. Twenty till five. Bank would be closing soon.

*Unbelievable,* thought Arlo, *Or was it?* Come to think of it, he'd never met a banker he liked. He also knew banks were one of the few industries left that could still get away with dismal customer service. He imagined wealthy reps from the Top Ten Worst Industries in the U.S. sitting in a billiards room, fat asses filling Victorian chairs, laughing at the expense of everyday Americans. There was King Cable, sipping cognac and telling some whoppers. The Banking Bros. sat by the fire, counting their fees and plotting ways to add more. The Insurance Czar was the king mackerel, puffing on a fat cigar, quiet amongst a room full of loudmouths. No need for him to brag; when it came to billfolds, he knew he had 'em all beat.

The scene playing out in Arlo's head was the last straw. If they didn't want his business, he would take it elsewhere—simple as that. He stood to leave when a loan officer rushed out from one of the offices. He walked briskly to meet Arlo, apologizing as he closed in.

"I am so sorry, Mr. Vaughan," the young banker said. "We've been behind schedule all afternoon; I'm sure you know how it goes."

"Ah, don't mention it." Arlo's demeanor quickly cooled the moment the man extended a hand.

"It's a pleasure to meet you, Mr. Vaughan."

"Pleasure's all mine, Mr. . . ."

"Webber. Daniel Webber."

"Well, Mr. Webber," Arlo said, glancing at the clock, "looks like we'd better get a move on."

"Right you are. Follow me, please."

The two stepped into the office. Arlo noticed the sign on the door: COMMERCIAL LOAN DEPARTMENT.

His heart skipped a beat. This was it.

Arlo took a seat in front of the massive oak desk and popped open his briefcase. Inside was everything but the kitchen sink. His original birth certificate, the fifty-five-year-old document faded a yellowish brown; checking, savings, and investment records covering the last decade; a detailed list of assets, current value taken into account less depreciation. With the help of Kerry's meticulous pen, the Vaughans had put together a flawless application package no loan officer in his or her right mind could deny.

That didn't ease Arlo's nerves in the least. He sat and watched as the lender turned over page after page, jotting notes on some, licking his finger to gain traction for the next page after the previous scores had dried it out.

"Uh huh," the lender said.

Arlo leaned forward, hands crushing the armrests. "Everything all right?"

"Yes."

"Got everything you need?"

"Mmm hmmm." The banker uttered without looking up.

Arlo leaned back and checked his watch. Two minutes to close. He looked at the lender—the man didn't seem the type to work late. No sooner had Arlo made the assumption, than the banker laid down his pen.

"Well, Mr. Vaughan. Looks like we're going to have to

continue this tomorrow."

Arlo tried not to look disappointed. He asked, "So how's it looking so far, Mr. Webber? Everything squared away?"

"We won't know until tomorrow. It's taking a little longer than expected to get the results back from your credit report, but I wouldn't dwell on it too much. These things tend to happen late in the day. We'll have a better idea of where we stand in the morning." Webber stood and buttoned his coat. "Will you be able to come by, say, ten, ten thirty?"

"Of course, of course. No problem. I'll make it work." He donned a smile, but inside he was hurting. 10 a.m. was well past his bedtime; days like this made him loath the night shift.

Webber said, "Okay, then. We'll see you tomorrow morning."

Aldo nodded, took his briefcase, and left.

***

The drive home was a rainy one. Afternoon showers on the Georgia coast had a tendency to pop up without warning, and by the time Arlo turned down the two-lane leading to the south side of town, the sound of heavy sheets of rain hitting the single cab drowned out the radio.

*Fitting*, thought Arlo. He hit the wipers. They smeared across the windshield of his old pickup, the dirt and bugs and water forming a thin, clay-colored paste that was almost impossible to see through. *Even better.*

He rushed to roll the window down, squinting through the muck while reaching for a handful of fast-food napkins to clean the windshield with. After a few circular wipes and a soaking-wet arm, he made a spot clear enough to see through.

He tossed the soiled napkins in the floorboard and cursed the day. Arlo was usually a positive guy, one to keep his head up when the going got tough. That's why everyone at work liked him. He didn't complain—just got things done.

But what irked him about the loan situation was the fact that he had to borrow money to begin with. Everything he owned, he had worked hard to pay off. As it currently stood, the Vaughans owed nothing to no one. The house—while modest and dated—had long been paid off. So had Kerry's car, and his truck, too (although the latter wasn't saying much; Arlo had driven the same truck for nearly two decades).

The Vaughans had worked their entire adult lives to become two self-sufficient, self-made citizens with little to no debt; no bill collectors calling at 2 a.m.; no liens or foreclosure notices or threatening letters in the mail. The feeling of living debt-free was pure liberation, especially after working so hard to pay off the countless bills that burdened them early on in their marriage. Living without debt was a relief. A blessing.

And now they had to ask for money again.

He didn't like it, but he had little choice. Harry had even said it was now or never, that other investors would be along soon, that a location like that wouldn't last long on the open market.

Arlo hit his blinker and turned down his street. Suddenly, a dark, four-legged blur jetted out in the road in front of him.

"*SHIT!*" He hit the brakes.

The truck sailed across the wet asphalt as Arlo worked the wheel. He turned in the direction he was sliding and prayed he didn't hit anything. Finally, the truck skimmed to a stop in the center of the street.

He checked his mirrors and looked for cars. No one in

sight. *Thank God*, he thought. He could have easily killed someone, and for what? To dodge some damn cat or dog or coyote running out in front of him? He put the truck in reverse, backed into his lane, then put it in drive.

But he didn't move.

In front of his truck, about twenty feet away, stood a black lab. The dog was looking Arlo's way, panting heavily, but otherwise relaxed considering it had come dangerously close to being roadkill.

Arlo leaned forward on the wheel, face almost touching the inside of his windshield.

"Naw . . ."

He took his sleeve and wiped the fog off the glass.

"*Samson?*"

As soon as he uttered the name, the dog took off. Arlo hopped out in the rain and watched the lab run back up the street before jetting off into the woods. Then it was gone.

He stood in the rain and leaned on his truck door, baffled. His black lab Samson had died the year before, but for a moment, he was certain the old pooch had been resurrected from the dead. Big golden eyes. Slick black fur. Everything a black lab was supposed to look like, with a prominent feature that made him one of a kind.

Samson wasn't a purebred, noticeable by the cross-shaped patch of white fir on his chest. The top rose up just under his chin, with the horizontal mark extending mid-shoulder.

There was no mistaking the mark, but Arlo knew better. He had buried Samson himself the summer before, underneath the Spanish-moss-draped oak tree in the backyard.

No way it was Samson, but damn did it look just like him.

"How 'bout that," he pondered. Then he got back in his

truck and drove home.

***

The front steps to the old house creaked, and Kerry knew Arlo was home. She rushed to open the door, a hopeful smile bright on her face.

"Well?" she asked as he sauntered up the steps. He looked up, and Kerry sighed.

"They want me to come back tomorrow, but I don't know. I don't think they're too interested in giving poor Mr. Vaughan a loan." He walked past Kerry, and she followed a trail of wet footprints inside.

"What did they say, Arlo?"

"A whole bunch of nothing," he said, hanging up his coat and hat. "Kept me waiting till damn near five o'clock. Then some wormy little pencil neck ho-hummed around, stalling till closing. Maybe I'm wrong, maybe I'm overthinking it. But I feel like he's kinda hoping I don't show up tomorrow."

He stepped into the kitchen and opened the fridge, searching for nothing in particular. Kerry stood in the doorway, hand on her hip.

"Well, with that kind of attitude, what do you expect?"

He didn't have an answer.

"So he told you to come back tomorrow. Big deal. You go back tomorrow, put a smile on your face, and hope for the best. It's all you can do. If things don't work out, Arlo, then it just wasn't meant to be."

Arlo smiled, took out a Coke, and closed the fridge. Kerry always had a way of making him feel better; he just needed a little encouragement from time to time. He popped the top and sat down at the kitchen table. Kerry sat beside him.

She said, "You worry too much, Arlo. Trust me: after tomorrow, everything's going to be fine. You'll see."

He took her hand. "We've just been dreaming about this for so long, Kerry. And to think, everything comes down to whether or not the banker's in a giving mood tomorrow. Just doesn't seem right, does it?"

Kerry laughed playfully. "Honey, if I didn't know any better I'd think you were born yesterday. Who ever said anything about banks being on the right side of anything?"

"Yeah. Guess you got a point there. Still, I hate even asking."

"Don't you worry about that, Arlo. We all need a little help every now and then. And if we're going to run a business, taking on a little debt is just going to be a fact of life."

Kerry seemed full of sound advice on the surface, but underneath all that positivity she was reeling like a duck on water. They sat in silence as Arlo stared blankly into the kitchen table.

Finally, Kerry asked, "You working tomorrow?"

"Yep. Seven P to seven A."

"Lord, Arlo. I don't know how you do it sometimes. Are you going to come to bed with me tonight?"

"Don't think I'll be able to, sweetie. It'll wreck my whole schedule."

"But if you've got to be at the bank at 10—"

"I won't get any sleep. I know."

Kerry rolled her fingers on the table. "I don't know why you won't just take your sleeping pill. Situations like this are exactly why you got them in the first place."

"I know, I know. They just . . . I don't like the way they've been making me feel."

"Rested? Relaxed? Rejuvenated? Well, I can believe it. You've never been any of those things in your entire life."

Arlo chuckled. "No, it's not that. They do work, but they make me feel funny sometimes. That's all. Plus . . ."

He was about to tell Kerry about the dog he'd almost turned into roadkill; the dog that had looked just like Samson. Hell, for a moment he'd almost convinced himself it *was* Samson, back from the dead. But, he stopped short of adding another worrisome thought to the list.

She asked, "Is there anything I can do to persuade you to come to bed at a reasonable hour?"

He looked up from the table. Kerry was sporting her bedroom eyes, then a wink. Both had aged quite a bit from their first summer of love, but Kerry's eyes had stayed the same. Tempting. Seductive. The primal glance took Arlo back to his youth.

Smiling, he said, "I suppose I could come to bed early this evening. You know, for my health and all."

"Uh huh," she replied, then turned to walk in the bedroom. She cast a single glance back, and Arlo was hooked.

He stood from the table, eyes fixed on the hallway leading to the bedroom. Then he thought about trying to sleep at a time he was usually at work.

His bottle of Ocula was still in the medicine cabinet—for emergencies only. This was one of those times.

*Guess I could take that pill tonight*, thought Arlo. *Hell, what's one little pill gonna hurt?*

# Chapter 9:
# Bajos, Part Two

The road to Bajos del Toro was notoriously treacherous. Chunks of road broke off from the shoulder and tumbled down the steep hills to each side. Potholes were deep enough to send wheels flying off their axles. In some places, the narrow, cracking, worn-out strip of asphalt connecting San José with the rural farmland to the north seemed less like a road and more like a vehicular graveyard; the rusted cars and rotting ox carts of the less fortunate coming to their final resting places at the bottom of the hills below.

Fortunately, Alejandro knew the road well. He drove while Claire rode shotgun, keeping her eyes peeled for wandering cattle and other pitfalls. One glance over at her and he couldn't help but smile. A man of his caliber always had a security detail close by; it was an occupational necessity in Central America. But with his daughter away at private school, he had been able to ask security to sit this one out, embarking on a two-day getaway alone with his Yankee crush in the passenger seat.

They crested a hill and watched as the last orange trace of sunlight peeked through the clouds before falling below the mountaintops to the west. Alejandro noted the time. It would be dark soon, and this was no road to be on at night.

Claire asked, "What do you think—ten, fifteen minutes?"

"Sooner. This road rides the ridgeline all the way into Bajo"—he made a downward motion with his hand—"and we're already heading down. Should be getting close."

She nodded and turned to look out the window. The scene was like watching a movie in letterbox, clouds capping the top of the frame, rolling green hills speckled with ceiba trees and high grass at the bottom, and the last light from a setting sun right in the middle. She had only been in the area once in her life, passing through in the opposite direction with nothing but moonlight to show off the rural landscape. The scene then was much different.

It was then that she thought about Roberto; the third wheel in the back seat who had abruptly woken her up while making his midnight escape. She wondered if he'd made it out of the jungle; if he was one of the facility technicians who'd raised such a fuss with the media in San José; if he really had told them everything he knew about Ocula 2.0.

*Doubtful*, she thought. An innocent scientist would have had every reason to stick with the escapees to San José—only a guilty party would have bailed like that. Not to mention the countless tails Claire had had to shake in Atlanta. Someone had tipped off Tanner's henchmen, and Roberto fit the bill better than anyone.

They rounded a blind curve as Claire looked ahead, just in time to see a cow standing in the middle of the road.

"*HAN!*"

Aguilar jerked the wheel and cursed, tires screeching, the momentum throwing him shoulder-first into the door. Claire grabbed the dash as the suburban rocked left, then right, before righting itself on the southbound side of an oblivious cow.

Aguilar stopped the car and wiped his forehead. He turned to Claire. "It really is a nice drive, no?"

Claire sighed and shook her head while Aguilar's nervous laugh played off his excitement. He slowed the car to take a breather, then pointed ahead.

"Look."

The small mountain town of Bajos del Toro lay in the valley just down the road, a modest enclave of rural homes surrounded by barbed-wire fences and farmland. They had arrived.

***

"How do you know this person again?" Claire asked, referring to the red board-and-batten farmhouse a hundred yards down a driveway of gravel and mud.

"He works for me."

"Up here? Doing what?"

"Exports."

She raised an eyebrow.

"Nothing illegal about exports, Claire."

She put up her hands. "Okay, okay. No need to get testy here." They pulled up to the house. It looked empty.

"So, where's the homeowner?"

"Exporting." He parked and jumped out, retrieving their bags from the back before Claire had a chance to finish an irritating game of twenty questions. He walked with her to the front door, quietly wondering if there was a journalist out there who could settle for not knowing everything about everybody.

The farmhouse was a structural patchwork, built with whatever building materials were available at the time. A tin gable roof covered the house; asphalt shingles hung over the porch. Barkless log pillars held up the exposed rafters of the crooked porch, the smell of motor oil heavy the moment their feet hit hardwoods.

Aguilar noticed Claire's nose crinkling. He said, "Motor oil, mixed with a little gas. It preserves the wood."

"Jesus. That seems incredibly . . . stupid. You didn't bring any cigars, did you?"

"No. I assure you, Claire. It's fine."

They stepped inside. Aguilar set the bags down by the door and found a light switch.

"You sure we've got Internet access here?" Claire asked.

"Of course. Would be kind of hard to talk to Miguel without it." He looked around the large main room, dimly lit, with the wall studs showing. Puzzled, he said, "Although, I'm not sure where the router is."

"I'll let you hop on that," Claire said. "I'm going to break these images back out. We need to go over everything a couple of times before heading out first thing in the morning."

Aguilar nodded and commenced the search for a line out while Claire cleaned off a place on the table for them to plan their route. She lined up the satellite images, piecing together a mosaic that collectively displayed the entire Poás Volcano National Park from 10,000 feet.

The photos were dense with information. Security patrols were outlined and categorized by foot, vehicle, and air. Naturally, the roads were off-limits, with Costa Rican police setting up checkpoints north of the town. Outposts were marked with red squares, with each zone transparently colored red, yellow, or green. Red zones were hot. Green zones were not.

Claire noticed an S-shaped strip to the west of the volcano; the green zone marked the safest route. She called Aguilar over.

"What do you think about this, Han?"

He looked over the images and cupped his chin in his hand. The bottom-right photo featured a legend, complete with dates, coordinates, and a map scale.

"Hmmm." He laid his index finger by the scale. "If it's a mile to my knuckle"—he used his finger as a ruler—"then it's at least seven miles to the facility. In this kind of terrain, that could take a full day. Even longer if we get held up by patrols."

"I never said it was going to be a cakewalk."

"Yes, I know."

"Do you think the route is legit?"

"Appears to be," Aguilar said. "Moving southeast into the park puts us away from the heavy patrols to the north and into the trees. We can follow the creek here to the west side of the volcano before cutting north. If we avoid these clearings here, we should be okay."

He paused, then said, "This is good intel. Who is your source in the state department?"

Claire smiled. "You know a good journalist never reveals a source."

"Right . . ."

She changed the subject. "Is the Wi-Fi hooked up yet?"

Aguilar looked toward the living room. A solid green LED lit up a white box by the TV.

"Looks like it." Claire's phone screeched out three chimes in succession. Aguilar said, "Sounds like it, too." He grabbed his backpack and stepped into the living room, checking his gear for tomorrow's hike.

Claire checked her phone. Three missed calls from three different numbers. No messages.

"Hey, Alejandro. You wouldn't know where a 530 area code is from, would you?"

He shook his head no.

Just then, her phone rang. It was a 541 number.

"What the hell?"

"Better answer while you can. Going to be phones off for the next few days."

Claire nodded and answered. The voice on the other end of the line was anxious.

"Hello?"

"Claire? Thank *God* you finally answered."

She almost didn't recognize his voice.

"Paul? Is that really you?" She put her hand over the phone and motioned to Aguilar that she was stepping out. He looked up and nodded, then went back to packing.

Claire walked out on the porch and found a post to lean on. Then she said, "I haven't heard from you in months, Paul. What's going on?"

"We can't run anymore," he said.

*You couldn't run in the first place,* thought Claire. She asked, "Has something happened?"

"I got pulled over. Six Rivers National Forest."

"Okay . . ."

"Northern California. We've been lying low, trying our best to stay off the grid. Camping. Cheap motels. Even slept in the car more nights than I can remember." He took a breath, then said, "That was before I was pulled over today. First time I've had to show my license to anyone in months—"

"And you're worried you're on the radar now."

"Exactly."

"I'm not sure what you want me to say here."

"You don't have to say anything." There was a pause, then Paul said, "Look. I know I should've stayed in touch. Tried to help out in some way. It's just—my family, Claire. These people tried to kill us, and all I could think about was keeping them safe. Away from Atlanta. From Asteria—"

"You don't have to explain yourself, Paul," she said. "Everyone ran. After the volcano exploded, we had nothing to take to court—or to the public. Just a handful of technicians who were quickly labeled by the Costa Rican government as quacks. We had to split up. It was our only move. But, it would have been nice if you had kept the burner phone I gave you."

"What can I say, Claire? I had every reason to be paranoid, then and now."

Paul's voice was riddled with apprehension, but Claire was calm and collected. "You've got nothing to worry about, Paul."

"Nothing to worry about? Have you lost your mind?"

Claire pulled the phone away, giving Paul's piercing comment somewhere to go besides her inner ear.

She said, "Hear me out. I'm not telling you to go back to Atlanta. Sturgis still has reason to worry about the missing outliers, and he may have his own people working the case. But as far as being a national fugitive is concerned, you really shouldn't fret."

Claire looked up to see Aguilar walking toward the screen door. She turned away. "Listen, I can't get into the details now, so you're just going to have to trust me."

Paul was silent. Was he following along? She didn't know, but she had to wrap it up quick. "There's something I've got to do tomorrow. Something big. If you don't hear from me in thirty-six hours, promise me you'll get in touch with this man."

Aguilar opened the screen. "Everything okay out here, Claire?"

She turned. "Everything's fine. I'll just be a minute."

Suspiciously, he nodded and walked back inside.

Claire said, "Paul. Did you get the name?"

"Yeah, I've got it. But how are you going to contact me? I can't exactly wait for two days by a rest-stop payphone."

*Right,* Claire thought, gently smacking her forehead. "Do you still have Ford's number?"

"Yep, unfortunately."

"Get in touch with Ford. I'll call him to check in. Sound like a plan?"

"Sure. I'll do it for you." He let out a heavy sigh, then said, "Hey, Claire. Whatever it is you're about to do, take care of yourself, okay?"

"You don't have to worry about me, Paul. But thanks."

She hung up the phone and walked back inside.

# Chapter 10:
# Crisis of Faith

"Fenton? Man, I haven't seen him in like a year." Fenton's ex-roommate Teddy spoke through a cracked apartment door while Dawa Graham took notes.

"And you said he was spooked in the days leading up to his disappearance. Why?"

"Something about being followed." Nervously, the stoner looked back into his living room, then to Dawa. The detective's eyes were dark and tired. Teddy said, "I already told the police everything I knew when he disappeared. I mean, don't you need like a warrant or something?"

"Would you like me to call a judge and get a warrant, or would you rather just get what I asked for?"

Teddy nodded and disappeared into a hazy apartment. Dawa tilted his head to the side, peering past the gold chain lock and into the living room. A girl lay on the couch playing video games, wearing nothing but her underwear and a headset.

Dawa checked his watch: 10 a.m. on a Tuesday. *What is wrong with some kids today? Can they not see past their own temporary enjoyment?* He thought about the dark side of things he encountered almost daily, and then he thought about the light. His students came to mind. They were on the right path, for the most part. Thomas could be troublesome, but he was still young and had much to learn.

Perhaps that was the difference between getting high on a Tuesday and living a fulfilling life: the pursuit of wisdom. The desire to seek knowledge. Striving daily to become a better human being.

The pale millennial unlatched the chain and opened the door just enough to stick a shoebox through.

"Here's everything that's left of Fenton's," Teddy said, handing the box to Dawa. "His family got most of his stuff last year, but they didn't seem to care too much about his old hard drives."

Dawa's brows drew together. Teddy explained, "I think they were convinced he just took off. Never seemed to care about finding him; just came for his clothes and TV and left. I think they thought computers were part of his problem. Fenton was kinda weird, man, so I get it."

"How was he weird?"

"You know, man. Like he would always be up all night hacking or whatever." His eyes widened. "I mean, not like illegal stuff, just—you know, on the computer all night."

Dawa anxiously shook his head. *Move it along, young stoner. Time is of the essence.*

"Then he was in some drug trial," Teddy said. "He was having these nightmares—said it was because of the drug company. So he started trying to go without sleep. Man, that guy looked like a walking zombie for weeks. Was saying shit like people were out to get him. Then one day he just disappeared. Haven't seen him since."

"No idea where he would have gone?"

"Dude, didn't I, like, *just* tell you?"

"Actually, you didn't." Mockingly, "You, like, *just* told me you hadn't seen him since."

"Whatever, man. You've got the box. That's all I know, okay?"

That was one thing Dawa could agree on. He thanked Teddy for his time, then walked back to the empty elevator bank on the seventh floor.

The private ride down gave Dawa a moment to check out the shoebox. He opened the lid and looked inside. It was a jumbled mess. Old hard drives. Batteries. Precision screwdrivers. Photos and papers and three packs of sunflower seeds. It appeared to be little more than a box of junk. He sorted through the contents and found the bottom. He felt something hard and rectangular under a wad of papers.

A flash drive.

Dawa looked it over, then slipped it into his shirt pocket as the elevator chimed and opened. He walked back to his car and debated whether or not he should head home. A homicide had kept him up most the night, and he was only a couple of miles away from the office. He could catch a quick nap there before his shift, or risk sitting in traffic for the next two hours trying to get home. It was a decision he had to make far too often—especially when people decided to shoot one another in the middle of the night.

By the time he got to his car, his mind was made up. Even if he hit traffic, he rationalized, a few hours in his own bed beat a yoga mat behind his desk any day of the week.

He caught a glimpse of his reflection in the window as he unlocked the door. Boy, did he look tired. He hadn't shaved in three days, the gray hairs on his head crowded out the black, and dark circles under his eyes looked painted on. His spiritual temple was crumbling. Between work, his students, and harboring a fugitive, life was taking a heavy toll.

The shocks sank a little more than Dawa would have liked as he got in the car. He had always been a stress eater. And for the last six months, he'd had plenty to be stressed about. He sat staring through the windshield at the blur of traffic whooshing by the apartments, and thought about the fourth precept.

*I vow to avoid false speech.*

Technically, Dawa had not violated the precept by hiding his friend. But the way things were going, it was only a matter of time. He thought about a story his mother had taught him growing up. How a young man was called into his village to testify about his knowledge of a crime. Rather than elaborate on the details, he resolved to state that either he had knowledge of the crime, or he did not. By omitting the truth, he walked the technical line of the fourth precept, but stopped short of being a reliable steward of honesty.

This was no path to enlightenment. Living by the fourth precept meant speaking with honesty and promoting trust; avoiding the kind of false speech that bred hostility and affliction; having the strength to speak out in defense of the truth—even when it meant putting one's own life and well-being in harm's way.

Did that mean he was in serious violation of the very precepts he had devoted his life to? For the first time in his life, Dawa wasn't sure. He knew the world wasn't black and white; that the veracity of stories was like a layer of an onion, the truth usually revealing itself once the skins of fear and greed and aggression were shed. And the more Dawa was able to peel back the layers of Donny's story, the more Asteria Pharmaceuticals seemed to be involved in activities that had to be brought to the light.

That didn't change the simple fact that Dawa was sworn to protect and serve based on laws that were very much black and white. He'd taken an oath to uphold the law, and every day he hid Donny away in his monastery was another day he failed to do so.

As he turned the key to the ignition, he had to remind himself to stay focused on the big picture. The absolute truth. The simple fact that breaking man's law in the pursuit of what was right and just far outweighed the spiritual consequences he would face if he turned Donny over to the police. That would have been the quick fix; a selfish solution to his internal conflict. Ford would be arrested, tried, and likely sentenced to life (or worse) for two murders he most certainly had not committed, all while Asteria went free to distribute its poison to the masses.

Turning on Donny wouldn't be the pursuit of the truth. It would be an act of cowardice.

Dawa was no coward.

# Chapter 11:
# Tough Choices

If the pressures of governing on the federal level weren't enough to test the mettle of every legislator on Capitol Hill, the summer heat was sure to bring representatives and senators to the brink of their boiling points. But inside the office of newly appointed CIA Director Margaret Lancaster, heads were relatively cool and collected. She sat behind her desk and listened to Atlanta Station Chief Stephen Cline fill her in on the Asteria situation while Colin Kovic sat next to Cline, his head in the clouds.

Things had certainly changed since the last time Kovic had been in the director's office the year before, starting with the nation's new leadership. 2020 had been the year of a contentious presidential election, with a referendum on the previous administration that was swift and indiscriminate. Most appointees from the previous administration had been given marching orders, regardless of their competencies. CIA Director James Bennett had been one of the first to be axed.

It was a new era at the agency, and Margaret Lancaster was leading the way. Tall, lean, and in better shape than most women her age, Margaret could work a room full of misogynists and leave with a pocket full of allies. Her wits were as sharp as the streak of silver cutting a vertical line down her jet-black, shoulder-length hair; her olive skin was rhino-thick from surviving years in Washington politics; her diamond face and thin, almond eyes would have made her an excellent swallow in her prime, but seducing enemy agents in the field was never an interest. She had worked her way up from within the agency stateside, starting as an analyst straight out of college and putting in twenty-two years before her confirmation. She was experienced, qualified, and tough. And she sent a message things at the CIA were going to change.

The director wasn't the only change in the room. A traditional oak desk had been replaced with a black, high-gloss workstation, centered in the back of the room. Cup lights in the ceiling were brighter than Kovic remembered, the bluish LED bulbs replacing the soft yellow incandescent lights that used to give the room its welcoming glow. To the left, smoked glass panels replaced wood interior walls, mounted a half inch off the wall and casting rectangular shadows on the light gray wall behind them. To the right, the reinforced window casings had changed, but the view remained the same: Washington, D.C. in the distance, just over the Potomac, with the Washington Monument and Lincoln Memorial standing prominently in the center of a panoramic view.

Kovic panned around the room while his bosses talked, looking for some semblance of the Agency of Old. Finally, his eyes stopped on something that hadn't changed: the large gold-framed American flag hanging on the wall behind Lancaster. His mind wandered as he gazed at the flag, counting the stars, admiring its craftsmanship. It was the same flag the previous director had had hanging in the office before the massive renovations. The seams were stressed and the edges were tethered. It must have been at least thirty years old—

"I'm sorry, Colin," Lancaster said, fingers intertwined and resting on her desk. "Are we boring you on this fine afternoon?"

"No, ma'am. Not at all." He reengaged and cleared his throat.

"Well, then," Lancaster said, "I think Stephen's done a fine job of bringing me up to speed on the dissolution of the joint venture with Asteria Pharmaceuticals from the agency's side. Tell me how things went yesterday in Atlanta."

"Could have gone better."

"Okay," Lancaster gestured, "This is the part where you elaborate."

"Well, for starters, he's not keen about a buyout."

"Did we make him an offer?"

"Didn't have a chance. Said no amount was worth it, then immediately got on the phone, started making calls."

Lancaster leaned forward and propped her chin on the heel of her hand. "That's not much of a surprise. Although, a buyout would have made things a lot easier." She turned to Cline. "Are we prepped for tomorrow's Senate hearing?"

"I believe so," Cline said. "Given that it's a routine review, I compiled a list of line items that are likely to be put under the highest scrutiny, with Project THEIA topping it off."

"And what's our official stance on that?"

Cline shuffled papers in his lap and found the summary, then read it aloud. "Project THEIA was an exploratory program carried out in cooperation with Asteria Pharmaceuticals to determine the efficacy of antisense therapy to influence the neural pathways of biological systems. Studies were conducted in clinical settings using volunteers provided by Asteria Pharmaceuticals. After nine months, results of the studies were deemed inconclusive and the project was terminated."

Lancaster pondered the language, then said, "Let's take out the part about influencing and replace it with something a little less indicative of a mind-control project. Something like, 'a program to determine the effects of antisense therapy on neural pathways.' We don't want this thing to look like another MK Ultra."

"At least that didn't happen on your watch," Kovic said.

"That may be true," she said. "But you know as well as I do how much the ripple effect can stonewall intelligence spending for years on end. The Senate Intelligence Committee leaks worse than a screen door. We don't need the details of this little arrangement getting out, regardless of who was in charge at the time. Something of this magnitude could tarnish the entire agency."

Lancaster stood and walked to the window, arms crossed. "Which brings me to the next issue," she said. "The situation with Asteria is beyond complicated. A source at the FDA contacted me last night to inform me that George Sturgis was digging for intel, trying to find out if the CIA had any unspoken leverage over at the FDA. The man can't be bought, and it doesn't look like he's going down without a fight."

"He won't," Kovic said.

"Then there's the obvious problem—national security. Less than a dozen people in the entire world know how dangerous Ocula is, present company included. I don't think I have to tell you how devastating this product can be. Every day it's on the open market is another day a catastrophe could happen without any way to gauge where or when it could occur, or on what scale. Women knocking off cheating boyfriends is one thing, but an outlier influencing a government official? Would be an absolute disaster, the likes of which we've never seen before."

She turned and faced the two men sitting in front of her desk. "We're going to have to make some tough calls in the coming days, and I need to know you two are all in."

"Of course," Cline said.

Kovic nodded. "Yes, ma'am."

Lancaster returned to her desk. "Now before we leave this room today, I want to know what our options are. Cline, we'll start with you."

"Well, we've got a few," he said, shifting in his seat. "The first is to run a smear campaign warning the general public about the effects of Ocula. Social media, press leaks, high-traffic blogs, the works. We've done it before, with measurable results."

Lancaster said, "You're talking about the MMR operation carried out in the late 90s. The op that put Sturgis and company on the radar."

"Precisely. Vaccine safety was immediately called into question. We could run a similar campaign here. A few convincing write-ups in a handful of prominent medical journals will drastically reduce the amount of product prescribed."

"I love the irony," Lancaster said, "but I think we're tackling a completely different animal here. First, even a highly effective smear campaign would take months to catch on, while leaving more Ocula on the market than I'm comfortable with. Second, the anti-vax paper you're referring to was quickly debunked, putting most people's minds at ease. It did wonders for Asteria's competitive line of vaccines, but provided few long-term results. We have to remember: this isn't about keeping some of the product away from consumers. This needs to be a complete and total elimination of access to Ocula to the general public."

She turned to Kovic. "What've you got?"

"We focus on the national security risk. Tomorrow's hearing is closed doors—"

"That doesn't equate to confidential," Lancaster said.

"Still, we shouldn't take coming clean off the table. With the FDA and DEA in Asteria's pocket, swaying the Senate

Intelligence Committee could be the best chance we've got to get the drug pulled from the market."

"By saying what, Kovic—that Ocula is giving people superpowers? Making their dreams come true?" Lancaster shook her head. "First, they'll laugh us out of the room, then they'll pull this year's budget request, then they'll have our jobs. Sorry, Colin, but in this case taking the honest approach is about the worst thing we can do."

Cline looked over at Kovic while speaking to Lancaster. "There is another option."

Kovic's eyes urged Cline to shut up.

"I'm listening," Lancaster said.

"Project THEIA. It hasn't been completely shuttered yet. Everything is still in place at Skyline, excluding the participants. Once we have them transferred back up from Guantanamo, we can have the project back up and fully operational within the week."

Lancaster's eyes narrowed. "What exactly are you suggesting, Stephen?"

"We use Ocula 2.0 to influence the head of the FDA to issue a recall for the formula on the market. If we can't sway opinions over at the drug administration, we'll go to the head of the DEA and convince him to classify it as a Schedule I drug."

Lancaster looked over at a concerned Kovic. "What are your thoughts?" she asked.

"I don't like it. Synthesizing the drug is one thing, but actually using it is something else entirely."

Cline looked over. "What good is the weapon if we can't ever use it?"

"You could say the same thing about the nuclear arsenal."

"That's completely different. You're comparing a weapon

of mass destruction to a sniper rifle."

"A sniper rifle is as accurate as the operator using it. Ocula is a shotgun at best. And I've seen you shoot, Stephen."

"Okay, gentleman. That'll be enough." Lancaster rocked a pen between her fingers and thought. She had to agree with Kovic—from a moral standpoint, anyway. She'd known Project THEIA had the potential to be catastrophic the moment she had been debriefed on the venture, which was exactly why she had ordered the project terminated. In the last several months she had worked to sever ties with Asteria; shut down the Skyline facility in Virginia; stockpile what remained of Ocula 2.0 under heavy lock and key; and put away any memories of the Costa Rican connection—the latter of which still remained a thorn in her side.

She didn't like the idea of bringing Ocula back, but when it came to actionable solutions, she was drawing a blank. And here was Stephen Cline, right in front of her, offering up a state-of-the-art weapon that could solve their problems within the month. Her moral compass was swerving.

She asked, "Who would run the operation?"

"I would," Cline said, "with Roberto Ramírez in charge of clinical intervention."

"You mean Doyle's assistant?" Kovic couldn't believe it. "That guy's a bigger sociopath than Dick ever was."

"I think you forget your place," Cline said. "Besides, no one knows the program better. No one who's still alive, anyway."

"And why did we lose so many people in that operation, Cline? Have you already forgotten about Doyle and Tanner's inability to control the outliers? One slip up, one mistake, and BOOM! This time it could be you eating a bullet from your own gun."

Lancaster said, "That's why I want you there, Kovic. Working with Ramírez. Making sure everything runs smoothly."

Kovic went slack-jawed.

Lancaster continued, "Cline will handle the Costa Rica situation from here on out. You need to get to Skyline as soon as possible. Get everything operational within the next forty-eight hours. Stephen can handle your asset in San José."

"She's never going to go for that."

"She doesn't have a choice. And just so we're clear, Kovic, neither do you."

Kovic swallowed hard. He wanted to tell her Cline was dead wrong to bring Ocula 2.0 out of storage; that she knew better than to revive a dangerous weapon the agency had worked so hard to cover up; that using Ocula 2.0 as a means to eliminate the original made about as much sense as stopping a country's nuclear program by firing off a dozen warheads. Unfortunately, Kovic had used up all of his political clout for the day. He kept his mouth shut and played the good soldier.

"Will that be all for the day?"

"That will be all," Lancaster said. She checked her watch. "You've got a busy week ahead of you. I suggest you get started."

Kovic stood to follow Cline out the door. Lancaster stopped him halfway. "One more thing," she said. "About the situation in Costa Rica: do you think we can trust this in the hands of a journalist?"

Kovic nodded. "She's kept us up to speed on the situation so far."

"And you're convinced she can get us what we need and keep it contained?"

"The Costa Ricans are at the same stage of the development process we were when Paul Freeman wreaked havoc on the facility. If she sticks to the plan, we should be able to get in, get out, and finish what the volcano started."

Lancaster patted Kovic on the shoulder and sighed. "For our sake, Colin, I hope you're right."

# Chapter 12:
# Bruma

Alejandro Aguilar splashed into the middle of the shin-deep jungle stream, his combat boots muddying the clear water and testing the nerves of his hiking companion who was following close behind. He bent down, faced upstream, and cupped his hands to splash the cold mountain water on his face.

Claire said, "What did I say about keeping quiet?"

Aguilar wiped his face with the bottom of his shirt. "Come on, Claire. It's scorching out here. Plus, you said so yourself: there's no one around for miles."

Claire didn't like Aguilar's cavalier attitude, but he did have a point. A thick jungle canopy formed high arborous walls on both sides of the creek that cut across the flatlands and split the clearings between Bajos del Toro and the west side of Poás Volcano. The surrounding area was open Costa Rican terrain, giving the helicopters that passed overhead a clear line of sight to any movement on the ground. But if they stuck near the creek, there was no way spotters could see what was hidden beneath the trees.

She checked her wristwatch. Almost 9 a.m. They had left the cabin just before daybreak, and already they were halfway to the facility, moving much faster than they had anticipated the night before. If the two trespassers kept up the pace, the hidden path would lead them within a mile of the facility by noon.

That was, if Aguilar could stay out of the water.

"Okay," Claire said. "Just hurry up and fill your canteen so we can keep moving."

Aguilar signaled. "Throw me yours."

"I'm all topped off, but thanks."

"Claire," he said in his drawn-out fatherly tone, "I warned you about not drinking enough water—"

"And I warned you a long time ago about lectures. Let's just get moving, okay?"

Aguilar nodded, capped his canteen, and walked back to shore. The two continued north, straddling the narrow line between the foliage and the fields. The path was thick, with rocks and roots and knee-high ferns hindering Aguilar's effort to walk alongside Claire. He charted a clear stretch of path, then his eyes wandered from the trail, coming to rest on Claire. He had seen that face before. Resolute. Focused. And above all else, the face of a woman who didn't feel like talking. But that had never stopped him before.

"Tell me, Claire. Why are you so determined to keep things from me?"

"What are you talking about?"

"The call last night. The hushed tones. Whispers from the porch. Are you afraid I can't handle everything that is going on with you these days?"

"Plausible deniability," she said, still looking forward. "The less you know about Ocula, the better."

Aguilar laughed. "Plausible deniability? Claire. Dear. Drink some water. The heat is taking its toll on you."

"Come again?"

"I've been harboring you for the last six months. Set you up with a new identity. Stayed up all hours of the night waiting on you to return from secret meetings with mysterious contacts. Now we're trespassing on government soil, looking for some secret facility we have no business looking for. But yes, should the police forces find us, what then?" He raised his hands mockingly. "I'll cry out, '*No se nada!*' and then be on my merry way? Innocent and free?"

"What did I say about keeping it down?"

"Okay. You're right. I'll be quiet now. As quiet as a reporter speaking to secret sources from the porch of her host—"

"Jesus Christ, Han. You want to know who I was talking to? It was Paul Freeman, okay? Feel better now?"

Aguilar pondered the name. "Your friend from the facility?"

"The one and only."

"I thought he had broken ties with you months ago."

"He did. Had. I mean, last night's call was the first time I'd heard from him since Atlanta."

"What did he want?"

Claire was stone-faced.

"This is the man I lent a car to, correct? A car I was very fond of, by the way. And you won't tell me what he wanted?"

"It was a piece-of-shit Mercury, Han."

"The car had sentimental value, Claire. Besides, you've never had trouble muttering your grievances about Donny Ford. Why so tight-lipped about this Freeman character?"

No sooner had the question left Aguilar's lips than Claire's left arm clotheslined his chest, bringing the sauntering chatterbox to an abrupt stop. Shocked, he looked at Claire. Her finger pressed her lips, her eyes motioning to the clearing in the distance just beyond the break in the trees ahead.

She whispered, "One o'clock."

Aguilar nodded, then looked ahead to see two soldiers standing in front of a camouflaged jeep parked in the field about a hundred yards out. He could barely make out the symbol on one of the doors, but he already knew it was the Costa Rican police force. They had anticipated dodging the watchful eyes of helicopter patrols overhead, but running into the police force miles from the beaten path was a bit of a shock.

He whispered to Claire, "I can't see a road. Was there a road on the map?"

She shook her head. "If you're talking about pavement and little white lines, no. But this area is littered with pig trails. Either way, they're off the reservation."

They watched patiently as the two men loitered in the distance. The tall one appeared to be doing his job to some extent, rifle in hand, peering into the trees in a slow 180-degree motion. He panned their way, prompting both hikers to pivot behind their own respective trees for cover.

Claire held her breath for half a minute before she realized she wasn't breathing. She could feel a set of instinctive eyes burning holes through the bark on other side of the tree she was hiding behind. *Did we just blow this whole operation?* The thought of failing to make it to the facility was inconceivable. Everything Claire had worked toward for the last six months was riding on the next twenty-four hours.

She knew she had to be careful, but she couldn't hide forever. She looked toward Aguilar, and the two slowly peeked out to assess the situation.

They were in the clear.

The soldier had lost interest, focused now on yelling at his shorter, more inept partner, who was busy smoking and watching the clouds move overhead. The short one answered, dropped his cigarette, and stormed toward the driver's side of the jeep. In a moment they were off, leaving a long cloud of dust in their wake.

Claire and Aguilar decided to sit and wait for a good ten

minutes before making a run for it across the field. It was a decision Claire almost immediately regretted the moment Aguilar picked up right where he left off.

"So, this Freeman. Is he someone I should be worried about?" Aguilar asked with a raised eyebrow and a crooked smile.

"Worrying would imply you and I were an item, Han. You should know better."

"I love your spirit, Claire. Always the feisty one." He fidgeted with a stick in the dirt before turning serious. "Did you tell him where we were going?"

"Kind of had to, Han."

"And why is that?"

"I think you know why."

"Because he was with you since the beginning?" Aguilar said. "So was Ford, and look where that's gotten you. How many of these gringos are you going to babysit while you do all of the heavy lifting?"

"That's not why I told him about the facility," Claire said.

"Then why?"

Impatiently, "Because there's a very high likelihood we're going to die out here, Alejandro. And if something happens to us, the other outliers need to know about this place. They need to know what the government is doing here. That's why."

"Now why would you talk like that, Claire? Putting a hex on the whole operation. I certainly didn't come out here to die. Did you?"

"Of course not. I would very much like to live, but the way things have been going it would be naïve to think that death wasn't a very real possibility. I mean, look around you, Han. This isn't exactly a trip to one of your island cabanas."

Aguilar snapped the stick in two and tossed the pieces

aside. "Well, I know it is not a possibility for me. I'm not dying in the middle of some jungle."

"Oh, really? And how can you be so sure?"

"Because, Claire. When I was just a boy, I saw my death in a dream once."

Claire did her best to hide her amusement, pursing her lips and nodding with feigned interest.

"You don't believe me?" Aguilar asked.

"I didn't say that." Claire looked to the field. The dust trail left by the jeep was faint, but still visible. She looked back to Aguilar. "Okay then, let's hear why we're going to make it across the clearing, into the hills, to the facility, and back to San José in one piece, all because of some whimsical boyhood dream. May be just the motivation I need right now."

Aguilar started in. "I remember the night of the dream like it was yesterday. June 7th, 1982. I was twelve at the time, and spending the summer with my grandparents on their farm in the country. They were sharecroppers, my grandparents, harvesting everything from coffee to cattle in exchange for the promise of the title to the farm in the distant future. It had been their lifelong dream to own their own land. Sadly, it was a dream they never saw to fruition."

"I'm sorry to hear that, Han."

Aguilar tossed a hand. "Ah. Such is life, my dear." He continued, "Two days before my premonition, my grandfather had been working the rows of coffee in the field farthest from the house. No one knows exactly what happened, but I like to think he had a moment to take his midmorning break, sipping his water and wiping the sweat from his brow under the shade of his favorite ceiba tree before it happened. A brief moment of rest to contemplate a day's worth of hard labor—that's when he was happiest, you know."

Claire listened intently.

"He was a man of routine, my grandfather. So when he didn't show up for the lunch bell, my grandmother began to worry. She walked out into the field to investigate, leaving me napping on the front porch swing none the wiser. That was until I heard the shrill of an elderly woman echoing from the far reaches of the field in the distance.

"To this day, I still cannot remember running to see what was the matter"—he moved his hand across an invisible plane—"it was as if I floated from the porch to the coffee fields in the blink of an eye, experiencing no passage of time between my abuela's scream and the scene that followed."

Aguilar paused to collect himself, then said, "My grandfather lay on his side, lifeless. Blood soaked the soil where he laid what was left of his head. His entire right temple had been marked by a deep crescent indention, fractured red-stained bits of skull visible for all to see. My grandmother almost fainted. She would have fallen flat had we not caught one another, the two of us sobbing and embracing one another as we fell to our knees. It was then that I looked up, my eyes set on the hill rising above the back field. That's when I discovered who the murderous culprit was. Or rather, what."

Claire cocked her head as Aguilar explained, "The family horse. Bruma. She had been acting up for a time. My grandparents had suspected rabies, but my grandfather didn't have the heart to put her down right away. Back then, all one could do was wait patiently and observe, or hurry up and kill." He sighed, then said, "Looking back, it seems as though my grandfather's compassion for Bruma had only led to his demise."

"No child should ever have to see a loved one like that,

Han."

"I agree wholeheartedly. There's no doubt the experience had a profound effect on the rest of my life, beginning with that night."

"The dream?"

"That night? No. I didn't sleep. But two nights later, my life would be changed forever. You see, Claire, family tradition held that the spirit didn't cease to exist. Rather, it would live on in the afterlife."

"That's a pretty widespread belief, Han."

"You didn't let me finish. My grandparents were raised by their grandparents to believe that passage from this world to the next was not immediate. Instead, the spirit of the deceased would linger in this world for several days, tidying up loose ends and answering to unfinished business before making the final journey to the other side.

"Now, I can only assume as to what led to a dream detailing my own death in the distant future. But, had my grandfather seen the terror in my eyes upon looking at his mangled corpse, and his spirit remained on this side, I would imagine he would do whatever he could to assure his young grandson that no such death awaited him in this life."

"You think the spirit of your grandfather gave you a vision of some kind?"

"Yes. Two nights after his death. It was the first night I had slept since the accident, and it was only from pure exhaustion. I remember falling asleep just after midnight, and almost immediately waking in a bright, sunlit room. I opened my eyes to find myself sitting at a desk, pen in hand, paper in front of me. I was writing a letter, although I'm not sure to whom. To this day, that simple fact bothers me, but that's how dreams go, isn't it? Everything is vivid, everything real in the moment. And then we wake, and what are we left with? The vague recollection that something real is slipping through our fingers with each passing second, never fully understanding what we've seen, only knowing that it must have been something important."

"Vague is right. I mean, no offense, but that dream could mean anything."

"Perhaps, had I not noticed the elderly hand holding the pen. Nothing like that of a twelve-year-old boy. Old and weathered, with more sunspots than I'd like to admit. A few melanomas here and there, but nothing to worry about at that stage in the game. The aged skin startled me, so I immediately checked the other hand: equally as old, and ugly, too. Then I looked ahead to the large pane-glass window in front of me. Faint outlines of buildings lined the bottom portion of the window. Obviously, a city skyline, though it looked nothing like downtown San José.

"But my focus was not on the buildings. No, it was on the old man in the reflection of the glass looking back at me. His eyes were tired and drooping, his beard a frosty gray, his thinning hair disheveled. He must have been eighty years old, maybe older. A white-collar version of my grandfather, his twenty-first century counterpart. I could even spot the chicken-pox scar on my forehead, a conspicuous scar I've carried since grade school.

"I gazed into the reflection, completely at peace with what was to come. My right hand relaxed and dropped the pen I was holding. My eyes grew heavy and my vision blurred. Sometimes I think I even smiled, but details have a way of fading, you know. Then I saw a light, bright and unyielding."

Claire said, "You mean, *the* light?"

"Yes. And God, was it bright, bright enough to burn the

retinas, but I couldn't stop looking into it. The white light flooded the scene, and that's when I woke up."

"You think the old man in the reflection was you?"

"It must have been, Claire. That dream was a gift from my grandfather, assuring me I would die an old man—and wouldn't suffer the same violent fate as he."

Claire looked back to the field. The dust had settled. She listened for signs of patrols and motorcades and helicopters overhead, but heard nothing that would indicate soldiers were nearby. It was time to make a move.

"Well I'm glad you're confident we're going to make it through this," Claire said. "Because honestly, I haven't had much faith in my dreams of late."

Her eyes stayed fixed on the field ahead while she waited for Aguilar to ask what she had dreamed about in predictable fashion. Only her statement was met with silence.

"Han?" She looked his way.

A gun was to his head as one of the soldiers from the field pushed the pistol muzzle forcefully into his temple. Claire wondered where his shorter sidekick was when she felt a cold steel barrel shove into her back. A voice spoke from behind.

"Los matamos?"

"No. No podemos," the other soldier said. The two continued to talk to one another while the taller flipped through a ring-bound photo deck in one hand, his gun still pressed firmly into Aguilar's head with the other. Claire's Spanish was decent, but the hushed tones were hard to decipher. She looked to Aguilar for answers.

"What are they saying?"

"Well, they're not going to kill us."

Claire breathed a sigh of relief. She whispered, "That's a

bonus. What else?"

The taller one had stopped on an image. The soldier pointed to it, then to Claire. Aguilar listened for a moment. Finally, "They say they've been looking for you."

# Chapter 13:
## The Morning After

*Mercy, mercy, mercy . . . what a night.*

On most days, six a.m. meant Arlo Vaughan still had another hour to go until the next shift change. Then he'd punch the time clock, saunter off to his pickup, and watch the sun rise over the salt marshes of Savannah on his morning drive home. Tired, but relaxed.

But on this morning, an act as simple as brushing his teeth had gone from routine to rigorous.

He spit in the sink and cursed, temples still throbbing from the once-in-a-lifetime headache he'd had the night before. Arlo wasn't prone to having headaches; in fact, as he gazed into the mirror at his own bloodshot eyes, he couldn't remember the last time he had had one. Must've been years. Decades, even.

Last night had started off as the confidence boost he had been looking for. It was bad enough his appointment at the bank the day before had been cut short, but his wife Kerry always had a way of making his worries slip into oblivion.

That was before he took his sleeping pill.

The Ocula prescription was an older one, and he wasn't the type to take a pill every night. Kerry, on the other hand, had quite the nightly regimen, and often encouraged her reluctant husband to jump on board. *Everyone needs a little help now and then*, she would always say. Hearing her voice in his head made Arlo laugh, then wince, every little movement a pain-inducing endeavor. *Would've been better off just getting drunk.*

No point in getting bent out of shape though. When Kerry had suggested the sleeping pill she was only trying to help, and even Arlo had hoped Ocula would do the trick, sending him straight to dreamland with time to spare.

Instead, the pill seemed to do the opposite. Thirty minutes after taking it, Arlo was tossing and turning under the covers. An hour later, he was hugging the toilet as round after round of vomiting quickly turned into fruitless dry heaves. He sat on the bathroom floor most of the night, wedged between a toilet and a tub, sweating and shaking and thoroughly exhausted.

*Tomorrow's gonna be awful. Just plain awful.*

And it was awful. He splashed water on his face and toweled off, thankful the worst of his headache had receded but worried about his appearance. His mid-morning bank appointment was slowly creeping up and there wasn't much he could do about the way he looked. No amount of face washing or teeth brushing could hide the weariness on poor old Arlo's face.

Kerry heard the water running and walked in to check on her husband. "Up most the night?" she asked.

Arlo nodded. "Don't know what happened," he said. "Everything was fine before I took that damned pill. Wasn't long after I was hugging the toilet."

"You've taken Ocula before, Arlo," she said as she checked her own look in the mirror. "Think it may have been something else? I've seen what you take to lunch with you most days, and it isn't pretty."

"Maybe," he said, pondering yesterday's meal. "That ham sandwich did seem a little funky at the time."

"I keep telling you to check the expiration date on that nasty sandwich meat you seem to love so much." She felt his forehead with the back of her hand. No temperature. "Probably just something you ate. How are you feeling now?"

"Better, but tired. I don't know how I'm going to carry on

through the day like this."

"Well, you better suck it up because your bank appointment's in two hours."

Arlo forced a smile and asked, "Is the coffee on?"

"You know it is," Kerry said.

The two continued their morning routine of fighting for space in a cramped bathroom (Kerry was typically getting ready for the day about the time Arlo was returning from work), then they made their way to the kitchen. Arlo poured a cup of coffee, black, then sat down to sip on the hot elixir in the hopes it would take the edge off the dying pangs of last night's headache. Kerry fixed her own cup, then sat beside him.

"Everything ready for your meeting with the bank this morning?"

Arlo nodded toward the briefcase propped by the door. "It's all in there. Honestly, I'm not even sure why I'm having to go back through this mess. They should've either given me an answer yesterday, or called this morning. But they insisted we wrap it up at the bank."

"Maybe they want to give you the good news in person."

"Possible, but with our luck, who knows." He was about to reminisce on a series of nonspecific unfortunate events when suddenly it hit him:

*The dream.*

It must have been early, perhaps two or three in the morning, shortly after his headache had begun to ease off a bit. That's when he had fallen asleep by the tub, slipping away from reality and into the most lucid dream of his life. He remembered sitting in front of the loan officer at First National Bank of Savannah and checking the time.

*Almost five o'clock again. Again?*

He watched as the hallucination of Mr. Webber flipped through a stack of papers, eyes down, quietly muttering a melody of uh-huhs as he checked off page after page, taking sips from a "Come See Savannah" coffee mug in between. The stack towered above Arlo as he sat in his lowly chair—no way Webber would ever make it through the three-meter-high stack of papers.

He'd never get a loan like this, not with Webber wasting his damn time again. He would have jumped up to smack the bowtie off the pompous lender's neck if he hadn't felt bound to his chair, almost paralyzed, forced to watch the scene play out without being able to get up and shake some sense into the man.

Arlo's body was frozen in place in a kind of sleep paralysis, but at least his mouth still worked. Impatiently, "Jesus, son. Since when does it take this long to figure out whether or not someone deserves a loan?" He counted his points out on his fingers. "You know I work, you know my income, you know how successful every business on River Street is . . . Why the hell can't you just sign the money over? You know I'm good for it! Every damn time I try and—"

The rant was cut short by something hard rattling around in Arlo's mouth. Startled, he moved the rigid object from the back of his cheek with his tongue. Then he spit in his hand.

A tooth. Molar, to be exact. Root and all. *Good Lord, what's happening to me?*

Two rosy cheeks and a pair of sweating palms made it impossible for Arlo to hide his embarrassment. He tried to hide the tooth, but the hope that Webber wouldn't noticed was dashed the moment the pearly white was purged from his lips.

The lender stopped flipping pages, eyes now fixed on the blood-stained tooth Arlo held in the palm of his hand. Webber stared at the tooth for what seemed like an eternity.

Finally, he asked, "How much do you need, Mr. Vaughan?"

Arlo cocked his head, not quite sure how to answer. He had originally asked for $50,000—that's what was on the loan form. Didn't Webber know that? Had he forgotten?

Arlo pointed to the form. "Isn't it right there on the front page?"

The lender adjusted his glasses. "Yes. I see. $50,000." He looked up at Arlo and asked, "Do you think that will be enough to cover everything?"

"I reckon. I mean, that's the number me and Kerry came up with."

The lender shook his head. "Running a restaurant isn't cheap, Mr. Vaughan. You need more."

"I do?"

Webber reached under his desk and pulled out a leather suitcase. He laid it in front of Arlo and unsnapped the latches. Inside were stacks of cash, hundreds packed neatly in $10,000 bundles.

"Oh, my," Arlo said, raising his hand to his mouth. He stuttered as he searched for the words before finally asking, "H-How much is in here?"

"$100,000. That should be enough to get you started."

Arlo reached for the briefcase but stopped halfway. This was simply too good to be true; this kind of good fortune had never happened to him. Not once. He couldn't even remember the last time he won a free lotto ticket on a scratch-off. Something was up.

"This is double what we asked," Arlo said. "Just why are you doing this for me?"

The lender stood and referenced the tooth in Arlo's hand.

"You're worried, Arlo. Worried about getting older, worried about doing something good with the rest of your life. You've been through the ringer, Mr. Vaughan, but today's your lucky day. Simple as that."

Suddenly the office erupted in a series of cheers. Arlo turned to see a huge crowd packing the bank lobby behind him, dusted in the confetti that was falling from the ceiling, smiling and clapping and congratulating him as if he were the winning contestant on a game show. He slowly raised his hand to say thanks when the faces in the crowd faded and blurred like images behind a frosted pane of glass—

"You all right, honey?" Kerry placed her hand on top of Arlo's.

"Yeah," he said, snapping out of his daze. "Just thinking about the dream I had last night."

"Was it a good one?"

"Oh, yeah," he chuckled.

"Wanna tell me what it was about?"

"Ah, just the meeting with the bank today."

"You got the loan?" Kerry said, smiling and nudging her husband's shoulder.

"*We* got the loan. But yeah. I had a dream about getting the loan. More than we asked for, actually. That'd be something, wouldn't it?"

"Something? Where's your faith, Arlo? A dream like that is a good sign!"

"It was just a dream, Kerry."

"Maybe. But dreams have a way of telling us things we just can't believe when we're awake. You remember my Aunt Ruth's witchy feeling she'd get when there was a death in the family? She'd get that feeling early in the morning, fresh off a bad dream. She'd refuse to leave the house for the day, and sure enough, by dinnertime the phone would be ringing with the bad news."

"Best I recall, your Aunt Ruth would also get that witchy feeling every time she was running low on port."

"Well, say what you want, Arlo. But if you ask me, I think that's a good omen for today." She stood up and walked to the fridge, pulling out eggs and bacon before lighting the stove. "And if it's not meant to be, then it's just not meant to be."

Arlo nodded in agreement, but the statement did little to comfort him. He got up and went over to Kerry, wrapping his arms around her from behind and craning his neck around to give her a kiss on the cheek. "*Que sera, sera*, huh, Kerry?"

"Something like that," she said, and kissed him back.

***

Daniel Webber's office had been brighter in Arlo's dream. In reality, the loan office was dim, uninviting, even downright depressing. *Maybe that's the point,* Arlo thought. *Keep folks from getting their hopes up.*

A brass lamp sat on the right corner of Webber's desk and cast long shadows of books and office clutter on the wall to Arlo's left. Blinds were drawn over the only window in the room to Webber's back as he sat behind his desk in deep concentration, flipping through papers and crossing T's and dotting I's.

Arlo noticed Webber squinting down at the paperwork and spoke up. "You think maybe we should turn on the overhead—"

"No. Absolutely not," Webber snapped, then composed himself. "That is, if you don't mind." He rubbed his temples and

Arlo took the hint.

"Headache?"

Webber nodded.

"I had one of those last night, too. Strange really. Hardly ever get 'em. Guess we were both worried 'bout wrapping this thing up today."

Webber forced a smile and continued his paperwork. Arlo gave the spiral-bound notebook in his lap another firm two-handed twist. Things were not working out as he had planned.

*No,* thought Arlo, *That's not an honest assumption.*

A more accurate statement would have been that things weren't working out the way they had in his dream the night before. In reality, Arlo had never expected to get the loan. Kerry was the dreamer; the better half who always pushed her husband to think positive thoughts and hope for the best. But that just wasn't how Arlo was built. Too many experiences over a lifetime of disappointments had long ago taught the man the only mantra he could ever rely on: hope for the best, but prepare for the worst. And in this case, the worst was not getting the loan.

Arlo could already see the answer in Webber's bloodshot eyes. The lender was in no mood to be there, cringing with every rustling paper, scowling every time a phone rang from another office or an eighteen-wheeler roared down 8th Street just a few yards from the only window in the office.

The scene that played out was nothing like the dream. No glowing faces and positive vibes. No cheerful loan officer offering up double what the humble borrower had asked for. And no tickertape parade waiting outside the door to congratulate the new owner of the finest creole restaurant on River Street. Arlo turned around to look over his shoulder toward the door, double-checking that last notion just one more time. Nothing but stained oak.

Perhaps dreams didn't come true, but there was one thing Arlo did recognize: that stupid "Come See Savannah" mug sitting on Webber's desk. Sure, Savannah was a popular tourist destination, with mugs and T-shirts and postcards featuring every hot spot from the bars on River Street to the historic-district mansions in full, vibrant color. But why on earth would someone have a mug like that from the town they lived in? Wouldn't it make more sense to see some cheesy mug from Hawaii, or Paris, or wherever the hell bankers went to get away from the stress of turning people down for loans forty hours a week?

Arlo didn't have time to finish the thought. Webber shuffled the papers together, gave the stack three quick taps on the desk, and laid them neatly to the side.

"Well, Mr. Vaughan. It's with great regret I have to inform you that after reviewing your loan application—"

"Spare me the time, son."

"Excuse me?"

Arlo stood up and buttoned his coat. "You've been dragging your feet, jumping through the hoops, making a show, with no intention of ever approving this loan."

"Mr. Vaughan—"

"Now, I ain't mad. Honestly, I was expecting this. I'm just done wasting time talking about it, that's all. So why don't you spare us both the formalities and let me be on my way. If I'm not opening a restaurant, I'll need to be getting back to work."

Webber sighed as his head dropped, unable to make eye contact with the man standing over his desk. "Fair enough, Mr. Vaughan." He stood to shake hands, but Arlo was already halfway to the exit.

That's when the door swung open from the other side. A secretary stood in Arlo's way, holding a stack of papers.

Webber's arm went up to shield his eyes from the sudden burst of light flooding the room. "Jesus, Susan. Don't you know how to knock?"

"Sorry, sir. But it's your son."

Webber's face morphed from disgust to distress in half a second. "My son?"

"The school just called. They're saying your son got in a fight."

"Is he hurt?"

Susan sighed, then said, "It's nothing detrimental, but he is at Lakeside Hospital. Apparently he's missing a few teeth."

"Excuse me?"

"Two, to be exact. At least that's what the vice principal told me. He's been going at it with Frankie Finch for the entire school year, fighting over the affections of Erin Page."

Webber stared inquisitively.

"Anyway," Susan continued, "things came to a head on the playground during sixth-grade recess. Words were spoken, feelings were hurt, and fists started to fly."

Webber wasn't impressed with Susan's apparent fervor in telling the story. He stood quickly to grab his coat and hurried toward the door, breezing by Arlo along the way.

That's when he stopped.

It was as if the space on the floor in front of Arlo were an unseen patch of quicksand, with Webber knee-deep in the muck and no way to put the other foot forward. Vivid images of blood and teeth besieged his mind's eye, bringing with them a despairing sense of impending doom. His chest tightened and his pulse raced. Feelings of angst and guilt grew thick and heavy with every attempt to move closer to the door, as if some invisible, unanswered compulsion was holding him back. Then a voice, powerful and direct, asked—no, *demanded*—something from Webber.

And it wasn't going away. Webber was stuck, with only one way out. He had to answer. He turned to Arlo to speak. Solemnly, "About the loan, Arlo."

"Yes, Mr. Webber?"

"How much was it again, $50,000?" the banker asked as he briskly walked back to his desk.

"Yes. That's right."

"That's not enough," Webber said. He flipped back through the stack of loan papers, searching for every occurrence of the amount. Arlo watched over his shoulder as Webber crossed out and replaced each $50,000 with a cool $100,000, writing the new figure out to the side.

"Mr. Webber, I'm not sure I understand—"

"Of course, this figure is unofficial, as we'll need to draft new paperwork"—Webber initialed each line item while he spoke—"But, this is just for your reference. We'll get everything finalized when I get back, if that's convenient for you."

Webber marked one last item, tossed the pen on his desk, and made for the door, light-footed and relieved of the unseen burden.

Arlo spoke up as the banker raced off to check on the chivalrous boy sitting with a mouthful of gauze at Lakeside Hospital. "Just why are you doing this?"

Webber turned. "What can I say, Mr. Vaughan? Today's your lucky day."

# Chapter 14:
# Back on the Bottle

Diesels roared and jake brakes squealed as eighteen wheelers geared down to turn off the highway and into the Happy Jack Truck Stop in Cheyenne, the last place for long-haulers to fill up their tanks and stock up on smokes and Cokes for the next hundred miles. A new day was breaking as the first rays of burnt-orange sunlight peaked above the eastern horizon and spread across the golden Midwest plains, reflecting off every piece of chrome in the parking lot and creating a minefield of potential headache triggers for anyone caught amongst the sea of semi-trucks without sunglasses or a wide-brim hat. Paul had neither, but did his best to shield his eyes with his cup of coffee while keeping his head down as he walked from the gas station back to the car.

He hopped in the idling car and handed Michelle her coffee. She thanked her husband with a halfhearted nod, then looked away. *The silence continues*, he thought. Par for the course. He turned the key and pulled back onto I-80, eager to get back on the road and out of Nebraska.

The drive from northwest California hadn't been a bad one, but the ride through Nebraska was proving to be a boring stretch of highway. California redwoods and skyscraping Rockies were soon replaced with fruited plains and long straightaways, parting harvested fields and endless fences. At least the Pacific Northwest had provided winding roads and crisp mountain air to keep Paul awake on the journey back south. Nebraska, however, was about to put him to sleep.

Or maybe that was just the exhaustion talking. Paul gave

his eyes a rub and turned on the radio. Michelle reached for his hand to stop him but it was too late.

"Have you lost your mind?" she whispered forcefully.

"What?"

"You're going to wake up—"

The radio crackled, and a cry emerged from the backseat.

"Great. Just great, Paul. Aaron's going to be ill as a hornet."

"Sorry, dear. I wasn't thinking."

Michelle unbuckled her seatbelt and leaned in the back to fix Aaron a bottle. She spoke while she worked. "By the way, isn't there something you should be thinking about instead of what's on the radio?"

Their eyes met in the rearview mirror, but Paul didn't say anything. He knew exactly what she was talking about, and she was right. He had been putting off making the call to Donny Ford ever since he'd talked to Claire the day before. Now he was just delaying the inevitable.

He wasn't without his reasons. Paul had known exactly what kind of person Ford was from the moment he first ran across one of his late-night infomercials. Conman. Charlatan. Snake oil salesman. For every nasty euphemism you could think of that applied to a particularly duplicitous showman, Donny Ford fit the bill every time.

And there was something else Paul had never understood: why Claire thought Ford would have been an indispensable asset in the effort to take down Asteria. The man's very M.O. was self-serving and egocentric—a showman in love with the spotlight, infallible to a legion of fans salivating at the very sight of a fearless leader with all the answers. But to Paul, he was a narcissist and a crook. How Claire couldn't appreciate the risks that went hand in hand with an ally like that was beyond him.

The Donny situation had also gotten a lot more complicated since February. In a matter of months, Donny had gone from the hottest ticket on the self-help circuit to a high-profile fugitive. Every law enforcement agency in the country was looking for him, and it was only a matter of time before he'd get himself caught.

That was unless someone turned him in first. Paul drove on autopilot and considered the notion, rubbing his chin with one hand and steering with the other. The thought had crossed his mind more than once, but it wasn't much of an option. Sure, it might rid him of an untrustworthy ally, but it would mean certain incarceration for Claire and Dawa—and that was only if the authorities got to them before Asteria. Everyone involved in the Ocula trials was in it together. If one person went down, they all went down.

Michelle was already buckled up and back in the front seat by the time Paul ran through his options. Her knee bounced while her eyes split hard glares between her husband and the phone resting peacefully on the console.

"Well? Are you going to wait all day, or do I need to call him?"

Paul sighed, shook his head in defeat, and then picked up the phone.

*** 

An anxious fist rapped on the solid oak door to Dawa's bedroom, echoing through the empty monastery and provoking an irritable grumble from the other side. Donny waited impatiently for a coherent response.

Finally, "What do you want?"

"Sorry to wake you, Dawa. But it's about Claire."

Donny heard a click from within and the soft yellow lamplight beamed from under the door. A few choice words and footsteps later and the two men were face to face.

Dawa tied his robe and asked, "Do you have any idea what time it is?"

"Um, yeah. It's lunchtime." Donny cocked his head. "You feeling okay these days, Graham?"

Dawa squinted and rubbed his forehead. "Yes. Of course. I was just trying to catch a quick nap before my next shift. I must have lost track of time." He stepped out of his room and closed the door. "You mentioned something about Claire?"

"That's right. I wouldn't have woken you if it wasn't important."

"So, she finally answered one of your calls."

"Not exactly," Donny said. "I got a call from one of the other Ocula outliers. Paul Freeman."

Dawa thought on the name. "Freeman . . . Claire's friend from the facility."

"That's the one. Apparently he's been hiding out west for the last six months. He called Claire after getting spooked, and now he wants to meet up. Personally, I don't like it."

"Oh?" Ford's apprehension piqued Dawa's interest. "And why is there cause for concern?" He walked away and Donny followed, footsteps echoing hastily down the shadowy hallway until the two passed under the maroon archway leading to a well-lit kitchen. The faint morning sun that typically eased in from the skylight above the island where Dawa ate breakfast was now directly overhead, heating the room with a bright rectangular column of light that reached down from the ceiling and illuminated every floating speck of dust in its path.

Donny crossed his arms and leaned back on the counter. "This guy calls and says he's been in touch with Claire, only Claire hasn't mentioned him for the last six months. He says Claire is supposed to contact me to check in by tomorrow, only she never said anything to me about it."

Dawa filled a kettle and set it on the stove. "You did say she was dodging your calls, Donald."

"True, but she was supposed to contact me with any updates, including any leads she got from the other outliers out there. She assured me she'd keep me posted. Now her phone's going straight to voicemail."

The news did little to take Dawa away from his waking routine. He grabbed a mug from the cabinet and tore open a tea bag while Donny watched him impatiently.

"Well?"

"Well what, Donald? Did it ever occur to you Claire is out of service? Her battery is dead? Perhaps she has met someone, and she is out on a date."

"I'm serious, Graham."

"So am I."

"Well, you sure as hell don't act like it!" The cavalier attitude of his old college roommate flustered Donny to the core. He stood and waited for a response, fingers tapping his forearm, veins swelling on his forehead, his patience quickly evaporating. Dawa almost always had an answer for everything, of that he could be sure. But sometimes getting to it was like pulling teeth.

This was one of those times. The tea kettle hissed as Dawa leaned on the counter by the stove, his attention held hostage by the gentle puffs of steam that rose from the metallic spout, paying no mind to the man with all the questions. Donny stared and waited, eyes burning holes into his old friend.

Dawa could feel the tension. Finally, he sighed, then turned to speak.

"Donald. My friend. You never were one to think things through."

"What's that supposed to mean?"

"Paul told you over the phone that Claire would be contacting you by tomorrow with an update, correct?"

"Yeah. So?"

"So, Donald. By tomorrow you will know whether or not you can trust Paul"—he turned back to the stove—"and if that's the case, then we are one outlier closer to building a solid case against Asteria Pharmaceuticals, wouldn't you agree?"

Donny squinted and nodded as the obvious slowly sank in. Dawa asked, "Do you know where Paul Freeman is now?"

"Yeah. He said he was somewhere out west. Nebraska, I think. Anyway, he's on his way here, and he wants to meet."

Dawa tilted his head to glance behind the kettle. The clock on the stove flashed 1:47. He thought about a road trip he had taken to the Grand Canyon some years back. Then he said, "I don't believe he will be here within the day. Maybe by this time tomorrow, if he drives nonstop. But it seems to me that he will be arriving about the time you are expecting a phone call from your dear friend to the south. Yes?"

The water boiled and Dawa turned off the stove. Once again, Dawa had shut him down in his trademark calm-and-collected fashion. It was a tone Donny had always found condescending, regardless of the guru's benevolent intentions.

Donny glared at the man steeping his tea and cursed under his breath. *He thinks I'm incompetent. He's always treated me like I was incompetent.*

The houseguest was tempted to blow up on his benefactor, but now wasn't time. He took a deep breath and composed himself, then said, "Yes, Dawa. You're right. There's no sense in jumping to conclusions until tomorrow."

He started to leave the room when Dawa spoke. "Did you give him my address, Donald?"

"Not yet. Like I said, I still don't like any of this."

"We don't have many options here, my friend. Sooner or later, we are going to have to trust someone. If the man says he has been in touch with Claire, go ahead and tell him to come here."

"What if he's lying?"

Dawa took a sip of tea, then said, "We are big boys, Donald. If he is lying, then we will handle it."

The phone rang, and Dawa instinctively patted where his pockets should have been only to feel a pocket-less bathrobe. The cell chirped and vibrated on the counter closest to Donny. He slid the phone over.

"Thanks." Dawa read the screen. "I have to take this. Are you good for this afternoon?"

Donny nodded. Dawa answered the phone and jumped into work mode while his roommate shuffled back to the confines of his domestic purgatory.

***

Hairline cracks spidered across the sheetrock ceiling of the guest room Donny had called home for the last six months. His eyes followed the crooked lines from one corner to another and then back again. He could have easily traced images in his mind's eye of people or animals or perverse fantasies worthy of being featured on the finest shrink's inkblot cards. But as Donny lay on his bed, staring at a blank canvas at three in the morning, the only imaginary image he could see in the ceiling was an oversized cartoonish fist wrapped tightly around his old friend's neck.

Of course, he didn't seriously mean harm upon his friend. Ever since college, Dawa had been like brother, and brothers had a way of getting under each other's skin. In those days, any mention of using Tummo meditation rituals in any capacity other than for personal enlightenment and progress had quickly earned Donny a lecture from the surrogate sibling in the Graham Family Code of Ethics.

But what good did it do to keep such a powerful, life-enhancing method to one's self? To Ford, the notion of esoteric Tummo was selfish and wrong. Should a sect of humanity make a discovery that would be beneficial to all, it would be wrong to keep such information to themselves. Hell, downright sinful. The world needed Tummo, and Donny was going to give it to them.

Donny kept staring, eyes starting to burn, when the lines on the ceiling disappeared and faded in the pale white sheetrock. He rubbed his eyes and blinked, and the lines quickly returned. *Troxler's fading.* He remembered the concept from college, how staring at a certain point for some time caused everything around it to disappear—just like his good sense at the moment. Spreading Tummo to the masses was one of the reasons Donny was in dire straits to begin with.

He sat up in bed and took a few deep breaths to clear his head, dismissing thoughts of violent outbursts and bitter sentiments toward the only person he could count on; the one person keeping him from a six-by-six cell; a person who could very well be sharing a cell next to him if their plan went south.

Still, he couldn't get over the idea that no matter what he accomplished in life, Dawa would always regard him as inferior. He was the eternal apprentice, insecure, greedy, and jealous, unable to see that his negative emotions and self-serving character traits were the very reason why Dawa would always be the superior practitioner of Tummo.

But Donny knew he wasn't a screw-up. Or incompetent. Or a pitiful albatross forever hung from Dawa's neck.

No, Donny could do some things right.

He reached in the nightstand by his bed, rummaging through the clutter to find something in the back.

A pill bottle. Ocula.

He had long ceased taking it; the drug was far too dangerous for casual use. This, however, was not a casual occasion. In fact, it was something he had planned since he'd learned about the volcanic eruption in Costa Rica—an eruption that just so happened to coincide with the death of Ryan Tanner. Ford had dreamed about both events occurring simultaneously only moments before Claire's call confirming the news. One or the other showing up in Ford's dreamscape might have been coincidental, but Ford was a gambler who always played the pot odds, and this was no coincidence. He knew better.

His thumb flicked the cap and the lid popped open. Donny tapped a single pill out into his hand, looking it over and admiring the power of such a tiny little pill.

Then he swallowed it. *Won't be much time now*, he thought. A minute, maybe two. Just enough time to deploy a pre-sleep meditation technique he'd recently picked up during his newfound downtime at the monastery.

He laid back on the bed, closed his eyes and thought:

*Dawa isn't the only one with a few tricks up his sleeve.*

# Chapter 15:
# Dos Jefes

A set of all-terrain tires plowed into the shallow stream, creating a pair of muddy wakes that tailed the Jeep through to the other side where the riverbank looked steep, but climbable. The driver geared down on the approach and told his partner riding shotgun to hang on. The two hostages in the back braced for impact while the 4x4 climbed the riverbank, sending a rooster tail of thick mud sailing behind it before leveling out at the top. Soon it was out of the mire and back to the dusty Costa Rican trail.

Aguilar looked over at his friend and spoke, voice jostled by every bump and pothole. "Don't worry, Claire. If they wanted us dead, they would have left our bodies in the jungle."

"Do I look worried?"

Of course she didn't. She'd seen far worse situations than Alejandro Aguilar could imagine, but that never stopped him from trying to console her. "No offense, Claire. But you don't have to act so tough *all* of the time. It's okay to be vulnerable every now and then."

She ignored the comment. "Where do you think they're taking us?"

"That's what confuses me," Aguilar said, peering out the back window. 'The sun's behind us, when it should be in front of us. It appears as though they are taking us deeper into the jungle."

"Toward Poás Volcano?"

"Cállate!" The soldier's voice roared from the front, ordering the two in the back to shut up. He lit a cigarette and mumbled something as he continued to drive. His partner rode shotgun and glared at the two in the back for what seemed like an eternity, then turned back around to watch the trail ahead.

The Jeep trail was choked with underbrush and thick jungle flora—an indication it was rarely (if ever) used. Combined with a dense canopy overhead, the greenery formed a tight jungle tunnel just barely big enough for the Jeep to get through. For all Claire and Aguilar knew, they could be heading anywhere.

Suddenly, Claire noticed flickers of sunlight making brief appearances on her lap. The light steadied, and soon they were driving out of the canopy and back into the open Costa Rican countryside. The hostages in the back leaned toward one another to get a better view out of the front windshield. The northern summit of Poás Volcano was in full view.

"There it is," Aguilar whispered. He nudged Claire and said, "If I had known we'd be getting a free ride, we could have left these burdensome backpacks behind, no?"

"You, maybe." She minded the guards, careful not to speak too loudly. "But if I don't get a message out today, this place will be leveled by lunchtime tomorrow." Aguilar looked confused, but Claire was reluctant to explain. "No matter what happens, Han, promise me you'll locate the other outliers."

"Claire, you know I don't like when you start talking crazy—"

"Just promise me."

Aguilar nodded, then turned to look out the window to hide the concern on his face. Claire's mind had been through the ringer over the last six months, and the Costa Rican aristocrat was worried about his friend.

The Jeep slowed, the sounds of tires plowing across mud and puddles and roots replaced by the low roar of crunching gravel. The hostages looked ahead to see three Hummers parked on the side of a gravel road that led to high razor-wired fences surrounding a concrete compound on the other side. A dozen men stood by, with the apparent leader standing in the middle of the road a few feet ahead of them. His hand went up and the Jeep stopped.

Tight knots in Claire's throat were making it hard for her to swallow. After six long months, she was back at the facility—a place where she had been tormented and tortured for weeks on end. A place worse than the war-torn streets of Estonia, or Baghdad, or Mexico City, or anywhere else she'd covered over the course of her journalistic career. A place where she'd realized there were far worse things playing out in the mind than the most vile and violent locations on Earth.

The half-doors on the Jeep swung open and the soldiers hopped out, then ordered their captives to crawl out. The two obeyed as they stumbled out of the vehicle, hands zip-tied behind their backs. The rest of the soldiers advanced in quick steps, their rifles zeroed in on the two intruders, itching for one of them to make the wrong move.

Safeties clicked off as the soldiers halted, holding the line as the leader approached, hard-sole shoes grinding the gravel beneath a confident stride, his long shadow crawling up the captives' feet before spreading across their faces. The two squinted in the man's direction as the bright yellow orb washed out the scene behind him, leaving his face in the dark.

Finally, the three were face to face. The man towered over Aguilar (who was already tall by Costa Rican standards) as his hands filled the pockets of his dark slacks. His off-white button-down, silk black tie, and silver cuff links quickly caught Claire's attention, the white-collar uniform more fitting for a desk jockey than a field agent assigned to jungle duty.

He leaned down to face Aguilar, the stub of a smoked-down cigar caught in the clenches of his canines. "Well, well. If it isn't Alejandro Aguilar." Prado studied his prey, his calm and baritone voice resonating from under a thick mustache. "You're a little way from your home. What brings you to the jungle, patrón?"

Aguilar looked up defiantly. "Bird watching, señor."

Prado laughed, then looked to Claire. "And what about this one? Are you here for the birds, too, señorita?"

"What can I say? The majestic call of the wild toucan gets me weak in the knees."

"I see, I see." Prado's amused grin softened. "Well, I hate to ruffle your feathers"—he motioned for one of the soldiers to hand over the ring-bound rolodex—"but it appears our files say you are someone we've been looking for." He flipped through the photos, then stopped. He turned the photo for Claire to see. "Yes, here it is. Ms. Claire Connor. That is, unless, you have a twin sister. Do you have a twin sister, Ms. Connor?"

Not a word.

"I did not think so. Well, this is a most fortunate turn of events, isn't it?"

Aguilar spoke up. "What do you want with Claire?"

"That's none of your concern, señor," Prado said, stroking his thick mustache. "But, since we're going to be working together for the foreseeable future, I might as well fill you in now. Tell me, Alejandro"—he nodded back to reference the facility behind him—"how much do you know about the installation here?"

"I know enough, Prado."

"Sí? Did you know it is the product of the continual

Yankee invasion into the affairs of a sovereign Central American country? The result of a company too afraid to test new technology on its own soil; too afraid to show its people the ugly side of capitalism; too afraid its citizens might cringe once they see the true cost of the products they so dearly crave. Tell me, Alejandro: does it feel good knowing your friend's Yankee countrymen are using Costa Rica to do their dirty work?"

"And how much did they pay you, Prado?" Alejandro asked. "You think I don't know about your history with the CIA? With Ryan Tanner?"

"A man like yourself should know there is a difference between keeping the enemy close and selling out one's own country. I never gave up intel that would harm the homeland, cabrón. Only enough to keep the back channels open. Security forces were set to raid the facility when the volcano erupted. That is an indisputable fact."

Claire asked, "So why is the facility still standing, Prado? And what do you want with us?"

"Yes, Prado," Aguilar said. "You never answered my question."

The government official sighed, then said, "When the smoke cleared, we realized the building was still intact. The exterior and upper level was heavily damaged by the wildfires, but the installation below was spared from the volcano's wrath. Once inside, we discovered a foreign technology no government could pass up."

"Because every government wants to rule the world— Costa Rica included," Claire quipped.

"No, Ms. Connor. Because every government is responsible for the well-being of its people. It's easy for you gringos to criticize the way things are done here when you get to go home to your dancing stars and football and safe suburban homes. But you are not going to stand there and tell me the United States would not jump at the opportunity to harness a weapon of this magnitude.

Prado shook his head in disgust. "Puta madre . . . Your government has been on top of the world since 1945, all thanks to a weapon not unlike this one. Almost 200 countries in the world today, and only nine have the ability to wipe the rest of us off the planet. And not a *single one* of them from Latin America. Well, no more. Now is the time for Costa Rica to rise up and claim its rightful seat at the table of world superpowers."

A fire was in Prado's eyes that Aguilar knew all too well. It was the fire of a man on a mission, one who would stop at nothing to achieve his goal. Still, he had to try and reason with his captor.

"Prado. Jefe. What lies in the basement of that facility isn't some arsenal of nuclear warheads or smart bombs or nerve agent—it's unlike anything we have ever seen before. Do you have any idea what the human cost could be just from deploying this technology even once?" Aguilar motioned toward Claire. "Without the outliers, Ocula 2.0 is useless. What about them? Can you live with yourself knowing you must kidnap and torture innocent civilians just to have the tools you need to use your weapon? And what happens to these tools once you no longer have a need for them?"

"The same thing that happens to every soldier once the campaign is over, cabrón. They get discharged."

The callous omen triggered Aguilar and he had to act. He lunged toward Prado with the force of a linebacker, yelling to Claire as he drove his forward-leaning body into Prado's chest.

*"RUN, CLAIRE!"*

The impact sent Prado crashing into the gravel behind him as the guards closed in on the chaos, yelling and dropping their rifles to pull Aguilar off their boss. Everyone was distracted by the ensuing dogpile, including the guard holding Claire's arm. She turned into him and planted her knee deep into his gut, doubling him over before pushing him into the mix.

Then she ran.

It took four soldiers to pull Aguilar off Prado. They grabbed the assailant by the arms, and with one fluid motion hurled him off his target and into the front of the Jeep he'd ridden in on. Aguilar slammed into the grill back-first and let out a painful yell before sliding down and coming to rest against the front bumper.

Prado rose to his feet to see Claire disappearing into the tree line. "STOP HER!"

One of the guards raised his muzzle, only to have Prado grab the barrel and yank it toward the ground. "You fool!" he said, "We need her alive!" The soldier kept his weapon lowered and gave chase. Two more followed, but it didn't matter. Prado already knew she was gone.

He dusted his shirt off, his furious eyes returning to his attacker's. "You sanctimonious *hijo de puta*. You stand here preaching your concern for innocents, yet you have no problem colluding with Yankee bitches to sabotage the best interests of your own countrymen. You think I know nothing of your family's wealth, or how they acquired it? You're nothing more than a narco, amigo. Your hands are not as clean as you would like to think."

Aguilar sat in the gravel, exasperated but pleased with himself. He looked toward the jungle, satisfied Claire would make it to safety. Then he looked back to his captor. "No one will stand for this, Prado. What you are doing here is a crime against humanity. The people of Costa Rica will never stand for it."

Prado replied, "What the people don't know is what makes them the people, Aguilar."

"They will know, Prado. You won't be able to keep this quiet forever. And you cannot expect me to carry your dark secrets once you have finished playing God here."

Tensions mounted in a silent stalemate, the cool breeze rustling the leaves of surrounding trees not strong enough to clear the conflict from the air. Prado paced in front of Aguilar, hand cupped over his chin, finger tapping his mustache in contemplation. Finally, he stopped, reached behind his back, and pulled a pistol from his belt.

"You know something, Alejandro? You're right. I would never expect you to keep quiet."

Aguilar spit on the ground as Prado raised the muzzle to his head. Time slowed down and the world went quiet as the aristocrat watched Prado's index finger wrap around the trigger. He closed his eyes and silently recited The Lord's Prayer, "*Padre nuestro, que estás en el cielo, santificado sea tu nombre . . .*"

That's when they heard it, the sound halting both Aguilar's prayers and Prado's half-pulled trigger. It was a strange sound overhead, one that could have easily been mistaken for a single-prop airplane had they not been in the middle of nowhere. But it couldn't be a plane—it was too subtle, softer than any propeller-powered device he had ever heard before. It whirled and hummed from above as the noise grew louder.

Prado knew the sound all too well. He turned to look, and that's when he saw it.

"*DRONE!*"

He packed his pistol back into his belt and took off

running, screaming at his men to get as far away from the facility as possible. The soldiers panicked, not sure where to run, some dropping their rifles and sprinting down the gravel road while others made for the trees.

Aguilar, on the other hand, didn't move a muscle. He sat still and waited, saying one last prayer for Claire's safety, and then another: that soon he would be with his wife again. He closed his eyes once more and the missiles fell, the all-white flash from the blast followed by a shockwave that knocked Aguilar unconscious long before the flames ever reached him. Soon the entire area was being devoured by hungry red-orange clouds that billowed outward from ground zero and consumed every living thing in sight. Fast and merciless. Nothing was spared.

It appeared that Alejandro Aguilar's boyhood premonition had been little more than a dream after all.

***

In the distant jungle, no more than a mile from the facility, Claire heard the sounds of a massive explosion in the direction she was fleeing from. She dove behind a log to take cover in case the airstrike continued. Immediately, she thought of the bombings in the Baltics, how the powerful blasts could be felt from miles away.

This one was worse. The ground shook and the jungle reacted as birds fled their nests and animals rustled through the dense underbrush in search of higher ground. It was utter chaos as the deafening blast climaxed, then fainted and echoed into the distance, then disappeared.

The stillness of the jungle returned, and Claire thought about Han. *My God. No one could have survived that. No one.*

She lay by the log, arm bent and resting on top. She buried her face in the crease of her arm and began to cry.

# Chapter 16:
# Premonition

The warm mid-morning sun shone through a set of thin and dingy curtains covering the plate-glass window in Donny's room, creating a greenhouse effect that, on most days, would have been more than enough to wake the hot-natured houseguest from his slumber. But this morning was different. It was getting dangerously close to noon, and Donny was still asleep.

On a typical day, Donny would already be up well before seven, with most of his chores around the monastery finished by lunchtime (Dawa was all for charity, but would never suffer his old friend to live as a freeloader). He would spend the afternoons reading and meditating, then cook a meal for supper that he usually wound up eating alone. With his belly full and the day winding down, he'd return to the seclusion of his bedroom to finish up a few more chapters before calling it lights out around eleven. This had been the routine for months, with few exceptions.

This was one of those exceptions.

When Donny finally opened his eyes to glance at the clock on his nightstand, the green flashing numbers brought a crooked smile to his face. *11:15 a.m. Exactly eight hours since I took Ocula. Incredible.*

The efficacy of the gene-altering drug never ceased to amaze him. His entire career had been spent on what critics called pseudoscience: techniques that couldn't be verifiably quantified or proven. That's where the pitch came in. Creating a presentation to convince followers that his pricey programs were the answer to their problems had taken years of trial and error to perfect—and just as much time finding the right target market. Middle-aged women, 45 to 54, annual income between $25,000 and $50,000, and most importantly: women of faith. It was faith that transformed those buyers-on-the-fence into lifetime customers. True believers. Folks who would follow Donny Ford to the ends of the earth, if he so desired.

But with Ocula, no faith was required. You took the pill, and it did exactly what it said it would, down to the minute. It didn't need a sales pitch or persuasive ad copy or even those annoying minutes-long television ads—it just worked.

He lay awake in bed for a few minutes and collected his thoughts, then he got up and got dressed, throwing on a fresh T-shirt while thinking about his past experiences with medications. He remembered the first time he'd gone under general anesthesia after reporting to the ER for abdominal pain. The stress of life on the road had caught up to him in Phoenix, and after a few hours in a sleep-induced state, he'd awoken to learn a half-dozen ulcers had perforated his stomach lining, wreaking chaos on his abdominal cavity.

It had been a harrowing experience, but the strict diet, abstinence from alcohol and caffeine, and the months of recovery that followed weren't the first things to come to Donny's mind when someone mentioned ulcers. No, instead it was the general anesthesia that stuck with him. Propofol, the stuff made famous at the turn of the century by a questionable California doctor who had put one of the biggest pop stars in modern history to sleep for good.

*Potent stuff,* Donny thought as he buttoned up a Hawaiian shirt, trying not to dwell too much on the pain in his hand left over from the auto accident. *Pretty effective, too.* It was the only other drug Donny could think of that did exactly what it said it would. But it was given under the strict direction of an anesthesiologist—a medical professional with no less than twelve years of higher education standing at bedside from start to finish. One mistake, one miscalculation, one drug as innocuous as an herbal supplement a patient failed to mention prior to surgery, and the milky white solution creeping through an IV could be the last thing a patient ever saw.

That's what made Ocula so different. Revolutionary, even. Instead of applying the sweeping effects found in opioids or statins or anesthesia, Ocula found the specific source of the problem—a single sequence in the genetic code—and fixed it. And once the gap in the line of code was fixed, no amount of Ocula could result in an overdose; what patients didn't need simply took a one-way trip out via the renal system.

*If only I had thought something like that up, maybe I wouldn't be in this mess.* Dreaming about a career in biotech was a stretch for someone like him, but it was a nice thought nonetheless. He took one last look in the mirror, then left his room just before noon, making his way to the kitchen to scramble up something for brunch. Dawa had gotten in just before sunrise but would probably be up soon, given that the man had been running on catnaps for the last six months. It was crucial for Donny to get his ducks in a row before explaining to the detective why they needed to hit the road as soon as possible.

Unfortunately, Ford had little time to hatch up a story. He stood in front of a stove that wasn't even hot yet when Dawa walked in.

"Good afternoon, Donald. I trust you slept well?" Dawa asked as he walked past the amateur chef and straight toward his favorite mug.

"Slept great. And you?"

"Oh, you know me. I find long slumbers give the mind too much time to forget the knowledge acquired from the day before." The guru was already dressed, his empty cup dangling from his finger as he stared at the empty stovetop. He looked at Donny, eyebrows raised as if to inquire about a missing tea kettle.

"Sorry, Graham. You know I typically don't sleep in like this."

"That is quite all right, Donald. So long as it does not become a habit. I know how much you have been through, but you have come too far to slip back into a depressive state of mind. We cannot let that happen, my friend."

Ford nodded in agreement as he set the kettle and a frying pan on the stove. Dawa took a seat on a stool at the large oak island in the center of the kitchen.

"So, Donald. How is the leg?"

Curiosity arose on Donny's face. His old friend wasn't one for small talk. He shook his head and affirmed, "It's good, Graham. Still got the limp, but it's not too bad most days. Other than that, it's all good. Thanks for asking."

"And the hand?"

A spatula was nearby and Donny snagged it, twirling it in circles and showing off his range of motion. "Good as new . . . Say, Graham. No disrespect, but what's with all the health questions? Worried I'm gonna croak before we get a chance to nail these Pharma Bros.?"

"No, of course not. I am just concerned for your well-being, that's all. I have not seen you sleep this late in months."

"Well, with all due respect, you're usually still at work by the time I get up."

Dawa couldn't disagree there. Work was taking a toll; harboring a fugitive even more so. He knew he couldn't keep up the pace forever. He rubbed a set of bloodshot eyes and waited patiently for the water to boil.

"So," Dawa said, "if you are not in any pain, and everything is all good, as you say, then what kept you in bed half of the day?"

Two eggs cracked on the edge of a cast-iron pan, and Ford started in. "I'm glad you asked that, Dawa,"—he glanced back at his friend, then continued cooking—"and, I'm also glad you're sitting down."

"Do you have something important to tell me, Donald?"

"Yeah. Actually, I do. Do you remember the dreams I told you about when I first came to the monastery last February?"

Dawa remembered.

"Well, I've had a lot of time to think about everything over the last few months. Especially some of the things we first talked about; how you thought the pill couldn't possibly have an effect on reality; how you thought my dreams were little more than maddening montages of my worst fears and anxieties."

Dawa was tired and reluctant to engage. He had made it crystal clear in the past that he didn't believe the combination of meds and meditation could grant a user the ability to hold power or persuasions over other sentient beings. It also appeared his old friend hadn't changed his mind one bit. He took a deep breath, then asked, "Where are you going with this, Donald?"

Donny set the spatula on the counter and turned around. "I know where we can find Fenton Reed."

Dawa's eyes flickered and his brow pushed inward. The man who always had all the answers, who could always be counted on to deliver a wise or witty or instructional retort, was at a loss for words. Finally, almost afraid to ask, "How do you know where Fenton Reed is, Donald?"

"Because I had a dream about his whereabouts last night."

A deep sigh of relief escaped Dawa's chest as he breathed again. He smiled and shook his head. "Donald. My friend. We have discussed this. There is no way your dreams have any true influence on reality. It simply is not possible. You would do better to spend all of this time and energy focusing on the precepts, on the here and now, instead of these preposterous claims of mind control from afar."

"That's just it, Dawa. I'm not talking about mind control." The tea kettle began to whistle. "Tea, Graham?"

Dawa nodded yes, and Donny filled his mug. The guru was officially intrigued. "So you have abandoned the old notions of meditative influence and mystical powers. That's good to hear, Donald. I was beginning to really worry about you. But, if you are not alluding to nudging Fenton in the direction you want him to go, how could you possibly know where he is?"

"Because I've seen him."

"When?"

"I just told you. Last night, in a dream."

"The dreams again, Donald?"

"Just hear me out here, Graham. Unless you've got some place to be."

Dawa checked his phone. Sarcastically, "No. Not for a moment, anyway. I guess I could give you five minutes. Maybe six."

"Okay, so do you remember the Himalayan yogis we stayed with the summer between our sophomore and junior year of college?"

"Of course I do. Family friends. In fact, Tashi was the first person to introduce me to the ancient Buddhist tradition of

Nyingma." He eyed Donny suspiciously. "This has something to do with the mindstream, doesn't it?"

"You said it, Graham. Not me. But you can't blame me for looking further into these ancient methods of tapping into the so-called sacred streams of enlightenment, especially after what happened in February."

Noise from the grease popping on the stove had died down, signaling to Donny a well-done breakfast. He fixed two plates of bacon and eggs, slid one over to Dawa, and took a seat at the island. Dawa stabbed his eggs, but couldn't take a bite yet. He had too many questions.

"So you've taken an interest in the Nyingma tradition. A tradition based on ancient teachings that were supposedly revealed to Buddhist masters through their dreams. Is it safe to assume you believe the location of Fenton Reed has been revealed to you through the dream you had last night, Donald?"

"Yes. I believe so."

"But you were also convinced Ocula played a role in your troubled state, correct? And you have not taken Ocula in months . . ."

The look on Donny's face told Dawa everything he needed to know. "Donald! You have taken Ocula once again?"

"I was going to tell you—"

"Unbelievable! After everything we have been through, all of our hard work to bring this toxic pharmaceutical company to justice, you decide to experiment with this mind-altering drug once more?"

"If you would just let me explain—"

"What did I tell you when I agreed to hide you from the authorities? No drugs and no alcohol, Donald. None. Once again, you have completely violated my trust." His weathered fist slammed into the table and rattled the plates. "I should have known better!"

"I understand you're upset . . . " Donny paused and searched for a bargaining chip as Dawa steamed in front of him. The Buddhist master was no stranger to moments of backsliding, but this time was different. His face raged a deep red, balled fists shaking and looking for a reason, any reason, to strike. Donny had never seen him this upset before. He decided to risk it all.

"You must know that I know how upset taking anything would make you, right?"

The stone man across from him didn't flinch.

"I must have had a good reason to take it. And I did, Graham. I really did. So, please: let me tell my story. If you're still angry by the time I'm finished, I'll turn myself in today."

Through the anger, Dawa mustered, "You will turn yourself in. Just like that, Donald?"

Donald snapped his fingers. "Just like that. You won't have a thing to worry about, either. I'll say I've been living in the woods or out of a fast-food dumpster for the last six months. It's worked for other guys on the Most Wanted list before." He scratched his five-o'clock shadow, then moved up to his shaggy head. "Hell, I even look the part."

He didn't like being deceived, but Dawa had to hear him out. What did he have to lose? If this was another one of Donny's schemes—which was a very good possibility—then he could finally send the pitchman packing straight to the front office at Atlanta P.D. to turn himself in. It took a moment to register, but Dawa suddenly realized Donny's stunt could very well bring an end to six months of stress and deceit and moral ambiguity that very afternoon. He hid a smile, then said, "Okay, Donald. Let's hear what you have got to say for yourself."

Donny breathed a sigh of relief. "Good. Thank you. Although, it may take a little longer than five minutes." He tapped his fingers, looked up and thought aloud, "All right, where were we?"

"You took Ocula last night."

"Right. So I've had a lot of time to study here, as I'm sure you already know. What you don't know about is the research I've conducted into Nyingma, primarily the teachings that illustrate a spiritual channel that, with the right mindset, can be accessed by people across the globe."

"I always said we were connected, Donald. But I think—"

"I saw Fenton on this spiritual channel, Graham. Last night, after taking Ocula. I saw him and I saw exactly where he was—right now, at this very moment." He leaned forward. "He's in Savannah, just a few hours from here."

"Hold on a minute, Donald. You slept until noon today, remember? And you say you took Ocula last night? But in the past you told me you only had these prophetical dreams when you *didn't* sleep well. You said they only occurred after being up all night, stricken with illness."

"Yeah, the headaches. You're right, Dawa. But here's the thing: I started looking into other meditative practices and found something called lucid dreaming. It's basically like falling asleep with willful intent. You lie down in bed, begin your meditative practice, focus on what's important to you, and pretty soon you're fast asleep and in the midst of the topics *you* choose. Like, say, the whereabouts of Asteria's outliers, perhaps?"

"How could the willful intent to dream lucidly eliminate the physical side effects of Ocula, Donald? Every one of the outliers we know of, including yourself, spoke to how debilitated they were each time they had one of these dreams. Now you're not affected?" He sighed and shook his head. "It just does not make much sense to me."

"Honestly, it doesn't make much sense to me, either. I mean I haven't even had a lot of time to think about it. Maybe it's got something to do with letting go of everything and not resisting the effects of the drug, like the difference between a bad psychedelic trip and a good one. Meditation can be a pretty powerful drug itself, Graham. But like I said, who knows. The important thing is that we know Fenton's in Savannah, and we need to get there as soon as possible."

"Paul Freeman is on his way here now, Donald. We should probably speak to him first before embarking on a road trip to the coast, wouldn't you agree?"

Dismissively, "Yeah. Sure, Dawa. You're right. But I'm just saying, after that. We need to hit the road."

Dawa stood from his chair and crossed his arms. "There is just one problem, my friend. While I would like to believe you have had contact with Mr. Reed, there simply is no proof. Nothing. And without proof, I do not think it would be wise for us to hit the road together." He chuckled at the thought. "Just think: a first-grade detective and a federal fugitive, caught searching for another fugitive linked to unsubstantiated claims of Big Pharma corruption. And of course, what kind of conspiracy theory would this be without getting the CIA involved?"

Once again, condescension from the Tummo master had clouded the monastery air. He didn't mean anything by it, and Donny knew that. It was just his way. But, that didn't change the fact that Dawa's way could turn most people sour in just a few short quips. It was time for Donny to cut the comic relief short.

"Where's the jump drive, Graham?" Donny asked.

Dawa's joyful face quickly turned stoic. He paused, then

said, "How could you possibly know about Fenton's jump drive, Donald?"

"Because I saw it. In the dream. Fenton showed it to me."

A small rectangular bulge showed through Dawa's shirt pocket. He placed his palm over it, still speechless. Finally, "But how—"

"I don't know, Graham. I really don't know. The whole reason I've been practicing lucid dreaming for the last several months was in anticipation of a lead, a name, a picture . . . something I could cling to before taking Ocula and entering a lucid dream state. I thought this would help me have more influence on Fenton, persuade him to go where I wanted him to go, even.

"Only, it didn't. Instead of the other dreams like with Stevens and Tanner, where I just kind of witnessed everything folding out in front of me, this one was different. I was *there*, Graham. So was Fenton. In Savannah, River Street, to be exact, eating Baby Ruths and sipping on Cokes—which was kinda weird, now that I think about it. I don't even like Baby Ruths . . ."

"Let's rein it back in, Donald."

"He told me we should meet. He also said you'd never believe me." Donny pointed to Dawa's shirt pocket. "So, he told me to ask you about the drive."

The shock of such a revelation took Dawa aback. He fell back into his chair, arms still crossed, evaluating the situation like any good detective would. Was any of this possible, or was this one of Donny's parlor tricks? Had Donny snuck into his room and found the jump drive he'd picked up from Fenton's old roommate the day before? *No, that couldn't be,* thought Dawa, shaking his head. How could Donny have known the drive belonged to Fenton, or even to look for a jump drive in the first place? Not to mention Dawa's room policy: the door stayed locked 24/7, home or not.

The midday light shone down through the skylight and traced out the shadow of the jump drive protruding from Dawa's shirt pocket. Had the legendary pitchman Donny Ford caught a glimpse of the hardware and simply used that as a faux prop in an elaborate story to break out of seclusion and escape back into the real world? Dawa couldn't say for certain, but something wasn't quite adding up.

"So, what do you think?" Donny asked, breaking Dawa's concentration. The guru wasn't sure what to say, but before he could open his mouth to answer the doorbell rang, followed by five heavy knocks.

"Dawa Graham? Ford? Is anyone home?" The man outside sounded exhausted and desperate.

"It's me. Paul Freeman."

# Chapter 17:
# Southern Hospitality

The foyer of the Vajrayãna Monastery had been transformed from an empty-vaulted entryway to a kiosk for camping supplies in less than five minutes. Dawa and Donny looked at one another as Paul continued to unload the car, dumbfounded as to how the young couple could fit so much junk into the back of a Mercury sedan.

"Sure you don't need any help?" Donny asked as he held the front door open.

"No, thanks. I think we've got it." Paul entered the foyer toting a storage box, and Michelle followed with Aaron in tow. Dawa bowed and greeted the road-weary couple.

"Mr. and Mrs. Freeman. How good it is to finally meet you both." He relieved Michelle's shoulder of Aaron's hefty diaper bag, and she thanked him for his hospitality. He asked Michelle, "Would you like me to show you to your room?"

She nodded, and the two walked toward the back of the monastery. Paul pretended to put his belongings in order while Donny stood by, waiting for a proper introduction. There was no avoiding it. Finally, Paul looked up.

"Heard a lot about you, Donny Ford."

"Likewise," Donny replied, hand extended. Paul looked down to address the dreadful salutation. He knew he was now a guest in Dawa Graham's home—not Donny's—and the urge to deny the gesture was strong. He decided on peace, for now, and shook Donny's hand as half-heartedly as he possibly could.

Donny said, "It's good to have you here, Paul. A friend of Claire's is a friend of mine"—he referenced Dawa, who had walked toward the back—"well, ours. You do know Claire saved my life, right? If it weren't for her, I'm not sure I would have ever made it out of that hospital—"

"You said likewise," Paul interrupted. "What do you mean you've heard a lot about me?"

"Well, just from Claire. You two went through some shit together, and over the last few months we've stayed in touch," his eyes narrowed as he continued, "but you already knew that, didn't you?"

Paul agreed, making his dislike for Donny's suspicious tone apparent. He picked up his backpack and threw it across his shoulder. He looked at Donny stone-faced and pointed down the hall. "Our room's down here?"

"Yeah. Three doors down on the left. Watch your step; this place is old and some of the floorboards are a little uneven and loose."

The wood floors creaked and footsteps echoed as Paul made his way down the narrow hall toward the back of the monastery. Donny stood and stared at the back of a person he didn't trust. He let Paul get halfway down the hall before saying, "Hey, you know why you're here, don't you?"

"Sure do," Paul answered without turning around.

"Good. That's real good. Because if I don't get a phone call by tonight . . . "

Paul stopped and turned. His face was tired yet stern, effectively expressing a lack of patience for any of Ford's bullshit. "If you don't get a phone call then what, Ford?"

"Look, Claire's a friend. And frankly, I don't trust you. You've been gone for six months, with neither one of us sure of your whereabouts. For all we know, you could be colluding with the enemy. And I haven't gone through all of this over the better part of a year just to get caught or killed because my benevolent friend is kind enough to let a fox in the hen house. Get where I'm coming from?"

The floors creaked again, only faster this time, as Paul quickly returned to meet Donny face to face. "Yeah. I get exactly where you're coming from, Ford. You're an opportunist who's looking out for himself, worried more about someone turning you in than bringing Asteria to justice."

"You don't know a thing about—"

"No? You said it yourself, Don. The last thing you're going to do is get caught or killed. Tells me everything I need to know about you, pal."

"You're one to talk," Donny scoffed. "If you were so concerned about bringing down Asteria, then why'd you run in the first place?"

"Unlike some people, I didn't have a benefactor to keep me in hiding."

"No, but he did lend you his car—"

"That will be enough!" Dawa yelled as he emerged from the back and confronted the two. "I did not invite either of you into this home to cause a commotion. There are great matters at hand that we must discuss, bigger problems to address than who is the alpha in this situation." He walked toward the meditation room. "Besides, is it not obvious that I am the one in control?"

***

Golden shrines and Tibetan murals wouldn't have been Paul's first decorating choice for his little family's starter home in the burbs, but for an estate called the Vajrayāna Monastery, he expected nothing less. He was supposed to be meditating alongside Dawa and Donny, who were sitting close by with legs crossed, eyes closed—but Paul couldn't resist looking around. High maroon ceilings. Tall oaken columns. Buddha statues and Asian artwork . . . It was Graham's own little piece of Tibet, packaged neatly into a two-hundred-acre lot tucked away in the wooded flatlands south of Atlanta. The man had a passion for Tibetan Buddhism, and he'd done everything in his power to incorporate his beliefs into his daily life, right down to the smoldering incense and wallpaper. Claire had mentioned Dawa's first-grade detective accolades, but she hadn't talked about the man's profound faith. Paul was impressed.

Dawa, however, was not. Paul's twisting and turning to look around had broken the absolute silence of the room, and the guru took notice. He opened his eyes to see Paul turned backward and facing the far wall.

"Ahem," Dawa groaned.

Paul turned back swiftly. "Sorry, Mr. Graham. I was just admiring all of the artwork here."

"Please, call me Dawa." His hands cupped his knees, eyes closing again. "Now, if you will join Donald and I, we can get back to our meditative session."

The new pupil obeyed, and for the next ten minutes the three men sat with little more than the sound of their own breath. It was a practice Dawa required of all his guests; especially when stressful situations were sure to follow. In such cases, the detective knew how important it was to have a clear mind before facing tribulations like crime scenes or corrupt companies or ghosts from the past. That's why Dawa had meditated more in the last six months than ever before.

Soon a pleasant bell chimed, marking the end of the meditation session. The men opened their eyes, squinting and blinking while they readjusted to the daylight coming in through the tall windows at the front of the room. The two guests waited for him to speak. His attention was on the newcomer.

"I think it is important to acknowledge the bravery Paul has displayed by coming out of hiding to help us bring Asteria Pharmaceuticals to justice."

"I don't think I'd call it bravery," Paul replied. "Although I do appreciate your willingness to take in a stranger. I can't begin to thank you enough for your hospitality."

A soft smile arose on Dawa's face. "Now, Paul. There is no need to thank me for anything. The mutual friendship we all share with our friend Claire Connor is validation enough."

"Speaking of Claire," Donny quipped, "isn't she supposed to be giving me a call any minute now?" He took out his cell phone and placed it on the floor in front of him. "Or a text? An email? Anything to let us know you're not toying with us, Paul?"

Dawa's stern expression grew out of his distaste for Donny's attitude, but he did make a valid point. They had no idea who this Paul Freeman really was—only stories from Claire about their escape from Costa Rica. After that, the Book of Paul seemed to head into a tailspin. Claire had had a plan (albeit a flimsy one) to take down Asteria, and Paul had pretended to go along with it, right up until the point he'd stolen her car and headed for the hills.

When Donny would bring this up during their sporadic long-distance phone calls, Claire would always take up for Paul, saying he'd had no other choice but to flee with his wife and kid, that she would have done the same thing had she had the well-being of her family to think about.

This never sat well with Donny, and Dawa knew it. It also wouldn't be the first time he had to play the good cop for the sake of moving the mission along. "Please forgive us for asking such questions, Paul. But I am sure you already know how sensitive this situation is."

"Of course."

"Can you tell us when was the last time you spoke to Claire?"

"Monday night. I got myself pulled over earlier that day, and I panicked. I had been off the grid for the last six months, and I was convinced my license was going to show up on the radar. So I turned to the only person I knew I could trust."

"The same person you left hanging in Atlanta last winter?" Donny asked. Paul's eyes cut over toward the aggressor, but he ignored the remark.

He addressed Dawa. "Claire filled me in on everything she'd been through over the last six months, although most of it I already knew. She was living with Alejandro Aguilar in San José and looking into the whereabouts of the other outliers while doing her best to keep a low profile. What I didn't know was that she'd taken a keen interest in the site surrounding Tanner's facility—the facility that was supposedly destroyed in the Poás eruption."

"And now she's not answering her phone," Dawa replied. He turned to Donny. "Perhaps she has ventured into dangerous territory, Donald."

"That's what I think," Paul said. "She told me she was hiking into Poás National Park first thing Tuesday morning, said it would take at least a day to confirm whether or not the facility had been completely destroyed. She also told me if I didn't hear from her within 36 hours to contact this man." Paul reached in his pocket and handed Dawa a wadded piece of paper. "His name's Colin Kovic, currently with Central Intelligence. He was

Claire's contact for this little operation she had undertaken."

Donny jumped to his feet so fast he would've lost his shoes had they not been laced up right. "*THE CIA*? These are the same bastards who have been trying to kill us for the last six months? And you're telling me Claire was working with them? Sorry, pal, but I call bullshit."

"Look, she couldn't tell me much because she was with someone. Probably Aguilar or one of his guys. And I don't like this anymore than you do. This Kovic guy is the last person I want to call. Honestly, I hadn't even given it a thought. I was convinced she would have rang Donny by now."

"Jesus"—Donny looked down at Dawa—"tell me you don't believe any of this shit!"

The man sat and thought. Then said, "Honestly, Donald, at this point I am not so sure."

"Well, I am," Donny said, pointing a firm finger at Paul. "This guy's flipped, and he's going to end up leading Tanner's old CIA buddies right to us!"

Paul hopped up, and once again he was in Donny's face. "Listen, asshole. I've had about enough of your lip. You think because you made a career out of telling lies that everyone else is as untrustworthy as you?"

Donny grabbed Paul by the shirt with one hand and drew the other back to take a swing. Paul cocked his arm in return, but neither had time to strike a first blow. Dawa was just about to break the two apart when the phone rang. Everyone froze in place, eyes only moving to look down at the flashing cell vibrating on the meditation room floor.

It was Claire.

# Chapter 18:
# The Kovic Connection

"Claire? Where are you? Is everything okay?" Donny was in a panic, frantically asking questions while Dawa crowded in to get closer to the phone. He silently mouthed for Donny to put it on speaker, and with the touch of the screen Claire's voice echoed from the phone as if she were calling plays to the three men through a distorted megaphone.

She said, "I'm fine now, Donny. A little shaken up, but I'll be fine."

Heavy static and garbled tones on the line led Dawa to believe she was on a satellite phone. Odds were whatever trouble she was in, she was still in the thick of it. He leaned in and said, "Claire. This is Dawa Graham. It is good to hear your voice."

"Likewise, Dawa."

"We have Paul Freeman here"—he motioned for Paul to come closer and say something—"and he tells us you two have recently been in touch."

Paul chimed in, "Hey, Claire. Glad to hear you're all right."

"Thanks, Paul. And Dawa, you're right. Paul contacted me a couple of days ago and I asked him to do me a favor. If he didn't hear from me by today he was supposed to contact a man by the name of Colin Kovic."

Paul cut his eyes over toward Donny again, silently telling him *I told you so*. Donny ignored it and asked Claire, "Why would you be in contact with the CIA, Claire? These people want us dead. How can you trust anyone out of Washington?"

"One question at a time, Donny. This isn't a press conference."

Dawa said, "I think it would be wise to fill us in on the agency connection, Claire, so we can move on."

"Right. About the CIA. The reasoning was twofold. First, I had good intel from a source within the agency that higher-ups with knowledge of Tanner's post-retirement project had detailed files on the remaining outliers. We went back and forth for a few weeks, only to catch wind of rumors going around that the outliers had been located and detained."

"Sounds like they picked up where Tanner and Doyle left off," Paul said.

"Exactly. I also received some vague information on some state-owned land in the Virginia mountains, but details about the relevance to our case here never came through."

Dawa asked, "What happened?"

"My source at the CIA disappeared into thin air."

A moment of silence halted the meeting. Finally, Dawa said, "You mentioned a twofold approach . . ."

"Yes. With my source missing in action, piecing together this intricate puzzle came to a stalemate. Nothing was adding up, and I needed fresh intel. So, I decided to contact—no, *had* to contact—the agency directly and divulge some of what I already knew in exchange for cooperation in Costa Rica."

"What kind of cooperation?" Donny asked.

"A black op, one with only a handful of players involved, Kovic and myself included. The agency didn't know what the condition of the facility was, let alone what kind of information Tanner and Doyle had left behind. They knew the former company men had a project in place that was well-advanced from what they had been trying to accomplish, but weren't sure if any of their research survived the volcanic blast."

Paul asked, "So why send you?"

"Because I was the only person alive who had seen the inside of the facility and made it out in one piece." She paused, then said, "Well, you did too, Paul. But I'm pretty sure their calls kept going straight to your voicemail."

"Hysterical," Paul groaned.

"Anyway, the goal seemed simple enough: I was to infiltrate the facility, gather whatever evidence survived the eruption, then escape to the nearby hills to complete the mission from there. That meant laser-painting the facility so F-22s could lock in and level the place once and for all."

Paul said, "But that didn't happen, did it?"

"No, of course not. I got Aguilar to go with me because he knew the area well. We had no trouble getting past the guards on the outer parameter, but we got caught a couple of miles from the facility. That's when we discovered the facility didn't just survive the op, but was being brought back online by the Costa Rican government so they could use Ocula for themselves."

"You're kidding me," Paul said as he crossed his arms and shook his head in disbelief.

"I wish I were. But according to my sources inside the Costa Rican government, the discovery had become the country's number-one priority. It was like an atom-bomb kit, complete with materials and instructions, had landed on the government's doorstep. That's why, as bad as I hated to, I had to contact the CIA. I needed help, and the entire connection was simply a tool to get close to the facility to make sure it was destroyed for good. I had already planned to keep any intel I found to myself. Plus, I knew that the agency's involvement was limited to aerial surveillance and reconnaissance from above, so I would have had a good chance of escaping on foot, especially with Aguilar's help."

"Well, what about Aguilar?" Paul asked. "He still bitching about the Mercury he loaned me?"

Claire didn't speak for a moment, then her voice cracked. "Han . . . I mean, Aguilar. He didn't make it, Paul."

The boys' end of the line went silent again. They stood in the meditation room, hovered around Donny's phone, disturbed by what they were hearing. Paul was the only one who had met Aguilar—the man who had lost his life. But all three of them were sickened by the amount of pain their friend Claire had suffered, not just in the last three days, but for the better part of a year. All at the hands of Asteria.

Finally, Paul offered his condolences, and the rest of the men followed. Never one to dwell on her thoughts for long (mainly because so many of them were too damn painful), Claire solemnly thanked them, and then continued. "After we were captured, we were held at gunpoint just outside of the facility by a man named Gabriel Prado. He said he was the head of Costa Rica's security force. He revealed the government's plans to weaponize Ocula using what he called the Yankee facility, and that's when Alejandro attacked. It gave me a chance to escape, but I didn't stop to think about what his fate might be until it was too late . . ."

Dawa said, "There is no way you could have known, Claire. Alejandro Aguilar decided to take action in a way that would increase his friend's chance of survival. What he did was very brave, Claire, and he did it for you. His last hope was for your safety. Do not be ashamed of honoring his wishes."

They couldn't hear it, but Claire was wiping tears from her eyes. She had grown accustomed to her thick skin, but the thought of Aguilar's death wouldn't let up and weighed heavy on her soul. "Anyway," she pushed forward, "Kovic obviously screwed me. I was supposed to make contact with them around the same time I was to call Ford, but my slight delay obviously resulted in some itchy trigger fingers. It wasn't ten minutes after my escape that I heard bombs being dropped on the facility."

"And you're sure it's destroyed this time?" Paul asked.

"Positive. I could see the flames rising into the sky from my position, followed by the largest tower of smoke I've ever seen in my life. The ground shook so bad from where I was standing that I had to sit. The entire north side of the volcano must have been leveled. Yeah, there's no doubt that place is little more than a smoldering quarry by now."

"And where are you?" Donny asked.

Claire hesitated, then said, "I'm safe. That's all I can tell you right now."

A thought crossed Dawa's mind. "Claire, listen to me. This is very important. Have you contacted this Kovic person since your escape?"

"Of course not! Double-crossing son of a bitch tried to blow my ass to kingdom come."

"Good. Very good. You see, Claire, your contact at the CIA must think you are dead, or at least suspect it. Is that safe to surmise?"

"Yeah," Claire said. "Unless they had eyes in the sky. Either way, it doesn't matter. Satellite surveillance can do a lot of things, but it can't cut through Costa Rica's thick jungle canopy."

Dawa said, "Perhaps we can use this knowledge to our advantage. Tell us, Claire. Will you be able to return to the States soon? With Paul and Donny here at the monastery, your return would bring together almost all of the outliers—at least the ones we know about. That would certainly put us in the best position to move forward with our case against Asteria."

Claire picked up on a word. "*Almost* all the outliers, Dawa?"

"Yes. There is another outlier we have located. A young man by the name of Fenton Reed."

Claire asked, "Who's Fenton Reed?"

# Chapter 19:
# A Cabin in the Woods

It was the middle of August in the humid Virginia mountains, and Colin Kovic was steaming in more ways than one. It had been less than two days since CIA Director Lancaster took him off the Costa Rica assignment; now he was baking in the western Virginia hills while overseeing a black op he wanted nothing to do with. All because of Stephen Cline's big mouth, and his incessant need to impress the new director.

*Brownnosing bastard.*

Kovic lifted a handkerchief from his pocket and dabbed his forehead, a ritual he was forced to repeat every five minutes. He stood on the porch of an old cabin and watched a woodpecker working on a home for itself halfway up a pine tree by the dirt road leading in to the site. He wondered how the creature had the energy to work in this heat, because he sure as shit didn't have any. It was hot, humid, and no place the middle-aged field agent wanted to be.

Kovic was stuck at Skyline, and he was pissed.

There was a good reason the thirty-by-thirty cabin-slash-decoy was made to appear rundown, rustic, and unwelcoming. Like many of the CIA's safe houses and black sites, it was designed to hide in plain view, with a dreadful, almost haunted ambience meant to discourage hunters or hikers or wandering woodsmen from snooping around. The cedar-shingled roof was sagging and covered with moss; horizontal wallboards were full of knotholes with plenty of sawmill-grade wood to keep the carpenter bees busy; and the rotten front porch had more holes and gaps exposing the braces and dirt below than it did walking space.

In front of the cabin, a hog-wire fence with old pallets patching the gaps wavered as it ran its crooked lines fifty feet out from the cabin, then thirty feet across the front where it met the trail coming in. Bleached-out varmint skulls and whitetail deer tines hung from fence posts and trees around the perimeter, with *No Trespassing* signs, Confederate flags and lethal-force warnings rounding out the rural decorations.

It was an ominous, secluded stronghold; the kind of place parents told their kids to be wary of, and everything the average person would do anything in their power to stay away from.

And, it was all for show.

In reality, the exterior cabin was a kind of rural shell, wrapping up a top-secret compound in the woods in a not-so-tidy white-trash package. Surveillance cameras and thermal sensors were scattered across a five-mile radius, hidden in the trees and stumps and rocks and fence posts. The area surrounding the site was under twenty-four-hour satellite surveillance to keep an eye on anything moving into the area. Even the cabin windows were bulletproof glass, with dirty curtains covering faux scenes of rural interior living on the other side. It was another aspect of the facility that would have never passed the smell test under close scrutiny, but that only reiterated the point of the clandestine site: to ensure no one stumbled across it to begin with.

The stateside facility was also much larger than it appeared from the outside. Instead of burrowing hundreds of feet below the surface like the Asteria-funded Costa Rica facility, the CIA's Skyline cabin backed up to an undisclosed mountainside and ran the length of two football fields—plenty of space to house labs and employees and equipment . . . even a few illegally-held detainees.

It was enough to make Kovic sweat—along with the wretched humidity. He looked up from the cabin porch and cursed the sun, now high in the sky and cooking anything on the forest floor unlucky enough to be left out of the sparse shade of the surrounding skinny pines.

Kovic lifted his handkerchief and wiped the sweat from his forehead one last time, then turned back toward the door. A crooked NO SOLICITING sign hung by a single nail. Kovic lifted the sign and revealed what looked like just another carpenter bee hole.

It wasn't. He inserted his finger and a button clicked. Immediately, the heavily weathered board-and-batten door slid into the left-side doorjamb, exposing a sleek, steel-reinforced door that came complete with a keypad and thumb scanner. Kovic entered the code and placed his thumb on the touchpad, and soon he was in.

The small lobby just inside the front door made up the first chamber of the facility. Toward the back, an armed guard sat at a desk behind a pane of bulletproof glass and barked instructions. Kovic complied and stepped forward to the retinal scanner. A horizontal laser painted the whites of his eyes red before a pleasant chime and automated voice confirmed his identity.

The guard said, "Okay, Mr. Kovic. You may proceed." The agent nodded, and moved forward into a large fluorescently lit room. This was what the other agents called the bullpen. Almost two dozen desks filled the central space, separated by glass-pane cubicles once occupied by the agency's top scientists.

That was until Asteria had snatched away the cream of the crop, offering them better pay and incentives to take a Costa

Rican vacation in the name of groundbreaking research. Once Tanner and Doyle had had the power of George Sturgis's checkbook at their disposal, the government's copycat project had quickly come to an end.

Kovic walked past the desks and computers, pondering the recent shutdown. The general public had a habit of thinking the government had the funds to finance any project, no matter the size, no matter the scope. What they didn't realize, however, was that the real power players of the twenty-first century were large multinational corporations—especially companies like Asteria.

Corporate advantages over government agencies were profound—especially in the pharmaceutical industry. The CIA had a long history of relying on off-the-books ops to raise revenue for their slush funds; ops that were high-risk, time-consuming, and often resulted in more blowback and scandal than reward. But for companies like Asteria Pharmaceuticals, raising revenue was simply a matter of raising prices on products customers had to have; products like drugs used to treat toxoplasmosis or anaphylactic shock or muscular dystrophy. And unlike government agencies which had to answer to the people, companies like Asteria only had to answer to shareholders. Without being subject to the same stringent guidelines, rules, and regulations that publicly-funded agencies were, Asteria was free to scalp government contractors as it saw fit.

Kovic looked around the room and wondered how Lancaster thought they could even begin to turn a ghosted project into a fully-functioning operation again. It had already failed once, and as Kovic ran his finger across a dusty desk, he already knew there was little chance the reboot would succeed.

Until he saw the lab in the next room. While the bullpen

was empty, the laboratory was in full swing. A few men in white coats had eyes fixed to microscopes while others were talking amongst themselves. Computer screens were flooded with incoming data; Kovic didn't recognize the software on display at all.

Another group of scientists was at the far end of the lab, peering into the other side of a large pane of glass while holding clipboards and taking notes and whispering to one another. These were the people who caught Kovic's attention. He walked past the workstations to the observatory glass to see what all the fuss was about.

That's when he saw the patient.

The woman was strapped to a hospital bed on the other side of the glass, her IV pole and vitals monitor close by. Other than the necessary hospital equipment, the room was white, spotless, and almost seamless. In fact, Kovic could barely make out the rectangular lines marking the crease in the door leading into the room. On the surface, it appeared to be the ultimate cleanroom, but Kovic did notice something near the lights in the ceiling. It was shiny and metallic, like an inverted eighteen-wheeler antenna turned upside down and hanging from the ceiling. It was right above the woman, about two feet from the top of her head.

*The woman.* She was either asleep or sedated—Kovic couldn't tell. She was middle-aged, no older than forty-five, with a good inch of dark brunette roots showing at the base of her tussled blonde hair. Kovic found a gap in the white coats standing nose-to-glass and wedged himself in between two scientists to get a closer look. It wasn't long before his suspicions were confirmed.

*Julie Anne Griffin. One of the first.*

By first, Kovic was referring to the original outliers from

the Ocula clinical trials. Out of exactly 2000 participants who had participated in Phase Three of the FDA-regulated clinical trials, twelve had been classified as outliers. Those were the only participants who had experienced any negative side effects from the drug. Specifically, the onset of debilitating migraine headaches. What Ryan Tanner—and subsequently, Colin Kovic— had later learned was that the headaches were only a precursor of a power far more sinister; a power that gave a dozen patients the ability to dream up scenarios that led to real-world consequences.

Julie Anne Griffin was one of those patients.

There she lay, fresh off a return trip from Guantanamo Bay, bouncing from one CIA black site to another in the name of national security. It was obvious to Kovic (and anyone else in the know) that Julie's newfound abilities could wreak havoc on the people closest to her, especially when her dreams were a complete and total coin flip from one night to the next. Still, she was an American citizen. A mother of two. And now, according to a five-month-old missing person report, she was just another statistic.

*Eyes on the big picture, Kovic.*

It was tough for the agent to stand there and witness an innocent civilian being used as a government-sanctioned guinea pig for the purpose of completing an operation. But he also knew that if it worked, Ocula would be completely removed from the government formulary. Without international patents in the works, Asteria Pharmaceuticals would have no choice but to pursue other interests or close up shop altogether.

That didn't bother Kovic in the least. For him, bringing George Sturgis's company to near bankruptcy was a small price to pay for a nation that could sleep well at night. He watched as another dose of the opaque yellow fluid crept down the IV line leading into Julie's arm. The solution hit, and the patient turned from comatose to chaotic in half a second, raising off the bed and aggressively testing her restraints while her blood pressure and heart rate rose to dangerous levels.

Kovic had seen the violent reaction to Ocula before, but he never got used to it. He turned away for a moment when he felt a hand placed on his opposite shoulder.

"Mr. Kovic. And how are you doing on this fine day?" It was Roberto Ramírez. His bright and crooked smile looked more like a carnivore showing off his canines than a fellow human being extending a benevolent greeting. "Director Lancaster told me to be expecting you."

"That's right," Kovic said, a little shaken by the events taking place in the other room. He composed himself and nodded toward the torture chamber on full display. "I see you've got the program back up and running in record speed."

"Sí," Ramírez said. "The four outliers from Guantanamo were flown in last night."

"Four? Weren't there seven at Gitmo?"

"There were, Kovic. *Were* being the operative word."

"Jesus. What happened?"

Ramírez motioned for him to keep it down. "This is not the best place to talk about such things. Come, I'll show you to the offices."

Ramírez turned to leave and Kovic followed. The two walked to a secure door at the far end of the lab. Ramírez scanned his thumb and punched in some numbers, and soon they were on the other side.

The corridor leading to the remaining underground space was poorly lit, the unfinished concrete walls drawing a stark contrast from the sophisticated research laboratory.

Outdated yellow cup lights hung from a cracked and leaky ceiling; just one of the costs of running an underground operation. Rooms lined both sides of the cold and damp hallway, with windowless doors hiding their contents.

Kovic already knew most of them were empty.

They came to a stop at one of the metal doors near the far end of the corridor, and Ramírez invited Kovic inside. A cheap metal folding chair sat in front of Ramírez's desk, while Ramírez helped himself to the plush leather upgrade behind it.

"Wow, Roberto. You really know how to treat your guests." Kovic settled into his seat, the metal legs scratching across the concrete floor like nails on a chalkboard.

"What can I say, mi amigo. Budget cuts are a real pain in the ass, no?"

Kovic agreed, then asked, "About the three outliers who were unaccounted for . . . "

"Of course," Ramírez said. "I didn't want to say too much in the laboratory, but yes, three outliers lost their lives shortly after we had the group transferred to Gitmo."

*No one told me anything,* thought Kovic. *Fucking Cline.* The man had a reputation for keeping his closest confidants in the dark, and this was no exception. It also explained why Cline had placed Kovic on babysitting duty monitoring George Sturgis in Atlanta for the last six months.

Kovic sighed, muttered a few choice epithets directed at his superiors, then asked Ramírez to fill him in.

"For starters, a lack of communication led to some terrible outcomes in Cuba," Ramírez said. "As I am sure you already know, the Project THEIA facility was built under a very strict set of parameters. To the outside world, some of the most important features of the facility may have seemed wasteful and pointless. But for the safety of anyone who may be within electromagnetic range of an outlier, those features could mean the difference between life and death. It appears such oversights are exactly what led to the shooting at Guantanamo Bay last spring."

That was something Kovic did know about. While the underlying cause remained well-hidden (even to a lowly CIA field agent), a shooting at a foreign military installation was impossible to conceal. Four Marines had lost their lives following an intense firefight that was chalked up by the media and military as another unfortunate case of workplace violence, effectively placing the blame on an innocent serviceman.

In reality, four Marines had woken in the early hours of a cool April morning, marched to the holding cells for special cases, unlocked the doors, then promptly turned their guns on one another and started shooting. When nearby Marines had responded to the gunfire, all seven outliers had run from the crime scene. One of the outliers had picked a pistol off a fallen soldier, and that's all it had taken. The firing had commenced, and when the smoke cleared, almost half of the outliers and a handful of Marines had been put to rest for good.

Kovic remembered the reports well. "The shootings had nothing to do with the official report and everything to do with Project THEIA."

"I am afraid so, señor."

"Let me guess: they skipped the Faraday cages."

Ramírez nodded in approval. "You know your government all too well, Mr. Kovic. We sent strict instructions to our intelligence liaison at Gitmo, and he effectively took everything into consideration. File Thirteen, otherwise known as the wastebasket. That's where I suspect our instructions went."

"And without housing the outliers in prison cells lined with electromagnetic shielding—"

"—They were free to dream at their hearts' content."

Kovic propped his legs on the desk, put his hands behind his head, and watched the scene play out on the concrete wall behind Ramírez. "Damn. Can you imagine being on the opposite end of someone's sadistic nightmare like that?"

"I can, señor."

"*That's right*. You were in Costa Rica when all hell broke loose." A pause, then, "But that facility was state of the art . . ."

"That was different," Ramírez said. "A freak accident during transport. Paul Freeman had yet to be verified as an outlier. Tanner was taking him to the surface when he attacked one of the guards. The other knocked him out cold outside of the protected cells, and that was when he apparently dreamed of his escape."

"Never ceases to amaze me," Kovic said. "To have that kind of god-like power. You know, I tried Ocula once. Best sleep I ever had, but no dreams at all. Reminded me of anesthesia. Out in a flash, back awake eight hours later with no sense that any time had passed at all."

"It is an incredible drug, and a valuable weapon. That is for sure." Ramírez leaned forward. "Which brings us to the Sturgis situation. Couldn't the agency just buy the man out?"

"Believe me, Roberto, if there was a way we could make this go away with a check, we would." Kovic looked around the dimly lit concrete bunker Ramírez called his office. "Personally, I think this entire operation is destined to fail. A Hail Mary. One last desperate attempt to get Ocula off the market."

"Lancaster believes swaying the chiefs at the FDA and DEA is the only way to get the drug blacklisted. This is the first true long-distance test of Ocula's power. You should be excited to be a part of this." Ramírez seemed quite pleased with himself, his soft smile communicating his true intentions. It was clear the man loved playing the mad doctor.

Kovic put his feet down and got serious. He asked, "But do you think Lancaster's objective here is even possible?"

"Oh yes. It is very possible. There are just many, many variables we are trying to work through now."

"Such as?"

"Conditioning is a big one. For the last forty-eight hours we have subjected the remaining four outliers to a nonstop barrage of propaganda involving the dangers of Ocula. It's enough exposure to drive anyone mad, but there is still no guarantee our stream of content will play out in their minds according to plan. By their very nature, dreams are notoriously unpredictable."

"Trying to control the uncontrollable. It's what got Tanner and Doyle killed."

"Perhaps," Ramírez conceded, "but our government simply cannot ignore such powerful technology."

"What about range?"

Ramírez waved a hand. "Not an issue. That is the beauty of Skyline, jefe. The converted television tower at the top of the mountain will give us the ability to broadcast the outliers' neural activity up to one hundred and fifty miles away."

*That's cutting it close,* thought Kovic. "Both the FDA and DEA heads live in D.C. That's almost three hours away—"

"It will work, Mr. Kovic. We are taking every precaution to ensure a satisfactory result."

Kovic stood up to leave. "Well, at least you're confident, Roberto. Let's hope this isn't all for nothing."

"You worry too much, señor. Believe me, by the time this is all over, George Sturgis won't even know what hit him."

# Chapter 20:
# The Run-In

A soft breeze rolled across the Savannah River, rippling the murky water's surface before gusting inland toward a crowded River Street. The summer tourist season was wrapping up, but the waterfront was still bustling. Crowds gathered around street musicians blowing horns and strumming guitars. Bar patrons ate and drank and laughed as they packed the ironclad balconies overshadowing the cobblestone street below. A rail split the main drag, with trolleys making their north-and-southbound journeys every twenty minutes. It was still hot on the coast, but the nominal drop in the mercury signaled to the locals that soon the summer would be gone—along with the tourists.

*Michelle would love this,* thought Paul. Now he was kicking himself for not bringing her along. It probably wouldn't have been the best thing for Aaron, and this was definitely not a vacation (something he'd had to remind her of at least three times before he left), but he still wished she were there instead of cooped up in Dawa's monastery with some monk he didn't even know looking after her. Not that she needed looking after in the first place, but Dawa had insisted she stay behind with his quote, "Most reliable and trustworthy friend." Paul thought on the quote and then glanced at Donny. *Reliable. Trustworthy. Guy sure knows how to pick 'em.*

Paul's wife loved the fall colors, but hated the cold. So did Savannah business owners. Dropping temps sent a signal that things were about to slow down until the next tourist season, but that didn't bother the group from Atlanta. The historic town's three newest arrivals found the cool air a refreshing change from the state capital's stagnant summer climate. The men stood in a circle by the Savannah waterfront, Paul and Donny listening to the game plan while Dawa laid out the specifics. He held out his phone as they looked over a map of the riverfront.

"We are here," Dawa said, "in front of the old cotton exchange on River Street. This is near the halfway point of the river walk, so it should be a good starting point. Donny, you will walk east toward Morrell Park. Paul, you will walk west. When you get to MLK Boulevard, turn around and come back. I will hold down the surrounding area and let you both know if I see anyone matching Fenton's description." Dawa handed out wallet-sized photos of the pimple-faced teenager. Then he asked, "Does this sound like an effective plan to you, Donald?"

Donny took the photo and looked around, then nodded. "Yeah, Graham. This looks a lot like the place I saw in my dream. If everything plays out the way it did night before last, then Fenton should be close by."

Paul questioned the statement. "It *looks* a lot like the place, or *it is* the place? I hope we didn't just drive all the way down here to chase a ghost."

"He'll be in Savannah, Paul. I'm sure of it."

That was one fact Dawa could confirm. He'd seen Donny's deceitful side many times before. This was not one of those times, and the investigator knew it. The mannerisms. Confidence. An unwavering belief the higher plain had actually been reached. If Donny was wrong about Fenton in Savannah, he didn't know it.

The three men split up to case the one-mile stretch of riverfront real estate in search of a teenager none of them had ever met, armed only with cell phones and a faded booking photo from Fenton's cybercrime arrest two years earlier. The plan was simple: find Fenton Reed and convince him to come back to Dawa's compound south of Atlanta. If Donny's dream was accurate—and Fenton's hacking skills were everything Floyd County authorities said they were—they might have on their hands the key to bringing Asteria's offenses to light well before the Sunday shows aired.

The picture in Paul's hand was from two years prior, and teenagers had a tendency to grow like weeds. He squinted down and analyzed the kid's features, then looked up and into the crowd. People were everywhere. Kids held balloons while parents did their best to keep them corralled. Retirees walked in groups and took pictures of every single brick building and ironwork and barge they passed. Young couples held hands and strolled down the cobblestone street at a snail's pace.

The crowds moved slowly and were in no hurry to get to the west side of the street. Paul stepped on his tiptoes to look over a sea of heads. The crowd was massive. Finding a pale teenager in this mess would be like finding a needle in a haystack.

Toward the east, Donny took the sidewalk opposite the river, sticking close to the towering brick buildings that housed coffee shops and restaurants and bars and books. The ironwork balconies were filled to the brim with tourists and provided a little shade to the sidewalk below. He watched lines of people steadily moving in and out of each storefront and marveled at the masses.

One look down at the faded police photo of Fenton Reed, and the same doubts that had overwhelmed Paul soon filled Donny's head. *What if the dream was bogus?* He didn't want to believe it—especially considering minute details like the jump drive he had been instructed to mention to Dawa. But then there was the possibility that Donny had concocted everything in his head without even realizing it. After all, he already knew Dawa was going to check Fenton's old apartment for signs of life, and it wouldn't be a stretch to think the investigator would return with a jump drive or some other piece of electronic evidence.

What had been a surety just moments before was now causing Donny serious doubts. He continued squeezing through the crowd and peering into storefronts, looking for a face similar to dozens he had already seen. Even the recollection of his dream—vivid and vibrant at first—was now feeling more and more like a distant memory.

He came to the entryway of a semi-vacant space. Two painters were inside, one taping off the windows while the other laid a plastic drop cloth over the bar. A radio sat on the bar and blasted "Take Me to the River." Donny stepped inside, coughing a little from the amount of dust in the air. Tables and chairs were stacked on one wall, with toolboxes and ladders on the other. Two signs were propped up by the door: one badly weathered that read "Mary Lou's," the other a brand-new metallic plaque promoting "Kerry's."

A worker emerged from the back. Donny asked, "Hey, man, have you seen this kid?" He held out the photo as the worker approached. The man looked it over, then said, "Nah. Never seen him." He grabbed a toolbox, then returned to the back.

Just a few minutes in, and Donny was already discouraged. He looked around the empty restaurant under renovation and cursed. *This is pointless,* he thought. *If I really made contact, why is this kid so damn hard to find?*

He turned quickly to exit just as a tall black man was walking in, a box of dinnerware weighing heavy in his arms. The two collided, startling both parties and causing the man to drop the box. He watched in horror as several stacks of plates shattered on the sidewalk. When the noise subsided, he looked up at Donny, expecting some sort of apology.

Donny didn't have time for that. "Watch where you're going, pal." Then he stepped over the broken mess of plates and left.

Arlo Vaughan stood in disbelief and watched the stranger disappear back into the crowd, not so much as a *sorry* or *my bad* or any acknowledgement he'd just cost the man a chunk of change. He yelled, "Who do you think you are?"

There was no verbal response. Instead, Donny hung the finger behind him, too busy to take the time to turnaround and properly flick off a stranger.

"That son of a bitch!" Arlo muttered. A thought crossed his mind and he considered chasing the man down, but he wasn't the type. He hung his head, disappointed in the human condition, and began picking up the pieces to his plates.

# Chapter 21:
# A Woman Scorned

"Which one is this?" Kovic asked, staring through the soundproof glass at the sedated patient on the other side.

Ramírez checked his clipboard. "Diana Everly."

"What's so special about this one?"

Ramírez looked up, lips pressed, then returned to his clipboard. "Nothing, really. Ms. Griffin would have done just fine, but the outliers tend to get exhausted after a single round. Ocula 2.0 really takes it out of them."

"We've got a man in holding who is an outlier, too." He thought of Claire's experience at the Costa Rican facility. He asked, "Tanner seemed to prefer using women. Any reason why you're doing the same?"

"Actually, yes. From a biological standpoint, women don't sleep as well as men do."

Kovic cocked his head. "Isn't the whole point of this to get them to dream?"

"Yes, but therein lies the problem with using men to influence dream sequences. Men are naturally better sleepers than women. They tend to sleep longer, while females have shorter circadian rhythms. Some scientists think this is because women are responsible for childbirth and by their very nature have to sleep in shorter spurts to take care of their offspring.

"At any rate, women work better because they are less likely to experience R.E.M. cycles on their own in conjunction with the drug, which can lead to additional content that is uncontrollable and disruptive."

"So you're saying men are more likely to dream what they want?"

"Precisely. Women respond better to what we give them, which in turn helps to broadcast more convincing messages."

"Makes sense. Women are naturally better listeners."

"Uh-hum. The men, however, have been a mixed bag in the past. When our content collides with what they may already be dreaming about, it causes an internal conflict in the mind of the outlier. Messages then become convoluted and are often forgotten by our target—useless. Like a vivid dream that flees your memory the moment you wake."

The woman on the other side of the glass was resting peacefully. It wouldn't be long before the dose of Ocula 2.0 was administered. Then the first stage of Project THEIA would officially be underway.

Kovic and Ramírez stood and watched as two lab techs entered the room to prep Mrs. Everly. They tightened her restraints, checked the IV port of her arm, pressed fingers into her wrist and checked her pulse alongside the machines to verify accuracy. Everything was in working order.

One of the techs returned to the observation room adjacent to the lab with Kovic and Ramírez. Inside, a control panel stretched below the observation glass. A score of buttons and switches and touchscreens covered the counter-height panel.

"We should be ready to begin," Ramírez told him. He nodded, noted the time, and then began the process of turning Mrs. Everly into a mind-altering broadcast television.

A button was pressed and Kovic watched as the antenna hanging above Mrs. Everly's head descended from the ceiling. "This is the way out?" he asked Ramírez.

"In a manner of speaking, yes." Ramírez pointed to the

antenna that was now inches from Mrs. Everly. "See the small orbital globe at the end of the antenna? That's the same type of high-sensitive receptor used in brainwave experiences conducted at cutting-edge universities like MIT and Virginia Tech. The receptor amplifies everything we are putting in, and then transmits it to the broadcast tower two-thousand feet above us at the top of the mountain. This gives us the ability to transmit signals at a range far greater than we could in Costa Rica."

Kovic crossed his arms and nodded, impressed. He had kept up with the progress at the Costa Rica facility through Ryan Tanner, but they were still in the very early stages and had not yet determined a way to broadcast further than twenty miles. That was the reason the Dawkins operation in the Costa Rican jungle had been one of their first targets. It was also why Claire Connor had been picked up to begin with. Not only had she been identified as an Ocula outlier shortly after the clinical trials— she'd also had a personal connection to Dawkins that could have made influencing his behavior a much easier task to accomplish.

Putting unfamiliar content into the heads of complete strangers in the hopes of getting others to do your will, on the other hand, was a little bit trickier. Kovic knew this, and hoped that Ramírez had made some progress in the months he had been left in the dark.

His concern was soon lifted as he watched the tech still at Mrs. Everly's bedside fitting what looked like a virtual reality headset over her eyes.

"What's this?" Kovic asked.

"The content delivery system. We always called it THEIA, named for the Titan goddess of sight and light."

"Interesting. I just assumed you guys pulled these project names out of your asses."

Ramírez grinned as they watched the tech secure the headset across Mrs. Everly's face. He tightened two side straps, plugged a cord in, then flipped a switch. A green light shone a ring around the device, outlining it on the patient's face. Then the tech left, securing the door before stepping back into the observation room.

The four men stood and watched the room for what felt like an eternity. Ramírez played it cool, but in reality his heart was beating out of his chest. Kovic was nervous, too, but for other reasons that had nothing to do with the project outcome. He didn't like any of this. He had worked hard to shut the program down at the onset of Lancaster's appointment, and at the time she had been completely on board. Now they were bringing back a pariah; something that could ruin the agency for good.

And there were other consequences, too. Kovic knew how dangerous Ocula was. He also couldn't ignore how valuable such a powerful weapon could be in the hands of a responsible superpower. But the difference between possessing a potentially catastrophic weapon and actually using it was stark.

While Ramírez and Kovic had their apprehensions, the two techs working on the groundbreaking and top-secret project were eager to get started. They looked to their superiors. "We're initiating content now." Under normal circumstances, Kovic might have asked why a peacefully sleeping patient was being fed visual content, but he already knew the answer. As soon as Ocula hit her veins, she would be thrust into one of the most intense experiences she'd ever felt.

The overhead lights in the observation room went out, leaving the green glow from the headset the only visible thing in the room. The men squinted as they looked inward through the glass, watching the light from the headset as it began to flicker at rapid speed. Subliminal messages had been transmitted through the headset and into Mrs. Everly's eyes and ears for almost twenty minutes while the patient remained sedated.

"We've found running content prior to the delivery of the medication heightens the chances of the desired thought patterns playing out in the cerebral cortex," Ramírez said.

"What's on the menu?"

"A rather basic selection of anti-Ocula propaganda directed at Anthony Hoover."

*The head of the FDA,* thought Kovic. It was a good place to start. Lancaster had a few trustworthy sources at the DEA, but she had always been close to Hoover. When it came to getting someone to take action against Ocula, he was the best chance for a quick turnaround.

Ramírez continued, "We had originally hoped to incorporate a small team of CGI developers to come in and create visuals and audio based on our content briefs. We would then deliver this content through THEIA while dosing with Ocula." Ramírez sighed, "Unfortunately, this was a rush project, and we didn't have time to prepare the way I would have liked."

"Well, if it works, at least it's a step toward ridding the world of Ocula." Kovic took a deep breath as the two men looked inward toward Mrs. Everly. The pale yellow drug was beginning to cloud her IV line as it made its way toward her arm.

"But that's a big if."

***

Smuggling drugs for a living had its benefits. But as Claire chewed her thumbnail and stared out the window of her friend's private jet, she couldn't escape a single thought of

Alejandro Aguilar.

Below were the waters of the Gulf of Mexico, a sea of pure blue with streaks of twinkling diamonds stretching as far as the eye could see. It was a scene that would've taken most people's minds off their daily troubles, at least for a moment or two. But even the sparkling surface thousands of feet below reminded Claire of the tennis bracelets and necklaces and earrings the lonely aristocrat had tried to woo her with in the months after his wife passed.

Now a daughter was without a father, and a long list of extended family members, close friends, and business associates were without a patriarch. Alejandro Aguilar was dead, killed during an expedition Claire had talked him into going on.

Her eyes welled up as she looked away from the window, desperate to escape her guilt. She took her sleeve and dabbed her eyes, then asked the pilot in the cockpit ahead, "How much longer?"

"About three more hours, give or take."

Claire nodded, then returned to staring out the window. Over and over, she repeated the events leading up to her escape— and the subsequent explosion at the facility that killed her friend. *Why would Kovic order a strike before making contact? And why did I even ask Han to tag along to begin with?*

There were no easy answers, but as her analytical brain started ticking again, she did come to a few conclusions. First, making a deal with the CIA had been her biggest mistake. It was a sham proposal offered up by Colin Kovic after Claire made contact a month earlier. On the surface, the deal had sounded simple enough. Claire would infiltrate the Costa Rican facility, collect any intel she could gather on the Ocula program, then give the go-ahead to have the facility destroyed. Apparently, Kovic had missed the part where she was supposed to escape first.

In Claire's mind, however, this was never a legitimate offer. Putting her trust in the intelligence community would have been akin to a battered wife returning to a house of abuse. It wasn't in her nature to forgive and forget things like illegal kidnapping, torture, human rights violations . . . basically everything that kept Tanner ticking. She was well aware that technically speaking, Tanner wasn't officially CIA while playing in the jungle. But, once a company man, always a company man. And there was no way she was trusting anyone with a past or present affiliation with Langley.

Which brought her to her true intentions: infiltrate the facility, let the CIA obliterate it into a bad memory, then disappear again with as much intel on the Ocula program as she could carry out. But wasn't the intel just as valuable to Kovic as it was to her? If they really wanted her dead, and the promise of a pardon was just the bait needed to lure her out of hiding, wouldn't it make more sense to wait until she had delivered the goods, and *then* have her killed?

Her feet tapped, her fingers danced, and her nerves were shot. The turbulence wasn't helping, either. Soon she would be back in the United States, and without a solid game plan, it would only be a matter of time before Kovic discovered she hadn't been killed in the blast. Unless Claire went back into hiding, but that wasn't happening. This wasn't about her life anymore. It was about all of the innocent lives that had been affected by Ocula. All of the murder and corruption and turmoil it had and would continue to cause.

If there was any good news to be had, it was little. But the fact remained that the blast at the facility was no small bonfire. Claire had seen destruction like that before, only from much further away. The sheer force of the explosion had shaken her to the core, and easily incinerated any trace of human activity in or around the secret jungle compound.

That also meant Kovic likely thought she was dead. Mission accomplished. One more loose end wrapped up in a pretty little bow.

That's when it hit her.

Claire looked at the puffs of clouds overshadowing the gulf waters and made a host of promises to herself. She would avenge the deaths of friends lost, no matter what it took; she would bring down Asteria and any civilians affiliated with the illegal program; and then go after CIA both past and present.

They were all going down. No one would be left unaccounted for. Everyone would be brought to justice.

And she knew exactly how she was going to do it.

# Chapter 22:
# Come See Savannah

The old-fashioned streetlights cut on as the setting sun wedged in between the Talmadge Bridge and the Savannah River, marking the end to a busy day on River Street. The crowded streets thinned out as patrons dispersed into nearby restaurants and bars for dinner and drinks while a few stragglers smoked their cigars and took pictures and held hands and strolled across the cobblestones.

Dawa Graham checked his watch. A quarter past eight. The long August day should have been plenty of time to locate Fenton Reed; that was, if he had ever been in Savannah to begin with. Dawa shook his head, disappointed but not surprised. It would be dark soon, and in their search for the young Ocula outlier, the Atlanta crew had turned up nothing.

To the west, he could barely make out Paul, who was walking his way. He looked east; Donny was also making his return visit. He held his hands out as if to ask from afar if they'd found anything.

They both shook their heads. They hadn't.

*Worth a try*, thought Dawa. The trip might not have turned up anything, but perhaps Fenton's absence would finally be the proof Donny needed to realize he held no godlike control over the nature of reality. The very thought of it irked Dawa to no extent, and went against everything he believed involving spiritualism and Buddhism.

Ford should have known better. Maybe now he'd finally shut up.

The two men drew closer to Dawa, and he said, "No sign of Fenton Reed."

Paul said, "If he's here, he's not on River Street."

"He's here," snapped Ford.

"Okay then, Mr. Ford"—Paul looked west, then east—"maybe you'd like to fill us in again on where he's hiding. Because if you ask me, this entire trip was nothing but a waste of time."

"You know, Paul, I'm really starting to question your role in this whole thing in the first place."

"What the hell is that supposed to mean?"

"You say you've had these experiences, these dreams. But if you really were an outlier, then why in the fuck are you so eager to doubt everything I'm telling you?"

"Because you're a charlatan, Ford. I've known people like you my entire life. Regardless of what you say, there's always a catch."

Ford started to step into Paul's face again, but Dawa was quick to intercede. "Boys, boys," he said. "This solves nothing. We are all tired. We cannot afford to focus our energy in such a negative way." He looked at Paul. "I know you have your doubts about Donald, Paul. But I have known him for a long time. Yes, he has made mistakes. Yes, he has tried to monetize every noble thing he has come across."

Donny's face scrunched as he waited for his old friend to say something positive. "But," Dawa continued, "I do not believe Donald is a malicious man. Misguided at times, yes. But not evil. Whether his dream was real or not is of no consequence. If he said he dreamt Reed was in Savannah, we have to take him at his word." He put his hand on Paul's shoulder. "And, my young friend, you will get the same benefit of the doubt. Should you have the conviction Donald has, I will be more than willing to see it through.

"So here is the bottom line," Dawa said. "We cannot afford to continue this infighting any longer. From this moment forward, we must stick together. Agreed?"

Paul and Donny looked at one another, then down to the ground like two brothers scolded by an older, wiser father. Then Paul looked to Dawa. "You're right. This is getting us nowhere." He extended his hand to Donny. "Water under the bridge?"

Donny feigned hesitancy for a few seconds, then stuck his hand out to shake Paul's. "Yeah, Paul. So long as you at least give me a chance to prove to you that I'm not crazy."

The two men shook on it and smiled, but Paul's eyes wondered. A pale, lanky figure emerged from one of the bars down the street. He was redheaded with slouched shoulders, and wearing a backpack. He also looked like he hadn't slept in weeks. He stepped into the street and stopped to look around, and that's when his eyes caught a glimpse of Donny Ford.

Paul couldn't believe it. He reached into his pocket and pulled out the mugshot. Then he looked up again toward the wild-eyed kid just outside the bar.

It was Fenton Reed.

***

The front steps creaked and sagged in their predictable manner that signaled Arlo Vaughan's return home. Kerry was standing at the sink and heard him walk in the front door, but didn't take her eyes up from the dishes. He hung up his coat and stepped into the kitchen.

Kerry asked, "What's cooking, good looking?"

Arlo grunted, then walked to the fridge. Kerry took note

and turned the water off, then reached for a towel to dry her hands. She asked, "Everything okay downtown, sweetie?"

"Oh, yeah, everything's gonna be fine. It was just one of those days. That's all."

"Did something happen?"

Arlo grabbed a couple of Cokes, then the two sat down at the kitchen table. He slid one to Kerry, then started in. "You know, the nerve of some people just never ceases to amaze me. Here I am, bringing in another load of dishes to the restaurant, when out walks a guy I've never seen before in my life. The man runs right into me, knocks the box out of my hands, then takes off down the street like nothing happened."

"Wait," Kerry said. "Are you talking about *my* dishes?"

While waiting on the water to get shut on at Kerry's Restaurant, the couple had decided to caravan loads of dinnerware back and forth to stock the cabinets for the grand opening. That meant Kerry had worked her fingers to the bone getting supplies ready for the River Street restaurant. Arlo wasn't the only one putting in the work.

"Yes, dear. It was the load I just left with."

Kerry shook her head. Irritated, "And he didn't say a word? Not so much as an apology?"

"Just wait. It gets even better. Not only does the man bust every dish in the box, when I call him out on it he gives me the finger!"

Kerry's jaw dropped. "The finger? That man shot you a bird?"

"Mm-hmm."

"Good Lord, Arlo. No wonder you're in a mood this evening!"

He nodded and sipped his Coke. "Ah, it's not that big a

deal. World's full of assholes. Just put me in a funk, I guess."

Kerry leaned in toward her man and held out her arms. Playfully, "Hear, hear, baby. You sound like you could use a hug. Besides, with that big loan you got from the bank, we shouldn't have any trouble getting more plates. Now if something happens to the building . . ."

"Don't say it! You'll put a hex on the whole damn thing!"

Kerry grinned. She loved getting a rise out of Arlo, but she decided to call a truce for the time being. They rocked in each other's arms as they embraced one another at the table, and Arlo finally smiled.

***

*Lord, I've got a lot to do tomorrow.* Arlo looked at the clock. It was almost midnight. He tossed and turned in bed as Kerry groaned in displeasure on the other side. He did some quick math in his head. *If I take one of those little pills now, I'll be up by 8 a.m.*

He sat up at the edge of the bed and looked toward the bathroom. There were plenty of Ocula pills in the cabinet.

Then he remembered the headache.

It had only happened once. In the past, the sleeping pills had worked right as rain. But last time . . .

"Shew, lawd," he whispered as he shook his head. Taking a pill would mean taking a big chance. But maybe it wasn't the pill that gave him the headaches after all. It would have made perfect sense; one headache for every dozen or so doses. If the last time was a bad reaction to the sleep medication, wouldn't every dose have caused him to puke through the night?

It could have just been the stress he was under, too. He'd

been worked up for weeks in anticipation of the meeting with the loan officer. He was also the type of person who could work himself up into a headache over anything, like running into that jerk on the street earlier that day.

*That son of a bitch,* thought Arlo. *What kind of grown man behaves that way?* It had been years since someone like that had blatantly disrespected him for no apparent reason, other than the belief that one man's affairs were more important than another's.

Guess the world hadn't changed much after all. Arlo thought about that man in the ridiculous Hawaiian shirt on River Street and began to rub his temples.

And there he was, working himself up all over again. He nodded and agreed with his original conclusion. It probably wasn't the pills last time. And if it was, then this time he would know for sure whether or not he could rely on them for nights like tonight, or if he needed to flush every last one of them down the toilet.

He slipped on his house shoes and tiptoed toward the bathroom. Using Ocula again felt a little like playing Russian Roulette, but if it meant getting a little shuteye, Arlo was willing to take a chance.

# Chapter 23:
# Dangerous Liaisons

Anthony Hoover sat up in bed at 6:30 a.m., gasping for air, clutching his chest, and sweating up a storm. His wife immediately rose up to his side and grabbed the nearest shoulder.

Anxiously, "Anthony, Anthony! Wake up, Anthony. You're having a nightmare."

He continued to panic, trembling hands strangling a wad of sheets, eyes lost and confused as if he were a man waking from a thirty-year coma. "Wha—where am I? What is this place?"

"You're home, honey. You're with me. You're just having a bad dream."

*A dream.* Anthony heard the words and reality slowly began to set in. *It was all a dream.* The notion gave him almost immediate relief as he was finally allowed to breathe, but it also gave rise to another question: *what was I dreaming about?*

Anthony looked over to his wife, Cheryl, and forced a smile. He patted her arm and said, "I'm sorry, dear. I don't know what got into me."

Cheryl said, "Me neither. You haven't woken me up like that in years. Is everything okay at work?"

"Ah, just the same old, same old. Nothing out of the ordinary, or stressful. Well, nothing *too* stressful."

Cheryl got out of bed and grabbed her robe. "You've always been pretty good at handling stress," she said as she tied it. "Do you think you may have drunk too much last night?"

Anthony Hoover did like his nightcaps. And since being

appointed head of the FDA, what used to be a weekend ordeal had turned into a nightly habit. Working long hours meant taking extreme measures to wind down. Some nights, downing four doubles on the couch in the study was the only way he could get to sleep.

Now his anxiety was through the roof. It appeared his habits were starting to catch up to him.

He rolled out of bed and shuffled to the bathroom. Cheryl was already at the sink and brushing her hair. She asked, "What were you dreaming about that got you so upset?"

Anthony rubbed his eyes and shrugged his shoulders. "That's just it, Cheryl. I can't remember a thing about it."

She gave him a suspicious look, but he was telling the truth. Obviously, *something* had sprung him out of bed like a terrified jack-in-the-box, but the more he tried to remember the events of his dream, the further he drove them away. The fear had all but diminished too, replaced with an unfamiliar lingering sensation in his mind that something was wrong, a problem had to be solved—he just wasn't sure what. Strange sensation, indeed. He just couldn't quite put his finger on it . . .

Doubt. That was it. An intense feeling of doubt.

She asked, "It wasn't about another woman, was it?"

He half-grinned and assured her, "No, dear. Believe me, if it had been about another woman, I think I would've woken up in a better mood."

"You bastard!" She cupped her hand at the running faucet and slung a handful of water Anthony's way. He was quick to block it with a hand towel. He was about to retaliate when Cheryl said, "Stop it! You're going to make me late!"

The two smiled and laughed off the strange morning they'd had, then continued getting ready for work.

***

Anthony Hoover sat in his office at the Maryland branch of the FDA, shuffling papers on his desk and checking his email in between answering a phone that seemed to ring every five minutes. It was early on a Friday—a day he was typically checked out mentally to begin with. But today was different. No daydreams of weekend boating or fishing or cocktails on the golf course. Instead, Anthony kept returning to the dark wickedness that had launched him out of bed just before daybreak.

The same question whirled in his mind, playing on repeat: *just what in the hell was I dreaming about?* What kind of scenario could cause such early-morning trepidation—especially a scenario he couldn't even remember?

It was the strangest feeling, knowing he had been host to a handful of horrible thoughts, and not being able to recall any of them. His scalp tingled as he consciously tried to spark a memory within the delicate pink-and-gray muscle housed in his skull, hoping the right set of neurons could take him back to the early morning hours, back to the images behind his inquietude. He knew something bad had happened, something that felt quite alien. Foreign. A false memory that had been implanted. One he could never in good conscience take ownership of.

He just couldn't remember what.

The mental torment lasted through most of the morning. Finally, just before lunchtime, the sensation left him, evaporating into thin air. Maybe it was the countless barrage of calls and emails and the heavy workload getting in the way of the impending weekend. Or maybe his brain just gave out. Whatever the reason, Anthony was suddenly able to let go of the incessant need to have an answer and get on with his life.

Clear-headed and feeling like his old self again, he picked up the phone to dial his secretary, Hailey, for lunch ideas. He knew it was probably inappropriate to meet a female coworker for lunch so often, but there was a connection there that he couldn't deny. Still, both parties were married, so they made it a point to keep their midday rendezvous down to once every two weeks or so.

Always on a Friday. Always a good half-hour drive from the office.

This was one of those Fridays.

***

"Have trouble finding the place?" Anthony asked as he shut his car door. Hailey was parked right beside him. She smiled and said, "No. Navigation led me straight here." The two locked their cars and walked toward the restaurant.

Inside, the sweet aroma of barbeque smoldering in the back made Anthony's mouth water. Hailey wiggled awkwardly in her chair, looking around the joint and surveying the rustic surroundings. Skeptically, "This place is . . . different," she said.

"What do you mean?"

She pointed toward the black cook fixing plates in the back, then to the rebel flag hanging above the cash register. She looked back at Anthony and deadpanned.

"What can I say? Isaiah knows his clientele."

"What's that supposed to mean exactly?"

"Well, if you want to run a barbeque joint in the sticks, you've got to make a few concessions." Anthony looked to the back and waved at Isaiah. The jovial cook tossed up a quick hand, then got back to running a kitchen swamped by the busy lunch-hour rush.

The gesture didn't impress Hailey in the least. She pushed her silverware away from her across a red-and-white checkered tablecloth. "I find this entire establishment offensive. I don't think I can eat here."

"Hailey," Anthony said, "I promise you right here and now that once you've had a taste of this man's barbeque, you're going to forget all about that flag up there"—Anthony checked his watch—"not to mention we're already thirty minutes from the office. I may be able to get away with two-hour lunches. But you, my dear, will be sorely missed."

Hailey sighed, then caved. "Okay, Anthony. I'll try the damn barbeque."

'That a girl." The two waited while the sounds of a bustling kitchen and clanking plates and sizzling grills resonated from the back. The restaurant was always busy on Fridays. The locals would pile in just before noon, saving the limited seating for friends and family and coworkers who were on the way. Couples leaned in to one another across wooden tables and chatted. The blue collars guffawed and chortled and ate their ribs without a care in the world—or a napkin. The more Hailey looked around, the more uncomfortable she became. This was not her kind of place.

Isaiah walked out from the kitchen with two plates piled high with barbeque, pork and beans, potato salad, and Texas toast. He approached the couple and served up the meals.

"Well, well, well. Mr. Hoover. And what brings you in here on this fine day?" Isaiah didn't walk out plates for just anybody, but Anthony Hoover was one of a few exceptions.

"Thought I'd show my coworker here what real southern

barbeque was all about."

"Well then, you came to the right place," Isaiah said as he waited for Anthony to introduce his lunch date. Hailey looked away as Anthony spoke up. "This is Ms. Hailey Roderick. She's an administrative assistant who works with me at the FDA."

Isaiah said, "Well, it's a pleasure to meet you, Ms. Hailey. Name's Isaiah." The owner-operator extended a hand, but the woman ignored the cordialities. Isaiah grimaced and turned to Anthony for answers.

"Hailey can be a little shy sometimes—"

"Actually," Hailey said as she turned to Isaiah, "I'm not shy at all. I just can't understand why you've got that hateful flag hanging up in your place of business."

"Hateful flag?" Isaiah said as he looked around confused, eager to identify the point of contention.

"Yes, *that flag*. My grandmother was a Freedom Rider, and she would be rolling in her grave if she saw that symbol of hate hanging from the rafters of a restaurant some 50 years later."

Isaiah made the connection and billowed with laughter. "Ms. Hailey, let me tell you a little something about *that flag*. See, that flag up there don't mean shit to me. Not a damn thing. And I think it's clear it don't mean shit to you, either."

"Then why do you have it hanging up in your restaurant?"

Isaiah pointed to the walls decorated with old license plates and pin-up posters and animal heads and newspaper clippings. Then he said, "My daddy opened this place in 1966. Half this shit's been up since then. People like familiarity, that's all."

Hailey scoffed. "Doesn't make it right."

"Doesn't have to be right," Isaiah said. "But I'm a business owner in the boondocks, Ms. Hailey. I can stir the pot and watch my customers walk over to Merle's for lunch, or I can just let some things be."

"You know, Isaiah," Anthony said as he chewed on a rib, "You could probably take half this shit down and no one would even notice." He marveled at his plate, then said, "I mean come on, pal. The food speaks for itself."

"You may be right," Isaiah said. "Thing of it is, I don't notice half this stuff anymore, either." He tipped his cap to Hailey, then walked back to the kitchen.

Hailey was appalled. "Jesus, can you believe that guy?"

Anthony continued gnawing on his ribs, indifferent to the outrage. She went on, "The pursuit of familiarity . . . is that any reason to hold on to bullshit ideals, or an era that was full of inequality and injustice? I mean seriously, Anthony. You don't have a problem with that flag flying overhead?"

He shrugged his shoulders and kept eating.

"How can anyone rest easy at night knowing they're using a symbol of racism and hate to bring in these hillbilly customers?"

Anthony dropped his rib, the sound clanging the half-empty metal plate like a small gong. *Rest easy at night . . .*

The words shook him to the core. He said them out loud this time, "Rest easy at night . . ."

"Hmm?"

"You said, 'rest easy at night.' Isn't that the motto for Ocula?"

Hailey said, "The sleeping pill?"

"Yeah, from Asteria."

She thought on it a second, then said, "Something like

that. I think it's actually 'rest easy with us.' Why do you ask?"

"Just curious." But it was more than curiosity driving Hoover's questions. Once again, the terror that had awoken him that morning had returned. His ribcage grew tight and constricted with every laborious breath. Arteries in his neck bulged and pulsed painfully as they fought to accommodate the sudden spike in blood pressure. He'd ordered his ribs mild, but by the beads of sweat that were beginning to rise on his forehead, they could have easily passed for Cajun-style.

He reached for his glass of water and took several big gulps. Concerned, Hailey asked, "Are you okay?"

"Yeah, yeah. I'm just fine. It's just—"

He couldn't finish his sentence. He excused himself, then ran to the bathroom. He picked out the stall in the back, then retreated to it and latched the door behind him. He had just enough time to throw his tie over his shoulder.

Then he puked.

He couldn't believe how quickly the nausea had come on. It was also so much worse than any sour stomach or morning after a bad batch of sushi he had ever experienced. This was his nerves talking, and they weren't happy with how they felt.

Soon he had heaved all he could, and there was nothing left in the tank. He collapsed on the toilet seat, hugging the ivory throne with no regard for how filthy it must have been. He didn't care. In an instant, he had been drained of every ounce of energy he had. He was utterly exhausted, and closed his eyes to rest.

And the visions came.

They seemed innocuous at first. A montage of men and women of all ages wearing pajamas and nightgowns and taking their Ocula pills before tucking themselves comfortably into their beds. Nightlights and side-table lamps were clicked off, and in an instant the actors were fast asleep. Restful. Peaceful. All of them, sleeping like babies without a care in the world. They were anonymous at first, but soon one of the blurred female faces began to clear.

It was his wife, Cheryl.

Anthony opened his eyes and searched the bathroom stall, trying to escape the scene in his head, but that was impossible. He looked forward to the blank wall behind the toilet only to see his bed at home as his wife lay in it, tucked in under the large comforter and fast asleep. The first dim light of dawn glowed behind the curtains as she stretched and began to wake. She squinted and looked up, smiling at her husband.

"Hey, sweetie. What are you doing up so early? Did you forget to take your pill last night?"

Anthony didn't speak. She sat up in bed, her smile quickly turning to concern. "Is everything okay?"

A chef's knife was in Anthony's hand. He lunged forward, sticking the piercing steel blade into the left side of her slender neck before pulling the razor's edge up and across, slicing veins and arteries before hitting her trachea. The rigid tube put up some resistance, but Anthony muscled through. She started to scream, but the noise was soon muffled by the sound of a terrified and confused woman gurgling in a river of her own blood. Her eyes met her husband's. She didn't speak, she couldn't. But her eyes said it all:

*Why?*

Back in the bathroom stall, Anthony screamed. His fingernails dug into his scalp so deeply that it brought blood; a desperate attempt to dig out the horrific thoughts straight from the source. The sound was deafening and caught the attention of everyone in the restaurant. Couples stopped eating. Blue collars stopped drinking. All eyes were fixed on the entrance to the men's bathroom.

Isaiah dropped his plates in the sink and rushed in to see what was wrong. "Mr. Hoover! What's the matter, Mr. Hoover? Everything okay in here?" He approached the locked stall.

There was no answer.

With the strength of a scared parent, Isaiah grabbed the top of the stall door and jerked it off its hinges. He let the door fall to the side as he tried to understand what he was seeing.

Hoover lay by the toilet in the fetal position, grasping his own arms and shaking all over. He mumbled something, and Isaiah leaned down to get a better listen.

"Mr. Hoover? I think I'd better call 911."

Anthony quickly grabbed Isaiah by the arm. "No!" he said. "Don't call the police. It's not the police." He let go and returned to rocking on the floor. "The police can't help her now."

Confused, Isaiah asked, "Then what's the matter? Everyone in the restaurant heard you screaming in here."

"It's—*Ocula*." Just uttering the word made Hoover want to vomit all over again.

"Ocu—what? Mr. Hoover, I'm just not sure I understan—"

*"YES! OCULA! IT'S GOING TO KILL HER!"*

Isaiah fell back and gave up all efforts to comprehend what was going on. A waitress was standing at the door with a dozen other people behind her. "You want me to call the police?" she asked.

"Yeah. I think we'd better get an ambulance up here."

A small crowd stood slack-jawed at the door, Hailey included, not a single one of them sure of what they were witnessing.

But Anthony Hoover knew. He also knew what he had to do to stop it.

# Chapter 24:
# Voices

Three men and a teenager sat in the crowded lobby of the Savannah Inn on Friday morning, drinking coffee and Red Bulls in an epic battle to stay awake after a sleepless night. Their eyes were bloodshot, and the caffeine was doing little to take the edge off. At first glance, they could have easily been mistaken for a bachelor party: two middle-aged men and their teenage son, spending all night on the town, trying to show the groom-to-be a good time before taking the plunge. Had that been the case, the only thing they'd have had to worry about that morning would be how they were going to sober up before the wedding.

Instead, the group was hunched over the table, trying to let the dire news the young computer hacker was telling them sink in.

"Let's go over this again," Dawa said. "The Costa Rican project was not the only location Ocula was being used illegally?"

"That's right," Fenton said between sips of his energy-drink-on-ice. "What kicked this entire debacle off was a total coincidence. Tanner had retired from the CIA to try his hand at a high-paying pharmaceutical company. Doyle's the one who got him the job. His ties to George Sturgis go way back."

"This is Richard Doyle?" Dawa asked.

"Yeah, Dick. The one and only." Fenton continued, "Apparently semi-retirement wasn't in the cards for Tanner, because once he caught wind of the weird side effects coming from some of the Ocula trial participants, those old CIA gears started turning again. Sturgis funded the project, hoping that letting Doyle and Tanner run their experiments would land him a government contract."

"Greedy bastard," Paul said.

"No doubt. You know those Big Pharma fuckers are making bank to begin with, feeding us pills we think we can't live without before sending us a bill that looks more like a mortgage payment—"

"Let us return to the task at hand," Dawa said, interrupting the over-caffeinated teenager. "You said Tanner was playing both sides?"

Fenton nodded. "For sure. Tanner took one out of the George Sturgis playbook and cut out the middleman, deciding to sell the highly synthesized Ocula 2.0 to the federal government himself. A few calls to his old buddies at the CIA and the feds were well on their way to developing their own facility in Virginia."

"Jesus," Donny chimed in. "It's bad enough the plain-Jane stuff's out on the open market, but another facility working on the sequel? Owned and sanctioned by the federal government? I mean really, fellas, what the hell are we supposed to do now?"

Dawa said, "I am not surprised, Donald. Nor should any of us be. We all knew Tanner and Doyle were ex-CIA. We also knew they utilized old CIA contacts to do their dirty work. It makes sense this conspiracy rises to a very high level, but that does not mean there is nothing we can do." He turned to Fenton and asked, "All of this you are telling us, Mr. Reed. Do you have hard evidence?"

Fenton patted the backpack sitting in the chair next to him. "Yep. It's all right here. What'd you think I've been doing for the last six months? Running up pay-per-view tabs?"

That's exactly what Paul had assumed. The kid looked like the last person on Earth to blow the lid off a government conspiracy, but there was no denying he was proving his worth. Cooked books. Illegal overseas slush funds. Communications between parties linked to the Costa Rica facility and Asteria Pharmaceuticals. If everything Fenton said he had was truly on his computer, then they would have everything they needed to bring the guilty parties to justice.

That didn't mean it would be easy. While the hacked documents, files, and records would shed light on the conspiracy of the century, none of it would be admissible in court. If this was going to go anywhere, the case would have to be tried by the media. Paul drummed his fingers on the table and thought of Claire. *Really could use her help right about now.*

The three men sat back in their chairs and looked at one another. Finding Fenton Reed in Savannah had been a godsend. The discovery was also something Dawa and Paul were having trouble wrapping their minds around, but Ford was far from surprised. His conviction that Fenton Reed was in Savannah had been unwavering from the moment he'd envisioned the scraggly teenager inviting him to River Street. Ford was eager to talk about it, but none of them wanted to spook the teenager away. The task at hand was to get Ocula off the market—not reminisce tales of loopy dreams and extraterrestrial contact from the higher plane. There would be plenty of time for that later.

Still, Donny couldn't help hinting at it. "Still can't believe you were here, Fenton," he said, drawing a couple of glares from Paul and Dawa that urged him to shut his big mouth.

Fenton asked, "How'd you guys know where to find me again?"

"Put out an APB in Savannah," Dawa quickly answered.

"Foot patrol spotted you, and we followed up."

"But aren't you guys from Atlanta? How'd you know I was in Savannah?"

"Your old roommate from Atlanta gave us a box of your old stuff. Information obtained led us to search the Savannah area."

Fenton squinted inquisitively. They were hiding something, and he knew it. Plus, he couldn't for the life of him recall anything in his personal possessions that would have led them away from his friends and family in the Atlanta area to search a small town some three hours away.

What he could recall, however, were his own bizarre dreams that seemed to melt into reality. The apartment visit from Mr. Buzzcut. Free room and board at various motels across the state. The unexplainable compulsion to take the 7:30 Greyhound to Savannah the night before. He had developed a heightened sense of awareness through dreaming, and he wondered if one of them—or all of them—had the same ability, too.

It was clear their official story didn't add up, but he opted to ignore the details for now. "Well," Fenton said, "the important thing is that we bring these guys down. I've been on the run for the better part of a year, and I'm tired of running from a bunch of stooges in suits who are trying to kill me."

"You're talking about the Consultants," Paul said. He looked toward the bright lobby windows and thought of Alex. The same people who had murdered his brother were trying to exterminate this poor teenager sitting in front of him. And Donny Ford, too. The latter of which, Paul supposed, wouldn't have been quite so bad. Claire had told him Tanner's stooges were off the radar. But Paul wasn't about to let his guard down.

He looked at Donny, who was sitting across the table

from him. "You know all about the Consultants, don't ya, Don?"

Donny didn't answer. He stared into space out of the same window Paul had been focused on seconds earlier.

"Donny?" Paul asked. "You okay over there, man?"

His expression was hollow and blank. He continued to stare, eyes fixed on an imaginary horizon. Dawa and Fenton noticed too, but remained silent. Finally, Paul leaned over and snapped his fingers, and the trance was broken.

"Yeah," Donny said, startled. "Wait. What were we talking about?"

"The Consultants."

"Yes, of course. Whew . . . Bad people, those guys."

It was clear Donny hadn't been paying attention, something Paul found easy to ignore and move on from. He turned to talk to Fenton about the information the teenager had uncovered by hacking databases from Atlanta to Virginia.

But while Paul was engaged in conversation with their new young friend, Dawa's attention remained on his old friend. Something had Donny in distress, some psychological pain that had taken the reins in less time than it had taken Fenton to down a Red Bull. The pitchman's sharp eyes glared into the distance, teeth grinding, hands gripping the edge of the table as if he were trying to tear off a piece or two.

Dawa leaned over and whispered, "Donald. Is everything okay, my friend?"

Defensively, "Sure. Why wouldn't it be?"

"You seem nervous. Like something is bothering you."

"No, no. Nothing's bothering me."

"Perhaps you have had too much caffeine? Maybe an ice water would help calm your nerves?"

Donny shook his head in agreement, then stood up from

the table. "Sure. Ice water. Sounds great, Graham. How 'bout you order me one. I just need to step out for a bit. Get some fresh air."

Everyone looked up. "Where are you going?" Dawa asked.

"Just for a quick walk." Donny sensed the concern around the table—and the need to downplay his behavior. Casually, "Hey, guys, I'm fine. Just need to stretch my legs for a minute. Being holed up in a hotel room all night'll do that to ya, am I right?"

"I'll go with you," Fenton said, scooting his chair back.

"No!" Donny said. "I mean, come on, kid. This is a lot to process. Sometimes the grownups just need a minute alone, kapisch?"

Fenton nodded and sat back down in his chair as Donny left. He let the man get out of earshot, then said, "That's weird. Think he's got diarrhea or something?"

Paul shrugged without saying a word as the three men at the table watched Donny Ford walk hastily toward the door.

***

*What in the hell is wrong with me?*

Donny looked out over the Savannah River, trying to focus on the boats and the bridge and the people walking by, yet unable to escape a single terrifying thought. He looked down at his hands, palms up. Sweaty and shaking. He clasped them together, holding tight and trying to keep them still.

*Great. Now it's just two hands shaking like crazy.* He shoved them in his pockets and stared out toward the water, trying to process the noise in his head.

It was an utterly wicked thought, one that had caught

him completely off guard, bringing with it the kind of fear he hadn't felt since the car wreck six months earlier. It was so vivid, so clear. And the noise . . . God, was it loud! Where had such a thought come from? He tried to ignore it, but ironically that only made it worse. Clearer. Louder. Even when he got away from himself for a moment—using the practice of mindfulness to separate himself from such a wacky train of thoughts—it was always on the back burner. Always right there, waiting to tell him something was amiss. Something was off. And something had to be done to fix it all.

He muttered to himself, "Just don't think about it, Don. It'll all go away . . ."

*Jump in the river, Donny.*

He grabbed his forehead and moaned with disapproval. *Jesus, would you just stop it already?*

Silence for a second or two, then the internal argument started again.

*Jump in the river, Donny.*

*Fuck off!*

*It's the only way, Donny. The only way.*

Insanity. That's what this was. Years on the road, working impossibly long hours, and the occasional drug use had finally taken its toll on the traveling speaker. Again,

*Just do it, Donny.*

Who knew thoughts could hurt? It was as if a person were standing by his side, hand cupped, whispering into his ear.

*Jump on in, Donny. The water's fine.*

A devil in his mind, the Great Tempter. Sent by some ominous force to convince the man the thoughts were his own.

But they *were* his own, thought Donny. They must be. It was all in his head, after all. His heart fluttered and his chest weighed heavy. He put a hand to it, fingers searching the flesh over his breastbone. A nervous lump shuddered up from his chest and filled his throat. Breathing was getting tough now—all because of the voice. He couldn't stand it. He wanted it gone. What would it take to get it to leave? He tried to shake it loose (even catching the attention of a few pedestrians nearby who in turn pulled their kids in closer and sped past), but his efforts were futile, and only strengthened the thought:

*You're a horrible human being, Donny. What kind of man treats people the way you do? Best if you just climb over the rail up there and jump in the river. Best thing for everyone.*

Donny stood motionless now, caught up in the firm grip of his mind's eye. The voice continued, *Just do it, son. See that bridge up yonder? Pick you out a nice little spot, stroll to the top, and step off. Let that tide carry the trash on out to sea.*

Donny checked his surroundings and saw exactly what the voice was referring to. Half a mile up the river was the Talmadge Bridge, a cable-stayed bridge spanning the aquatic gap between Georgia and South Carolina. The bridge could be accessed from River Street, just a short walk away. It was high near the top, too. Plenty of space to get him out over deep water . . .

*WAIT . . . What in the hell are you even thinking, man?* A war brewed in Donny's head, the two vastly polarized sides determined to overtake the other. Had Donny paid more attention to Dawa's eternally dismissed teachings, he would have known it was better to ignore thoughts like these rather than entertain them. They were like schoolyard bullies: show any sign of weakness during a barrage of taunts and you'd earn yourself a group of personal tormentors for the rest of the year. Ignore the bastards, on the other hand, and they'd likely move on to the next untrained prey.

Unfortunately, Donny was proving he was quite the novice at fighting the demonic thoughts within.

It wasn't just the voices that bothered him, either. More frightening than the horrific commands going off in his head were the *feelings* that went along with them. Shame. Remorse. Guilt. Self-pity. A sense that everyone's problems were rooted in his shortcomings, and the lives he'd affected would be better off without him.

What did he have to bring to the group, anyway? To an outside observer, the obvious answer would have been that without his help the whereabouts of Fenton Reed—the one outlier who seemed to have the drop on Asteria and company—might never have been known. But to the new Donny Ford, there was no positive, only negative. He couldn't rationalize; couldn't be pragmatic; couldn't take a step back and realize the chatterbox going off in his head was nonsensical and foreign.

No. The only answer he had for the current situation was to jump off the bridge and kill himself. Soon he was walking at a steady pace, eyes locked onto his final destination. He looked around at the people passing by and wondered if they knew his intentions. Nope. No way. Just another guy taking a riverside stroll on a Friday morning.

Shorebirds chirped and the brackish water sloshed with the outgoing tide. The sky was blue and the incoming breeze was refreshing. Donny took a big breath of the fragrant salt air. It hit his nostrils and filled his lungs, and what was once panic quickly turned to peace. Warmth filled his chest, and in that moment he knew everything was going to be just fine.

He floated toward the bridge, finally able to understand what he had to do. It felt like salvation. The same burden that had overtaken him moments earlier was lifted, vanishing with the faint morning fog into the cool coastal air.

*Just do it, son.* The voice was benevolent now, like a wise old man speaking soothing parables to a wayward son.

He stepped off River Street and started the long walk up to the top of the Talmadge Bridge. A thought occurred to him, and then he smiled.

*Just a few more steps and the voices will stop.*

# Chapter 25:
# Turncoats

Chatter through the grapevine moved quickly between the FDA and Big Pharma; a side effect of the long-standing culture between the government watchdog and private-sector pharmaceutical companies. Industry insiders called this the revolving door policy, where FDA employees maintained fruitful relationships with Big Pharma in exchange for future high-paying jobs at the same companies they once oversaw. You scratch my back, and one of these days, I'll scratch yours.

For George Sturgis, a thick rolodex of back channels to the Food and Drug Administration had typically meant getting the jump on competitors; gaining insight into potential clinical trial barriers; and learning how to get the strictest FDA reviewers to loosen up and move a drug forward for approval. On most days, such phone calls and email correspondence usually led to good news for Sturgis and company.

This was not one of those days.

The double doors to the boardroom burst open and slammed into the walls on both sides as Sturgis stormed in, effectively silencing every mouth in the room.

"Did anyone else know about this shit?" he asked as he hastily walked to the head of the table at the far end of the room. Halfway, he tossed a memo on the table, the closest board members leaning forward curiously for a peek. A bright yellow Post-it note was stuck to the front and read, "Thought you'd want to know—J.D."

One of the members removed the note and read:

## FOOD AND DRUG ADMINISTRATION

**This is an internal document and not intended for public use.**

MEMORANDUM

**DATE:** Friday, August 19th, 2021

**FROM:** Anthony Hoover
Commissioner of Food and Drugs

**SUBJECT:** Federal formulary blacklist revision

**TO:** Dorothy Adams
Deputy Commissioner for Regulatory Operations and Policy

Deputy Commissioner Adams,

Previously undisclosed information has led me to believe that the recent approval of the sleep medication Ocula from Asteria Pharmaceuticals needs to undergo an emergency investigation into the recent approval of the drug. This includes, but is not limited to, setting up employee interviews, reviewing clinical trial policies and procedures, and most importantly, putting an immediate stop to the clinical supply chain to limit further distribution of Ocula until the investigation can be completed.

I'm sure you'll have questions regarding the basis for the

blacklist request, and I plan on explaining to the remaining leadership first thing Monday morning. In the meantime, please draft the necessary documents needed to move the formulary blacklist request forward and have it ready by 9 a.m. Monday.

Best,

—  Anthony Hoover, M.D.
    Commissioner of Food and Drugs
    10903 New Hampshire Avenue
    Silver Spring, Maryland 20993
    (555) 555-8423

The memo was passed around the boardroom while Sturgis sat at the head of the table in silence, arms crossed, face full of consternation, waiting for everyone to take it all in. The last board member read the note, then everyone sat back in their chairs, confused, and waiting for Sturgis to tell them more.

Finally, "Everyone's read the memo. Now I want to know which one of you knew about this."

Everyone was silent. A few held their breath, afraid to draw the slightest attention from the raging CEO.

"Well, someone must have known," Sturgis said. "Otherwise, what 'previously undisclosed information' is Hoover citing here?"

Shoulders shrugged and faces were blank.

"For God's sake, people. Don't any of you have any kind of clue as to what's going on here? *Someone* has given something to the FDA; information that is causing the man at the top to question our recently approved mega-drug. Now if you people don't start talking here, heads are going to roll. So," he leaned forward, "who's first?"

Jillian Penn raised her hand.

"Ah, Jillian. Ironically, the only female at the table is also the only person here with any balls. Would you care to shed some light on the developing situation here?"

Slightly irked by Sturgis's penchant for the politically incorrect, she answered, "I *may* have an idea." She looked around the table. "I think it's clear most of us are just as shocked as you are right now. Honestly, this seems more like a bad joke than a revelation set in reality . . ."

Sturgis shook his head no. The threat was real. Jillian continued, "That said, maybe it has nothing to do with new information at all. Have you considered the possibility that one of the FDA reviewers is trying to extort the company?"

"If that's the case," Sturgis said, "they've got a funny way of going about things. Usually, one would contact the people they were extorting *before* going to their bosses. If someone involved in Ocula's approval is looking for a payday, they'd do well to pick up a copy of *Extortion for Dummies*."

Jillian asked, "What about your other sources at the FDA? Is anyone else talking about this memo?"

"No. No one. And it was drafted today. Not last week or last month. Today. Now what the hell has happened in the last twenty-four hours to make this son of a bitch want to throw a wrench in the one product that's keeping this company afloat?"

Another board member, vice-chair Gary Larcen, worked up the courage to speak. "Maybe it's the higher-ups looking for a payday," he said. "It would make sense, because the company was over-extended throughout the entire clinical trial process. Conventional FDA payoffs dried up, and we all know that didn't go unnoticed. We had to play by the rules on this one, which is exactly why it took so long to move this drug through the approval process to begin with. Now that every stock analyst in the country is stampeding to pick up shares of the hottest biotech offering on the market, maybe a few rogue FDA officials are looking to get their dividends paid in full, directly from the source."

Sturgis nervously tapped a pen on the table and considered Larcen's statement. Maybe Hoover was looking for a little under-the-table payback now that Ocula was the launching Asteria into unforeseen financial territory. The company was already up double digits year-to-date, and they were barely into quarter three. If Asteria's line chart continued to climb on the Nasdaq, they'd be breaking biotech index records by Christmas. If there was ever a time to extort the company, this was it.

"I guess it's a possibility," Sturgis said. "Tell me, Larcen. Have you"—he looked keenly around the room—"or anyone else in here heard about this from other sources?"

They had not. They couldn't have heard anything, either. In Hoover's hasty effort to shoot off an email to Deputy Commissioner Dorothy Adams at the FDA, he had forgotten to carbon copy the other deputy commissioners and leadership. It appeared the commissioner's nervous breakdown in a barbeque-joint bathroom had led to an ardent belief that now had him calling for a federal ban on a sleep medication with barely a year of exposure on the open market.

Unfortunately, Sturgis had no way of knowing the true motive behind Hoover's unforeseen and expedient Ocula reversal. He lowered his head and sighed heavily. "Ladies and gentlemen, I think it goes without saying that this drug isn't just another product manufactured and sold by Asteria—this drug *is*

Asteria. Without it, we'll be shuttering the windows and locking the doors within a month of it being pulled from the market."

He looked around the room again, desperate for answers, but consented to receiving none. Defeated, he told the board members to keep their ears open, and then called the meeting to a close. Soon, George Sturgis was the only person left in the room.

He sat and wondered just why in the hell Hoover would do this now. Was it just about the money? If so, why write the memo? For better leverage on down the line? And why hadn't he heard anything from his backchannels at the FDA yet?

Nothing made a lick of sense. Sturgis leaned back in his chair and looked out of the window toward the Atlanta skyline. He watched a plane ascend from the busiest airport in the world before turning to head north. It climbed and then disappear into the distance, and that's when the thought of Colin Kovic's recent visit hit him.

*Kovic. That double-crossing bastard must've gotten to Hoover.* The CIA field agent had already warned Sturgis days earlier that Director Lancaster was pushing to have the market version of Ocula banned from the government formulary. But that was before Sturgis got on the phone with his associates at the DEA and FDA. Hell, Hoover had assured him just two days prior that Asteria had nothing to worry about. Now the man was sending memos deeming the drug a potential threat to public welfare? What had happened in such a short period of time?

And what about the DEA? Would they be the next federal agency to go full turncoat on Sturgis? The CEO fidgeted and cursed and ruminated on the lack of loyalty in the world today.

Suddenly, he was still as stone as a thought, a question, rocked his very consciousness, causing him to call into question everything he'd believed about the world. Convictions he'd held his entire life. Values that had held true throughout a highly successful professional career in medicine and biotech. It was the question that Tanner and Doyle and Kovic had all raised at one point or another from the onset of the Ocula project:

*Do you still believe our research is nonsense?*

For the first time in his life, George Sturgis didn't know what he believed.

# Chapter 26:
## Take Me to the River

From a distance, the tourists that packed the deck of a Savannah riverboat floating downstream couldn't tell the silhouette standing between two steel cables atop the Talmadge Bridge was about to jump into the chocolate-milk-colored waters below. Up close, however, his intentions were clear. Donny Ford was about to plunge to his death, and nothing was standing in his way.

The unstable apex of a two-hundred-foot tall moving overpass should have been enough to make him rethink his decision. Cars rushed by and rocked his body, pushing him out before sucking him back in with every break in the traffic. His grip was white-knuckle tight around one of the cables—it had to be. The wind howled in his ears as the waters churned below. The top of the bridge was pure chaos, loud and unsettling, but for some reason, all of the doubts and apprehensions and what-ifs that had plagued Donny his entire life were gone. Now his choice was clear. This was the answer to everything. He thought he should feel worse, even tried to drum up some sense that stepping to an inevitable death was the wrong thing to do.

*But everything feels so right.*

He inched forward a little more, still grasping to one of the cables. He imagined being knocked out cold by the impact of a 185-foot drop; then he thought about living through it. *Unlikely. A plummet from this height would be like hitting concrete.* But if it *did* happen, he'd quickly be sucked under by the current. It would be cold, but probably wouldn't take too long. Two or three minutes, tops. Then this whole charade would be over.

It would be worth it in the end. He just knew it.

He let go of the cable and stared down. The wind continued to blow and the bridge rocked under his feet. The dizzying view forced his eyes closed. With no sign of second-guessing, he went to take one last step, but something stopped him from behind, leaving one foot hanging mid-air over the river below. He tried to push himself forward with the other, but the resistance coming from his back collar wouldn't let go. A hand grasped his Hawaiian shirt firmly before jerking him back onto the sidewalk.

"Jesus, Donny!"

The journalist yanked the pitchman away from the edge so hard he fell on his back. She dropped to her knees as he lay there, dazed and in shock.

"Claire? What are you doing here?"

"I think the bigger question is what the hell are *you* doing here?"

He sat up and rubbed his forehead. *Come on, man. Think.*

"I'm not sure," he said.

"What do you mean, you're not sure? Because from this angle, it looks like you were about to high-dive into the Savannah River." She drew closer to analyze him. His eyes told the story. He didn't know what he was doing.

She asked, "What's the last thing you remember?"

"I—I remember . . ." *Nothing,* thought Donny. But then there was something.

"The hotel lobby," he said. "I was in the lobby with Graham and Freeman and Fenton Reed. We were up all night talking about what Fenton had on Asteria and the CIA connection. I was pretty drowsy. Even drifted off a little, but I thought I was just dozing. Next thing I know, you're body-slamming me to the sidewalk."

"You have no idea how you got here?"

"Not a clue, Claire. One minute I'm talking to the guys, the next minute I'm about to go for a swim."

*This is bad.* Claire had a good idea about what Donny had just experienced, because she'd been there herself. That feeling. That witchy, intrusive, uncontrollable feeling, where it didn't matter what you wanted to think, because the worst thoughts you could imagine were going to happen to you, regardless.

It was a total loss of control only Ocula could cause. Donny had made someone's nighttime to-do list, and he had just felt the effects firsthand. Losing control like that was a terrifying ordeal only a handful of people in the world had gone through, and the journalist in Claire was eager to pick Ford's brain.

But there was no point in frightening Donny any more than he already was. Not yet, anyway. She helped Donny to his feet and dusted off the back of his shirt.

"You gonna be okay, Donny?" she asked.

He looked around and shook his head. "Yeah. I think so. Just a little freaked out at the moment." He paused, then said, "You don't think this has anything to do with Oc—"

"Don't even say it," she said. She took him by the arm and they began to walk down the bridge back toward River Street. "Come on. Let's get you back to the hotel."

***

In the lobby, three members of the Atlanta crew sat around a small square table sipping coffee and checking the time, each one of them wondering where Ford had stumbled off to.

"It's been almost an hour," Paul said. "Think we should go look for him?"

"Maybe," Dawa said. "If he is not back here in the next ten minutes, we will split up and search. But he is probably just clearing his head. This is a lot to take in, and we all handle these situations in different ways."

Fenton said, "If by situations you mean diarrhea, then yeah. He's gonna be a while."

"Come on," Paul said.

"What? You saw his face." Fenton gulped his Red Bull, then said, "Classic diarrhea face. A face no man can hide."

Paul and Dawa shook their heads while Fenton crushed his can and looked around for a trash bin. Across the lobby, he saw Donny returning with a pretty redhead by his side.

"Hey, speak of the devil," Fenton said. Paul and Dawa looked up to see the couple walking in.

"Claire?" Paul couldn't believe his eyes. He stood to greet her as she approached. "What are you doing here?"

"You guys didn't think I was going to wait in Atlanta, did you?"

"How did you get here so fast?" Paul asked.

"Aguilar Airlines. How else?"

Paul sunk his head, then said, "I'm sorry about your friend, Claire. I know you two were close."

Claire nodded and pressed her lips, then said, "Thanks, Paul. I don't think it's really set in yet. And honestly, I don't want it to. That wouldn't serve any purpose for Han's memory. No, what I want to do is find the bastards who did this."

Paul looked back at the boys. "Trust me, Claire. So do we."

Dawa pulled up an extra chair for Claire as the rest took a seat. The square table in the corner of the hotel lobby had become their provisional war room. Fenton had printed documents and penciled scribblings scattered across the table. Aerial maps of the Skyline facility. Schematics for interior construction. Blueprints for the tower on top of the mountain designed to connect the underground facility to the rest of the world. Dawa picked up an internal memo and silently read through it. Nothing was redacted. Everything the CIA had on Project THEIA was at their disposal. He passed the memo to Paul, who immediately recognized the name of the author.

"Holy shit, Claire. Check out the name here." He handed the document over. She couldn't believe it.

"What did you find?" Dawa asked.

"This guy heading up the project," Paul said. "Roberto Ramírez. He worked for Tanner at the facility in Costa Rica. After the incident he helped us escape by hotwiring one of the Jeeps. He tried to convince us he was in the dark about the extent of Tanner's experiments, but that argument went out the window the moment he bailed out of the Jeep halfway to San José."

Claire said, "I knew something was up with the guy from the get-go."

"What is interesting," Dawa said, connecting the dots, "is that the facility in Costa Rica was funded by Asteria and operated by *former* CIA agents."

Fenton said, "Ryan Tanner and Dick Doyle."

"Yes," Dawa said. "Now it looks like the agency has borrowed from their playbook and picked up right where Tanner and Doyle left off. This facility in Virginia, the same people working for Tanner . . . It can only mean one thing."

"Tanner was playing both sides," Claire said. "Using Asteria to fund the project while selling information to his old CIA buddies."

"Precisely." Dawa laid the memo down and said to Fenton, "This is incredible. How did you ever find a way to obtain this information?"

"That's the beauty of government security," Fenton grinned. "The private sector has been gobbling up cybersecurity jobs for years now, because they pay better. When the best hackers in the world work for telecoms and banks, it means government cybersecurity falls one step behind. And as fast as the Internet evolves, one step is all it takes."

Dawa nodded and pretended to follow what the young hacker was saying. He said, "I think it goes without saying that none of this is admissible in court." The detective turned to Claire. "Do you think there is anything here we can take to the press?"

"Honestly, no. Everything I see here was obtained illegally. Sure, it would catch the attention of conspiracy theorists and guys with tinfoil hats. But no self-respecting media outlet is going to touch any of this."

Paul said, "And it would expose us. I don't think the risk is worth the reward."

"With you on that one," said Donny. "I mean, what, we're gonna wave our hands and basically beg these guys to come after us? After what happened today? No way."

Fenton leaned in. "What exactly did happen this morning, dude?"

"It's hard to explain," Donny said. "It was like a blackout. One minute I'm sitting here with you guys, the next I'm about to go for a swim with the fishes." They all looked toward the Talmadge Bridge, visible from the tall lobby windows. "And the weirdest thing is that I can't remember a thing. I mean, I know deep down something incredibly fucked up was going on in my head. Any of you ever wake up knowing you had the most insane dream of all time, but you just can't remember it? It was something like that."

Claire knew just where Donny was coming from. "This is not good news," she said. "This kind of behavior doesn't just happen out of the clear blue sky. What Donny's describing here sounds exactly like the Ocula effect. Either an outlier had a dream about Donny going hara-kiri on himself, or someone intentionally planted the thought there."

Paul asked, "You think the CIA is going after the remaining outliers again?"

"It's a possibility," Claire said. "Kovic assured me the search was off, but that was before he betrayed me in Costa Rica. It would certainly explain why my mind's been at relative ease, since he likely thinks I died in the blast." She asked Fenton, "Anything popping up on your mental radar?"

"Not a thing. Not that I know of, anyway."

Donny's eyes sharpened as he scrutinized the response. Either the kid was a great actor, or he was telling the truth; the latter of which meaning he had no knowledge of the dream that had led the team to Savannah to find him in the first place. But if that were the case, what about the jump drive Fenton had pointed out during Donny's lucid dream? What were the odds of Donny randomly dreaming about Fenton's jump drive, only to have Dawa return from Fenton's old apartment with the device in hand?

The scenario reminded him of the volcano incident six

months earlier. Suddenly, Donny was uneasy again. In the beginning, the orthodox science behind Ocula had made a lot of sense to him. Gene therapy led to weird side effects in a small number of patients. Those patients had amplified brainwaves during R.E.M. sleep; brainwaves that were then picked up by other organisms nearby. A far-out theory, but something he had come to accept.

But volcanoes weren't organisms, and the case of Fenton Reed only exacerbated his anxiety. The way Claire had explained it to him, Ocula was supposed to be a one-way street: Electromagnetic radiation—brainwaves—sent messages to targeted minds nearby. Those messages influenced others to take any number of actions. Anything the brain could dream up was fair game. But in this case, Fenton had told him about a jump drive, and Dawa had delivered. So many things weren't adding up, but one thing was certain: there was no way this was a series of coincidences.

Donny took his eyes off the ceiling and regrouped. "What about the outliers we don't know about?"

Fenton asked, "What do you mean?"

"Let not our troubled souls forget that Ocula 1.0 is still just as dangerous as the new and improved version. It's what got us here in the first place. What got my business partner killed. Remember?"

"He's right," Paul said. "There were 2,000 participants in the original clinical trial, and a dozen outliers were reported. Fast forward to today and Ocula's been on the open market since March. How many people are having these same side effects that we don't even know about?"

Disturbed, "I didn't even think about that," Fenton said. He did the math in his head. "That's about half a percent."

Paul said, "But multiply that by a few million users—"

"—And you're talking thousands of people potentially dreaming up crazy shit from coast to coast."

They all sat back in their chairs as the demoralizing reality sank in. They looked at one another, then Dawa said, "Well. Anyone have any ideas?"

"I have one," Claire said. "And I think it's our only play."

"Let's hear it."

She took a deep breath. "I can make contact with Kovic. Turn myself in."

The table erupted before she could finish. "Are you out of your mind, Claire?" Paul said, loud enough to get several hotel guests to look over. Paul waved to say sorry, and they returned to their own affairs.

Claire continued. "Hear me out. According to these documents, the new facility has the capacity to influence people within a 150-mile radius. The place is like its own news station, complete with the ability to broadcast whatever message it wants to straight to dreamers for miles. If I can get in there and use the machine myself, we can broadcast our own message to thousands, maybe millions of people."

Fenton said, "It could work. I didn't print off everything here, but there's a folder on my jump drive titled 'Project Scope Statement.' Inside there's a whole bunch of stuff about the goals of the project, like creating a system that could guarantee an effective reach across the entire D.C. area."

"For obvious reasons," interrupted Donny. "Give the CIA the ability to sway the politicians, and they'll be free to do as they please."

"What I'm saying is," Fenton said, "if this thing can reach D.C., then there's a good chance the right people will hear whatever you've got to say, Claire. If you need any help, you can count me in."

Dawa asked, "What about the element of surprise, Claire? It is safe to believe that Colin Kovic thinks you are dead. There must be some way we can use this to our advantage . . ."

"How? By sneaking me into a CIA black site?" Claire shuffled through Reed's documents and found a blueprint. She slid it over to Dawa. "Check out the security at this place, Dawa. Entrance codes. Retinal scanners. Armed guards—the works. It would take about two seconds before the project lackeys realized I'm still alive, and just a few seconds after that to take me out for good. The only way we're getting in here—the only way we can get the word out about Asteria in a way that is sure to bring them down—is if I turn myself in and agree to meet Kovic at the site."

"How do you know Kovic won't kill you on the spot?" Paul asked.

"I don't. But do you guys have any better ideas?"

They didn't.

# Chapter 27:
# Done

Skies were clear on a Friday night, giving a bright gray moon the freedom to shine down over the Vajrayãna Monastery without a single cloud getting in the way. Inside, Michelle lay in bed wide awake, arm under her pillow, eyes locked on a moonlit window that was putting her in an irresistible trance. Panes of glass filled the window in her room and were outlined in soft silver as the moon outshined every star around it.

The last two nights locked up at the Vajrayãna Monastery had become the pinnacle of a six-month stretch of high anxiety, fear, and frustration for the young Mrs. Freeman. Kidnapped by a psychotic ex-CIA agent; uprooted from her home in the suburbs for a life in hiding; and driving nonstop from one coast to another (only to be left alone in an unfamiliar place with a friend of Dawa's who frankly creeped the poor woman out) was enough to drive anyone mad. This wasn't living. Just surviving.

And, a new marriage was already on the rocks. While her husband Paul was off playing soldier (like he'd always wanted) and trying to save the world, she was effectively on house arrest. Left behind once again. Of course, the last time she and Paul had been apart it was against his will, and Michelle felt guilty for insinuating in her mind that he could have done anything about it.

Still, it felt like some cosmic force was doing everything it could to pull the two apart. Even when Paul had called to check in earlier, it had felt like he was doing it out of obligation, in a hurry to get back to the mission. What had started as a promising high school romance had blossomed into the perfect little marriage, complete with a house in the burbs and a newborn—only to wilt at the first sight of a serious challenge.

Few marriages could survive the duress the Freemans had been put under, and in that respect, Michelle could stop beating herself up for a moment. It didn't help that Paul was still convinced she'd drugged him to begin with either; the man's trust issues dated back to high school. But just like Michelle hadn't made out with Paul's arch nemesis Jason Young at Jessica Reilly's Sweet Sixteen party, Michelle had also had nothing to do with Paul's acquisition of Ocula. Oh, the fragile early years of marriage, where resilience is tested and doubts are aplenty.

She turned to face away from the window and prayed for drowsiness. Even with her anxiety working its way out through a pair of restless feet kicking the covers off the bed, she could start to feel her eyes burning that burn that came right before that inescapable kind of sleep that arose out of pure exhaustion.

But Aaron cried, and visions of sugar plums and counting sheep by a cozy fire quickly dissipated. She sat up and threw her pillow across the room, hitting a lamp on an end table and almost knocking it off. It rocked left, then right while Michelle watched in angst, seconds feeling like hours, before it came back to rest on the table, only slightly out of place. She breathed a great sigh of relief, thankful the expensive-looking lamp hadn't busted all over the hardwood floors and roused Dawa's Asian friend with the wandering eyes. Then again, he was probably standing just outside the door.

Michelle flipped on the lights to find her young son had rolled off his pallet of comforters and blankets. Her cold feet hit the floor and she thought *no wonder he's awake*. She picked him up and rocked him back to sleep, then put him in the bed next to her. She was trying to ween him off the need to sleep in Mama's bed every night, but what the hell. The first year of Little Man's life had been less than conventional, and even though his vocabulary was mainly limited to Mama and Dada and baba (kids learn real quick how to ask for a bottle) he still probably had some understanding of the trauma they had gone through.

But unlike the worries and stresses that tend to nag the fully developed minds of adults, Aaron's upset didn't stick too long. Soon he was right back to sleep, back in the comfort of his loving mother. She lay there for a few moments after the last sign of wakefulness, checked to make sure he was sleeping well now, then slowly eased out of bed. A drink was calling her name from Dawa's kitchen, even though she figured him for a guy who only stocked his fridge with juice and water. With any luck, she might find something a little stronger.

She opened the door and looked down the hall. Dawa's friend Tsomo was sitting in the foyer at the end of the long corridor in khaki slacks and a button-up, one sharply-dressed foot propped on the other, and reading a book. She tried to step out quietly, but as soon as she was in the hallway, he looked up.

"Ah, Mrs. Freeman," he said, folding his book shut. "Such a pleasant surprise this evening."

*Busted. Dammit.*

"Hi, Tsomo," she said, disappointed she'd been caught. The kitchen was closer to her room than the foyer. If she was fast, maybe she could get there before Tsomo had the opportunity to rise from his chair. Just a little haste . . .

No such luck. Michelle took the first step and Tsomo was already getting up to walk her way.

"Is there anything I can help you with, Mrs. Freeman?"

"Just going to the kitchen, Tsomo."

Hopefully, "Perhaps I'll join you?"

Tsomo had been a friend of Dawa's for his entire adult life; Michelle had been a guest for barely two days. She could hardly say no.

She motioned for the thirty-something to come on. "Sure. Why not. Hell, maybe you can help me find the scotch."

"Scotch?" Puzzled, "I didn't take you for a drinker, Mrs. Freeman."

"You've known me two days, Tsomo. Stick around much longer and I'm sure you'll find I'm full of surprises."

***

The bottle of Sauvignon Blanc was a pleasant surprise to Michelle, especially after Tsomo had assured her that the monastery was a place free of drugs and alcohol. Her instincts told her otherwise, armed with the knowledge that Dawa loved to cook. One look in the back of the pantry, nestled behind the cookies and sodas that were surely Donny's, and the bottle was spotted.

Michelle wasn't a heavy drinker, but such a find was a lifesaver on a sleepless night. She searched through one of the drawers and found a bottle opener, and within minutes she was sitting on a barstool in front of the kitchen island, sipping room-temperature wine and listening to her new acquaintance explain how he had come to know Dawa Graham.

"Atlanta's about the last place I thought I'd wind up when I was a teenager," said Tsomo as he sat across from Michelle, sipping hot tea, elbows propped on the island. "I was born in San Francisco, lived there my whole life. All my friends were there, my school was there . . . life was good and I had no reason to think we'd leave. We didn't travel much; no vacations or weekend trips or anything like that. So when my dad came home from work one day and told me and my mother and my little sister we'd be moving within the month, it didn't exactly go well."

Tsomo ran his hand through his dark and carefully parted hair, and Michelle could tell the memory made him uncomfortable. Concerned, "We don't have to get into it if you don't want—"

"No. That's okay. It's all in the past now anyway. Let's just say I became a little hard to handle, especially after we arrived at our new home in Atlanta and the reality set in that we were here to stay."

"Hard to handle? Pssh, sounds like your average teenager to me."

"I assure you, it was a little worse than that. Unruly and disobedient at first, yes. But by the time I was a sophomore in college, I had already become quite fond of alcohol and weed, and was beginning to move onto bigger and better things." Tsomo shook his head, disgusted with his past behavior. "I'd try anything anyone handed to me. Pain pills. Speed. Acid. Ecstasy. If it was illegal, I wanted it. Partly because I was turning into an addict, yes, but mostly just to get back at my dad for uprooting the family a decade earlier."

"That's a lot of time to hold onto resentment," Michelle said, gently swirling the wine in her glass.

"You're not telling me anything I don't already know, believe me. I was a mess, my grades were sinking, and I was about to flunk out of school. So, when I came home for summer break between sophomore and junior year, my father had had enough. He told me he had found a man by the name of Dawa Graham who had just recently opened a center focused on the teachings of Tibetan Buddhism. I became one of Dawa's first students. He helped me turn my life around, and I've been trying to pay him back ever since."

"Sounds like an incredible man," Michelle said.

The comment raised a red flag for Tsomo. Curiously, he asked, "How did you say you know Dawa again?"

"College!" Michelle blurted out, caught a little off guard. She lowered her tone. "I mean, I went to Georgia State. Took transcendental meditation as an elective. Had to write a paper on Dawa's work here at the monastery." The more she rolled on with the concocted story, the worse it sounded. *Stop talking. Start drinking.*

Tsomo said, "I would love to read this paper one day."

"Mmm-hmm." She took a long sip of wine and looked away.

Tsomo took the hint and dropped it.

"So," he said, "your husband is helping Dawa with an investigation?"

"Yes, he and—" She was so close to naming Ford, with no clue as to how much Tsomo knew about the situation. She looked at the wine and checked herself. *Careful not to ramble, Michelle.* "—and one of Dawa's coworkers. They're looking for some teenage hacker who broke into some government system. I think he's wanted by the FBI; I can't remember. Anyway, that's all they told me."

She briefly analyzed Tsomo to see if he bought the story, then retreated back to her wine. Sure, she knew Dawa and Tsomo were close, but the detective never mentioned Ocula around his old student. Instead, he'd told Michelle to tell Tsomo they knew one another from college. The little white lie seemed innocuous at the time, but could only signal that Dawa was hiding things from Tsomo. And if that were the case, odds were he didn't know all the juicy details behind the Savannah trip.

The conversation went silent for a moment—something that would have made her extremely uncomfortable without the help of a little vino. Now, the quiet didn't bother her so much. Her hair draped like a dirty-blonde curtain between her and her glass as she twirled it to pass the time.

Tsomo couldn't ignore her beauty, but he was doing a good job of hiding his approval (for the most part). There had been a couple of times over the last two days where Michelle had caught her newly-acquired bodyguard checking her out, but he was always quick to avert his eyes. It was only human nature, and Michelle wasn't going to hold it against him.

He broke the silence as he stood to refill his tea, asking along the way, "Did Dawa mention when they'd be back?"

"He didn't tell you?"

Tsomo shook his head no. "There have been a few times over the last decade or so where Dawa's asked me for help, but each time's the same. I don't ask, and he doesn't tell. Honestly, I like it that way. I basically owe the guy my life, so when he needs something, who am I to start asking questions?"

*Someone who could be implicated in a laundry list of felonies,* thought Michelle. And weren't Buddhists supposed to strive for honesty and avoid deceit anyway? Maybe Dawa was slipping. Michelle was about to play judge and jury, but she quickly stopped herself. Dawa was probably just looking out for Tsomo to begin with. The less he knew, the better.

"Well," Michelle said, "it's very nice of you to stay with me. But really, I *don't* need a babysitter. I'm a big girl who's seen a lot of shit. Believe me, I can take care of myself."

Hearing Michelle cuss brought out Tsomo's giddiness.

"Seen a lot of shit, huh? Go on . . ."

"I was an E.R. nurse for five years before taking a leave of absence to take care of Aaron."

"Oh, really? What hospital?"

"Grady. Downtown."

"I know the place. That's a rough scene." His eyes drifted to the ceiling. "Man, I bet you really have seen some shit."

"Stab wounds. Gunshot wounds. Auto accidents. Husbands beating their wives and wives beating their kids. All in a day's work."

The two took a moment of silence as they both sipped their drinks. Finally, Tsomo asked, "So how are you and Mr. Freeman? I noticed you two didn't talk much before he left."

Whatever feeling of comfort Michelle had had in the room evaporated immediately. She stood up, turned up her wine glass for that last remaining sip, and proceeded to the archway leading back into the hall.

"Listen, Tsomo. No offense, but I'm not going to sit here and go down this road with someone I just met—"

"I'm sorry"—Tsomo turned and put his hands up, blushing, and feeling like an absolute jackass—"I really didn't mean to offend you."

"It's okay. I'm not offended. I'm just not going to talk about it." She got a little further and Tsomo piped up.

"Wait. Before you leave. Let me make it up to you."

Even that sounded creepy.

"Excuse me?"

Tsomo stood but didn't move closer. Just stood by the island while nervously trying to figure out a way to salvage the situation; make up for his antisocial comments; and get rid of this damn embarrassment that was washing over his body and making him sick. He saw the empty wine bottle and blurted it out.

"The wine. I can run to the store. Get you another bottle. Would you like another bottle, Mrs. Freeman?"

Michelle stopped and turned. *Get another bottle. As in, no more bodyguard.* She nodded in agreement, hiding cheerfulness behind stern eyes and a straight mouth. "Sure. Another bottle. That would be very kind of you, Tsomo."

"Okay. Good. Great." He looked around frantically and patted his front pocket for his keys and his back pocket for his wallet. Everything was there. "Okay, I'm going to run, Mrs. Freeman. I'll be back soon. And please, I'm really sorry if I intruded—"

"No need to keep apologizing, Tsomo. Better hurry, before the stores all close."

"Yes. You're right. I'll be on my way then." He rushed out the door and left Michelle standing at the entryway to the kitchen. She waited to listen for Tsomo's car to crank up and head down the driveway.

Soon, the monastery was silent again. She looked down the empty and dark hallway, then back toward an empty kitchen, and thought of being left behind once again. A flood of emotion almost overwhelmed her, but she cut it off short. After everything she'd been through, she knew she was stronger than that.

"Fuck this," she murmured.

She sped-walked back to her room where Aaron was sleeping and called to him,

"Aaron! It's time to wake up, sweetie!"

# Chapter 28:
# Junk Food

"Pull over at this exit," Fenton said as he sat wedged in between Paul and Claire in the backseat. Dawa hit his blinker to get over while Donny rolled his eyes. "Jesus, kid. What'd I say about you having to piss every thirty minutes? If you can't hold that golf-ball-sized bladder of yours, then lay off the Red Bulls. Got it?"

It was just after midnight on I-95, and already Dawa had wheeled into half a dozen gas stations on the dark northbound road to Skyline, Virginia, easily turning an eight-hour drive into a trip closer to ten just to appease a teenager's unhealthy soda habit. They were supposed to be using their time on the highway to polish up Claire's plan, but three hours into the overnight drive and they were still coming up short. Maybe that's why Dawa had no problem pulling off the interstate at Fenton's every ridiculous thirty-minute request. For whatever reason, everyone kept looking to the detective for answers. Unfortunately, he had none, and stopping at every other gas station took the pressure off him to come up with a feasible plan (if only for a minute or two).

The car veered off the exit before turning into the brightly lit twenty-four-hour Speedtrack gas station, coming to a stop in a space near the front door. Dawa threw it in park and looked over his shoulder. "Make it quick, Fenton. We have a lot of miles to cover tonight."

Fenton nodded, then crawled over Paul before he had a chance to move out of the way. "Sorry, dude," he said as he opened the door and piled out of the car. Paul shook his head and wondered if he had been that annoying during his teenage years. "Just hurry up, Reed. We can't keep stopping like this."

Bright fluorescents contracted Fenton's pupils the moment he walked through the automatic door. A sign hung from the ceiling that pointed to the bathrooms in the back. He walked between two candy aisles, browsing the shelves on the way, stopping short near the endcap. Something to his left caught his eye. There, among an endless selection of chocolate bars and gummy bears and bubble gum, lay his favorite guilty pleasure of all: an almost-full box of king-sized Baby Ruths.

He picked it up with his left hand, checking his pocket for loose change or a wad of cash with his right. The feel of the white plastic wrapper thinly draped around a bar of bumpy peanuts and nougat brought a sense of revelation to the forefront of his consciousness. Suddenly, he wasn't in the store anymore. He looked up and into the bright fluorescent lights, searching for something *here*, in the gas station, not *there*, in his mind. But, it was no use.

A wave of vertigo set in as he turned around to find himself back on River Street, back in Savannah, talking to Donny Ford and shooting the breeze like old friends while munching on Baby Ruths and sipping on twenty-ounce sodas. The scene was lucid, unclouded, plain as day, as real as anything Fenton had ever experienced on this side of life.

And as suddenly as it had come on, it was gone. The warm sunlight faded back into fluorescent white as the sounds of River Street were traded for cheesy elevator music playing inside the convenience store. The tall brick buildings lining the Savannah riverfront morphed into a long stretch of beer coolers, glowing that bluish white and humming refrigerated tones that spoke to cold refreshments just a few steps away.

Fenton turned to look out of the store window and back at the car to make sure Donny hadn't been transported to River Street. Sure enough there he was, still sitting in the passenger seat of the sedan, tapping his wristwatch and saying something Fenton couldn't hear (but was almost surely something along the lines of hurry the hell up).

Fenton nodded, put down the candy bar, and walked to the bathroom. Inside, he rid himself of his last two Red Bulls, then walked to the sink to wash up. Looking in the mirror, he thought about the vision.

It was a repeat of the dream he had had days earlier. The dream where he'd met Donny Ford in Savannah. The dream where he'd told Ford how to find him. About the files. About the jump drive in Dawa's possession.

Donny and Fenton had spoken to one another in a dream. As the teenager let the cool water from the tap cascade over hands shaking with excitement, he knew exactly how they could get to the CIA. How they could take down Asteria. How they could all get their lives back.

He shook his hands dry, running out of the bathroom without grabbing a paper towel. He'd had an epiphany, and he couldn't wait to tell the others.

***

"And how is Mrs. Everly on this fine Saturday morning?" Ramírez stood next to the dazed patient and gently nudged her arm as she slowly regained consciousness.

"Where—where am I?"

"You're safe, Mrs. Everly. That's all that matters." Ramírez began to break down the equipment, starting with the headset, then her monitors, then her drug port. Kovic stood back in the room, cupping his chin and keenly observing the new process.

Mrs. Everly licked her lips, then asked, "Is it time for my cookie now?"

"In a moment, Mrs. Everly. After we get you back to your room. Then you'll get your treats."

"Milk, too?"

"Of course, Mrs. Everly. What would cookies be without a little milk to go along with them?"

Mrs. Everly smiled and closed her eyes. Ramírez looked back at a confused Kovic, and nodded in assurance that everything would be explained in due time. He returned to Mrs. Everly and bid her goodbye, then called two techs to come and escort her back to her holding cell. No need for handcuffs or shackles or armed guards.

Kovic followed Ramírez out, and when they were back in the main laboratory and out of earshot he said, "Okay, you're going to have to explain to me what that was all about."

Ramírez chuckled, "That, my friend, is how you properly handle an outlier. In the beginning, we would just put patients to sleep using a narcotic cocktail once they returned from an Ocula-induced event. But as I'm sure you know, people dream on narcotics, too. This led to the incidents with the detainees in Costa Rica and Guantanamo. So, we elected to treat the remaining four outliers in a way that would ensure something like that would never happen again."

"By doing what, lacing their milk and cookies with coke?"

"Close. MDMA."

Shocked, "You're giving them Ecstasy?"

"It sounds unconventional, but the treatment has worked

so far. Patients get a nice little high the moment Ocula wears off, then they eventually fall asleep. And the icing on the cake, compadre? We don't have to worry about them dreaming when we don't want them to."

Kovic was well aware of the fact that mind-altering drugs like LSD, Ecstasy, and cocaine led to dream suppression due to their inhibitory effects on R.E.M. sleep. He was also aware that as soon as withdrawal from these drugs set in, vivid and nightmarish dreams were sure to follow.

"Aren't you worried about withdrawal effects? Contraindications?" he asked Ramírez.

"At this point, no. They are only taken off the meds when they are being prepped for an event. Ocula is running through their veins long before any withdrawal symptoms would take place. The treatment is working, and until we find a better way to keep the outliers under control, this is how we handle it."

Kovic nodded, and together he and Ramírez began preparing for round two of Project THEIA: Ramírez with a renewed passion for the project, and Kovic with a soldier-like obedience that was in direct conflict with the voice in the back of his head telling him he should be completely freaked out.

In a nutshell, round one of Project THEIA had been an extraordinary success. They hadn't even reached the twenty-four-hour mark following Mrs. Everly's carefully managed dream sequence, and already the head of the FDA was legitimately spooked, trading internal memos and freaking out in restaurant bathrooms and working to remove Ocula from the government formulary. The content of the CIA broadcast had effectively reached its intended target almost a hundred miles to the east by way of poor Mrs. Everly's beautiful brain. Skyline had received confirmation late Friday night, and by early Saturday morning they were already prepping Mrs. Rogers for their next target: the head of the Drug Enforcement Agency.

Ramírez was like a kid on Christmas morning, going over the next steps with the other lab techs and doling out high-fives and sneaking off to his office every hour to take a pull off the high-dollar tequila hidden in the bottom drawer of his desk.

Kovic was a different story, only going through the motions and pretending to be fully involved in the process. Didn't matter; Ramírez and Co. seemed to know what they were doing anyway. The way he figured, he was only there to supervise the project—not become another working gear in a machine that had become far too powerful for any government to safely deploy.

The lab buzzed like a beehive, whitecoats scurrying to and fro, some with their heads in their tablets, others swiveling in their rolling stools from one work station to the next. Ramírez returned from his office with tequila fresh on his breath and noticed Kovic staring off into the distance near the observation area. He wiped his mouth (as if that would've masked the smell), walked up and gave him a nudge.

"No time for daydreams, Colin. We've got work to do."

Kovic blinked hard and shook his head. "Of course. It's just been a long one."

"Venga ya," Ramírez grumbled in his native tongue, telling Kovic to give him a break. "You've had it easy, strolling in at halftime. As for me, I haven't had a wink of sleep since I got here." Ramírez turned to face Kovic and lowered his voice. "Which reminds me: how did everything go in Costa Rica?"

"How do you think it went? I was forced to hand off my asset to Cline. The guy hasn't worked in the field in over a decade."

"What about the facility?"

Kovic shook his head, and Ramírez knew that the Costa-Rican chapter of the Ocula saga was finally closed. "Well, at least we can put that place behind us. That is what's important, no?"

"To some extent, yes," Kovic replied. "But not at the cost of innocent American lives. I had a plan in place, and Cline blew the entire operation, calling in drones before giving my asset a chance to gather intel and get out in one piece."

"This asset," Ramírez replied coldly, "was his life more important than taking a necessary step to keep Ocula 2.0 out of the hands of a foreign government?"

"No, but her life didn't have to end the way it did."

"*Her?*" Ramírez's curiosity was piqued. "And who was this mystery woman?"

"That's privileged," Kovic snapped. Ramírez patted him on the shoulder and tried to break the tension, but his apathetic attitude and boisterous laugh only pissed Kovic off even more. He pulled away from the man and left the lab.

In his office, resources were scarce, but Kovic still had everything he needed to communicate with the outside world. He circled his mouse to deactivate his screensaver, then went straight to his email. He had dozens of accounts, many of them used only a handful of times before being replaced with another, cleaner, account.

But there was one account in particular that was on his mind.

He opened a new window, pulled up the throwaway account, and logged in. Right at the top, above a lengthy exchange of read messages, was a new email sporting that fresh bold text that was the calling card of unread messages, dated Friday, August 20th, 2021.

It was from Claire Connor, and she wanted to meet.

# Chapter 29:
# Preparations

An eight-hour drive up the I-95 corridor through Virginia was hardly considered the scenic route (not that it would have mattered anyway, since they had been driving through the night). But once the car full of outliers hit its exit and veered off onto highway 33, the pre-dawn sky was already painting the Saturday-morning sky with a burnt-orange horizon that blended upward into a palate of pinks and blues and purples that shed a mixture of warm and cool colors over the earth-toned Appalachians around them.

Dawa rubbed his eyes and checked the rearview mirror. Paul and Claire were both fast asleep in the backseat, heads propped hard against their respective windows, with Fenton wedged right in the middle, passed out and drooling on Claire's unsuspecting shoulder. The driver was tempted to wake them up, but that would've been cruel. They needed the sleep.

So did Donny, but sleep was the last thing on his mind. He rode shotgun, thumbs twiddling, restless in his seat, still wide awake after two nights without any meaningful rest.

Dawa had seen him like this before. He leaned over, never taking his eyes off the road, and whispered, "You are fidgeting, Donald." He nodded toward the passengers in the back. "Perhaps you should try and get some rest, too."

Donny deployed his classic what-are-you-talking-about look, a look he reserved for people he was trying to hide things from. Dawa knew it all too well.

"Come on, Donald. The twitching. Red eyes. Restless

legs."

Defiantly, "I'm not tired."

Dawa pointed to the mess in the passenger-side floorboard. "You are practically drowning in coffee cups and energy shots. If you are not careful, you are going to crash, just like the kid in the back. If this plan is going to work, Donald, I need you awake *and* coherent. Otherwise, we may be putting Paul and Claire in more jeopardy than they are already getting into."

"I can't believe this is the plan," Donny said.

"It is not the best situation. But like Claire said, is there any other way?"

Neither could think of any, which meant Claire and Fenton were calling the shots. It also meant their chances of surviving to September were about one in a million. The way the two had explained it was simple: contact Kovic, agree to meet him at the Skyline facility, then use their own technology against them to shed light on Asteria and the CIA's wrongdoings on a regional scale. Easy peasy, right?

Not so much. It was a long car ride; plenty of time for Donny to think of a dozen ways it could go wrong, with Dawa adding twice as many to the list. Kovic could shoot Claire on sight. Or maybe he'd find one more outlier too invaluable to dispose of, and opt to keep her detained for the rest of her life instead.

Even if she made it to the facility in one piece (odds few gamblers would ever have placed a bet on), the entire plan hinged on Donny's ability to control a dream in the same way he had to locate Fenton Reed. But dreams were about as predictable as the weather, and Donny had never had to perform under pressure before.

And a direct confrontation? Forget about it. This was a

top-secret CIA black site, complete with state-of-the-art security, heavily armed guards, and a handful of spooks who'd love to see every outlier either in a high-security prison or six feet under.

If the plan was going to work through to the end, Claire was going to have to give Kovic something, anything. That's where Fenton's files came in. Those would at least get her in the front door, post her buy-in. But staying in the game long enough, while relying on everyone else to work their magic, laid most of the risk at Claire's feet.

And that's one thing that made Dawa uncomfortable. Every element of their plan revolved around the ability to influence minds from afar—something Dawa had never been a believer in to begin with. Sure, the fact that Donny knew he was carrying Fenton's jump drive after returning from the teenager's old apartment gave him the creeps, but it wouldn't have been the first time a sheer coincidence played out in Donny's favor.

It also could have been one of the showman's countless magic tricks. After all, Donny had a knack for showmanship and misdirection. *Look over here while I do something over there. Pay no attention to the man behind the curtain.* Only this time, the man behind the curtain had accurately predicted that Fenton would be in Savannah.

*Even a blind squirrel finds a nut sometimes,* Dawa's colleagues would say when a case had been cracked against all odds. But Claire and Fenton both had confidence in Ford, enough so to persuade Dawa to reluctantly go along with a seemingly impractical plan. He just hoped he wasn't being misled.

He slowed the car and hit his blinker, turning off the winding two-lane and into the parking lot of the Little Bear Motel located in the township of Lydia, Virginia, just five miles south of the entrance to Skyline Drive. Off the beaten path and lying in the eastern shadows of the Appalachians, it would be the perfect staging area for the operation that was to come.

The passengers in the back felt the car stop as the therapeutic roar of the highway faded, rousing their senses. They carefully opened their eyes, squinting and stretching and dazed, like kids lost in an amusement park.

"This the place?" Paul asked.

"Yeah," Donny said. He looked around and noticed the parking lot was almost empty with the exception of a single car. He thought that was a good thing. "We should be able to stage everything from here." He started to open his door, but Dawa advised against it.

"You are still a wanted man, Donald. Let me check us in first, make sure the coast is clear." Dawa got out of the car and walked into the motel office while Donny stayed put. The rest of the passengers piled out and stretched their legs, casing the parking lot of the vintage motel and checking their surroundings.

The tan-colored building looked like it had been there since the 60s. It appeared to have ten rooms, maybe twelve, and backed into a steep mountainside scattered with resilient pines hanging on to whatever soil they could cling to in the erosion-riddled hills. A hip roof and dark shingles lay atop the long rectangular stretch of block construction, each room marked by a fire-engine-red door and the kind of old metal-frame jalousie windows lined with parallel panes of glass that could be tilted open from the inside (a feature that must have been a lifesaver for non-smoking wives shacked up with their pack-a-day husbands back in the day).

The motel was old—and quiet. Paul listened hard for people or cars or other signs of intelligent life, but heard little more than the occasional songbird along with a few squirrels scurrying around the trashcan in front of the motel office. Not another soul in sight.

After a few minutes in the office, Dawa walked out dangling a pair of old room keys. He handed one to Claire, and kept the other to himself.

"Room 11 . . ." It was Claire's old cell number at the Costa Rica facility, a number that would never set well with the journalist again.

Casually, Claire asked, "Which room'd you get?"

"10. Right next door," Dawa said.

"Wanna trade?"

"Sure. If you would like." They exchanged keys while the rest wondered what was up. Except for Paul. He knew.

"All right, then," Dawa said. "Let's go ahead and get everything set up in my room." He turned to Fenton. "How soon can we tell if Kovic received Claire's message?"

"Ten minutes, tops," he said as he scratched the back of his nappy red head.

"And if there is no response?" Dawa asked.

Claire said, "He'll respond."

Paul asked Fenton, "You're sure they can't find us here?"

"Yeah, man, I know how to cover my tracks."

Claire said, "I've used virtual private networks to communicate with anonymous sources before, but I don't have too much confidence in them anymore."

Fenton confirmed her suspicions. "VPNs are only as trustworthy as the company providing the service. Even the VPNs that are adamantly opposed to government oversight still have insiders feeding the feds log data. Not throughout every agency, of course. I mean, you're probably safe from local and state officials and maybe even some federal agencies, but when it comes to the CIA, NSA—"

"I think it is time to focus on the task at hand," Dawa said, cutting the talkative teen off short. Everyone agreed and they all went to Dawa's room, motioning to Donny that the coast was clear.

Inside the small room with the single queen-sized bed they began laying out everything they needed to get started. Paul found a corner chair, grabbed the folder with Fenton's documents and began thumbing through them, moving the relevant documents to the top of the stack. Fenton unpacked his equipment, plugged in his laptop, and set up shop on the small desk next to the television in front of the bed.

Claire emptied the go bag she had kept beneath one of the floorboards at Aguilar's San José mansion: a backpack full of emergency supplies saved for when the shit hit the fan. Passports. Cash. Two Glock 9mm handguns, six preloaded clips, and two more boxes of centerfires to spare. She popped in a clip, chambered a round, then set the gun aside with the same casual demeanor as a woman putting on makeup.

Fenton stopped what he was doing and watched Claire work, then looked at Paul wide-eyed, silently mouthing, "*HOLY SHIT.*" Paul's eyes drifted up to casually concur that *holy shit* was indeed right, then returned to the documents.

Dawa spread a map of the Shenandoah National Park out on the bed. The facility was located near the center of the 200,000-acre park adjacent to Skyline Drive: the two-lane road running north to south atop the Appalachian ridgeline that effectively split the park in half. Problem was, they weren't exactly sure where. The CIA had a tendency of going out of their way to keep black sites hidden, and the clandestine cabin in the woods wasn't on any map or directory or list of Top Ten Places to

See in the Virginia Mountains.

Paul sifted through Fenton's incriminatory stack of documents and found the satellite image of Skyline's cabin decoy taken shortly after construction, then laid the image to the side of Dawa's map to compare the surrounding landscape. It was apples to oranges: different scales, dissimilar foliage, with both images taken years apart from one another. The photos had little in common, but Paul knew there would be geological features that would take decades, even centuries to change. He looked for those, and pointed to a uniquely twisted valley running perpendicular to the two-lane.

"Looks like the same valley in both images."

Dawa leaned over the bed for a closer view and thought for a moment. "Hmmm. It is close." His head swiveled from the map to the satellite image and then back again, carefully comparing the two. Finally, "Yes. I think it is a match, Paul." He motioned for Claire. "What do you think?"

She stepped over and quickly she knew. "That's the same valley, all right. Any way to tell how far the facility is from the main road?"

Paul said, "Not exactly, but it can't be more than a mile or two."

"Just a walk in the woods," Claire said. She turned to Fenton. "Anything from Kovic?"

"Checking it now," he said, plugging away on his laptop. A few keystrokes and he had the preliminary barriers in place to comfortably check Claire's throwaway email account without getting pinched. Everyone had worked on the email before leaving Savannah, fine-tuning the short-and-sweet message to Kovic while making sure no detail was left out:

FROM: dorisday29@hotmail.com
SUBJECT: Alive, need to meet ASAP
TO: cohenforlife@yahoo.com


Kovic,


It's Claire Connor. Escaped strike in Costa Rica; back in the U.S. I know about Skyline, location, Project THEIA, the Asteria connection… everything. I have emails to backup claims (see attachments). Must meet at Skyline facility alone. The sooner, the better.


It was enough to get the point across: they were coming to Skyline, whether the CIA liked it or not. It was also sure to take Kovic completely off guard, considering the destruction of the facility in Costa Rica had likely put his mind at ease that every loose end south of the border had been taken care of.

They also knew they were taking a huge chance contacting Kovic, especially when a thousand things could go wrong. Kovic could set up a military perimeter surrounding the facility, denying them access to Skyline and shipping them off to a secret prison somewhere to rot away in a cell; they could be shot on-sight; or he might not reply at all while renewing the search for the original outliers and effectively forcing them all back into hiding. (Out of all the possibilities, that seemed like the worst one of all.)

Once Fenton was in, they had their answer.

"We've got something," he said, and the rest of the gang circled around the computer:

FROM: cohenforlife@yahoo.com
SUBJECT: RE: Alive, need to meet ASAP
TO: dorisday29@hotmail.com


Claire,


Glad you're alive. CR mission was compromised. Out of my hands. Meet me at the cabin in the woods to discuss. I'll be waiting.


*I'll be waiting.* Short, simple, and ominous. Everyone in the room felt the weight of the message and its implications deep in their chests.

This was it—the plan was a go. Dawa would make the twenty-minute drive into the heart of the Shenandoah National Park to drop off Paul and Claire. That's where the two would split up. From there, the team would rely on the pitchman and his adolescent accomplice back at the motel to penetrate the facility using a combination of Donny's newly-acquired skills and Fenton's tried-and-true digital acumen. Once Claire was inside, the operation would hinge on whether or not the rest of the team could come through at precisely the right time. If one link in the chain was broken, the entire plan would be a wash.

It was far from ideal—in fact, it was an epic long shot. If the plan worked, the wicked little partnership between Asteria Pharmaceuticals and the CIA would be exposed. Everyone could go home. Everyone would have their lives back.

But if they failed, the consequences would be dire.

***

"What's wrong, dear?" Ronald Linklatter's wife asked

him over Saturday morning brunch at one of D.C.'s finest restaurants. He tapped his fork on his plate, staring off into the distance with a discernible unwillingness to respond.

"Ronald? Honey?" She leaned across her muffin and oatmeal, trying to get his attention. But Ronald's mind was still a million miles away. Concerned, "Okay, now you're starting to scare me." She reached over and slapped his shoulder, and he returned to Earth.

Startled, "Yes! What is it, dear?"

"Did you not hear a word I just said?"

Ronald was still trying to figure out what had just happened. Where his mind had just returned from. And why his wife looked like she had just seen a ghost. "I'm not sure what you're talking about, honey." He shook the cobwebs from his head and stabbed at his eggs. "Let's just get back to breakfast, shall we?"

His wife was clearly rattled, and wondered for a moment if Ronald was having a mini-stroke. That's what her mother had called them anyway, right before the big one had sent her up to the spirit in the sky a week before her 80th birthday. She was worried, for certain, but didn't know what else to say. She watched Ronald scarfing down his eggs and bacon as if he hadn't missed a beat, then slowly returned to her own meal, sipping her coffee while wondering if she should make Ronald a doctor's appointment.

Ronald kept on eating like nothing had happened. But something *had* happened. Something had gotten in; a thought; an obsession; a neural pathway firing on all cylinders that wouldn't let up, couldn't let up until the acting head of the Drug Enforcement Administration took action.

He downed his coffee, stood up, and told his wife he had

to get back to the office.

There was a drug on the market that warranted his attention. A drug that could be a danger to the general public. To national security. To the future of the entire world.

A drug that had to go.

# Chapter 30:
# A Walk in the Woods

The winding two-lane known as Skyline Drive was cracked and aging, with bleached-gray asphalt and faded yellow-and-white lines that would have made nighttime navigation challenging, to say the least. Fortunately, it was the middle of a sunny Saturday afternoon when Dawa, Paul, and Claire loaded up the car and took off up the road for what could be the last time they all saw one another alive.

The drive was quiet in the beginning—and eerily peaceful. The road clung to the side of the steep mountain, white oaks covering the surrounding hills, their leafy limbs hanging over the road and casting a flickering patchwork of sunlight and shadows through the windows and onto the laps and faces of the outliers heading toward an uncertain fate. Every now and then the woods would open up to views of the Appalachians that stretched for miles, rolling pastures dotted with the occasional evergreen standing all alone in the middle of fields separated from the road by Depression-Era short walls constructed of river rock and mortar. The views were beautiful, and in their own little way, each person riding in the car that day thought that if this was their time to go, the scenery sure could've been a whole lot worse.

Dawa drove the car while Claire rode in the passenger seat, Paul in the back. Their bodies might have been buckled into a northbound sedan, but their minds were wandering far from the Virginia mountains. Dawa was lost in the hypnotic curves of a long and solitary road; Claire beat herself up by replaying every decision and judgement call she'd made leading up to Aguilar's death; and Paul wondered if he'd ever have a chance to see his wife and son again. She had long ditched her cell phone (part of the cost of living off the grid), and now she wasn't answering at the monastery. A few unanswered calls convinced Paul that Dawa should call his friend, but his phone kept going straight to voicemail.

Paul broke the silence and scooted over to the middle of the backseat, leaned forward, and asked Dawa, "Can I see your phone again?"

"Yes. Of course." He reached inside his jacket and passed the phone to the back.

Paul sat back in his seat and checked the service. One bar. *Of course there's only one bar.* He cursed his luck, only to watch the one-bar icon change over to NO SERVICE. "Unbelievable," he said.

Dawa spoke to him through the rearview and asked, "What is the matter?"

"The phone. We're now officially out of service."

"Bound to happen sooner or later," Claire said, still staring out the window. "Not much demand for cell towers and Wi-Fi in the middle of a national forest."

"I am sure Michelle and Aaron are fine," Dawa said. "You spoke to her yesterday, correct?"

"Yeah," Paul said, "but my mind wasn't in it. This operation, this plan . . . Guess the magnitude of this whole thing is just starting to set in."

Claire turned around to face Paul. "We'll be fine, Paul. So will your family. You need to trust me on this one."

"It's not you I'm worried about, Claire, or even Fenton. It's Donny. Think about it: you're going to be alone with Kovic and his cronies half a mile under a mountaintop, well-protected from any kind of electromagnetic interference. Can we really count on that guy to come through at precisely the right moment?"

Dawa answered first. "Donald's problem has never been incompetency. He has always had a gifted mind; it is what made him millions. But, like so many others tempted by their own talents, he strayed from the path of enlightenment, trying to feed the insatiable appetite of more. Fortunately, Donald saw his way back. He wandered out of the wilderness and found the path again." His eyes met Paul's in the mirror. "Once Donald gets his mind on something, he is unstoppable. Have faith, Paul."

"You know, you've made it pretty clear you don't believe in any of this mind-control stuff," Paul said, "and now you're telling me to have faith in Donny's ability to do just that. See the irony here?"

"I do."

"Then how can you sit there and tell me to have faith?"

Dawa paused, then said, "I will be the first to admit, I have had my doubts about some of Donald's claims. Claire's and yours, too, for that matter. But, there is a Buddhist concept, Śraddhã, that teaches us to have confidence in others, as well as confidence in our own convictions. Sometimes, Paul, you just have to surrender to the universe and hope everything works out for the best."

The winding road straightened at the top of the ridgeline where the trees thinned and all the cracks and crannies of the surrounding landscape could be seen without a troop of bark-covered columns to block them. Claire looked down the grassy hillside to the east where a low-cut pasture dipped into a thick tree line.

"There," she said, referring back to the map in her lap. "That's the valley." She looked at Dawa, then turned to Paul. "It's time."

They both nodded and grabbed their backpacks while Dawa slowed the car. A dense patch of tall oaks created an arborous tunnel up ahead, darkened by a thick canopy that refused to let the sunlight through—and hidden from the view of satellites overhead. It was the perfect place to drop off the passengers.

"Remember to act quickly," Dawa said. "There could be a dozen eyes glued to monitors and watching the area from above."

The car rolled into the shadows and the doors opened. Dawa slowed to a crawl and wished them both luck. They returned the platitude, then hit the ground running. As soon as Dawa confirmed the two made it out safely, he floored it. In seconds, the car was gone and all was quiet in the woods again.

"Just like old times," Paul said.

"Yeah. But this time, I expect you to stick this one out."

Paul looked down to the solitary woods toward the valley. A sea of green lay like a blanket atop the wooded hollows and rolling hills, with shadows of clouds for patchwork. Then he turned to look toward the top of the mountain. Just the sight of the steep grade stretching a half a mile toward the tower at the top made his knees weak. He tightened his pack, then asked, "So you going to be okay down there?"

"Oh, yeah. I'll be fine. Just make sure you get your ass up there before Fenton's bedtime."

The two grinned nervously, then held their arms out to synchronize their wristwatches. Paul said, "17:00 hours. And not a second late." Claire nodded to confirm. "Don't keep me waiting." Then Paul took off uphill.

Claire watched for a moment as Paul ascended upward toward the tower, pulling at saplings and using them for hiking poles to assist him on the slow climb up a steep and rocky grade. Soon he was out of sight, lost behind a veil of tall oaks and intertwining branches.

She threw her pack over her shoulder and started downhill toward the valley, looking for any trails or markers or signs that could point her to the facility. Of course, Claire didn't expect anything too obvious. CIA black sites didn't exactly advertise in the yellow pages or post up road signs saying SECRET GOVERNMENT FACILITY: 2 MILES AHEAD.

Not far into the tree line, a rustle in the trees ahead caught Claire's attention. She looked up to see a constable of ravens hopping from branch to branch, battling for limb space high in the forest canopy. It was startling, for sure, but nothing that would have sent her running for the hills.

*Paul, on the other hand, would have shit his pants.* She knew how easily this mission could go south; how she might not make it to sunset; how a bullet could come whizzing by at any second to take her away for good. The difference between she and Paul was the fact that Claire had come to terms with her mortality long ago, while Paul still had plenty to live for. It wasn't a death wish—that would have involved fantasy and indifference and all the things Claire didn't need in her life. But you didn't take the kinds of assignments and go through all the shit she'd been through without a sobering acceptance that one day it would all be over, you'd be dead, and you probably wouldn't even see it coming.

Twigs snapped and leaves crunched under her feet as she shuffled down the hillside. Halfway down, Claire stopped and saw a trail barely visible through the trees on the other side of the hollow. She whispered to herself, "An old logging trail. But we don't log in national parks . . ." She checked the map. The faux entrance to Skyline was past a huge dogleg in the valley about a mile from the main road. She looked up. *Dogleg left. Getting close now.*

Suddenly, a noise, steady and foreign. A truck, maybe a Jeep. Distant, but getting closer. She knelt behind a wide tree trunk and peered around, watching and waiting. Soon the source of the noise came into view as an antique CJ7 rolled down the old logging trail, swaying and rocking on the uneven path on its way down into the valley.

*CIA,* thought Claire. *Has to be.* With a little luck, following the dusty trail of a CJ7 down that logging trail would lead her straight to Kovic.

***

"I still don't understand this whole 'lucid dreaming' business," Fenton said, munching on a Baby Ruth he'd picked up from the vending machine in the motel lobby. "I mean, I *believe* it, I just don't understand it."

Donny lay on the hotel bed, hands crossed over his chest, rehearsing his new ritual. "You don't have to understand it, kid. You just have to shut the hell up and follow the plan."

"Just explain your end to me one more time, before we get started. I don't want to screw the pooch or anything."

Donny huffed, then said, "Okay, kid. One more time. It goes like this: I'm going to lie here and perform a meditation ritual that's going to help me dream lucidly, which means I'll know I'm in a dream. Once that happens, I can pretty much do what I want. The trick is to keep the mind from wandering to places it doesn't need to go."

"That's why you're surrounded by all this shit on the bed?" Fenton asked, referring to the photos and documents surrounding Donny. It was a montage of everything in Fenton's files related to Project THEIA, particularly information related to everyone thought to be inside the facility and working on the project.

"Yeah, that's why. It's also why I need you to play the Kovic recording while I'm repeating the mantra. He'll be closest to Claire during the event, making him our number-one priority."

Fenton ignored him, still uncomfortably fixated on the shrine surrounding Donny on the bed. "So when you lucid-dreamed your way to River Street, were you, like, surrounded by a bunch of pictures of me? Cause if so, man, that's creepy as *fuck*."

"Just get the damn recording," Ford said.

Fenton grabbed Claire's burner phone and clicked through a long list of recordings. VARGAS 1. VARGAS 2. FREEMAN 1. FORD 23. *Damn, she must've recorded everything.* Finally, he got to the Kovic call. He set the phone on the nightstand, the play button at the ready.

"I think we're all set," Fenton said.

"Good. Now let's just hope you can uphold your end of the bargain."

Fenton referred to Ford's makeshift shrine. "Um, shouldn't be a problem, dude." He took a seat at the desk and flipped open his laptop, a two-way radio lay next to a half-empty can of Red Bull on the corner. "I just hope he makes it to the tower without breaking his neck."

The idea to hijack the facility's broadcast transmitter tower had come to Fenton in a gas station in South Carolina just moments after he had been hit with the memory of the River Street meeting with Donny Ford. Paul had told him in Savannah that the drug was like an amplifier, juicing up already-oscillating brainwaves and broadcasting them like radio stations broadcast music and talk shows and those annoying advertising jingles that were near impossible to get out of a person's head. It didn't happen *every* time, but the longer an outlier had been taking Ocula, the higher the chance they would eventually transmit one of these amplified dreams from their minds to the minds of unsuspecting victims. And just like a radio station, the further away an outlier was from the subject of their dreams, the less of a chance their influence would make an impression.

That's where Skyline came in. By incorporating a high-voltage transmitter towering one-hundred feet above the highest peak in the region, the CIA could effectively take the brainwaves of Ocula-induced outliers and broadcast them across a hundred-mile radius (the signals naturally traveled even further than the guaranteed effective range, but at a diminished capacity, waning out over the next fifty or so miles).

Fenton knew if they could access the communications building next to the transmitter on top of Skyline Mountain, they could reverse the poles, so to speak, and transmit their own message deep into the mountain, all the way into the facility some two-thousand feet below—the kind of message he now knew Donny Ford could deliver by using the power of lucid dreaming.

It was the best way in, and the best way to beat the CIA at their own game—all thanks to the principles behind electromagnetic radiation. It came from X-rays and sunrays and microwaves, and was even a byproduct of naturally occurring neurological activity like brainwaves. But, brainwaves—without the help of Ocula—occurred at an extremely low oscillation. Typical brainwaves (outliers excluded) were a mild form of this type of oscillating energy. But in its worst forms, electromagnetic radiation could happen at frequencies so high that it damaged electrical equipment like computers, cellphones . . . even batteries.

No way the facility wasn't protected from the kind of electromagnetic radiation that came with an EMP or dirty bomb or any other type of nuclear attack. Getting to Kovic and the rest of the employees at the facility through traditional channels would be impossible.

But using their own tower against them was not.

"So I guess we just sit here and wait for Paul to contact us?"

"Yes, Reed. We wait."

# Chapter 31:
# Arrival

Stephen Cline swung the half-door open, hinges creaking as he stepped out of the 70's model Jeep and into the packed leaves in front of the cabin in the woods. His boots kicked up a cloud of pollen and dust that rose up past his dark slacks to a starched white button-up—hardly an effective way to blend in with the locals.

By contrast, Kovic was no stranger to rural Virginia. He sat on the front porch in worn jeans and a black Aerosmith T-shirt (Back in the Saddle Tour, 1984) and worked a noisy rocking chair, one leg propped on the other, all his attention focused on the half-eaten piece of beef jerky in his hand. Cline walked up and stopped just short of the porch, the Atlanta station chief waiting for some acknowledgement from his subordinate that the boss had arrived. But, Kovic didn't look up—he still had half a bag of beef jerky to kill.

"You going to say anything, Kovic? Or you just going to sit there drooling over that jerky like a teenager at a strip club?"

"Thought you were heading back to Atlanta . . ."

"Yeah, about that," Cline said, thumbs in his belt, "I wasn't quite convinced you were on board with the mission during our meeting with Lancaster. So, figured I would drive up here. Make sure everything was running smoothly. Only a couple hours from D.C. anyway." He walked up on the porch, looked at the door, then back to Kovic. "Why aren't you inside?"

"I'm waiting for someone."

"And who would that be?"

"An asset," Kovic said. He finally looked up, smacking on the salty snack. "An asset Lancaster told you to handle—not to get killed."

Puzzled, "Not quite sure where you're going with this, Colin—"

"So you wouldn't know anything about a premature airstrike in Costa Rica this week?"

"Who said it was premature?"

*"SHE'S ALIVE, CHIEF!"*

Cline gave Kovic a pass. It would be his only one. "Listen, Colin. I know you're upset, but a judgment call had to be made."

"Judgment call?"

"We caught wind of an American getting picked up in the restricted zone east of Bajos del Toro through one of our backchannels, said she was with a Costa Rican. Someone with money. We couldn't risk more intel about the CIA's ongoing involvement in Ocula getting leaked. So, we had to clean it up."

"*Clean it up?*" Kovic rose from the rocker. "One little hiccup in an operation, and your backup plan is to *clean it up?*"

"I really don't like your tone, Colin."

"Then you're *really* not going to like the report I plan on turning into Lancaster when this shit's all over."

Cline stepped into Colin and shoved his index finger into his sternum. He had a good four inches on him. "Listen, son. I think you're forgetting your place. Everything I do, every judgement call, every impossibly difficult decision is in the interest of national security. This job isn't about one American citizen, or two, or two thousand for that matter. It's about the greater good. The nation as a whole. What's best for the American people—all 340 million of them." He stepped back and gave Kovic some space. "If you can't handle that, then I think you chose the wrong line of work."

"The line of work I chose didn't involve killing off assets—especially Americans."

"Yeah, son. It did. The ability to make the tough calls is crucial to keeping the rest of the country safe and free to watch football and talk shows and all the other shit that makes them feel good enough to hang on for just a little bit longer so they can drag their asses into work the next day. If we didn't do what we do, society would fall apart long before you'd ever get your paperwork filed. But go on, Colin. File your little report if it makes you feel any better."

Cline could sense the disgust in Kovic's eyes, but he chose to ignore it. There was too much work to do. He looked around and surveyed the site. He was glad he'd come. The last five minutes with Kovic had only reaffirmed his decision. The Kovic who had had no problem rounding up outliers and stuffing them away in Guantanamo had become a crusader, an idealist; someone who believed he could serve his country without ever having to get his hands dirty. *Ignorant stance.*

Admittedly, Cline was a little depressed. Kovic had been a levelheaded field agent in the past. This new agent—the sanctimonious foot soldier—was wearing on the station chief's patience.

"Connor's on her way here?" Cline asked.

"Yes."

"She coming alone?"

"Didn't say."

"When did she make contact?"

"Late last night. Email."

"How much does she know?" Cline asked.

"Everything. She's got an entire dossier on the CIA's

connection to Asteria, the Costa Rican facility, Skyline. Everything."

"Jesus," Cline said, sighing and shaking his head. "What does she want?"

"Just said that she knows about Skyline, and she wants to meet here. She was adamant about that."

"Think she's planning something?"

Kovic laughed sarcastically. "After we dumped a half-dozen hellfire missiles on that place the moment she arrived? No, chief. I don't think she's planning anything at all." He stepped over to the NO SOLICITING sign by the door, lifted it up, and pressed the hidden button. The rustic board-and-batten door covering a steel-door entrance slid into the doorjamb, the mechanical whirl of the gears moving it startling a few birds dancing in the leaves nearby.

Kovic gestured toward the door. "After you."

"What, you don't want any company?"

"Probably be best if you were inside with the others"—he looked out into the big woods—"we certainly don't want to spook her, now do we?"

That was something Cline could actually agree on. Plus, he was tired of dealing with Kovic's insubordination. "Okay then, Colin," he said, wiping beads of sweat from his forehead. "I'll leave you to it. Too fucking hot out here anyway. Just make sure whatever you do, you get her inside." He paused and looked around the woods, then asked, "You've got spotters, don't you?"

Kovic pointed in no particular direction. "Cameras should be enough. I'm not too worried about it."

Doubtfully, Cline nodded. Risky leaving a single field agent alone to bring in a wily asset, he figured, but then again, there was plenty of firepower inside should something go amiss.

"All right, then. We'll be watching." He stepped up to the keypad, punched in the code, and stepped inside. The doors closed, and once again Kovic was left alone to his rocking chair and beef jerky.

The bag crinkled as Kovic's hands searched for one more piece. Empty. *Son of a bitch.* He tossed the bag and sat back in the rocker, hands on the armrest, searching the woods for signs of life. Plenty of birds and squirrels and butterflies, but no Connor.

It was getting quiet again, and Kovic was getting that uncomfortable tingling feeling that twisted between his ears and crawled across his scalp when his mind was about to start racing out of control. It had happened earlier, before Cline showed up, but Kovic had written it off as a lack of sleep combined with an abundance of nerves.

Now it was happening again.

He stood up and paced the porch, walking off emotions long-thought to have been killed off after years spent honing his mind for the betterment of the CIA. Guilt. Remorse. Fear. Uncertainty. All the neurological responses that might have served some great purpose in the Stone Age—but did little to help a CIA field agent make the tough calls that got the job done in the twenty-first century—were beginning to infect him like a plague.

Kovic looked down at his hands, palms up, trembling and sweating, fingertips hot and flushed. He hadn't seen his hands tremble in decades (not since asking homecoming queen Valerie Foster to the senior prom). Each breath was more labored than the last, as if some invisible boa constrictor had taken a hold, twisting and tightening around its prey with each breath until there wasn't any breath left at all.

"What is happening to me?" he said aloud, then stopped

himself from saying any more. Cameras and microphones surrounded the facility. In all likelihood, several people were inside listening, watching. The realization shut Colin up, but did nothing to deter the voice in his head.

*This is wrong, Colin. All wrong.*

Over and over, the voice grew louder. That was the problem with getting voices in one's head, because no matter where people went, they had to take their heads with them.

*This operation. Ramírez. Cline. They're all wrong.*

It was insanity, thought Kovic. A decade's service in the CIA, and he was finally going insane. He'd heard of past agents going through the same ordeal. Some blamed it on the stress of the job; of making sacrifices for one's country only a handful of people at Langley would ever know about; of never being able to maintain normal relationships or a normal home life. But as Kovic paced and sweated and waged a war inside his head, the tiny sliver of rationalization that was faintly calling from deep in the back of his brain was blaming his mental state on one thing, one group:

*The outliers.*

But how could he be affected by anyone using the free-market Ocula way out here in the boonies? And what were the odds someone would be randomly dreaming about him in the first place?

That's when Kovic thought about the two closest outliers he knew of: Claire Connor, who was supposedly on her way to the facility, and the four outliers inside the facility. Mrs. Rogers and Mrs. Everly had already been tapped for Project THEIA, per Lancaster's orders, leaving the remaining two outliers fresh and ready to target whomever his colleagues inside pleased.

Had Cline lost faith in Kovic? Was Ramírez getting into

his head?

Unlikely. Kovic began to think it might be Claire, out there in the woods somewhere, more than close enough to deploy those pesky little brainwaves into the unsuspecting skull of her new nemesis at the CIA. Problem with that theory was the fact that Ocula 1.0 led to haphazard results that were random and oftentimes unpredictable—not unlike our dreams and nightmares.

The kind of skill it would take to use the first version of Ocula to target specific individuals was something Kovic (and Tanner and Doyle for that matter) had never encountered, hence the need to synthesize Ocula 2.0 to be more receptive to external persuasion.

Sure, there was also the chance that Claire could have influenced Kovic through coincidental dreaming, but that notion was quickly shot down the moment the crowd of voices ringing in Kovic's ears was interrupted by the crunch of leaves coming from the logging road ahead.

*It's showtime, Kovic. Get your shit together.*

Kovic put his hand up for a visor and looked toward the strolling figure moving closer and making brief appearances between the trees. He called out, "Connor? That you?"

"The one and only," Claire said. She drew closer, and Kovic noticed the 9mm attached to her hip.

"You know there's really no need for—"

"I'll be the judge of that," Claire said.

Kovic asked, "Why are you here, Claire?" He tried to mask the nerves in his voice, but the question leaked out clumsily before he could regain his composure.

Claire walked up the steps to the front porch, closing in on the field agent. Kovic knew he looked troubled. Bothered.

Sweating and nervous, like an amateur poker player trying to run a high-stakes bluff when he's got no business sitting at the table in the first place. She leaned in and asked, "Something on your mind, Kovic?"

It was the understatement of the year. Still, Kovic was a professional, and he wasn't about to let a guilty conscience get in the way of the task at hand.

"First off, I just wanted to apologize for the incident in Costa Rica. I know there's no way I can really—"

"*Apologize?*" Claire cut him off short. "You betrayed me, Kovic. Got Aguilar killed, all to cover your tracks. I'm lucky to be alive, and you want to *apologize?*"

"Now hear me out, Claire. The drone strike wasn't my call. I got word from the top that Project THEIA was getting a reboot and was reassigned to this hellhole in the woods. I never would've authorized a strike until I knew you were safe."

"So who made the call?"

Kovic sighed.

"Hello? Earth to Kovic—who made the call?"

Finally, "My boss. Stephen Cline." He looked over his shoulder toward the camera mounted in the corner of the porch and shrugged. Claire looked, too, picking up on the fact that every movement and every word spoken was likely being scrutinized by a room full of people inside the facility.

"Is this Cline inside watching right now?" she asked, never taking her eyes off the camera.

"Yeah. He's inside. So's your old buddy Ramírez."

"Well," Claire said as she walked to the front door, "who doesn't love a good reunion. Shall we?"

Kovic nodded, entered his codes, and the two walked inside.

# Chapter 32:
# Behind Enemy Lines

Inside the lab, the team of scientists and lab techs and physicians and field agents had been working nonstop since the reboot of Project THEIA. Mrs. Rogers and Mrs. Everly had produced an ocean's worth of data that had to be analyzed. A medical team reviewed the physiological effects of Ocula on patients from injection to half-life to full metabolism and expulsion. An engineer who specialized in electromagnetic consulting for federal contracts was brought in to gather radio data to determine just what exactly was going on across the airwaves when outliers began their R.E.M. sleep cycles. The CIA was there to manage the process and keep Langley informed. Computer fans whirled, centrifuges spun, and shoes clacked and shuffled across the spotless linoleum floor of a lab functioning at maximum capacity.

That was before Kovic showed up with his new guest.

The moment the steel door lifted and the two entered the lab, eyes widened, jaws dropped and the chatter stopped. The once-energetic staff had turned to stone statues, gray faces in long white coats frozen at the sight of Kovic strolling in with an outlier.

Not just any outlier, either. This girl was one of the originals, freshly poached from the wilderness, wild and untamed. Upright, conscious, and coherent. Not like the other four, who had been tripping on Ecstasy between Ocula doses for the last two months.

Those had been tainted. But Connor was pure.

Cline stood with Ramírez on the back wall of the lab, facing a six-by-six grid of monitors displaying feeds from the facility's closed-circuit security cameras. He noticed a change in the atmosphere behind him, but there was little need to turn and look toward the lab entrance some forty feet away. He and Ramírez had watched the entire scene unfold the moment they caught a glimpse of Claire walking under one of the infrared cameras mounted in the trees and lining the outer perimeter, about a mile up the logging road from the facility. They had also witnessed Kovic's strange behavior prior to bringing Claire inside, but weren't sure what to make of it. Heat exhaustion. Sleep deprivation, maybe. Either way, they both vowed to keep a close eye on him.

Kovic led Claire down the main aisle that split the lab in two as stunned workers looked on from their desks and workstations. Cline and Ramírez were at the end, finally turning around to greet their new guest.

"Hola, Ms. Connor," Ramírez said. "It's been a while, hasn't it?"

"Not long enough, you piece of shit." She fought against every impulse to strangle the double-crossing son of a bitch right then and there, but the feeling of Kovic's grip tightening on her arm reminded her that that would be a mistake.

Cline said, "Now, now, Ms. Connor. There's no need for that kind of language."

Agitated, "Why isn't she in handcuffs?" Ramírez asked.

"Aw, now there's no need for that," Cline said. "After all, we're all on the same team here. Right, Ms. Connor?"

"Oh, you mean the team that murders its own players the moment things don't go as planned?"

The Atlanta station chief had already known this was

coming. "Listen, Claire. About the Costa Rica incident. We cannot begin to tell you how sorry we are for your loss, and how appreciative we are for your resilience and tenacity during this trying time. Your country owes you a great debt of grati—"

"—Oh, for fuck's sake, Cline. Like I haven't heard that same cheese-dick line straight out of every bad war movie that's ever been made. You screwed me on this one, and you got my friend killed. You think a debt of gratitude is going to make me forget about all that?"

Cline shoved his hands in his pockets, head down, eyes and eyebrows up and looking at Claire. *Let her talk,* he figured. He was holding all the cards, after all. Of course, she had to know that, but it wasn't stopping her from venting a little. *So, let her vent. Then we'll proceed . . .*

"And another thing," she continued, "what's stopping me from blowing the lid off this whole operation? You know I've got files out the ass on this illegal use of taxpayer money. How do you think it would go over once the general public caught wind of illegal genetic experiments performed on American citizens and conducted by the CIA in cooperation with one of the wealthiest pharmaceutical companies in the world?"

"Told you we should have put her in cuffs, jefe," Ramírez said.

"No, no." Cline put his hand up. The chief was genuinely intrigued by Claire's wealth of knowledge, almost entertained. Life at the Atlanta station was mundane. Boring. A glorified desk job that amounted to little more than managing field agents and filing paperwork. This, however, was exciting. Cline was craving a challenge, and Claire Connor would do just fine.

"You've risked a lot coming here, Ms. Connor," Cline said. "What exactly is it that you want?"

"Only what I was promised to begin with," she said. "A full pardon. A clean slate. Give me my life back, and you can be assured those files will never see the light of day. Should something happen to me, I've got three colleagues working for the three biggest papers in the U.S. ready to release these files the moment I fail to contact them on time."

Cline pursed his lips, brows tense in thought. "A clean slate." He looked at Kovic, then Ramírez. "Well, it certainly sounds reasonable to me. Especially after all you've been through. I think we can find a way to put this all behind us." He stepped out of the aisle and gestured toward the end of the hall leading to the offices. "Would you mind joining us in one of the private rooms down the hall? We've certainly got a lot to talk about."

Claire waited for them to turn around, then snuck a smile as the party of four walked toward the entrance to the rooms beyond the lab. Reed's blueprints showed that each room from the offices to holding cells to storage was designed just like the holding cells in Costa Rica. Rooms that protected management from the outliers housed in the same facility. Rooms designed to prevent the kind of electromagnetic radiation the outliers emitted from getting out and harming susceptible minds nearby.

That also meant nothing could get in.

***

The wind gusted and howled at the top of Skyline's summit as Paul trekked up the last incline before the treeless mountaintop leveled off. He reached the high clearing and looked back, satisfied and relieved the arduous terrain he had just conquered was behind him. The last hundred yards had been fraught with loose rock that seemed slicker than ice at times, testing Paul's footing as he swept the precarious marble-sized stones back down the mountain with every step toward the top.

Out of every other mountain he could see below, Skyline must have been the steepest. The distant hills were also thick with greenery from the lowest valleys to the highest peaks—but not Skyline. The summit was bald and gray with scrambles of large granite boulders circling the peak and choking the path to the facility's transmitter. Just getting to the tower meant squeezing through a narrow thirty-foot pass at trail's end—or scaling over it.

Paul chose to squeeze. He threw off his pack and held it to his side, clothes wiping the rough granite clean as he carefully sidestepped through the narrow and shadowy pass. The stone walls were damp—a fact that likely helped Paul through more than a few places. It was a tight fit, but nothing a hiker fit enough to crawl up the mountain couldn't handle.

He emerged from the wall of boulders on the other side and immediately spotted the prize: the small six-by-ten communications building next to transmitter tower. He wiped his sweating brow with his forearm and breathed a sigh of relief. Finally, he'd made it. Directly below him (2000 feet below, to be exact) was the lion's den, where Kovic and his goons were planning to use outliers—American citizens—for God knows what. (It would be days before Paul would realize that Project THEIA was already underway and yielding unbelievable results from certain parties across the D.C. area. A lot was going to change between now and then.)

Paul set down his pack and pulled a walkie talkie from the front pocket. He tuned into Channel 30, then clicked to talk. "Okay, Fenton," Paul said, "I'm at the tower now. Do you copy, over?"

"Yeah, Paul. Loud, but not so clear."

Windy mountaintops weren't the best place to make calls. Paul cupped the microphone and huddled against the boulders. "Better?"

"Yeah, that's better. Can you tell me what you see, over?"

Paul scanned the area. "The tower is in front of me now, the base is probably twelve by twelve. There's a building next to it, maybe six by ten. It's metal, with a keypad next to the lock on the door, over."

"Anyone else around?"

The question made Paul's hand to drift down to the pistol holstered on his hip. He gripped the gun with his left hand, walkie talkie in the right, slowly stepping away from the wall of boulders toward the small metal building a few yards ahead. Without thinking, he approached the door, jiggled the handle, then quickly stepped out to the side, gun at the ready, waiting for a response.

Nothing happened.

He reached over and jiggled the handle again. Still, nothing. Either someone was inside, watching and waiting to make a move on their terms, or the place was empty.

There was no time for doubt or hesitation. He simply had to take a chance.

"I think the coast is clear," Paul said. "Now walk me through this keypad thing, over."

"Okay, do you see a port on the underside of the keypad? You may have to feel for it, over."

Paul swiped the underside of the metal box housing the keypad and felt a square hole near the corner. "Yeah, I've got it."

"That's where you're going to plug in the key logger. It's

going to run a sequence that evaluates the last several thousand keypad entries to determine what a valid code is. It shouldn't take but a second, over."

Following Fenton's instructions, Paul pulled the key-logging device from his pack, a bundle of wires dangling from its port on the bottom side. He worked through the bundle, trying to find the right connector for the keypad's socket, and coming up short. Just as he was getting nervous that maybe he'd hiked all the way up here for nothing, a plug fit and the program on Fenton's machine started running.

*Damn, that was close,* thought Paul. He radioed Fenton and said, "The machine's plugged in and working, over." On the screen, six columns of numbers blurred as they scrolled vertically at lightning speed. Within seconds, the far-left column stopped, locking in on the first number of the passcode. Paul relayed the info.

"Shouldn't take long now," Fenton casually replied.

Paul could make out the smacking jaws between his words. The teen sounded more focused on a candy bar than the mission at hand. "By the way," Paul asked, "where do you get these wonderful toys?"

Fenton answered with his mouth full. "Trade secret. If I told you that, I'd have to kill you."

Paul was about to tell Fenton he'd have to take a number, when the locked clicked. The light by the lock turned green, the deadbolt clanked and receded back into the door, and it slowly swung open.

Hesitantly, Paul peeked into the metal communications building. No one was inside. He breathed a sigh of relief and stepped in. The building was small, but not a single square inch was wasted. Every wall was lined with open metal cabinets full of humming box routers and battery packs and broadcast units connected by a web of colorful interwoven coaxial and fiber-optic cables, draping from the ceiling and branching off from larger bundles hung from the top. It was a room packed with heat-producing electronics—a fact the poor exhaust fans at the top of the rear wall didn't seem to be equipped for. Outside, it was a ninety-degree day. Inside, the temperature was easily in the triple digits.

"I'm in," Paul said, voice rising over the hums and purrs inside the high-powered communications shack working overtime. Fenton had jotted down a crude set of instructions detailing how to use the transmitter tower in their favor, just in case they weren't able to communicate. Paul took the note from his back pocket and unfolded it. Inside were scribblings and diagrams and some cursive-like language he didn't quite understand. One look at Fenton's instructions and he was glad the walkies were still working.

"All right, Fenton. You're going to have to walk me through this one step at a time, over."

Fenton leaned back in his office chair back at the hotel and dove in. "So there are basically two things we've got to do here if this plan's ever going to work. First, we've got to make sure the antenna portion of the tower is working so we can pick up on Donny's dream. Second, we've got to amplify the signal by piggybacking off the main transmitter's power supply so it sends Donny's message from the antenna *back* down the mountain and into the facility, over."

"And we've got to do all of this as soon as we know Donny's asleep and dreaming," Paul said. "You remember what to look for?"

Fenton said, "Yeah. Eyeballs jerking back and forth and

going nuts under his eyelids and shit like that. Rapid eye movement, over."

"You got it. Once it starts, that'll mark our best chance of getting through to the facility." Paul paused, then said, "Man. Hope Claire's got her watch on her."

"I'm sure she'll be fine," Fenton said.

"I hope so. Because you know what happens at three o'clock."

"Yeah, dude. The bastards are going down."

# Chapter 33:
# Headlines

Back at the Little Bear Motel, Donny and Fenton were preparing for the second stage of the operation. Out of the entire plan, this was the dicey part. It was on Claire to get into the facility; Paul to hijack the transmitter tower (with Fenton's help); and Dawa to get them both in and out safely. Then, at precisely five minutes before three o'clock, Donny would take a dose of Ocula, lie on a bed surrounded by a shrine of everything they had on Skyline (a collection of employee photographs, background checks, facility blueprints . . . even a recording of a conference call between Kovic, Cline, and Ramírez), and enter into a lucid dream. Hopefully.

Content overload, combined with monk-like focus, a unique genetic makeup, and the power of Ocula. It was the same way Donny had located Fenton Reed, so they both knew it could work. But, this time was different. This was the big game. No do-overs. No excuses. And if something went wrong, Donny knew he would essentially be leaving Paul and Claire hanging out to dry.

The pressure was on, and the last thing Donny needed was an inquisitive kid testing his patience. "So can we go over what you need me to do just one more time?" Fenton asked.

"Are you kidding me right now? We're doing this thing in two minutes!"

"Just sum it all up real quick."

Donny rolled his eyes. "Again, all I need you to do is to make sure there are no distractions. To make sure *you're* quiet and the *phones* are quiet and *everything* around us is quiet,

quiet, quiet."

"Even the recording?"

"Obviously, *NOT* the recording!"

"So, you want me to be quiet?" Fenton asked, a certifiable teenage smartass.

Donny ignored him. "Just make sure nothing distracts me, okay?" He leaned up in bed and pulled a couple of tissues from the Kleenex box on the nightstand. He tore off little pieces, rolled them into little balls and stuffed them in his ears. Then he asked Fenton to hand him his headphones, motioning toward the pair lying on the desk. Fenton tossed them over. The headphones went on, and Donny lay back in the bed.

"Now remember, when I'm done with the mantra I'll raise my index finger off my chest. That's the signal to walk over and place the pill in my mouth, then give me some water to wash it down. We need to keep movements to a minimum. Every thought in my head needs to be on the task at hand—not on this room or this motel or anything else that could lead to distractions. That means following through from start to finish with absolute silence. Got it?"

"Got it."

"Okay, then." He took a deep breath, checked the clock, then said, "Give Freeman the signal."

Fenton complied, radioing Paul and giving the go-ahead to flip the switch before signing off Channel 30 for the foreseeable future. Then he pulled up a chair and sat next to Donny. He pressed play on the recording and watched as Donny closed his eyes, crossed his arms back over his chest, and began the ritual:

*I know I am going to dream. I know I will see Kovic.*

*I know I am going to dream. I know I will see Cline.*

Fenton's lip curled, brows snapping together as watched the ritual. *That's it? That's lucid dreaming? Just repeating the same shit over and over?* He thought there would be more to it than that. But, when it came to mantras, the simpler the better. Anything extra, anything that could jump-start a racing mind, was a potential distraction.

One simple mantra. One goal.

Donny must've repeated the phrases thirty times, the monotony of the exercise losing Fenton's attention fast. He blinked hard and tried to stay focused. Just when the lure of closing his eyes was becoming a hard temptation to resist, Donny raised his index finger.

***

Claire sat in the holding cell across the table from Kovic as she watched him flip through a pocket-sized notepad in search of a blank page to scribble on. *A little old school,* she thought— especially for someone who likely had access to the latest 007 tech straight from the finest brains Langley had to offer. Then again, this was a field agent sporting a Casio watch and an Aerosmith T-shirt. Maybe there was a reason behind the low-tech approach; maybe he was afraid that being surrounded by outliers 24/7 would lead to short-circuiting cellphones and stopped watches. Or maybe he was just a little old school.

Kovic waved to the two-way mirror—Cline and Ramírez watched and recorded from the other side—and the interrogation commenced.

"Please tell us your name for the record," Kovic said.

Claire rolled her eyes and reluctantly played along. "Claire. Claire Connor."

"Ms. Connor, can you tell us who turned over the illegally-acquired Skyline files?"

"Sorry, Kovic. Reporter's privilege. I'm not revealing my sources. You should know that."

"*Sources*. So you're saying there's more than one?"

"I'm not saying anything, Kovic. I have the information. That's all that matters. Well, that and the fact that if I don't get a call out by 7 p.m. tonight then this operation will be the lead-in story for all the Sunday news shows. Sunday papers, too"—Claire poked at Kovic's dated wardrobe and interrogation methods—"You prefer the paper to the Internet, Kovic?"

"Sometimes," he answered without looking up, scribbling something on his pad. "So, tell me what you know about Paul Freeman."

"Freeman? What's he got to do with any of this?"

"Don't play dumb with me, Claire. We know you two were together at the old facility, together on the flight out of San José, together in Atlanta . . . we also know he was pulled over earlier this week just outside of Hiouchi in northern California. Know anything about that?"

"Why would I?"

"Because he was driving a car registered to a man named Antonio Gonzalez. Name ring a bell?"

*One of Alejandro's smugglers*, thought Claire. Quickly, "No, not at all."

Kovic knew she was lying. He leaned back in his chair and crossed his arms. "You know what I think, Claire? I think you've been in contact with Paul Freeman all along. In fact, I wouldn't be surprised if he were out there in the woods, popping

Ocula pills and hoping he can get inside our heads, just like back in Costa Rica." He looked into her face, full of doubt, as his eyes sharpened. "Is that it, Claire? Is that your big plan? Let Paul do the dreaming for you?"

"Yeah, Kovic. Paul's out there in the woods holding an Ocula-induced séance." Mockingly, "That's the big plan, all right!"

"Where is he, Claire?"

"Even if I knew, why would I ever tell you? And how can you even have the audacity to ask me a question like that? You already know Tanner went completely off the reservation bringing him into all this."

Kovic cocked his head. "I'm sorry?"

"Paul worked for Tanner in the marketing department at Asteria. Tanner sent him to a Donny Ford seminar with the device you guys use to detect nearby outliers, and when Paul brought it back, Tanner knew he was one of them. That's the reason he got kidnapped in the first place—wrong place at the wrong time."

The chair squeaked as Kovic leaned forward, propping his elbows on the table. "You think Tanner hired Paul based on his résumé? Have you *read* his résumé?" Amused, he shook his head, even laughing a little on the inside. "Claire, Tanner didn't hire Paul only to find out later that he was an outlier. He hired Paul *because* he already suspected he was an outlier."

It was clear Claire wasn't following, so Kovic explained.

"Paul's brother, Alex. He was a participant in the original clinical trials held by the FDA spring of 2020. Once Tanner had a lock on the twelve outliers, he started digging into their families, too. He had this theory of heredity that presumed the genes responsible for the R.E.M. effect were likely to occur in family members as well, just like skin tone and hair color and every other gene we pass on from one generation to the next. And in Freeman's case, he was right."

Claire was stunned, and for a moment, speechless. She'd always assumed the Freeman brothers' ties to Asteria were mutually exclusive: Alex on the consumer side, seeking a drug to help him sleep, with Paul on the corporate side, working to give consumers like his brother exactly what they wanted, one pill at a time. Claire kicked herself for failing to connect the dots. Perhaps she had gotten lost in the way Paul had told his side of the story. He'd always painted a picture of a bad coincidence—it had never occurred to Claire that Paul was only hired by Asteria to confirm some hypothesis Tanner had come up with.

A hundred thoughts raced through her mind, but one in particular stood out more than any other:

*Michelle didn't drug Paul. Tanner did.*

In retrospect, Claire knew it must have been all too easy. Slip him a pill here, or maybe even a liquid or an aerosol there. From nine to five, Monday through Friday, Paul and Tanner had occupied the same building, the same floor, giving the boss free rein over the new hire to experiment with him however he saw fit—while leaving Paul the Guinea Pig none the wiser.

Finally, Claire asked, "Did Tanner find any other family members who were outliers?"

"I know it's only your journalistic nature, but you don't get to ask the questions here," Kovic said. "Besides, what Tanner did or didn't do has no bearing on the situation at hand. We need to know . . . No, we *have* to know who all is involved here, who knows about Skyline."

Kovic read the cynicism in Claire's eyes and got ahead of it. "This isn't about a cover up, Claire. This is a matter of national security. If Ocula remains on the open market, it's not a matter of if it's going to harm Americans, but when. In all likelihood, there are already cases out there of murder and domestic violence and God knows what else that can be traced back to Ocula—we just haven't made the connections yet. All of our data say that one-half of one percent of the general population carries the same R.E.M. gene as you, Freeman, Ford . . . Meanwhile, the CDC estimates that 60 million people suffer from sleep disorders. You don't think a substantial portion of these people aren't going to try the latest greatest drug to hit the market?"

A briefcase propped against Kovic's chair. He picked it up and flipped the latches open, tossing Claire a manila folder. "Go ahead, take a look. Those are yours to keep."

She dumped out the contents, and a flurry of newspaper clippings came to rest on the table in front of her. "I knew you were a newspaper man," she said.

"Just read them."

She turned a rectangular piece over (she highly doubted Kovic wanted her to see the weekend sale on all pork products running at the Piggly Wiggly) and read the headline:

### 9 Dead, 12 Injured After Fire Roars Through Country Club

Dayton, Ohio—Members of the Seneca Hills Country Club are still in shock after one of its own members allegedly started a fire that claimed the lives of nine members as of this press run. According to several eyewitness reports, 39-year-old Barbara Webb was seen lighting the curtains draped over the ballroom windows during a private event late Saturday night. So far, no motive has been found …

"Strange," she said.

"It gets stranger," said Kovic. "Keep reading."

Claire read another clipping:

### Harrowing Honeymoon Turns Deadly

Tampa—What was supposed to be a honeymoon to remember turned deadly over the weekend, when 23-year-old Wade Bryant turned a knife on 22-year-old Erika Maddison-Bryant less than 24 hours after their wedding day. According to investigators, Bryant then turned the knife on himself, cutting his own wrists before passing away next to his bride in the honeymoon suite of the Tampa Ritz …

Claire said, "This kind of shit happens all the time, Kovic. World's a fucked-up place." She sifted through the pile of clippings. Must have been two-dozen stories, maybe more. "How did you link this to Ocula?"

"The government formulary. We've kept tabs on everyone who has been prescribed Ocula in the United States since the day it hit the open market. Some of those prescriptions were only filled once, putting those users on the list of former Ocula patients. When we started looking into why these patients were no longer filling their prescriptions, we took a closer look, only to find that the majority of them were deceased or incapacitated in some other way."

"Some other way?"

"You read the first headline yourself, Claire. Not every Ocula victim dies. Some just end up in the burn unit at Dayton

Medical."

A few major developments courtesy of the agent who was supposed to have her back in Costa Rica, and already Claire's resolve was beginning to crack. Before entering the facility, Claire had known exactly what she had to do, and that involved doing everything in her power to take down Asteria and the CIA in one fell swoop. Now, she was confused. These were still the people who'd betrayed her south of the border; still the people responsible for the death of Aguilar; still an organization of professionals who lied for a living.

Kovic also had a good point. Several, in fact. If everything they had on Asteria's connection to the CIA were leaked tomorrow, it would be a national-security nightmare. Bringing down Asteria was one thing, but indicting the Central Intelligence Agency on such an epic scale would cause America and its allies to lose what little confidence they already had in the federal government overnight. It would be a nightmare scenario: One of the largest pharmaceutical companies in the world in bed with the CIA, performing illegal genetic experiments . . .

The leaks would also do little (if anything) to get Ocula off the market. Claire hated to think she could ever cooperate with the same people responsible for Aguilar's death—she didn't do betrayal. Wasn't in her blood. But, in the near-term, putting the CIA aside for the time being, at least until Ocula 1.0 was off the market, might be the best play.

Maybe.

Claire was just about to concede that Kovic might have had some valid concerns when she noticed it in the cup of water sitting on the table. A shimmer across the top, breaking the placid liquid like a spring wind across the surface of a lake. It was gentle at first, then the ripples grew, reminding her of a scene in her favorite sci-fi movie about dinosaurs stomping through a park and shaking everything from water cups to the poor souls caught in the grips of their gnashing teeth—only these ripples didn't coincide with seven-ton steps. Instead, they were consistent. And they were getting bigger.

Claire checked her watch: 3:07 p.m. *Right on time.* Soon, the noise followed. A loud hum, distant at first, like the roar of a jet taking off from an airport thirty miles away. It got closer, louder. Kovic noticed it, too, and looked up to see fine particles of dust from the ceiling tiles drifting down like slow-falling snow from above. He wasn't quite sure what to make of it until it was too late.

And that's when the screams started.

A chorus of them, traumatic and agonizing, all coming from down the hall outside the interrogation room. Kovic went from conversational to high alert, like an anxious dog that had just heard a knock at the door. He kicked his chair out behind him, put hand to pistol, and stepped to the door. A small horizontal window reinforced with diamond-pattern wire was at eye level near the top of the entryway.

Kovic peered out, but couldn't see a thing. He turned to the two-way mirror, hands out in a kind of disbelief, and asked, "What the fuck's going on out there, Cline?" An intercom hung from the wall above the window, but there was no answer.

"Cline? Ramírez? Come on, guys. Tell me what's going on here." He looked back at Claire. She was way too comfortable with the events unfolding.

"What in the hell is going on, Claire? You'd better tell me *right now.*"

Claire shrugged. "Feels like an earthquake to me."

"Bullshit. Something's going on. Something you're not

telling me."

She deadpanned. She wasn't talking, and there was nothing Kovic could do about it. He turned back to the door and grabbed the knob, slowly turning it until the latch clicked. Then he looked back at Claire. "Don't you even think about moving."

Some might have listened, but not Claire. She never was one to take orders. She watched him intently, ready to act, her eyes fixed on his fist gripping the doorknob. She braced herself for what was to come. *It won't last. Only be a second or two.*

The door opened, and Kovic screamed. An ungodly force of charged particles roared down the hallways and into the room, the high-pitched noise piercing his eardrums while some unseen energy pressed hot on his skin. His first reaction was to fall back into the safety of the room, to slam the door shut, to stay inside until this unknown catastrophe subsided.

And he might have been able to do just that, had Claire not taken the initiative, waiting for Kovic to feel the full force of the electromagnetic radiation pouring into the hallway before jumping up to give him a push. One hard shove and Kovic slid across the linoleum floor and into the hall, far enough out of the way for Claire to get the door shut. She quickly grabbed the nearest chair and wedged the back under the doorknob, effectively locking Kovic out of the room.

For a moment, she couldn't see him through the horizontal window—something that came with the territory of being a short girl in a tall man's world. She was used to it. What she wasn't prepared for, however, was the look of horror on Kovic's face the moment it shot up from the hallway floor and pressed against the horizontal mirror. The noise outside thundered down the hall; there was no way Claire was going to hear what he was saying.

But she could read his lips. "*I'M GOING TO DIE,*" they said. "*PLEASE . . . YOU CAN'T LEAVE ME OUT HERE!*"

"Drama queen." Claire backed away from the door—the chair doing its part to keep Kovic and all the other bad things out—and watched the contorted face in the window. He wasn't going to die: that was something Claire was sure of. Maybe a little deaf in the end, even a few burns, but nothing worse than a day at the beach without the sunscreen.

Still, it did look like he was about to pass out, and that was a good thing. A great thing, actually. Because once he and the rest of the goons occupying the facility were out for the count, she could get to work.

# Chapter 34:
# Hail Mary

He was supposed to wait for Fenton's radio call, but Paul had been sitting in the same place for almost an hour now, and he was getting antsy. Even with the door open to a steady high-altitude wind, the communication shack at the top of Skyline Mountain was stagnant with thick, hot air that made it feel like breathing in a sauna. It was loud inside, too, but Paul had already acclimated to the sound of grinding hard drives and spinning exhaust fans that had quickly become little more than background noise.

He turned his wrist to check his watch. It was 3:17. Plenty of time for Donny's dream to get through. The plan had been to avoid radio contact until Fenton could confirm that Donny's eyes had calmed under their lids—a sign that he had completed the first R.E.M. sleep cycle of the session induced by Ocula (while the average person dreamt several times a night, only to remember the last dream before waking, lucid dreamers like Donny always found the first dream to occur immediately after falling asleep the most profound).

Fenton hadn't made the call yet, and Paul was tired of waiting. He turned the volume up enough to hear the static over the noise in the room, then played with the squelch to get it just right. "This is Paul. Fenton, do you copy?"

Static.

"Fenton, this is Paul. Do you copy, over?"

Finally, the static stopped and Fenton came through in trademark walkie-talkie distortion. "Hey, Paul. I read you loud and clear. Had to step out of the room before answering back."

"Donny still sleeping in there?"

"Yeah, man, but I'm pretty sure he's not dreaming. At least not now. *Dude*, you should've seen his eyes. It was like he was having a seizure or something. Is that how everyone looks when they're dreaming? If so, man, that's just trippy. I've never seen anything like that before . . ."

Impatiently, "Yeah, it's weird all right." Paul hadn't called to make small talk; only to get the confirmation he needed that Donny was through dreaming for the time being. He quickly began to walk back the steps that had channeled the transmitter's power supply into the high-frequency antenna. If Claire was going to get *her* signal out, they would need to get the original transmitter back online.

This was the part of the plan Paul liked the least.

That was because it was the one part that based the most crucial steps moving forward entirely on assumptions. Had Claire made it safely inside? Was she out of harm's way? Had she made it to one of the protected rooms in time, or had she been incapacitated by Donny's dream that rode the antenna line down into the facility before streaming into the minds of anyone not behind a wall of electromagnetic shielding?

They had no way of knowing—one of the realities of being in a facility meant to stay hidden from the rest of the world. Sure, Kovic and Ramírez had secure lines out to communicate mission progress to Langley, but Claire couldn't count on those to reestablish contact once the rest of the facility was unconscious on the floor—there simply wasn't enough time.

But that's just the way the plan had to be. Donny took the pill at 2:55 and got to work. At three o'clock sharp, Paul flipped the switch on the tower so the hundred-foot mast of reinforced steel could pick up on Donny's brainwaves and shoot them down two-thousand feet into the facility, debilitating anyone not protected from the intrusive signals. At 3:20, Paul was to shut off power to the radio-wave-receiving antenna, and route it back to the radio-wave-sending transmitter. That way Claire could broadcast the message before everyone else inside started to come to.

As if that sequence of uncertainty weren't bad enough, the worst part had been saved for last: getting the message out. The facility, in all its state-of-the-art technology combined with the power and pocketbook of the federal government, still relied on outliers to function. Seemingly normal people, school teachers and business owners and marketers and reporters, all with a unique (and unseen) genetic sequence that made them capable of accomplishing remarkable things, were the lifeblood of Skyline. Without them, the transmitter was just another hunk of towering metal, good for little more than broadcasting bad radio—and Ocula was just another sleeping pill.

And therein lay Claire's dilemma. Once Donny's transmission stopped, the occupants inside the facility would start to come to. Slowly, she hoped, but there really was no way of knowing how much time she had to get the Asteria message out. Their only hope meant counting on another outlier to be prepped and ready to go—after all, Fenton's hacked stack of insights had made it clear that's what Project THEIA was all about. But if no one was there to perform, Claire would have to hook herself up to the machine, take the pill she had hidden in the lining of her bra, and get the job done herself.

Paul knew that would mean eight hours of pure R.E.M. sleep. No escape. No way out. One go at the Skyline transmitter, and Claire would either wake up to the inside of a prison cell somewhere, or never wake up at all.

They couldn't let that happen.

Paul walked back the final steps, then said, "Okay, Fenton. The transmitter's back to normal. Claire should be good to go, over."

"All right, Paul. You've done everything you can. Now get your ass outta there, ASAP."

Paul stuffed the walkie talkie into his backpack and threw it over his shoulder, then left the communications shelter, planning to retrace his steps through the boulder pass and back down the mountain toward Dawa's rendezvous point on Skyline Drive.

But he soon found out that the boulder pass wasn't an option.

***

Inside the interrogation room, Claire let the commotion die down a bit before opening the door. The screams lasted only a minute or two; long enough for the people working inside to realize something was deathly wrong just before passing out. She put her ear up to the door and listened. Not a sound. She stepped out into the hallway like a deer methodically stepping out of the woods and into the open field, careful and wary of any hunters or threats that may have been nearby. One look down at Kovic and she realized the electromagnetic event was over—Donny's dream had worked.

She stepped over the field agent lying near the interrogation room door (who was still alive, but out for the count) and made her way back into the lab. The once-bustling facility had gone silent, muffled by powerful brainwaves that had worked on the medulla—the part of the brain stem responsible for controlling heart rate—to dramatically raise the blood pressure of everyone inside, right before dropping it off a cliff. Donny had thought of the idea in the car on the way up from Savannah. If he could use lucid dreaming to toy with the blood pressure of everyone left unprotected in the lab, then he could effectively knock them unconscious.

Claire stepped over more bodies in white coats on her way to the control panel by the observation room. She couldn't believe the plan had worked so well. Outlier dreams were notoriously unpredictable, so going after the most primitive part of the brain seemed to make the most sense to her. Other dream sequences required vivid input and heavy influence to target the frontal cortex—the part of the brain that made humans cognitive, responsible for everything from problem-solving and social interaction to memory and judgment. If Donny could simply get them to pass out, she figured, it would give her the best chance to get in and out alive.

She stopped to look around the lab, then smiled, even laughed like someone who was completely surprised by an unlikely outcome would laugh, shaking her head in disbelief. She'd never expected the plan to work.

The control panel of blinking lights and switches lit up the counter just below the observation room, with six LCD screens acting as window dressing above. Claire tried to process everything as quickly as she could, analyzing each knob and port and plug-in, and that's when she noticed her.

It was Mrs. Everly. She was on the other side of the glass, the poorly lit room brightened only by the tiny lights on the monitors and machines surrounding the hospital bed. Claire had to squint to get a better look. To Claire, the green glow of Mrs.

Everly's headset brought a little warmth to her soul in the cold underground bunker.

*It's still on. The feed's working.*

It was exactly what the team had hoped for. Fenton's stolen Skyline files had revealed the facility's primary method to ensure outlier dreams was controlled by uploading a steady stream of content to patients while Ocula was being administered. Claire remembered this from her time in Costa Rica all too well. No matter how hard she tried to fight it, how hard she pushed her mind to ignore the messages, they played out anyway, like thoughts she wanted so desperately to avoid— only to have them reoccur tenfold, over and over again, a broken record with no way to stop the music.

It was a horrible reality of Ocula, but in this case, Claire hoped she could use the little green and glowing head-mounted display attached to Mrs. Everly's face for the greater good (the greater good being a necessary distinction, since the wrongfully-imprisoned Mrs. Everly was the unfortunate catalyst necessary for the plan to work).

A USB port was grouped among a dozen other ports below the touchpad in front of her marked CONTENT SELECTION. Claire almost let herself feel stupid for asking aloud whether this was where the content was uploaded. Her finger found the touchpad and swiped it, looking around to see which screen was affected.

There. Right above her, above the observation room window was the main screen—the screen she could work from. *Now we're cooking with gas.* She leaned back on the counter and hiked up her leg, taking her foot in her hands and pulling down on the loose flap of rubber making up the sole of her shoe. The hidden compartment for the jump drive was Fenton's idea, and

Claire wondered if the only shows the kid had watched in the grimy hotels he'd been staying in for the last six months were Get Smart reruns.

She took the drive, flipped it open, and stuck it in the control-panel socket. The folder icon that appeared on the monitor above was labeled HAIL MARY (the unofficial name the group had given the operation). Claire double-clicked it. Inside were two files Fenton had created on the ten-hour drive up from Savannah to the Virginia mountains: one labeled CIA, the other titled ASTERIA.

Compared to the head-tracking, motion-sensing stereoscopic programs that the most state-of-the-art virtual reality headsets deployed, Fenton's movie-maker versions were primitive and crude. But they were still confident they could be uploaded into the headset prior to administering Ocula to get the point across, at least in the Asteria video. The CIA compilation was a little trickier, but they were short on time and resources, and beggars couldn't be choosers.

A few clicks in, and Claire had located the program responsible for launching Project THEIA. It was the program that ran content through internal systems straight into the outliers' headsets; monitored vitals like blood pressure and heart rate, even neural activity; and robotically released Ocula into the patient's IV at the time designated by the people behind the control panel.

Claire looked at both files—one for the CIA, one for Asteria—and knew she had a choice to make. She could buy into Kovic's diatribe about national security and looking out for the American people and public health and all that mess, or she could launch Fenton's CIA program—a program that could potentially expose every human rights violation the agency had shared with Asteria over the last two years. Or, she could run Fenton's rather incriminatory video.

Either way, Asteria was going down. But was launching *both* programs necessary at this point? Kovic's little spiel had stuck the same way a timeshare salesman pitched a bullshit deal. She knew it was just that—a pitch—but the charismatic field agent had almost convinced Claire they were on the same team; they could work together to take Asteria down; and they needed to leave the CIA's involvement out of it.

Yes, Claire was almost convinced.

Almost.

# Chapter 35:
# Damage Control

Paul couldn't get out of the communications shelter fast enough. He grabbed his gear and shut the door behind him (as if someone would've complained he was letting all that hot, stagnant air out), then turned to walk back toward the narrow boulder pass that led down the mountain.

That's when he heard it. A plunk on the metal wall of the communication shelter, then the report. He looked over and saw a curl of smoke rising from the bullet hole a mere foot from his head.

*Shots fired. Just run.*

He never got a good look at the silhouette blocking the mountain pass—just the black semi-automatic handgun pointed in his direction, firing shots in rapid succession, a wave of bullets whizzing by his head as he rounded the corner and dove behind the temporary safety of the communications shelter. The shots continued as Paul backed up tight against the rusty metal wall of the building separating him from the shooter. Breaths were shallow and panicked; his hands trembled like a man who'd had one too many cups of coffee.

This was not a good time to be nervous.

*Life or death, Paul. Get a fucking grip.* He fumbled to loose the gun from his hip, finally busting the latch on his holster, bringing the pistol up to chest level and chambering a round. Just as he'd hoped would happen before his attacker moved any closer, Paul heard a few fruitless clicks of the trigger, followed by silence.

*He's out.*

Paul leaped out from behind the building and met his attacker, face to face, less than twenty feet away. Startled, the man looked up, eyes wide on his fear-crossed oh-shit face, empty clip on the ground, the fresh clip still in his hand. Busted.

Then Paul fired.

It was pure survival instinct. He shot without thinking; he didn't have time to. The reality of at least three bullets punching little red blotches into the man's chest before knocking him on his ass didn't set in until much later. But in the moment, Paul didn't hesitate. A man was trying to kill him—life or death. And Paul wasn't one to roll over. Six rounds in and the man was already lying on the ground, face up, his last pained breath a mist of blood spatter rising from his mouth and creating a little red cloud that puffed into the air.

Paul's ears rang from the gunfire. But as he stood there over the body, listening intently for any signs of life elsewhere, he picked up on more noises coming from the south on the other side of the boulder pass.

Voices. Human voices. And they were headed his way.

He popped his pistol's clip release and checked his rounds. Only five left. *Fuck a duck.* He could make out more voices now, and there were at least two more goons making their way up the boulder pass, on their way to kill the outlier who had (unbeknownst to them at the time) just killed their colleague in self-defense.

Trying his luck in the southern boulder pass would be absolute suicide. He pivoted and searched for another way off the mountain. In front was the communication building, with the transmitter tower just to the east. Unfortunately, the eastern side of the summit was a two-hundred-foot cliff no man or woman could navigate down without the help of a rope and a harness. He looked west. More boulders.

His only option was to take his chances to the north, past the tower and communications building, where the plateau at the summit dropped off into a steep grade of crumbling hillside that would have probably been easier to sled down than to run.

But Paul didn't have a sled, and once again, shots were coming from the south.

No time to think. Just run.

***

Dawa sat in his car, windows down and engine off, waiting for Claire and Paul to meet him back at the rendezvous point near the entrance to the national forest. At first, the only sounds coming from the woods were serene. Peaceful. Like fat cardinals chirping to peers while sagging down small branches, or gentle gusts of wind that offered up just a hint of fall in between the idle stretches of the still and humid mid-August heat. Sounds of nature filled the air, and for a moment Dawa could close his eyes and breathe it all in and forget about the worries that had burdened him from the moment Donny Ford showed up on his doorstep.

Then he heard gunshots.

He knew the distinctive POP-POP-POP of semi-automatic gunfire well. *9mm handgun, thirteen-round clip.* Over the years, Dawa had become an expert at Name That Tune: Shots Fired Edition. He imagined that's what working Atlanta Homicide for so long did to a person.

But it was still hard to tell where the shots were coming from. Dawa swung the car door open and stepped out into the secluded two-lane road to get a better listen. Up the mountain, maybe a mile or so away, the sporadic firing continued. *Paul*, he thought. *He is in trouble.*

Dawa instinctively lunged forward, gun in hand, as if he were about to bolt up the hill and go rescue the man, but a single step in and he stopped short. By the time he made it to the top, he would be too late—especially with the spare tire he'd been packing around his waistline for the better part of six months. He racked his brain, searching for a better way to help. Was there anything he could do besides stand there and wait for the shots to cease?

If he had a moment to worry, it didn't last long. A car emerged from around the bend in the road ahead: a black sedan, windows tinted, speeding toward Dawa. Surprised, he quickly jumped out of the way just as the car came to a screeching halt where he'd been standing just a foot or two from his own car.

Startled and pissed, he reached for his badge, holding it out firmly as he approached the driver's side window. "Where did you learn how to drive? You could have killed me!"

The window came down, and Dawa stepped back. The man inside wore sunglasses, a black suit, his hair cut high and tight. He began to speak, and Dawa noticed a distinct scar from an old cleft pallet surgery. "Dawa Graham, I presume?"

Hesitantly, "Yes. That is my name. What is this all about?"

"Sir, you're going to have to come with me," the man said, arm casually propped on the window. Dawa hunched down to look inside; another man in shades and a black suit sat in the passenger seat. "I'd do what he says, Mr. Graham. Fast." The man checked the mirrors. "We can't be seen out here."

The door latches clicked, and the driver motioned for

Dawa to hop in. The detective's brain went into overdrive searching for solutions, but none were plausible. It appeared he had little choice but to hitch a ride with the two strangers who must have been either CIA, NSA, or some hybrid and diabolical combination of the two.

"What about my car—"

"Leave it. Just get in. *Now*."

Dawa obliged, accepting the uncertainty of his fate as his hand reached the door. He looked up the hill one last time, and said a little prayer for Claire and Paul. *Please make it back.*

He opened the door and stepped inside.

***

At first, Kovic wasn't sure why he was lying in the hallway, face plastered to the linoleum floor. The fluorescent lights flickered above him—a settling reminder that the power was still on. He rose slowly, his cheek taking with it a thin coat of wax and grit, then pushed himself up, stumbling to right himself and using the wall for support. He leaned against the hallway wall by the door to the interrogation room, rubbing his strained eyes before moving his hand down to address the painful knot in his neck as he gathered his senses.

The facility was still rather quiet—at least compared to a normal workday. But as each second passed, Kovic began to hear groans coming from down the hall, in the main laboratory, just one or two at first before quickly turning into what sounded like a chorus of zombies painfully rising to their feet.

Whatever had happened, it appeared to be over. And that's when Kovic realized something: *Claire.*

He busted open the door to the interrogation room.

Empty. Nothing but a table and two chairs. The captive was gone. It was then he remembered being pushed into the hallway, right after he opened the door and was blasted with some strange energy he'd never felt before, an energy that had driven into his head and into his chest and swelled within as if his entire body were about to explode into a giant red mist, completely ruling out an open casket funeral. His heart had pushed against his ribs, seemingly eager to escape his chest as his pulse had soared. Veins had bulged in his head and pressed against every last nerve wrapped around his skull as the pressure within continued to rise. Kovic was no stranger to pain, but the experience had been the most excruciating sensation he'd ever felt before in his life.

Then, it had stopped. Suddenly, like a game of tug-o-war where one team decided to drop the rope at once, sending the other team falling back on their asses. The rope dropped, and Kovic's vitals plummeted with him to the floor.

He was lucky to have woken up, but a period of grateful reflection was the last thing on his mind. He quickly paced to the room next to Claire's—the room on the other side of the two-way mirror. Inside, Cline and Ramírez were lying on the floor beneath the mirror, both unconscious. Kovic looked around the room and shook his head. *Unprotected. Because why would an outlier be on the wrong side of the glass?* Claire must have known exactly where she'd be protected from an outlier's attack—and what she needed to do to get there in time.

Kovic kicked Cline and Ramírez and yelled for them to get up, but his foot landed on motionless bodies. They were still out of it, and he didn't have time to wait. He raced toward the lab, busting through the door before entering a room full of dazed and confused lab coats rubbing their foreheads and swaying like a herd of drunk college students after an all-night bender. He ignored the techs—it looked like it would be a minute before they could coherently explain what had happened to them in the first place—and rushed past them to the observation window.

Inside the patient room lay Mrs. Everly, asleep and still, apparently unaware that anything out of the ordinary had happened. Kovic leaned on the control panel and breathed a sigh of relief. *She's still here. Nothing's changed.*

But a quick glance up at the monitor, and Kovic realized he had spoken too soon:

Project THEIA
OS V 2.14.50
File C:/desktop/Asteria/Asteria.exe
Program executed 08/21/21 at 15:12

"*Holy shit,*" Kovic said, the ominous epithet muffled by the hand covering his mouth. It must have been Claire. That had been the plan all along—to get into the facility and take everyone out just long enough so she could send out a message.

Kovic read the screen again. Whatever was in the Asteria file, it couldn't have been good. Kovic kept staring. His mind was still hazy, and it was taking a minute to process the words he was reading on the monitor. Then, a moment of clarity:

File C:/desktop/CIA/CIA.exe
Program initiated 08/21/21 at 15:18
In progress

Another program was running. Panicked, Kovic looked back into the observation room. *The green headset. The light was blinking.* How in the fuck hadn't he noticed it before? An emergency cancellation button was ten feet away on the far end of the panel. He lunged toward it, hammering it with a closed fist, but nothing happened—the button was unresponsive.

The banging continued as he turned his head to yell at the rest of the lab. *"JESUS, SOMEONE TURN THIS THING OFF!"*

A couple of techs came to and approached the control panel, half wanting to help, half wanting to go back to sleep. Kovic yelled, *"GET IN THERE, NOW!"*

Rattled, the techs stammered to the door and into the patient room where Mrs. Everly's subconscious was hard at work. They quickly pulled out plugs and flipped switches and yanked the headset off the outlier's face. She continued to lie there, eyes wide open, darting back and forth, following traces left of the rapidly evolving images in front of her as if she were still wearing the device.

One of the techs tapped her cheeks in rapid succession, and her eyes began to stop. Then, she closed them, back to sleep, drifting slowly away from the influence of anything coming through the facility's little green headset.

Kovic stood back from the glass, sick at the thought of repercussions to come. Had they stopped the program in time? What exactly was in the executable CIA file Claire had run to begin with? He looked around the room as everyone's wits were slowly coming back to them. It was time for damage control.

In a daze, Cline emerged from the back, rubbing his temples as he stumbled toward the control panel.

Kovic asked, "Where's Ramírez?"

"Still asleep. Whatever that was, it got him pretty good."

Cline watched the techs wheel Mrs. Everly out of the patient room and back to holding, then asked Kovic, "How bad is it?"

Kovic pointed to the monitor. Cline read the program list over, then cursed under his breath. It was bad.

# Chapter 36:
# Disconnected

A cloud of pollen followed Paul like a contrail down the mountainside as quick feet sprinted across the dried and brittle leaves toward the sanctuary of the valley below. The incline was slick and treacherous, with no clear path to the bottom through a thick maze of trees. Every ten or so hastened leaps down the wooded slope were halted by short, erosive drop-offs that formed the giant staircase descending the northern spine of Skyline Mountain. Paul would baseball-slide off the short brown walls of dirt held together by tangles of roots that spidered out from the soil, skidding off the four- and five-foot edges before landing on a clear stretch where he could sprint again.

Back up the mountain, Paul's pursuers were hot on his trail. While the two gunmen had lost sight of him the moment he'd leapt off the ten-foot drop surrounding the north side of the tower, the runaway wasn't hard to track—the summertime drought had turned dried leaves and twigs into woodland alarms that gave up the position of even the smallest creatures moving across the forest floor. Couple that with the ragged trail of shuffled leaves and snapped twigs he had left behind, and the trail might as well have been highlighted with neon signs pointing in his direction.

Still, Paul had put some distance between him and his pursuers. He found a thick-trunked white oak and dove behind it, catching his breath while fidgeting with his walkie talkie. He clicked over to channel twenty-nine, one channel down from Fenton's.

"Dawa. Dawa. Do you copy, over?"

The channel was silent. No response.

"Dawa. I'm in big trouble here. Had to take a detour, but should be near the rendezvous point soon. Do you copy, over?"

Still nothing. Paul toggled the squelch in search of chatter from truck drivers or hunters or hobbyists in the area, but the radio wasn't picking up a thing. He flipped it over in his hand, inspecting the back, then the front, and that's when he saw it.

Burn marks. Both the microphone at the bottom and the speaker near the top were fried. Now that he'd stopped running, the smell of burnt plastic rose to his nostrils as he sat back against the tree. The radio was busted. No calls in, no calls out.

Certain it was a loss, he threw the walkie talkie into the woods to the east, opposite the direction he was heading. He'd seen and heard of devices affected like this before, like the story Tanner had told him about an original outlier, poor Donna Edwards: the blind insomniac who had blown up an entire lobby's worth of electrical equipment after a night out with Asteria's hottest new sleeping pill.

Paul checked his wristwatch, just to test the theory. Sure enough, the digital numbers flashed all zeros. *Another bust.* There was little doubt now that Donny's amplified dream had produced an EMP powerful enough to knock out surrounding electronics—at least above the surface.

And if that were the case, it meant complete radio silence. No cellphones, either. Everyone in the field was completely on their own. Paul peered around the tree, looking up the hill and listening for signs of the people chasing him. Not a soul in sight. But the gentle breeze rolling down the hill carried the sound of faint footsteps kicking up leaves further up the mountain.

It was time to move again.

****

Claire lay on her belly and snuggled tight to the stone wall separating Skyline Drive from the field below. Earlier that day, she had crossed the same field on the way down to the valley in search of Kovic's secluded facility. Now she was returning, just as they had planned, to catch a ride back with Dawa and Paul to the motel. Everything seemed fine on the surface: she had escaped in one piece, and Dawa's sedan sat idly by on the shoulder of the two-lane asphalt less than fifty yards ahead.

And that was the problem.

Skyline Drive was by no means off-limits. In fact, a moderate amount of traffic still took the scenic route through the Shenandoah National Park—especially on the weekends. Between the CIA keeping a close eye on anything suspicious near its latest pet project and running the risk of getting towed for illegal parking, they had already decided that Dawa would return at a designated time: 5 p.m. If Claire and Paul hadn't made it back by then, the detective would drive back and forth, making a pass by the rendezvous point every thirty minutes so as not to attract too much attention by sitting still and waiting.

But as Claire peered over the mossy wall, it seemed like Dawa was doing just that. Sitting. Waiting. Sticking out like a sore thumb. The glare of the sun on the windshield made it impossible to see inside, but fortunately the wall ran parallel to the road and right past the broadside of the car. She lowered her head and started crawling, elbow to knee, core to the dirt, keeping her ass down so as not to get it shot off. (That final piece of advice Dawkins had given her years ago had saved her ass more than once.)

She kept her head down and hung tightly to the wall on her right until she felt like she was getting close. Slowly, she peered over the wall in search of the car. There, sitting only fifteen feet away, was Dawa's sedan. The engine was off. The detective was nowhere in sight.

Claire checked her surroundings. Empty field. Empty woods. Empty two-lane wrapped around the mountain. A few birds chirped and the wind rustled the leaves in the trees, but all else was quiet. The serenity of the Appalachians relished by hikers and campers and Sunday drivers tested Claire's nerves. Had Dawa been taken hostage? Had his car been left behind as bait? Was a sniper up there in the hills, scope homed in on the disabled vehicle, waiting to draw the nearby facility's number-one troublemaker out of the shadows?

She had no way of knowing, and little time to think it through. She looked left, then right, then hopped over the short wall and ran to the car. The driver's side window was down, and she leaned in to investigate. The front was empty. So was the back. A strange tingle crawled up her back, and she wondered if a set of eyes in the hills was upon her. She opened the door and hopped inside. Putting a little steel between her and the tree line may not have been a foolproof way to avoid getting shot, but it did give her some sense of security (however false it might have been).

Inside, something hit her right knee and jingled the moment she settled into the driver's seat. Car keys. They were still hanging from the ignition—Dawa had never taken them out. Claire wasn't sure what to make of it, but that damned familiar feeling of dread and guilt was starting to sink in uninvited all over again.

Maybe he was nearby, just pulled over to stretch his legs or find a tree and take a piss. After all, if someone had scooped him up, then why would they just leave the car unlocked with the keys still in it? There was no sign of a struggle, no blood or shattered glass or shell casings lying in the car or on the street. But did that really mean Dawa was safe?

And there she was again—worrying. She swallowed hard and brushed it aside as she turned the keys. *No time for that shit now. Worry about it later, Claire.*

She started the car and left it in park. Five minutes. That's all she could give the good detective. After that, she'd have to get moving again.

Just five more minutes.

***

There. Just up the hill, the steel-gray line cut horizontally through the trees a hundred or so yards up the steady incline. It was the road out. Had to be. The foliage was thick, with no clear view, but Paul could see the asphalt line peeking through the trees and highlighted by the sun beaming down through the strip of cleared canopy that opened over the winding stretch of two-lane.

Deliverance.

It might not have been the rendezvous point. Come to think of it, Paul hadn't a clue as to where on Skyline Drive he was emerging from the woods. (Running for one's life tended to sideline one's sense of direction.) But that didn't matter. Skyline Drive was the only road in Shenandoah National Park. As long as he kept the late afternoon sun to his right once he hit the road, he knew he'd be fine.

He trudged up a hill strewn with rotting logs and rocky obstacles and the long shadows of the trees in front of him as the lazy sun teased the top of the ridgeline ahead. *Westward bound.* That was a good thing, since Skyline Drive ran west of the mountain summit. With any luck, he'd be just a little north of the drop-off point. And if Claire had made it back in time, then she would (hopefully) be patrolling the area with Dawa, eyes peeled.

The hill was steep, but Paul made progress one foot at a time, using protruding quartz rocks and thick roots as steps wherever he could to avoid sliding on the leaves. *Slow and steady wins the race, or so they say.* Of course, Paul was sure when they said it that they didn't take into account armed gunman bringing up the rear, but he felt good about his prospects.

Until he slipped. A stepping stone had given way, and had it not been for the quick reflexes that led his nearest hand to the sapling on his left, there was no telling how far down the hillside he would have slid. He clung tight to the tree as he watched the rounded stone tumble down into the valley below, the prehistoric bowling ball taking long bounces and crushing sticks and stirring up leaves before finally coming to a rest near the bottom.

Paul waited for the sounds of the rock barreling down the mountain to subside, only they didn't. The rock came to a rest, and the leaves continued to crunch—and not in some haphazard way, either. Those were steps. *Human steps.* As suddenly as Paul had noticed them, they stopped.

Then the shots rang out.

Bullets met tree bark as Paul scurried up the steep hillside on all fours, using his hands and his feet to propel himself toward the top as fast as humanly possible, praying the entire time he didn't catch a bullet in his back. The spooks had made it to the valley below him almost undetected—an impressive feat across the noisy terrain. Now they were right on his tail, firing into the hillside.

Paul cursed the rock he stumbled on as he worked his way up, trying his best to avoid more obstacles. He was getting close now. The road was just ahead: only a few more yards away. He hunkered down to dip under a low-hanging branch, and that's when he felt a tug. A tree limb had snagged the top loop of his backpack and was holding him back. *Son of a bitch!* No time to detangle it. He wiggled out of his shoulder straps and let the backpack hang. Faster without it anyway.

And he was right. He hadn't realized just how much the backpack had slowed him down until he left it behind. Now he was able to make a serious sprint toward the road, feet lightened and arms swinging. He emerged from the tree line, hopping the guardrail and hitting the asphalt in a few short steps. But, without a way to radio Dawa or Claire or Fenton for help, he was far from out of the woods yet. There was one silver lining to the EMP, however, and that was the fact that *every* radio above ground must have been affected by Donny's dream. That included any radios or cellphones the goons behind him were carrying, too.

It was a modest advantage, but Paul would take it. He held tight to the white line and started to run to the south, pacing himself for what he imagined might be a long journey home. He worked to soften each step on the asphalt, trying to ignore the sound of his own feet while listening for cars.

*Cars.* He was certainly going to cross a few, and when he did, what the hell was he supposed to do? The plan had been for Dawa to patrol if they didn't make it back to the pickup location by five. Paul's watch was busted (that damned EMP) but judging by the late-afternoon sun it must have been going on six, maybe six-thirty. If Paul jumped into the woods at the mere sound of any oncoming cars, he would likely miss Dawa if he drove by. On the other hand, if the CIA was running patrols, he would be, in a word, screwed.

But he didn't want to think about any of that now. He was tired of asking questions; tired of worrying about what might happen; and most of all, he was tired of running. Not in the actual physical sense—that was something he actually found refreshing. Mind-numbing (especially when those endorphins kicked in), but in a good way. A way to escape the worries and keep the mind busy on simple things like breaths and heart rate and doing whatever it took to keep the body moving forward. A primitive exercise, away from the sophisticated frontal cortex, and into the lower parts of the brain stem, where everything was much, much simpler.

He settled into an eight-minute-mile stride, deciding not to worry too much about who might or might not be in the next car to come wheeling in from around the corner. If it was Dawa, great. He'd make it out in one piece. If it was someone else, well, he'd cross that bridge when he got there.

Fortunately, he didn't have to wait too long to find out if his brazen approach to road travel near a CIA black site was a mistake or not. As a car rounded the corner ahead and closed in, his heart jumped up into his throat, only to settle in its rightful place again.

It was Dawa's vehicle.

Only, Dawa wasn't driving. The car slowed, and Paul could see Claire in the driver's seat with the window down. She came to an abrupt stop alongside him.

"Get in," she said.

"Where's Dawa?"

"There's no time. I'll explain later. Just get in."

Paul nodded, ran around the front of the car, and jumped inside. Claire cut the wheel sharply to the left before performing a three-point turn that would face them south again, and in a flash they were off, back to the motel where Donny and Fenton were waiting.

With any luck, Paul thought, Dawa would be waiting there, too.

# Chapter 37:
# Voodoo

"Would you look at this?" Kerry said, passing the *Savannah Herald* to Arlo as the two sat in the kitchen eating breakfast on Sunday morning. Arlo held the paper out across the table and adjusted his eyes. On the front page, above the fold, Arlo began to read:

### Mystery Woman Saves Talmadge Bridge Jumper

River Street—An attempted suicide was halted Friday afternoon when an unidentified man was rescued near the top of the Talmadge Bridge crossing over the Savannah River. Witnesses say a woman in her late twenties or early thirties pulled a middle-aged man away from the edge just as he was about to leap into the river, which flows almost two-hundred feet below. Both parties have yet to be identified.

"Ain't that something," Arlo said, setting the paper back in the middle of the table as he sipped his coffee.

"Mmm-hmm. Sure is sad though," Kerry said. "People getting caught up thinking that's their only way out." She shook her head, then said, "Thank God for that woman, whoever she is. Good to know there's still people doing good in this world."

Arlo agreed as he forked his eggs.

Kerry asked, "Did you see the picture?"

"Nuh-uh," Arlo said, focused more on breakfast than small talk. Kerry playfully slapped his arm. "Well, take another look, you old goat! Who knows, you may have seen them outside the restaurant last week."

Arlo looked up from his plate and over to his wife, his warm smile signaling he'd play along. "All right, then," he picked the paper back up, "let's see what we've got here." He brought the paper closer in, sharpening his eyes to analyze the grainy cellphone picture that had made the front page.

A closer look, and Arlo's eggs nearly fell out of his mouth. *That's the guy. The man who ran into me on River Street. Made me drop the plates. Gave me the finger . . .*

*. . . The guy I dreamed would take a leap off that bridge.*

Shocked, he laid the paper back on the table, and fell back in his chair. Kerry raised an eyebrow as she watched her husband's solemn reaction. "Honey? You okay?" she said, head cocked. "You look like you've just seen a ghost." She looked down at the paper, then back up to Arlo. "You recognize one of them? Both of them?"

On the outside, Arlo was silent, wide eyes lost in the collector-plate-covered wall on the far side of the kitchen. On the inside, however, Arlo's mind was working overtime, retracing his every thought, every action from the moment that rude son of a bitch gave him the finger, to the next day when he was still recovering from the Ocula he'd taken the night before.

*The Ocula. The dreams.*

Slowly, he began to piece everything together. How he'd never dreamed much before Kerry insisted he start taking a sleeping pill; how when the pills did help, he didn't dream at all; and how the nights they made him sick, he'd walk straight into the most lucid dreams of his life.

For Arlo, it was as clear as day. The night before his meeting with the loan officer, he'd dreamed he'd get the loan. In fact, he'd dreamed he'd get twice the amount he'd originally asked for. He had.

Then there was the asshole on River Street. Following that encounter, Arlo had taken a pill to help him sleep. Then he got sick. Sick as a dog, up most the night, running back and forth from the bathroom. Finally, he'd fallen asleep. And when he had, he had had another dream, vivid as anything he'd ever seen or experienced in his waking life: that the man in the tacky Hawaiian shirt would try and kill himself. Drowning, specifically. Take a long walk to the top of the Talmadge Bridge and fly off its edge and into the river. And according to the *Savannah Herald*, it looked like he'd come mighty damn close to making that dream a reality.

*Sick as a dog . . .*

And what about that dog, the one he'd almost turned into roadkill a few days before. It had looked just like his old dog, Samson! Could it be, or was it just a sheer coincidence?

Kerry tapped his shoulder, hard this time as she tried to break the trance. "Arlo, honey. You're starting to worry me now." He didn't reply. He couldn't—not until he worked everything out in his head.

*What have I done?* He couldn't help but bear some of the responsibility for what had happened—regardless of how little sense it made. He tried to tell himself that people couldn't help what they dreamed; all those crazy stories and thoughts just sort of popped up on their own. So he'd dreamt about some asshole meeting his Maker by flying off the Talmadge Bridge . . . so what! Dreams couldn't possibly have an effect on reality, could they? The whole thing sounded like a bunch of nonsense. But that didn't alleviate the guilt and worry that was burrowing deep into Arlo's chest. He had done something horrible, he just knew it.

Now, he had to make it right.

Kerry smacked the table in front of her husband. "Arlo Vaughan! You stop this right now and listen to me!"

Startled, Arlo finally got out of his head and settled back into his chair at the kitchen table. He hemmed and hawed around, pretending like nothing had happened. "Yeah, um—I mean, no, Kerry. No, I don't know 'em."

"Really?" Kerry was incredulous. "Because from this side of the table it looks like that picture stirred up quite a reaction. Sure you don't recognize them?"

"No, Kerry. I said I don't know who they are." That wasn't exactly a lie—he'd never seen the woman before, and never caught the man's name down on River Street. Still, there was no denying the photo had struck a chord in Arlo, and he couldn't hide it. He quickly thought of a reason to excuse himself.

"It's just—" he desperately looked down at the paper. There, in the right-hand column. A preview of the stocks report:

### The One Biotech Stock to Watch This Week

"—it's just the financials here. Reminds me I've got to call Webber first thing tomorrow morning, make sure we're all lined up for our second draw."

"You sure that's all?"

"Of course that's all. You worry too much, sweetheart." Arlo stood from the table. "Now if you'll excuse me, I need to go get cleaned up."

He couldn't get to the bathroom fast enough. He rushed in and shut the door behind him, careful to not make too much noise clicking the lock. Kerry was already suspicious enough, and he didn't want her ear to the door. He turned to the mirror and braced himself on the sink.

The reflection staring back at him was worried and afraid. What had happened over the course of the last week? More importantly, how much had Ocula had to do with it? What had begun as a fortunate series of events following some incredibly influential dreams had turned into a living nightmare; some satanic ability where the worst scenarios to cross his subconscious mind after a night on sleeping pills were the ones that played out the day after. Sure, it all sounded like hocus pocus to Arlo—the kind of voodoo his grandmother used to warn him about, but nothing he ever took seriously. How could he? Witchcraft. Spells. Superstitions. None of it was based in science, in anything that made any kind of logical sense.

But that didn't change the fact that several strange events had happened over the last week; events with no rational explanation. Events that continued even into today—like the fact that Arlo knew the biotech stock to watch mentioned in the paper was Asteria Pharmaceuticals. He also knew it was a strong sell, and he didn't even have to turn to page D2 to find out. All of the events seemed wildly impossible. However, they did seem to have one common denominator:

Ocula. Arlo's sleeping pills.

It was a childish, silly, and superstitious idea that wasn't lost on Arlo. He even caught himself blushing in the mirror, almost ashamed that he would entertain such a sacrilegious notion. Harboring the ability to play God with a bottle of pills and a propensity for strange dreams sounded more like comic-book fodder than facts.

But, none of that mattered. Arlo thought about the bottle of pills in his medicine cabinet, and voodoo or not, he wasn't going to take the chance. He reached for the bottle, poured the pills in his hand, and stepped over to the toilet. He looked at them one last time, about twenty or so chalky white circles lay in the palm of his hand. Never had done him any good anyway. Maybe a few restful nights, but nothing a few fingers of whiskey couldn't cure.

He lifted the seat and tossed them into the water, a blurry cascade of aspirin-sized pills breaking the surface with a whoosh and a splash. Then he flushed. The water swirled and shrank as it made its way to the bottom where the pills were finally washed away, through the plumbing and down into the sewers where the most retched of mankind's messes seemed to wind up sooner or later.

The bathroom ceremony was fitting. In a matter of seconds, the wicked pills were gone, the toilet was empty, the tinted-blue water indicating everything was gone, everything had been sanitized, everything could be forgotten.

As he stood and listened to the hiss of the refilling toilet tank, he wondered if he could forget everything, too. Forget about a dream of good fortune and briefcases full of money. Forget about a nightmare centered on payback and petty vengeance toward an ill-mannered man with a horrible taste in attire.

Yes. Dreams had a way of fading over time. It wouldn't be long before this crazy week was far behind him. He was sure of it.

The water stopped, and the bathroom was quiet again. Arlo opened the door to leave, satisfied he'd taken the first step toward moving on, toward getting back to his old self again.

Back to a life without those little chalky sleeping pills.

***

Mondays were always busy at Asteria's Atlanta

headquarters, but nothing could have prepared the board members for a morning like this. Sturgis stood at the head of a full table and leaned in, palms down on the polished mahogany, poised like a lion setting its front paws just before an attack. To his immediate right, Jillian Penn sat and filled him in on the current real-time situation unfolding at the FDA.

They were halfway into what would turn out to be the longest meeting of the year (so far) when Sturgis asked, "Is there any word as to what's driving Hoover on this? What about your source, Jillian? Can someone please tell me why in the hell this is even an issue right now?"

They couldn't. The entire board had worked every channel they could think of over the weekend to determine what was behind the sudden desire to have Ocula blacklisted—a desire that was coming directly from the top at the Food and Drug Administration. Hoover was little more than a professional acquaintance to Sturgis, although they had golfed in a few tournaments together over the years—not an uncommon dynamic between federal regulators and the Big Pharma players who desperately craved their influence. Still, Sturgis felt like Hoover's actions were personal and unwarranted, especially since he had assured the Sturgis earlier in the week that Asteria had nothing to worry about.

Sturgis wasn't the only one baffled. The entire room was in a state of panic trying to figure out what had gotten into the feds. Jillian was glued to her phone, refreshing her inbox every thirty seconds, along with the rest of the board. Solemnly, "Still haven't heard back from my source. They're probably still in the meeting."

Sturgis looked over his shoulder to check the loudly ticking clock mounted on the wall behind him. 10:47 a.m. *Almost two hours now . . .*

Firmly, "This has gone on long enough. We're going on nothing here. No emails, no phone calls, no ransom notes or letters hinting at blackmail or extortion—"

The angry CEO was about to launch into one of his infamous and vengeful rants when the boardroom door burst open. A man barged into the meeting unannounced, catching everyone by surprise. It was Frank Grimes, general counsel for Asteria. He was exasperated and breathless, sweat beading on his forehead, oval pit stains protruding from under his arms and soaking his shirt. Sturgis figured it was the first time the man had run anywhere since grad school.

"Jesus, Frank. What's going on?" Sturgis asked.

"It's—it's Linklatter," Grimes huffed out. "He's flipped, too."

"Linklatter?" Sturgis thought on the name. "The DEA's Linklatter?"

"Yes, that one. He's—he's on board with the FDA—sources say he's moving to blacklist Ocula as we speak . . ."

Maybe the severity of the news hadn't set in yet, or maybe he just didn't care anymore. Either way, Sturgis stood there, listening to the devastating news, his reaction indifferent, almost stoic.

Finally, he asked Grimes, "Is that all?"

It wasn't. Without a word, Grimes reached over the far end of the table for the remote. He pressed a button, and a seventeen-inch flat screen rose from the center of the table. He turned it to market coverage, and there it was, plain as day, the news that had almost given Frank Grimes a heart attack (and still might, if the market trend continued):

## MARKET ALERT: ASTERIA PHARMACEUTICALS SELL-OFF LEADS BIOTECH INTO THE RED (NYSE: ASTR, -9.84% ↓)

The board was speechless. A room full of wide eyes and slack jaws sat in their thousand-dollar leather chairs, stunned and glued to the television. For the anchors who covered markets like sports announcers called ballgames, the Asteria news was the headline of the day. The talking heads chimed in:

*"Only a month off a positive second-quarter earnings report, the unexplained sell-off of Asteria Pharmaceuticals this morning has market analysts baffled. Several sources tell us some of the biggest names in investing have dropped Asteria from client portfolios, setting off a chain reaction that has echoed through stock exchanges across the globe. As of this report, Asteria is down almost 10 percent ..."*

Ten percent. Over a billion dollars in market value gone just moments after the opening bell. Even the analysts were puzzled, but the confusion didn't change the fact that confidence in the company had fallen overnight. It didn't take an army of naysayers to send a stock into the red, either. Just a few heavy hitters—money managers and investment firms—to send ripples through the market. Once smaller investors caught wind of a few big moves, it was all over.

No one sitting around the table could believe it, because the news was simply unbelievable. If the trend continued, that was it. The company would be finished, joining the ranks of all those other brave pharmaceutical companies who had risked everything for antisense in the past, only to send their companies into Chapter Thirteen.

Nothing special. Just another statistic.

It was Sturgis's life work, and it was crumbling away before his very eyes. His mind wandered to a sonnet he'd learned in college; one he had carried with him throughout his entire adult life: *Ozymandias. The Egyptian pharaoh who had it all, only to lose his empire to the sands of time.*

Nothing lasts forever; Sturgis knew that. But losing his company, his baby, like this? The news sickened him. He fell back into his chair, utterly drained from the worst week he had ever faced. Worse than his battle with cancer. Worse than the death of his college sweetheart (and the three failed marriages that followed thereafter). For a man who hung his hat on his company, the news couldn't get any worse.

But the investors had spoken:

Asteria Pharmaceuticals was finished.

# Chapter 38:
## Assets

Director Lancaster rocked her pen in one hand while reading over the report she held in the other. Every other line of it irked her to the core. *Unforeseen circumstances. Unavoidable consequences. Unaccounted-for agents.* Nothing positive. All negative.

Well, there was *one* positive, and for that Lancaster was relieved and grateful, even if it wasn't showing through her stern expression and half-rim glasses. Wall Street was tearing Asteria Pharmaceuticals a new one, all thanks to a signal sent out from Skyline the weekend before. By Monday's opening bell, the market was responding. Hard to ask for better results. If only the CIA was responsible . . .

Lancaster dwelt on that last part while Kovic and Cline filled the two chairs facing her desk, sitting and waiting in total silence, each of them apprehensive about speaking unless spoken to. She dropped the report on her desk, and then started in on Cline.

"So, let me get this straight. The asset you were supposed to handle in Costa Rica comes back with a vengeance after the death of her friend in a failed drone strike that you authorized?"

Cline looked up and nodded yes, then returned to counting stitches in the carpet like a kid being scolded by his mother, too afraid to look up.

Lancaster continued, "Then this asset, a journalist, threatens to expose the entire operation unless you give her a meeting at our facility, and you agree to it? Does that cover all the bases so far?"

"Director Lancaster, if I may—"

"You may not," Lancaster interrupted. "The only reason I signed off on Project THEIA in the first place was to keep this technology contained—not to let more people in on the CIA's botched operations. Your trigger-happy actions south of the border turned a valuable asset into an enemy, Cline. One who is once again on the loose and off the radar."

Cline couldn't defend his actions. Sure, he'd known what he was doing at the time, and had felt like he had good enough reason to make the call. It made more sense to clean up the entire mess in Costa Rica in one fell swoop rather than take a chance on a chatty journalist who wouldn't be able to resist running the story of the century after the fact. At least, that had been Cline's thought process. His M.O. had always been the same: eliminate the variables, ask questions later. Claire Connor was a variable, and Cline was just cleaning up Kovic's mess. Still, Lancaster hadn't given the order, and even though Cline had taken the lead on the Costa Rica operation, deviating from the plan by betraying an asset was something Lancaster would have never signed off on.

And, this was exactly why. Lancaster went over the report again, line by line, steaming with fury and ruminating on all the possible outcomes that could spell the end of the agency—and her career. "This program Claire ran before escaping," Lancaster pointed out in the report, "the CIA file—is this the same software she ran on Asteria before sending the signal?"

Kovic leaned forward and answered, "Yes, it's the same. It also points to her true intentions all along. After the underground shockwave knocked everyone below ground unconscious, she was able to escape from holding, use Project

THEIA to run her own programs, and broadcast those programs across the region."

"And you're convinced one of these programs is responsible for Asteria's sudden sell-off and negative press coverage?"

"Absolutely. The software was crude, but all signs point to the obvious. Hell, doesn't take much to spook investors these days anyway. Now imagine having a little voice inside your head screaming, 'SELL! SELL! SELL!' until the wee hours of Monday morning. What's the first thing you're going to do when you get to work and hear your colleagues saying the same damn thing?"

Lancaster asked, "What about the CIA file? Do we have anything to worry about there?"

Kovic said, "I don't believe so. The program hadn't been fully executed when we shut it down. These signals play on people's dreams, and can feel just as real as us talking here one minute, only to fade into obscurity the next. If anything were going to happen as a result from the CIA file she uploaded, we would have heard about it already."

Another positive. At least the run-in with the outliers hadn't been a total catastrophe. Still, the agency had plenty of cleaning up to do. Lancaster thumbed through the report and found the section on Claire's accomplices. "This Fenton Reed guy—how much do we know about him?"

"A lot, actually," Cline said. "Reed's got a juvenile record involving a computer-hacking scheme in his hometown. A couple of years later he's volunteering for the Asteria drug trials. Word is that Tanner tried to pick him up last year, but Reed escaped and has been on the run ever since."

"And we're sure he's working with Connor?"

"Lifted his fingerprints off a backpack our guys found in

the woods about a half a mile north of Skyline. Paul Freeman's, too. They're definitely working together."

"And Dawa Graham—is he cooperating?"

Kovic and Cline looked at one another. Then Cline sighed. "Not really. Graham's proving to be a hard egg to crack, but we're working on it."

"Maybe instead of cracking eggs," Kovic said, "we should be focused on getting him over to our side. This guy's Atlanta P.D. for Chrissake. Surely he can understand the magnitude of the situation; the national security risks; the importance of keeping this thing contained—"

"Give it time," Lancaster said. "I'm sure he'll come around." She checked the report again, then said, "Graham's not one of the outliers from the original clinical trials. Do we know how he fits into all this?"

"Not yet, but we're working on it," Kovic said. "If there's any connection between Graham and the clinical trial participants, we'll find out soon enough."

Lancaster sat back in her chair, still uneasy about the turn of events, but a little relieved nonetheless. "Well, at least we know Claire's on our side, whether she knows it or not. Between her message to stockholders and our message to Hoover and Linklatter, I think Asteria is going to be nothing more than a cautionary tale within the year."

"That's certainly a silver lining to all of this," Cline said. "I mean think about it. Ocula's getting taken off the market. That was the primary objective all along." Cline shifted in his seat as he downplayed his mistakes. "It wasn't the smoothest ride, but who cares how we got here? We still made it to our final destination, right?"

The statement sounded a lot like an excuse. Lancaster

hated excuses. "Yes, well. We still have plenty of loose ends to tie up, and plenty of work to do ahead of us. With so much at stake here and so many people out there fully aware of how powerful Ocula is, we can't afford to drop our guard. Not for one minute."

Cline leaned in. "Does this mean Project THEIA remains online?"

Lancaster rolled her fingers on the desk and thought on it. A promising appointment as the first director of Central Intelligence had quickly turned into a janitorial position cleaning up the mess caused by the previous administration. Everything about the project turned her stomach, from the illegal detainment of citizens deemed national security threats, to the covert production of a weapon of mass destruction. The nation—and the world for that matter—was better off without Ocula.

But, sometimes you had to fight fire with fire, and the CIA couldn't afford to give up their highly influential weapon just yet.

"Yes. The project stays, at least until we can get this threat fully contained. Do you two understand what that means?"

Kovic and Cline exchanged glances, then nodded. They understood.

# Chapter 39:
# The Call

The notes plastered to the front door of the Vajrayāna Monastery signaled to the four outliers stepping out of the car something they hadn't thought of until they had arrived back in Atlanta: they weren't the only ones looking for Dawa Graham.

They all stepped out of the car, hesitant to approach, wondering if anyone affiliated with local or federal law enforcement was waiting inside, ready to attack.

Except for Paul. He boldly walked to the door and pulled the yellow Post-it from below the peephole. It was from one of Dawa's coworkers:

*Missed you at the station today. Tried calling. Let us know everything's okay. — Phil.*

Paul crumpled up the note and glanced over the rest of the door hangers. There must have been a dozen notes stuck in the doorjamb and shoved underneath. He started collecting them, then used the key under the little Buddha statue by the door to get inside.

The echo of his feet hitting the hardwoods bounced off the maroon plaster walls and reverberated through the dark and empty foyer. He tossed the notes on the end table near the door and called for his wife and son.

"Michelle! Aaron! You here?"

No response. Only echoes called back from the hollow, cathedral-like building.

"Michelle!" He walked down the hall and to the kitchen, where he noticed a piece of paper lying on the island. Apparently, Dawa's friends hadn't been the only ones leaving notes. He picked it up and read:

*Paul,*

*Had to leave. I know the last six months have been rough, but Aaron and I aren't going to be placeholders in your life any longer. If you need me, you can reach me at (555) 555-3998.*

*—Michelle*

No terms of endearment. No cordialities. Short, and not so sweet. Paul had put his wife's needs on the back burner for months now, and she'd finally had enough.

He let the note fall out of his hands, then took a seat on the stool, shoulders slouched and head hanging low. Soon Claire walked in, followed by Fenton and Donny.

"Everything okay in here?" Claire asked.

"No. Not in the least." He stared down at the note lying face-up on the floor as a poignant wave of guilt came flooding in. *Of course she left,* thought Paul. *Why wouldn't she?* The stress. The danger. The life on the run and off the grid. It was enough to test any couple, let alone one barely two years into a marriage.

Donny stepped closer and eyed the note. "Damn," he said. "Really sorry to hear about that, Paul." Paul nodded with gratitude, even if Donny's condolences sounded about as sincere as one of his late-night sales pitches.

Fenton chimed in, too. "Yeah, man. That just—that just

plain sucks."

Claire saw the number scribbled on the note and asked, "You need a moment to give her a call?"

The question almost didn't register.

Finally, "Yeah. I'll step out here in a sec, once we figure out where we're going from here." He tried to regain some sense of composure, but making it back to Atlanta alive only to find out Michelle was gone had sent his mind into an uncontrollable tailspin. Dazed, he said to Donny, "You're still a wanted man, Ford. And judging by all those notes on the door, it looks like Dawa's APD buddies are getting a little worried. Maybe we need to get you somewhere that's a little more low-key. Hell, maybe we all need to get somewhere that's a little more low-key."

Donny agreed. "Can't stay here with cops banging down the doors, that's for sure." He thought about the deal he'd made with his friend and mentor; how he would gladly turn himself in to the authorities once Asteria was brought to justice. Technically, the downfall of one of the biggest pharmaceutical companies in the world was already playing out live on every cable news station. But with Dawa missing and the CIA still focused on weaponizing Ocula, Ford's run was far from over. No way he could turn himself in now. Not yet.

"You guys still think the CIA nabbed Graham?" Fenton asked the group.

Paul said, "It's the only explanation for his disappearance. For the car he left on the side of the road, keys still in it. Someone grabbed him fast—I just hope we hear from him soon."

The rest agreed, but no one was holding their breath. The most tragic part of Dawa's disappearance was the fact that out of the entire group, he was the only one who wasn't an outlier, who hadn't been wanted by the CIA and Asteria (at least in the beginning). Dawa was just a good detective, an even better man, eager to help those in need. Of course, he would also be the first to tell someone that no good deed went unpunished.

The good news—if one could even call it that—was that Dawa was worth more to the CIA alive than dead, especially after the Skyline incident. An Atlanta Police detective got caught nine hours from his stomping grounds near a clandestine CIA mountain compound that had just been attacked moments earlier . . . What was he up to? What did he know? And more importantly, who was he working with? Picking him up was no doubt a solid lead for Langley. The group could only hope his value would buy them enough time to find him and get him back in one piece.

Always the pragmatist at the expense of compassion, Donny chimed in. "Well, if Michelle's not here then I think we'd better head out. If the CIA's got Dawa, then it's only a matter of time before they send some of their goons here to snoop around. No point in sticking around for that."

Claire shot Donny a shut-the-fuck-up glare that could have cut through glass. *Insensitive prick.* Donny might have been right, but that was beside the point—Paul's wife had just dropped him a Dear John letter and skipped town with their infant son. Probably a good idea to give Paul a minute before voicing one's own concerns about one's own ass.

She hadn't forgotten the bombshell Kovic laid on her at Skyline, either. According to Kovic, Tanner was the one who had drugged Paul with Ocula to begin with—not Michelle. It was a revelation she should have picked up on from the beginning, but good investigative journalist or not, stress had a way of putting the blinders on. But there was little doubt now. Tanner hiring

Alex's older brother to see if there was a familial connection to the genes Ocula affected made a hell of a lot more sense than Michelle slipping Paul a comatose cocktail the night before his kidnapping.

She wanted to let Paul in on the truth right then and there, to let him know his wife's hands were clean, but the timing wasn't right. Claire recalled how Paul had suspected Michelle of drugging him from the very beginning. How would he feel once he realized he had placed all that blame and suspicion on his completely innocent wife? She watched Paul's face turn a pale white, his eyes welling up now. He was nearing his breaking point, and she didn't want to push him over the edge with a guilt trip like that.

*I'll tell him. Not now, but soon. When the timing's right.*

The room was quiet again as everyone stood circled around the kitchen island, each navigating their own deluge of whichever thoughts weighed heaviest on their hearts. Paul's eyes fixed on the note on the floor, lost in the emotional guilt of a marriage that appeared to be over.

Claire silently repeated the vow she made to Aguilar on the plane: *They're all going to pay. They're all going down.*

Donny found himself staring into a set of disappearing cracks in the sheetrock walls again. *Troxler's fading. Everything we think we see disappears sooner or later*—from his business partner Bill Stevens to his assistant-slash-lover Marci to that volcano down in Costa Rica. Give it long enough, and everything was certain to succumb to the void.

Then there was Fenton Reed, standing there and chewing his bottom lip, pretending to be deep in thought like the others, but focused more on catching quick and stealthy glances of Claire's backside in those tight blue jeans. She shifted her weight and his mouth curved into a smile—one he quickly had to reel in the moment Claire busted him out of the corner of her eye.

It was clear there were certain benefits that were inherent to the underdeveloped teenage mind, like the inability to take anything seriously—or take one's mind off sex—even in the face of imminent danger. But the grownups had few reasons to be excited. Sure, every indicator pointed to the fact that Asteria seemed to be finished, but it was still too early to call the game. Stocks rise and stocks fall, and while it didn't look the overextended pharmaceutical giant would pull itself out of the hole, stranger things had happened.

Still, no company could fully recover from such a hard sell-off. The financial impact would be felt in every department and in every lab across the globe. Further, the likelihood that investors would point to the company's riskiest asset as a reason for the plummeting stock price was high. Even if Asteria managed to stay in business, it would have to be without Ocula. And that, at least, was a silver lining in an otherwise shit situation.

A sliver of good news, but nothing that could take away from the fact that they'd lost one of their own, and they were the only ones who could get him back.

A battle at Skyline had been won. But the war was far from over.

An uncomfortable silence dragged on for what seemed like an eternity before Paul resolved to breaking it. He was about to speak up when the phone rang.

"Michelle!" He jumped up from the stool. The phone was on the other side of the kitchen, a cordless model set on the counter next to the sink. He picked it up and answered,

"Michelle, is that you?"

There was a long silence. Nothing from the other end. "Michelle?"

The line crackled and broke the caller's words up into an incoherent ramble, but the voice sounded eerily familiar—and it wasn't Michelle.

"Who is this?" Paul asked.

Finally, the line cleared and the voice answered:

"No, Paul. It's me. It's your brother, Alex."


**To Be Concluded ...**

<u>Resources</u>

This novel is a work of fiction, but several of the themes covered in this book have real-world ties. The following list of resources was put together to help anyone interested in learning more about the science, history and current events behind the book.

Breggin, Peter. "From FDA to GSK: The Dangerous Partnership between Government and Big Pharma." *The Huffington Post*, TheHuffingtonPost.com, 26 July 2008, www.huffingtonpost.com/dr-peter-breggin/from-fda-to-gsk-the-dange_b_115117.html.

Chow, Harrison. "The Emotional World of Propofol Dreams, Part I: A Personal Perspective." *California Society of Anesthesiologists*, 7 Nov. 2011, csahq.org/news/blog/detail/csa-online-first/2011/11/08/the-emotional-world-of-propofol-dreams-part-i-a-personal-perspective.

Draaisma, Douwe. "Why can't we remember dreams? The neuroscience of ecstasy and sadness." *Salon*, 1 May 2015, www.salon.com/2015/05/03/why_cant_we_remember_dreams_the_neuroscience_of_ecstasy_and_sadness/.

Herper, Matthew. "Why Did That Drug Price Increase 6000%? It's The Law." *Forbes.com*, Forbes, 10 Feb. 2017, www.forbes.com/sites/matthewherper/2017/02/10/a-6000-price-hike-should-give-drug-companies-a-disgusting-sense-of-deja-vu/.

Honan, Mathew. "How to Make Your Own Pirate Radio Station." *Wired*, Conde Nast, 3 Nov. 2015, www.wired.com/2015/11/create-your-own-pirate-radio/.

Hughes, Trevor. "NORAD's hidden bunker keeps the (Data) snoops out." *USA Today*, Gannett Satellite Information Network, 12 June 2015, www.usatoday.com/story/news/2015/06/12/norad-cheyenne-mountain-bunker/28689013/.

Hurd, Ryan. "The Link Between Depression and Dreams." *Dreamstudies.org*, Dream Studies Press, dreamstudies.org/2009/09/15/depression-ssri-and-dreams/.

Hussain, Nasser. "The Sound of Terror: Phenomenology of a Drone Strike." *Boston Review*, 5 Nov. 2013, bostonreview.net/world/hussain-drone-phenomenology.

Johnson, Tim. "Government in Competition with Private Sector for Cybersecurity Experts." *Govtech.com*, 19 Oct. 2016, www.govtech.com/data/Government-in-Competition-with-Private-Sector-for-Cybersecurity-Experts.html.

Knox, Richard. "Women's Circadian Rhythm Beats Faster Than Men's." *NPR*, NPR, 3 May 2011, www.npr.org/2011/05/03/135954176/womens-circadian-rhythm-beats-faster-than-mens.

Lupkin, Sydney. "A Look At How The Revolving Door Spins From FDA To Industry." *NPR*, NPR, 28 Sept. 2016, www.npr.org/sections/health-shots/2016/09/28/495694559/a-look-at-how-the-revolving-door-spins-from-fda-to-industry.

McNamara, Patrick. "Psychopharmacology of REM Sleep and Dreams." *Psychology Today*, Sussex Publishers, 4 Dec. 2011, www.psychologytoday.com/blog/dream-catcher/201112/psychopharmacology-rem-sleep-and-dreams.

Porostocky, Thomas. "Pro and Con: Should Gene Editing Be Performed on Human Embryos?" *National Geographic*, National Geographic Partners, LLC, 19 Oct. 2017, www.nationalgeographic.com/magazine/2016/08/human-gene-editing-pro-con-opinions/.

Reardon, Sara. "NIH reiterates ban on editing human embryo
    DNA." *Nature News*, Nature Publishing Group, 29 Apr. 2015,
    www.nature.com/news/nih-reiterates-ban-on-editing-human-
    embryo-dna-1.17452.

Reilly, Rachel. "People with high IQs really DO see the world
    differently: Researchers find they process sensory information
    differently." *Daily Mail Online*, Associated Newspapers, 27 May
    2013, www.dailymail.co.uk/sciencetech/article-2331580/People-
    high-IQs-really-DO-world-differently-Researchers-process-
    sensory-information-differently.html.

Wehner, Mike. "Scientists crack nightmare code with new
    technique to control dreams." *BGR*, BGR Media, LLC, 25 Oct.
    2017, bgr.com/2017/10/25/lucid-dreams-technique-research-
    method/.

Woodford, Chris. "How do antennas and transmitters
    work?" *Explain that Stuff*, 5 Mar. 2017,
    www.explainthatstuff.com/antennas.html.

About the Author

J.M. Lanham was born in Georgia in 1983. He currently lives in Florida with his wife and son.

Be sure to stay up to date with the latest J.M. Lanham news by visiting www.jmlanham.com.

www.ingramcontent.com/pod-product-compliance
Lightning Source LLC
Chambersburg PA
CBHW020644120726

47906CB00001B/111